THE COLLECTOR'S BAG

THE COLLECTOR'S BAG

Travellers' Tales from India
and Elsewhere

R. V. Vernède

COLIN SMYTHE
Gerrards Cross, 1992

First published in 1992 by Colin Smythe Limited,
Gerrards Cross, Buckinghamshire

British Library Cataloguing in Publication Data

A catalogue record for this book is available from
the British Library

ISBN 0-86140-352-5

Produced in Great Britain

CONTENTS

To Anne and Vivian

INTRODUCTION

The postman carries a miscellany of covers in his bag; the scattergun sportsman's tally includes a variety of game in his bag; the author, for his part, has gathered together a diversity of tales and verses in 'The Collector's Bag'. Most of these relate to India where I spent nineteen years in the Indian Civil Service. Because of this diversity, I thought it might be helpful to the reader if I included a synopsis in my Introduction. There is a Glossary at the end of the book.

The Talking Tree (Sub-title for six Hill Stories)

Sometimes it was men talking, sometimes the Tree, and sometimes both together. The men came to see me for various reasons and at many places during the course of my work or while I was enjoying my leisure, at my bungalow or tent, under the thatched porch of a village house, in the fields or in the forest, round the camp fire, at a wayside halt. The Tree was different. I was the visitor, not the visited. It was not always the same tree in the same place, but the same kind of tree and always just in the right place, more particularly in the Hills where all my touring was done on foot. How welcome on those steep hill roads were the wayside cisterns, bubbling over with cold spring water, and near them the stone platform built round the base and shaded by the talkative leaves of the roadside *peepul* tree. Here I would sit to rest and presently, by that oriental magic which never failed, I was no longer alone.

All six stories under this Sub-title have their setting in Garhwal, one of the three Hill Districts of the Kumaon Division in the central Himalaya, in what used to be known as The United Provinces of Agra and Oudh, or U.P. for short, now called 'Uttar Pradesh' — the Northern Province of independent India. I was lucky enough to be able to spend five years of my service as Deputy Commissioner in charge of Garhwal District.

The Garhwalis live in a country of majestic beauty, but it is a hard land in which to earn a livelihood. The area of the whole District, 5,629 sq. miles is about the same as that of Northern

1

Ireland — 5,452 sq. miles, but more than 2,000 sq. miles is moun-
tainous and unculturable. The valleys are deep and narrow, the
mountainsides steep and unstable as must be expected in one of the
world's youngest mountain ranges still subject to heavy erosion.
Despite ingenious and incredibly laborious terracing and walling,
there is not enough culturable land to support all the inhabitants
— 602,115 at the 1941 Census.

Luckily, men are moulded by their environment and many of
these highlanders have the qualities that fit them admirably for
military or police service. There are today twenty battalions of a
homogeneous regiment, the Garhwal Rifles serving with great
distinction in the Indian Army, successors of the Unit first raised
in 1887, expanded in 1891/92 and in 1921 re-named the 18th Royal
Garhwal Rifles. They were one of the eight regiments of the Indian
Army to be honoured with the title 'Royal' in recognition of their
records of gallantry in the First World War. In the Second World
War their record was just as fine, in Abyssinia, the Western Desert,
Italy, in Malaya and Burma.

The money sent back to their families by these Servicemen and
by Garhwalis in civilian jobs outside the District, helps materially
to pay for food and other goods imported from the Plains to make
up the local deficits. There are poor families but no abject poverty.
When these men retire and go back to their villages, their pride in
the Regiment, or in the Police, as the case may be, as well as the
economic factor, ensure a regular flow of recruits. During the last
war a very special recruiting campaign was organised. The total
male population of military age was just over 100,000. In the five
years 1941–1944 the combatant recruitment was 22,000 and the
non-combatant 4,000. The number of Garhwali batallions was
raised from five to ten.

The Six Hill Stories

The Path to Eternity (fiction) — A description of the predicament
of a small party of Hindu pilgrims cut off by a landslide across the
pilgrim path to the shrine of Badrinath. Such accidents did happen
and could have happened anytime before the motor road was completed up to Badrinath after the British left India.

The Bridge of Juma Gwar (fiction with historical background) —
This background was the mounting tension between India and
China from 1951 onwards over frontier adjustments which
culminated in China's invasion of India's northern frontier at both

ends of the Great Himalayan Chain in 1962. It is known that they sent small patrols over the high frontier passes between Tibet and India to reconnoitre invasion routes. During the long and bitter diplomatic exchanges there was little publicity outside India for China's claim for an adjustment of the frontier in the central Himalaya as well. In the actual fighting China never mounted an attack on this front. If she had done so with anything like the success achieved at both ends, Delhi itself would have been threatened. Again, though China's claim here may have been for only a relatively small area, it was particularly offensive to Hindu national and religious sentiment, since it included part of their holy land, Devistan, the home of their gods, the sources of some of the tributaries which join to form their most sacred river, the Ganges, and one of the holiest of their pilgrim shrines, Badrinath.

The hero of my story is a Tibetan thief, forced by a Chinese patrol to guide them over the high passes between Western Tibet and Garhwal during winter when they are normally considered closed. By the time they reach a damaged rope suspension bridge which holds up their further progress, Tombu has guessed what they are up to and foils them, though at the cost of his own life.

The Hermit of Hemkund (fiction) — A Sikh soldier deserts from the Burma Front in 1943, motivated not by cowardice, but by the mental affliction known as 'cafard'. He uses a Sikh legend relating to Garhwal to devise an ingenious scheme for evading arrest and Court Martial. He gives the local people the clear impression that he intends to spend the winter hibernating in a state of suspended animation, without food or heat, in a small hut beside a mountain lake at 15,000 ft. Actually he proposes to slip down undetected and assume a new name and identity. But he is not a mountaineer and makes no provision for unseasonable weather and this defeats him. When, in the Spring, the villagers go up to the lake and find no trace of him, the headman reports to higher authority that a reincarnation of a famous Sikh Guru has visited them but has vanished again.

Snow Tiger (fiction based on fact) — A retired Viceroy's Commissioned Officer of the Royal Garhwal Rifles returns to his village, lying at 8,000 ft., in the far north of the District, to find that two village women have been killed by a man-eater. When a third woman is killed in broad daylight, he suspects that the man-eater is a tiger and not a leopard as everyone else assumes. He considers it his duty to put his theory to the test. He sits up for the man-eater, sitting on the ground, over the body of the dead woman. But the animal does not come back to its kill until after dark, so that he can neither identify nor shoot it. He had just decided to fire one shot into the air in the hope that this would scare the animal away, when the moon rises over the canopy of trees and reveals an animal the size of a tiger but with a coat so pale it almost looks white. Instead of firing into the air, he aims at the tiger and kills it with one shot.

The Blood Feud of the Bishts (fiction based on fact) — Is the story of a blood feud (very rare in Garhwal) between two septs of the same clan. It is also a story of the personal tragedy of a man who started by trying to stop the feud but ended by becoming fatally embroiled.

The Law of their Fathers (fiction) — This is a story of intrigue leading up to murder and trial by a village court, set in the far north of Garhwal in the year 1857. The identity of the murderer and his guilt are discovered by the time-worn ritual of Ordeal. A young English District Officer witnesses and condones the methods used to reach the court's decisions, on the ground that there is insufficient evidence on which to obtain a conviction under British rules of Law.

At the beginning of the nineteenth century the Kingdoms of Kumaon and Garhwal in the central Himalaya were independent States consisting of areas later known as the Almora, Naini Tal and Garhwal Districts, Tehri Garhwal State and the Sub-division of Dehra Dun. The rulers were seldom in control of all their territories at any one time and war between Garhwal and Almora was endemic. In 1803 the Gurkhas from Nepal invaded and conquered the whole area, which they occupied for twelve years. The British had no conceivable trade interests in the region to justify intervention, but were alarmed at the rapid expansion of Gurkha power in Northern India. Provided with a convenient excuse in the frantic appeals from the ex-ruler and the inhabitants to be rescued from their ruthless oppression by the Gurkhas, the British invaded Nepal and Dehra Dun in 1814 and Garhwal in 1815. After some reverses and very tough campaigns, in which they first learnt to respect their redoubtable enemy, they finally defeated the Gurkhas and drove them out of Dehra Dun and Kumaon. The Directors of the East India Company restored to the Raja a State less than one third its original size, annexed Dehra Dun as a reward for their assistance and the rest of Kumaon in order to check any further inroads from Nepal.

There was no reason to establish and insufficient revenue-obtainable to maintain any elaborate system of administration in these newly acquired border territories in the hills. The result was a long period of personal rule by several highly individualistic and dedicated Englishmen covering over forty years. It is a curious reflection on the history of British rule that so often such men appeared on the scene, it would seem almost by chance, just when their particular qualities were required.

In time, and even before acceptance by the British Government in 1858 of responsibility for the administration of all the East India Company's acquisitions, regulations and principles of policy were laid down from above for the settled areas. But many of these did not apply to backward and border areas or to territories very recently acquired. Such areas, including, of course Kumaon, were designated 'non-regulation'. Even orders which were supposed to apply were not always followed locally. This was particularly true in the hill districts, where conditions were so very different from those in the plains. Some orders were quite unsuitable, some never reached the Deputy Commissioner in time when he was on tour for five or six months in the year.

Two further points require some elucidation, namely, the existence and position of Thokdars and the non-existence of regular police.

The title of Thokdar was hereditary in Kumaon and pre-dated the British occupation. They found it covenient to confirm the title to its holders, the privileged rent collectors, as they had already done in the plains for the Zamindars of Bengal and were to do later in respect of the Taluqdars of Oudh. But the British took away from the Thokdars their honorary position as heads of the hill police and their responsibility for maintaining law and order in their own areas, as they were found to be abusing their powers. As a result they soon declined in importance and prestige, though they remained in existence until the end of British rule.

It will be noticed that there is no mention of police in this story — for the very good reason that there were none, as normally understood by the word, in the hill districts of Kumaon. When, nearly one hundred years later, the British left India, the regular police in Garhwal were still only a handful, whose jurisdiction was confined to the pilgrim routes and the towns of Pauri, Lansdowne and Kotdwara, the capital, the cantonment and the rail-head respectively. The *patwaris*, or revenue accountants, whose main task was to keep up-to-date records of all rights in land, performed also the functions of a civil police force.

The Kumaon province was not affected at all by the revolt of 1857, except that, in Garhwal, the land settlement was interrupted for eighteen months to enable the Assistant Commissioner to raise a force of militia and to stay near the southern border to see that no gangs of lawless men invaded the district.

John Nevill in my story is a fictitious character. But his counterpart in real life at that time might well have had to deal with a similar situation. I do not claim that he would have dealt with it in the same way — but it would have been possible. After the disappearance of John Company and untrammelled personal rule, with codification of criminal law and procedure, it would, I think, have become more difficult, if not impossible, even though Garhwal remained a non-regulation district and for many years longer the Executive head of the district was also the district Judge.

Tales of a Tahsildar (fiction based on a core of fact) — A Tahsildar is, literally, the holder (i.e. the official) in charge of a Tahsil, the basic unit of revenue and civil administration in an Indian District. There were four to six Tahsils in a District, six Districts to a Division and eight Divisions or forty-eight Districts in the U.P. As a rough guide an average Tahsil was about the same size as an average County District in England; the average size of a District in the U.P. was slightly larger than the average size of an English County; the area of the U.P. is 107,161 sq. miles; the area of the United Kingdom is 94,211 sq. miles.

The Tahsildars served in the lowest grade of the Subordinate Provincial Executive Service, but it would not be a great exaggeration to say that the whole revenue and civil administration of the British Raj in Northern India hinged on the Tahsildar — the man who actually saw that the Orders were carried out. To give some idea of the variety of tasks required of him, he had, for instance, to measure the rainfall on the roof of the Tahsil building, the political temper of a dozen of the largest villages in his area, the damage done to crops by severe frost, storm, flood or drought. He might have to arrange for the extermination of locusts, a duck shoot for the Governor, or for fuel and hay for a Brigade on their way through his Tahsil. It was sometimes best not to enquire too closely through how many mouths an order passed before it reached someone so humble that he could pass it no further and so had to carry it out himself. The important thing was that the job was done and that everyone, including the Tahsildar himself, knew that he was the man responsible.

I doubt if things have changed much in this respect since the

British left India. There were dishonest and incompetent Tahsildars, but, on the whole, they were a worthy and resourceful body of men, the nuts and bolts of the so-called Steel Frame.

Two of these tales have their setting in Meerut, forty miles north-east of Delhi, the third moves to Afghanistan. They are portrait studies of a most remarkable Tahsildar who served under me in the early 1930s. Sardar Rahat Ali Shah was an Afghan political refugee of good family who had been given asylum and a job in British India. He was a square peg in a round hole if ever there was one, but by sheer strength of character he had got right on top of his job with the minimum of exertion to the exasperation of his more orthodox and hard-working contemporaries.

A Gentleman's Agreement (historical fact) — How Jawaharlal Nehru came to be released from jail for eleven days in 1934 in order to see his sick wife.

A Snake in the Grass (true story) — This is the story of how the Muslim landlord of a village eight miles east of Benares (Varanasi), a grand old man of seventy, whose tenants were all Hindus, came to learn, rather painfully, that he had been deceived and his tenants systematically cheated for twenty years by a rascally Hindu Agent. The story goes on to detail his revenge. The association of a Muslim landlord with Hindu tenants was by no means uncommon during the Moghul period and up to the end of British rule. I do not know if it has survived the division of India into India and Pakistan.

Fragrance of Cedar (fiction) — This story was inspired by a short stay in the Lebanon in 1932 on my way back overland to India after leave. In my story an Austrian Count, exiled to the Lebanon in 1903, visits the Cedars of Lebanon in 1913 where, quite by chance, he meets again the glamorous gypsy actress with whom he once lived as a young man in Vienna and whom he rashly introduced to the feckless Archduke Leopold Ferdinand. Leopold married her mainly to spite the old Emperor Franz Joseph. The Archduke was disinherited and Count Otto banished for this part in the affair.

The Last Enemy (fiction) — A romance which turned sour only because of war, set in the last days of the Hapsburg Empire, the First World War and the opening days of the Second World War in Poland.

The
Talking Tree

MAP OF UPPER GARHWAL
Showing the Locations of Stories of the 'The Talking Tree'

TO TIBET

R. Alaknanda

●MANA

△ RATABAN
20,100

●NITI

BADRINATH

△ GAURI PARBAT
21,750

CHAUKHAMBA
23,420 △

XHEMKUND
*(The Hermit
of Hemkund)*

△HATHI PARBAT
22,070

△
SATOPANTH

△
NILKHANTA
21,640

●PUNN

● MALARI

Bhyundar Valley

● JUMA GWAR
(The Bridge of Juma Gwar)

R. Alaknanda

●JOSHIMATH

△
DUNAGIRI
23,184

XPATALGANGA
(The Path to Eternity)

R. Dhauli

●
BINAIK
(Snow Tiger)

●GARUREANEA

X KUARI PASS

Birehganga

●CHAMOLI

Bireh Tal

△NANDAGHUNTI
20,700

NANDAPRAYAG

R. Nandakini

△ TRISUL 22,916
△ TRISUL 23,360

KARANPRAYAG

R. Pindar

LOWER GARHWAL

● SARKOT

●
DEOSARI

●
GWALDAM
(The Blood Feud of the Bishts)

ALMORA

Scale 1cm = approx 2.25 miles

THE PATH TO ETERNITY

The pilgrims advanced with infinite caution across the treacherous slope, in single file, hands linked and facing alternately inwards and outwards. The laden coolies in the rear followed independently, bent under the weight of their loads which swung out over space. As they moved forward, one step at a time, they tapped the path ahead with their short wooden crutches. Pilgrims and coolies alike went barefoot.

Their path lay up the left bank of the Alaknanda river, one of the main tributaries of the river Ganges, some 170 miles north of the point where the latter bursts in swift and splendid beauty out of the hills above Hardwar. Their goal was Badrinath, a dirty straggling little town, redeemed only by remembering what it stands for and by the beauty of its setting amidst the snow mountains at 10,000 odd feet above sea level in the vale of Badriban. This still lay thirty miles before them.

Their immediate objective was a narrow stone bridge half a mile ahead, which spanned the gorge through which a small tributary, the Patalganga, flowed into the main river. The valley here was deep and narrow. The slopes on the side where the pilgrim path ran were heavily wooded but, in spite of this, unstable and scarred with the passage of many slips. The pilgrim party had started to cross the worst of these now. Across the valley, the mountainsides rose steep and bare, a rich green above dark red cliffs. If they had cared or dared to raise their eyes, they would have caught glimpses above the rain clouds of the two great peaks of Hathiparbat and Gauriparbat dominating the head of the valley.

But this was no place for lifting one's eyes to the hills. On their right the crumbly blue shale stretched up steeply for 300 feet to join the yellow clay scarp over which the green lip of the forest curled, torn and menacing. Here and there a pine had slipped over the lip and leaned crazily out of the glistening clay, its roots exposed, its sap still running strongly. To their left the naked blue slope plunged almost vertically to a wicked chaos of boulders, through which the river foamed, red with iron, 250 feet below. A smell of sulphur hung in the hot heavy air. It had been raining recently and the whole slope glistened evilly. The path ran like a ribbon across it, never more than a foot wide and in some places less. There was a constant tiny movement down the slope of small particles of the gritty blue shale of which it was composed. Ahead of them another party of pilgrims was edging along in the same way, but they were nearly off this dangerous place.

This was the Patalganga slip, the most dreaded half-mile on the whole pilgrim route to the shrine at Badrinath. The month was August, towards the end of the rains.

If you were to ask the local people about the Patalganga, they would tell you that the gods were angry with the greedy hillmen of Garhwal who exploited the pilgrimage to Badrinath for their own material gain, charging the pilgrims exorbitant prices for food and fuel. One day, when their anger became too great to contain, they would cause two mountains, Nar and Narayan, one on each side of the Ganges, to fall into each other's arms and block the sacred river, so that it would turn back and find a new exit to the plains. Opinions in the district differed as to the exact site of these two fateful mountains. Some held they were further north, between Joshimath and Badrinath itself; and there were certainly two mountains called by these names opposite Srinagar, much further south. But the local people were firm in their belief that the gods had selected the Patalganga gorge for this manifestation of their displeasure. The natural evidence certainly seemed to support them, for the Patalganga valley, which protruded this crumbling flank into the main valley of the Alaknanda, was a veritable laboratory of nature. her ceaseless processes of erosion were displayed here nakedly and on a vast scale. The whole valley was in a state of dissolution.

Three years ago, the long narrow islands in the river bed, still covered with trees, had been part of the thickly wooded southern banks; in two or three years more they would be gone, washed away, but only to be replaced by other living fragments of the torn mountainside. Ugly gashes behind its present frontier marked the line of fresh subsidences. On the north bank all trace of vegetative cover had been stripped from a pale cliff three miles long. A permanent cloud of dust hung over it as over a limestone quarry in working. Throughout the rains the valley reverberated with the restless thunder of landslides; the waters of the Patalganga never ran clear at any season. The young Himalayan giant merely twitched in his sleep; what would happen when he awoke? It did not bear thinking upon.

Leading the little group of pilgrims was an elderly man whose bearing inspired confidence in his followers, though none of them had ever seen him before. His iron-grey hair was shorn close and he wore no covering on his head. He carried a bundle of cooking pots and spare clothes tied over one shoulder and under the other arm by two ends of the coarse cotton cloth in which they were wrapped. This left both his arms free, a necessary enough facility at any time in such a perilous traverse, and now essential to enable him to hold his strong but light bamboo alpenstock in one hand and to grasp the hand of the pilgrim immediately behind him with the other. From his clothes alone it was evident he was not a pilgrim from the plains. Instead of a *dhoti* he wore loose woollen homespun breeches of the jodhpur style; the fine oatmeal coloured shawl round his shoulders suggested he was a man of some consequence. His sort sturdy figure, slightly bandy legs and broad round head confirmed unmistakably that he was a hillman.

Gopal Singh was indeed a hillman and, more surprisingly, a hillman from Upper Garhwal, very few of whom were ever known to perform this pilgrimage, whatever shorter pilgrimages they might undertake in deference to gods who ruled before one stone of Badrinath was laid upon another. Yet Gopal Singh was neither a professional guide nor a contractor out to seek material profit from the pilgrims. To be precise, he was a Khassiya Rajput, headman of his village and greatly respected in his own locality. Ever since his only son had died, late in the previous winter, of the dread hill disease known as Mahamari, a kind of pulmonary plague, he was determined to perform the pilgrimage to Kedarnath and Badrinath. The more he brooded over the death of his son, the more importance he attached to the pilgrimage, until the obsession grew that he could never be reconciled to his loss until he had performed it. He had seized the first opportunity after the wheat had been harvested and when, owing to the rains, no important work could be done out of doors, to carry out his vow.

It had never occurred to him, nor to any of his fellow travellers, that he had thrust himself into the lead at this critical stage of their journey. He had taken it unconsciously, as of natural right, because this was his country, because he alone looked on this passage as a natural hazard of a day's journeying in the high hills.

It was very different with the others, pilgrims from the plains. They had been terrified or, in the few cases where physical fear no longer applied, non-plussed at the ordeal which faced them. Before Gopal Singh arrived on the scene there had been lengthy consultations. Some were for waiting till the next day in the hope that the slopes would dry out — but it was just as likely to rain again

heavily overnight: others were for returning to the last *Chatti* or
group of pilgrim resthouses, in order to take the three mile detour
which would enable them to pass above the slip. When Gopal
Singh arrived they asked his advice. He looked pointedly but
politely at their frail limbs and bodily infirmities and then up at the
great ridge towering above them.

'Certainly, there is a way round,' he said, 'but it will be long and
hard; it will take you all the rest of the day to reach the bridge
there, which you can see now at the end of this slope, the bridge
over the Patalganga river. Better let me take you over; in half an
hour, in twenty minutes perhaps, we shall be across.'

Six of them had agreed to follow him and a seventh, a very old
woman, too frail to walk, was taken without being consulted,
because the coolie carrying her wanted to stay with his mate, who
had been hired by one of the other six pilgrims to carry his
belongings.

Directly behind Gopal Singh was an elderly man of about his
own age, just under sixty, small and wizened. His delicate, mouse-
like features put the hillman in mind of a musk deer, shyest and
most timorous of all the mountain animals. He gripped his leader's
hand with desperate determination. This man, Bishn Narain, was
a petition-writer attached to a small causes court in one of the
remoter districts of the eastern United Provinces — not a very im-
posing profession perhaps, but one performing an essential service.
In addition to drafting petitions and pleas for presentation in court,
he did a fairly brisk business writing out letters on a miscellany of
subjects for anyone who applied to him and who was prepared to
pay four *annas*.

As he shuffled along, one part of his mind was paralyzed with
fear, but another part was actively engaged in a process of painful
introspection. As is alleged to happen in the case of a drowning
man, where supposition is easier to come by than fact, his sins rose
up before him with accusing fingers. There was, for instance, the
case of the widow, Rukmini Devi; there had been many others but
this one chose to fix itself relentlessly in his mind. He had charged
her one rupee for writing a letter to her son, in which she had
spoken urgently about the disposal of certain property.

'Tell him it is urgent, urgent', she had said, drawing her sari over
one side of her face as if to prevent her words being overheard by
anyone interested. She need not have bothered since it was Bishn
Narain himself who received a further rupee from Nannoo, *bania*,
the only person interested, for information as to the contents of the
letter. The widow owed Nannoo considerably more than she was

worth. Bashn Narain had had no compunction at the time in spite of the fact that the woman was some kind of a distant relation, but now he was assailed by doubts. He was only human after all, both in his fear and in his venality. In the circumstances should he have charged one rupee — four times the usual fee? He knew Rukmini well enough — and her worthless son; knew that the latter would ignore his mother's appeal, that the *bania* would inevitably have his way over her land. But one rupee because of the urgency? It had been too much; he had known it at the time and kept quiet; he knew it now and his soul shuddered at the enormity of his crime. Other cases came to mind, all involving the pettiest sums, but this was the only currency he knew, and he started to calculate the amount he would have to expend at Badrinath in order to appease the gods. Gopal Singh, glancing back at his face, guessed nothing of his inner turmoil, of these preoccupations which masked the face of fear, and marvelled at his composure.

Behind the petition-writer was a tall emaciated Brahmin who dragged one leg painfully after him. A cow-dung plaster was very crudely clapped over a festering sore on his shin. The dressing and bandage applied by the doctor at the last dispensary refused to stay on his skinny shank and had long since been discarded. Rudri Dutt was one of those men whose age and profession it was easy to guess at, impossible to determine from his appearance. He might have been anything from fifty to sixty, a retired schoolmaster, a government or railway clerk, a bookkeeper or a bank casher. The actual post was of little significance, only the fact that he represented a type — the humble clerical worker, industrious, anonymous, impersonal, the target of wit and caricature, the very stuffing of bureaucracy.

It seemed to him that he had already died many times on this fearful journey; he was past caring what happened now and walked like an automaton. This was his third pilgrimage, expiation for goodness knows what sins, yearning for who knows what consolations after the dull routine of his earthly career. He would come now every year till he died.

Behind Rudri Dutt came a woman just past middle age, dressed in white cotton *sari* and *dhoti*, her head shaved like a nun's, at first sight just like any of the other thousands of middle-aged and elderly female pilgrims. And your first impression would have been right — she was exactly like thousands of others — but no one of them was ordinary. In her eyes was a light, on her face an expression difficult to relate to her age and figure.

Tara Devi was the mother of six children, now all grown up; a woman of good family with a comfortable home, a widow for the last seven years. But all that past had been, as it were, erased from the mirror of her face by some magical elixir. Now she was only a pilgrim awaiting a miracle, another birth but this time a re-birth, the delivery of her own soul. She, too, was counted amongst the number of those who had put fear behind them. She, too, walked as if in a trance but resolutely enough to inspire confidence that she would reach at least her physical destination.

Not so the woman behind her. At every step her overburdened lungs wheezed and grumbled in protest at the task demanded of them. After every ten paces she would pause to recover her breath, only to be dragged forward inexorably by the woman in front, who seemed to be oblivious of her frailty. If she had halted longer the odds were she would have fallen over the edge from sheer fright. Three — perhaps as many as four — out of every ten pilgrims on the route were as feeble as herself; their passage excited the compassion of all beholders.

Gyanshiam, who followed her, was a young *sadhu*, dressed in the saffron shawl and *dhoti* of his brotherhood, a pleasant young man whose friendly smile offset the effect of a slight cast in one eye, which gave him rather a villainous look when he was not smiling. But he seemed to smile most of the time, he was a little simple in the head. He had offered to come with them to help the other pilgrims cross the slip. As he walked he sang softly to himself through his nose to keep up his courage and moved his head rhythmically to accompany his refrain. Gopal Singh doubted privately whether he would prove reliable in an emergency but welcomed his presence because he was willing and cheerful.

Behind the *sadhu* and, by his own choice, last of the little group of pilgrims on foot, was a solid, prosperous looking middle-aged man, carefully dressed in the correct white pilgrim clothes but wearing them in a way which conveyed the impression that he was still closely linked to the cares and standards of a middle class world — they wee spotlessly clean in contrast to the soiled and creased cotton garments of all his companions except the widow Tara Devi — an impression that was confirmed whenever he glanced back anxiously at the coolie following him. It was clear that the latter was carrying his possessions and that these were of considerable bulk and weight. Of value, too, for Baboo Lal was a well-to-do cloth merchant from Mathura. His business had flourished, he could now safely leave it in the hands of a son as thrifty and reliable as himself. it had seemed a fitting moment to render thanks to the gods for their favours — on account of course — for he had no doubt that further favours would be bestowed. In his judgement, too, the servants of the gods would not be averse to gifts of fine cloth and warm shawls. So he had packed a basket with fine pieces to present to the priests at Badrinath and at the various temples of note on the way.

At times, such as the present, he had regretted his decision to perform this pilgrimage, but pride and the persistence which had made him a successful business man, drove him on, however appalling the conditions and dangers. He was determined to complete his pilgrimage.

The two coolies in the rear were Dotials, professional carriers from western Nepal, whose tribe had almost the monopoly of carrying on all the pilgrim and trade routes in the central Himalaya.

The first was a muscular young man with rather a surly expression, in some part a reflection of his temperament but undoubtedly enhanced by the strain imposed on his features by the weight of the basket on his back, which he supported almost entirely by a broad headband. Whenever Baboo Lal looked back, all he could see of Bikram Singh was a greasy cotton skull-cap, the whites of his eyes and his mouth lolling open.

The basket he was carrying was made of split bamboo cane, broad at the mouth and tapering to a narrow flat base. it was roughly circular at the top but slightly flattened on the side carried next to his back. It was black with the smoke of many fires and the dirt of untold journeys. Besides his skull-cap, Bikram Singh wore a frayed cotton *kurta*, or shirt-waistcoat, sweat-stained and malodorous. It was cut low in front, revealing a square silver locket suspended round his neck on a thick black thread. In addition to the *kurta* and a belt in which he kept his money and tobacco, he wore only a loin-cloth, equally dirty, which exposed a pair of smooth muscular thighs and buttocks shiny with sweat. His feet were broad and business-like, turned in, with the toes widely splayed, as is inevitable in the case of all bare-foot load carriers. Though he showed no sign of nervousness and was in superb control of his straining body, he was, in fact, acutely conscious all the time of the insecurity of the track. He moved with the care of a well trained young elephant.

The second Dotial, Hardayal Singh, the last man in the line, was an older and a slighter man, well proportioned, wiry and remarkably good-looking. He was carrying the last pilgrim, a very old woman, in the shoulder basket on his back. This was a special pilgrim basket, very much like the other already described but with a square cut out of the front. The pilgrim sat in the basket with her back to her carrier and her legs hanging out through this gap. It could hardly be called a comfortable form of transport — the occupants had to be removed from time to time to restore the circulation to their limbs — but it had the merit for the carrier of immobilising the passenger. This reduced the risk of a sudden shift of weight which might upset the porter's balance and bring disaster on a tricky passage.

His passenger now sat so still in Hardayal's basket it was difficult to believe she was alive. Her eyes were shut, her face expressionless. Only her lips just moved ceaselessly in silent prayer. The skin was stretched so tight and fine over her shins it seemed almost transparent, like the finest parchment. Dried and wizened as a raisin, she might have been any age up to ninety or more; she was, in fact, only just over seventy. Her bearer carried her effortlessly, thankful for such a light load.

They had crossed about one third of the landslide when there was a sudden shout from across the river, followed by a cry of warning from the party of pilgrims in front of them who had just reached the bridge. Gopal Singh looked up — the whole slope had begun to move. The slip was only on the surface so far but at any moment the weight and momentum of the fine particles of shale might trigger off a major landslide. In any case it was sufficient to endanger their footing.

Gopal Singh stopped and shouted in a loud authoritative voice: 'Stand still! Stand still!'

They watched the creeping tide of death, it flowed over their feet and most of it spilled over to the river below but where they stood the path held firm. Undoubtedly Gopal Singh had saved their lives. When the mountainside stopped moving there was no path in front of them and, for perhaps fifty feet, no path behind. They were trapped. Gopal Singh knew from experience that it was only a matter of time before the precarious ridge on which they were standing would collapse. Their combined weight had pinned it temporarily, their legs like breakwaters had split the wave of shale whose direct shock must otherwise have carried the path with it. But it could not rest for long without firmer support. At the same time any hasty movement on their part would be fatal.

'Remain where you are,' Gopal Singh directed, 'but turn round one at a time, beginning from the rear.'

As they had been going, the Dotial, Hardayal, carrying the old woman, had been last in the line: when they had turned he was in front.

'Put your basket down carefully,' Gopal Singh ordered.

The man obeyed. They all held their breath while he lifted and fixed his wooden crutch below the basket and then bent back slowly till he could ease himself, first out of the headband, then out of each shoulder rope in turn, until he was able to turn round again and put the basket down carefully on the path. The worst moment of all was when he casually smoothed the loose shale off the path with his foot to make a level base for the basket to rest on.

'Good,' said Gopal Singh, 'now turn round again and test the slope in front of you, ever so gently — that's right, press the soil lightly but firmly; keep your weight evenly divided on your feet — that's the way — splendid!'

Step by step the coolie formed a link of human footprints until he was across the gap.

'Now come back and fetch your load,' said Gopal Singh. He said this firmly but in a most matter of fact voice, hoping that the habit of obedience would prevail over the power of reasoning or imagination. It was too much to expect; a long argument ensued. Gopal Singh pointed out that none of them could pass the basket without performing an acrobatic feat which was beyond their powers and that even to attempt it would upset the precarious balance of the slope. Only a brave and nimble *Dotial* like himself could shoulder a load which he had so skilfully off-loaded.

The Dotial pointed out with equal force that, even if the unstable surface he had just crossed would bear the extra weight, the feat of balancing a load over a track which only consisted of his bare footprints was beyond his powers, or, for that matter, the powers of any mere human being — he was not the Monkey God, only a human coolie.

Hardayal squatted on the end of the firm path which had not been affected by the slip and lit a *biri*. It was stalemate. They all stared at the basket and at the old woman sitting unconcernedly in it. Throughout these exchanges she had sat expressionless and without movement; perhaps she did not understand what had happened or her present predicament. Hardayal said bluntly:

'The only thing to do is to tip her out — no need to lose the basket though, it will be no weight or trouble empty; it is a good basket, I should be sorry to lose it.'

There was rather a strained silence, no-one could think of any other solution. The old woman had closed her eyes; she had stopped praying and appeared to be dozing. Across the Alaknanda half a dozen villagers had gathered; one or two had shouted advice at first but now all had fallen silent, helpless witnesses of the drama being played out opposite. Some twenty pilgrims, who had crossed the Patalganga slip without accident, had stopped to watch from the rough stone steps, hewn out of the living rock, which climbed steeply up the bluff beyond the Patalganga bridge, where the pilgrim path doubled back along the sharp promontory which divided the two rivers. They, too, watched silently, until someone thought the occasion suitable for striking up the Hindu dirge for the dead:

'Ram! Ram! Sat Narain!: Ram! Ram! Sat Narain!' whereupon they all took it up, beating their breasts at the same time. But they stopped when Gopal Singh protested that they were not yet dead.

The suspense was bad enough without that. The sun shone fiercely through a watery haze; there was no breeze to temper the oppressive heat. Gopal Singh felt the sweat gathering in his palms and trickling down his thighs. In front of him the pilgrims stood patiently. Each in varying degree had accepted the fact of their situation with the fatalism for which their religion and way of life had prepared them. The *sadhu*, Gyanshiam, started to call aloud on Siva in a high nasal sing-song.

'In a minute he will go mad and leap over the edge,' thought Gopal Singh and wondered with painful intensity whether this would happen before the path gave way and threw them all to their death.

Just in front of him a single pebble of shale had come to rest on the very outside edge of the path. He decided they were safe while it remained there, doomed as soon as it slipped over the edge. From that moment he could not take his eyes off the pebble, it hypnotised him. His eyes began to play him tricks. Twice he saw the pebble moving and was only just able to suppress an involuntary cry before he realised it had not changed its position. With a great effort he looked away from the pebble.

The sun beat down warmly on the old woman. It seeped through to her torpid blood and sent it coursing a little faster on its old familiar journey. She stirred once in her basket, then dozed again. She was dreaming of her adolescence, of a wonderful journey with her grandmother to Hardwar, where she had offered her young body to the ice-cold embrace of the river-god as he came past the bathing steps. She could hear again the cooing of the temple doves, the hypnotic intonation of the priests as they invoked the sun-god and sprinkled drops of the holy water over their naked bodies. She could feel again the fierce fire in her blood as she came out of the water, the kiss of the sun-god on her damp forehead and breast. Ah! — the days of youth in the sun, the days of innocence and desire, the days so long past and done with! Now she was the helpless prisoner of old age, caged in the basket of death — and in her dream she stirred feebly to escape.

Suddenly the other Dotial, Bikram Singh, gave a grunt, muttered something in their own tongue to his companion and started to lower the basket which he had been patiently supporting on his back all this time. When he had lowered it onto the path, he started to take its contents out. The cloth merchant realised his intention and protested vehemently but to no purpose. He dared not intervene physically to restrain him. One after another the Dotial threw his precious bales down the slope. When it was empty he picked up the basket and started to put it on his back again.

The others had all been watching this performance which came as a welcome relief to the strain, so that no-one noticed the old woman until she was half-way out of her basket. She had been too tightly wedged to climb out. Whether by accident or design, she had tipped the basket and it was now too late to warn or stop her. She did not attempt to struggle or clutch and she never uttered a sound. In a moment she was gone and the basket with her. Until she disappeared from view all eyes followed her and then switched immediately to the path where she had been. Would it hold?

Gradually all movement of the loose shale ceased. A long sigh went up from the spectators. Bikram Singh, who had been frozen into immobility with one arm half-way through a shoulder rope, now finished fixing his empty basket on his back. As he stepped forward to cross the controversial gap he shouted almost gaily to his mate:

'You've lost your basket, I've lost my load and we've both lost our wages now. But never mind, at least the old nanny-goat has obligingly helped to save our lives!'

Gopal Singh smiled grimly — the others had not understood for the Dotial had spoken in his own patois.

'Wait a minute,' he called out in Hindostani so that all could understand him, 'Is it your intention to leave these people to die here while you save yourself? You know as well as I do that none of them will be able to cross the gap without assistance. What sort of a man are you?'

He had spoken sharply. Bikram Singh half turned and looked at him sheepishly, took off his cotton skull-cap and scratched his head in embarrassment.

'Very well, I will try to help them,' he said sullenly.

'Good', said Gopal Singh 'take your basket over and leave it and then come back to help the first pilgrim. Make fresh footprints both ways as you cross — and perhaps your friend will assist too, now that there is no question of his carrying a load.'

Both men nodded their assent and Bikram Singh was again about
to start over when the cloth-dealer, Baboo Lal, who, apparently,
had not followed the implications of Gopal Singh's opening
remarks, suddenly understood their conclusion.

'Never!', he cried out vehemently, 'never will I entrust myself to
such a devil. he has already thrown all my gifts down the precipice;
no doubt it will give him still greater pleasure to throw me after
them.'

Gopal Singh tried to humour him:

'Well, then, I will ask the other coolie to come back to help you.'

'No, no, he is just as bad!' exclaimed the merchant, 'we have all
heard what he said about tipping the old woman out of her basket
and seen how he abandoned her to her fate without lifting a finger
to try and save her. I would rather go by myself, thank you, than
rely on such fiends.'

Hardayal gave a short laugh; Bikram gave the cloth merchant a
look black as thunder, shrugged his shoulders and set off. Gopal
Singh cursed under his breath. To run up against so many
awkward people in such a crisis! But all he said to Baboo Lal was:

'Very well, please yourself, but don't blame me if you fall off.
Wait till I tell you you can go and then be as quick as you can for
we others are also waiting on death and do not want to meet him
yet.'

Step by step Bikram balanced across the gap, making fresh footprints between those of his fellow Dotial, so that there was now
almost a continuous track, if such an exiguous link could be so called. Once over, Bikram sat down beside his friend, ostentatiously
lit a *biri* and paid no more attention to the pilgrims.

Gopal Singh drew a deep breath, the biggest test of all lay ahead:

'Now you go,' he said in a matter of fact voice to Baboo Lal. The
bania hesitated and then very gingerly set out. He had not gone
more than five yeards when he lost his nerve. He was too frightened to move or speak; in a moment he would lose his balance and
fall to his death.

'Hold on!' shouted Gopal Singh 'I am coming to help you,' and
he made to squeeze past the little petition-writer. But in that instant
he saw the older Dotial, Hardayal, darting back, sure-footed as a
goat. With great skill and firmness he helped the wretched man
across the remaining gap. After that he and his mate, with great
good humour, took it in turn to come back and escort the remaining pilgrims to safety. Finally, Gopal Singh crossed by himself
amidst the cheers of the onlookers.

When he had got off the slip and reached the safety of the broad pilgrim road behind the danger zone, he sat down suddenly, feeling weak and rather sick.

'I am too old,' he thought 'too old and foolish. I had no right to lead all these people into such danger. How shall I reach Badrinath?'

People came up to congratulate him on their escape. he bowed his head in acknowledgement and remained with his head bowed and his eyes shut until the nausea and giddiness passed off. He heard an argument start between Baboo Lal and the two Dotials but presently they drifted out of hearing and he did not learn its conclusion until he raised his head and opened his eyes. The pilgrims had gone but the two coolies were squatted on their haunches before him. They lit '*biris*' and offered him one, which he politely declined.

'Well?' he asked.

The older man made a gesture.

'Who will pay us our wages?' he asked.

Gopal Singh looked at him sternly but there was no unkindness in his voice.

'Why do you ask for wages? God has taken your fare but spared your lives — what more do you want?'

The Dotials considered this and then the same man replied.

'It is possible to die quickly, like that old woman; it is also possible to die slowly — of starvation. We have had no food today.'

Gopal Singh rose to his feet.

'Come, we will return to Garurganga *Chatti* for food. As for wages, there will be plenty of work for you two when the pilgrims hear that the path has gone and that they will have to climb the Patalganga ridge. And we must report the death of the old woman at the dispensary.'

As they turned to go, they heard a familiar sound and looked back quickly at the Patalganga slip. The little island where they had stood recently and the make-shift path by which they had escaped, together with the whole of the path this side of the original slip up to within a few yards of them, were slowly disappearing under a fresh fall of shale. They watched until it was all over, until there was nothing left to show that there had ever been a path at all.

With a last glance at the scene of their recent adventure, Gopal Singh murmured aloud the old proverb:

'All are free to enter, but only they may leave who have permission,' and, joining his palms before his face, he made a little obeisance to his gods.

THE BRIDGE OF JUMA GWAR

The cell was bare, bitterly cold and indescribably filthy. Inside, two men sat on the floor on their own rags, on which they also had to sleep. The stench was overpowering but neither man noticed it or gave any thought to the conditions in which they existed. They were both accustomed to prison life in Tibet and, after all, these conditions were only a few degrees worse than those in their own homes.

The tall thin man was a consumptive; death was already written in his face and advertised by the dry hacking cough which racked his spare body. He was a Jykpa, a member of a gang of professional bandits, who had been so foolish as to waylay and rob the Jongpen's wife.

The other man was strong enough, short, thick-limbed and villainously ugly. Every feature in his head was crooked. He had one wall eye, his nose and lips were flattened as if by a press, his ears, enormous and coated with dirt, stuck out of his huge ungainly head like the leaves of the wild rhubarb. His hair was coarse and filthy, cut short behind, where it stood on end; in front it was long, lousy and hung about in all directions. His right arm ended in a stump at the wrist, which had been cauterised by being dipped in boiling oil, proclaiming him an habitual and convicted thief. His name was Tombu; he had been in the Jongpen's lock-up for two months. The other man, Burphu, had only joined him two days ago. The Jongpen was away on a visit to Lhasa; when he returned there was still no certainty that he would deal promptly with them, they might languish in the lock-up for months.

The man called Tombu was boasting cheerfully to the other who listened perforce but with obvious ill humour.

'You Jykpas,' said Tombu, 'consider yourselves the most power-ful and dreaded robbers in Western Tibet, but you are wasting your time and energy. Once in a blue moon you are lucky enough to catch a wealthy Tibetan traveller, but it is the Indian traders who have all the wealth. They only spend a few months each year in Tibet, are tough customers who know how to look after themselves and have influence with the Jongpens. You are frightened to attack them because you know they would complain to their own rulers and this would cause a lot of trouble for the Jongpens who, in turn, would make it hot for you. But I know where and when to rob them with impunity. They think their villages over the border in Garhwal and Almora secure in winter because they are buried under snow and the passes are closed. But I know a way to get over in winter and then — why it is easy, you just help yourself from their deserted houses. If the Jongpen spares my life I shall be going over again this winter. Free drink too — plenty of it — just think of that! Wouldn't you like to come with me?'

'No,' said Burphu,' 'it doesn't attract me at all'.

'Ah well, never mind,' said Tombu, and then added as an afterthought, 'besides, I don't think, somehow, that you would be fit enough to accompany me after the Jongpen has finished with you, one needs at least one sound hand and two good legs for such a strenuous venture. Now, if you have only one hand, there are compensations; you can hold a begging bowl with the stump of the other arm — it is wonderfully effective in conjuring alms and food — and you can still pick pockets with your one good hand — like this' and Tombu moved closer to the Jykpa and started to do his begging thieving act in mine.

Burpha moved away with a gesture of distaste and said irritably: 'Bah! You are a jackdaw amongst thieves — never have I heard such a boastful and loquacious liar. The Jykpas would never tolerate such a one in their company — we are men of deeds, not words. The Jongpen will not harm me, he is too frightened of our power and influence. He pays us secretly to keep away from Gartok. How was I to know that his foolish wife would choose to travel abroad while he was away? His cowardly police would never have caught me if I had not been prostrated with fever.'

Tombu laughed uproariously.

'If I'm a jackdaw, you're a scarecrow — but you don't scare me! Well, if you don't like my company, it is just too bad as we are likely to be companions for some time in this homely cell.'

'I shall be freed as soon as the Jongpen returns — you will see,' said Burphu,' but as for your chances . . . you have lost one hand already . . . perhaps this time an ear, who knows?' And he shrugged his shoulders and spat on the floor.

They heard steps approaching. Their warder looked in through the grille.

'Catch,' he said and threw each of them a bone. The Jykpa made no attempt to catch his and let it lie where it fell. When Tombu had extracted everything he could from his bone, he went over and picked up the other one.

'To-morrow you will be dining with the Jongpen,' he said sarcastically 'here goes!' and he dealt with the other bone with relish.

The Jykpa scowled evilly.

'Dog's food for a dog,' he said. 'I wish you joy of it'.

This pleasant conversation was interrupted by the warder who looked in again to say.

'The Jongpen will arrive shortly; they say it will be a large party.'

Tombu groaned.

'Then we shall starve — no dinner for you to-morrow, Burphu — are you sure you won't change your mind about this bone?'

The warder still hung about outside the door.

'They say there are Chinese with the Jongpen,' he volunteered.

'No pigs or chickens in Gartok for a month!' exclaimed the irrepressible Tombu. 'Perhaps it is better to be in jail.'

In the evening they heard what certainly sounded a considerable party arriving to a welcome of shots and the discharge of firecrackers. Two days later they were both surprised, despite the Jykpa's boast, when he was called out to see the Jongpen. 'Too bad,' said Tombu, commiseratingly. 'He wishes to amuse and impress his guests at your expense first. Well, good luck, and leave me your blanket like a good chap — no point in presenting it to the hangman.'

Burphu gave him a dirty look as he went out and ignored his request.

Four men were seated round a table in the Jongpen's house. The Jongpen was proud of his table and chairs; they were the only ones in Gartok. His three guests were Chinese officers in uniform. Their leader was questioning the Jongpen.

'You say these Bhotias pay taxes — they are Tibetan subjects?'

'Most certainly,' said the Jongpen, 'they have always done so. The Bhotias of the Mana and Darma valleys pay Tibetan land taxes as well as trade tolls; we have always considered them as Tibetan subjects — and the other Bhotias too — but they dispute this on the ground that they live in India.'

'But do they live in India?' asked the Chinese officer, 'that's the point. I understand that you have never accepted the frontier as claimed by the British and now by the Indian government?'

'That's true,' said the Jongpen, 'and the frontier has never been demarcated.'

'How far do you claim that Tibetan territory extends in this area?'

The Jongpen was vague.

'At least as far as the most southerly of the series of frontier passes,' he suggested, 'but we have also claimed all land where the Bhotias live in settled villages.'

'How far is that?'

The Jongpen shifted uneasily in his chair.

'I am not certain, it is a matter of opinion.'

'On the contrary,' said the Chinese officer, 'it is a matter of fact.'

'The are a very nomadic people,' said the Jongpen apologetically. 'They are always changing their villages.'

He knew this was an exaggeration but this cross-examination was not to his liking and he was driven on the defensive.

'Never mind,' said the Chinese officer, 'let's put it another way — what are the furthest points in Garhwal and Almora to which these Bhotias have migrated to live?'

The Jongpen considered carefully.

'In Garhwal, at least as far as Chamoli,' he said, 'in Almora, down to Milam for certain, possibly to Mansiari in the Goriganga valley; to Khela and even perhaps to Dharchula in the Dhauliganga and Kali valleys — I am not sure.'

'But we must be certain,' said the Chinese officer, 'haven't you or your predecessors ever visited these areas to survey and stake your claims?'

The Jongpen wondered if they knew he had only crossed into Kumaon once, when he had heard of the Chinese take over in 1951 and had fled for fear of being arrested and removed from his post. His predecessor had acted similarly when the Khazzaks had ridden into Western Tibet ten years earlier. He hunched his shoulders and spread out his hands as he replied.

'My own people would think I was running away if I crossed the Himalayan passes. Besides, the border trade is lucrative and it was advantageous to keep on good terms with the Indians and with the British before them. For some reason, too, the British officers liked to come over to see me and my predecessors to settle any trade differences. Why should we trouble to go over to Bhot — it is a very arduous journey by any of the routes.'

The Chinese officer banged his fist on the table.

'That's the trouble with you Tibetans — too lazy and stupid to look after your own rights, or rather our rights as Tibet is a province of China. The British officers were spying, of course, and you only too happy to accept their presents! But we shall change all that now. For reasons of state it is urgent that we should make a precise survey of all Tibetan territory unlawfully occupied or claimed by the Indians. You must supply us with reliable guides at once.'

The Jongpen raised his hands in dismay.

'It is impossible at this season, the passes are all closed — no-one would be able to cross them till late next spring.'

'Not even if there was a monetary reward offered?'

The Jongpen considered the matter. These men were in earnest and ruthless, it would not do to thwart them. But he knew of no-one suitable for their purpose. He was only too anxious to get rid of them — preferably for good. he must find someone who could be relied upon to take them so far that they would never be able to return and take their revenge on him for their failure to cross the passes in winter. Suddenly he had an idea.

'There are two thieves in my lock-up,' he said. 'Two rascals who would probably be ready for any desperate venture for the sake of a reward. The reward would be cheap — their lives, which are worthless anyway.'

He was just about to add 'and serve them right too if they never returned', but remembered in time that this would hardly be politic.

The Chinese officer looked at him with contempt.

'Is that all you can offer us? Thieves indeed! How can they be trusted? Nevertheless, we shall see them; send them in at once.'

When the Jykpa saw the three Chinese officers he lost his head. The Chinese administrators, unlike the Tibetan, had a reputation for ruthless suppression of banditry. As soon as they had started to cross-examine him on his knowledge of the topography of the borderlands, he suspected they were laying a trap for him and denied all knowledge of the area, of any connection with the bandit brotherhood and pleaded his ill-health. To convince them he started coughing and spat up some blood. The Chinese leader looked at him carefully and then conferred with his fellow officers. When he had done so he turned to the Jongpen and said.

'This man is useless, he is a consumptive and a bad case at that. We are wasting our time. What offence has he committed and how do you propose to punish him?'

'He robbed a high official; I shall cut off his nose and his ears.'

Burphu threw himself before the Chinese officer.

'Hear me, lord! The high official was his wife; she was visiting the house of a low-born tinker — how was I to know she was the Jongpen's wife? Mercy lord and your justice, not the Jongpen's!'

The Jongpen started to protest but the Chinese leader silenced him with a fierce gesture.

'We shall be more merciful, scum, if you can produce an able-bodied man to guide us over the passes into Bhot.'

The Jykpa grasped at the straw.

'Lord, I know of such a man, the very man you want!'

'Who is he and where?'

'His name is Tombu, he is in the Jongpen's lock-up. He knows the passes and how to cross in winter.

The Chinese leader turned to the Jongpen.

'Bring in this man Tombu — and god help you if he is no better than this miserable creature.'

Turning to one of the other Chinese officers, he said.

'Take this man out and see that he is shot.'

Tombu in his cell heard the shot but did not give it a thought until the warder opened the door and threw a blanket inside.

'With the compliments of the Jongpen,' he said 'the owner will not need it any longer. And I doubt if you will have much use of it either, the Jongpen has sent for you too.'

Tombu looked at the blanket and recognised it, it had belonged to Burphu. He looked up slowly at the warder.

'He has been shot?'

The warder nodded.

'About five minutes ago, if I had not been right on the spot, someone else would have taken the blanket. Your turn next,' he added cheerfully.

Tombu said incredulously.

'But this is not a punishment used by the Jongpen — he would not waste the ammunition, even one cartridge is worth its weight in gold in Gartok.'

'The Chinese soldiers shot him. Come on, now, the Jongpen is waiting,' and he tied Tombu's left wrist securely to his own right wrist.

Tombu scratched his head thoughtfully with his stump as he accompanied the warder. Why, he wondered, were they all in such a hurry? Perhaps they wanted the cell for other prisoners they had brought with them?

When he reached the Jongpen's house, he was taken straight into the main room. There was no sign of the Jongpen. Three Chinese officers in uniform sat behind the table. One of them read out his dossier. Tombu listened complacently.

'H'm,' said the man who appeared to be their leader, 'decapitation, I think, do you agree, comrades?'

The others nodded their heads in agreement and their leader started to write out an order. Tombu flung himself at the officer's

feet with such violence that he pulled the warder down on top of
him and cried indignantly.

'Decapitation for only a third offence — it is too severe a punishment! I offer one ear, or even one eye, my head is too precious —
how can I earn my living without it?'

They were amused. The warder with many oaths pulled Tombu
to his feet.

'Untie him,' ordered the Chinese leader, 'and leave him alone
with us, we can look after ourselves and the prisoner.'

The warder reluctantly untied him and left the room. The senior
officer pushed the order paper aside.

'You know a route over the passes into Bhot?' he asked suddenly.

Tombu gulped and nodded — and however did they know this?

'You can cross in winter — now?'

Tombu became suspicious — were they concocting a capital
charge?

'I don't know,' he said, 'I have never tried.'

The Chinese officer pulled the order paper back and picked up
his pen.

'In that case we are wasting our time on you,' he said.

'What do you want?' asked Tombu quickly, his wits sharpened
by crisis. The Chinese leader leant over the table.

'We want a guide who will take us over the Niti pass into
Garhwal, we are in a hurry. If you are prepared to do this your life
will be spared.'

Tombu looked at him carefully. He sensed that the other two
Chinese officers were waiting expectantly for his reply, but the face
of the man in front of him was a blank mask. He could hardly
believe his ears, why should they be so eager to cross into Garhwal
in mid-winter? Pickings for the like of himself, yes — but what
could they be after? He had enough sense to conceal his curiosity.

'Done!' he said. 'When do we start?'

'I am glad you have chosen to be sensible,' said the Chinese officer. 'We shall start in two days' time.'

A Chinese soldier was called. Tombu was led away to be given
some better clothes, felt boots and a square meal. He was locked
up but in a better room. He congratulated himself on his good luck.
If he could have laid his hands on some liquor he would have got
drunk.

After he had left the room the Chinese leader rubbed his hands
with satisfaction.

'He will do, I think. He is not to be trusted far but, at least, he
seems to be a man of spirit.'

'He would scare the devil himself,' said one of his companions.

The party which set out two days later consisted of the Chinese officer who had led the interrogation and two Chinese soldiers, all disguised as Bhotias, three Tibetans dressed and equipped as traders and Tombu as their servant. He was kept on a rope. The Chinese carried rifles, their own modern army issue, the Tibetans knives. Tombu was searched thoroughly before they started and only allowed to keep his pipe and some tobacco. Once they had crossed the passes, if they met anyone, their story was to be that they had caught Tombu escaping over the border with goods looted from the Niti valley and were bringing him back to hand over to the Indian authorities.

Tombu led them willingly enough. The prospect of being able to loot over the border with an armed escort was eminently satisfactory. He was fairly certain they would not meet any Indian officials while engaged in their business, whatever that was, and, if they were unlucky enough to be stopped and questioned, he thought he might be able to turn the tables on his employers. At the worst he could count on a mild term of boring imprisonment, probably in better conditions than he had suffered in Tibet. He did not particularly like what he had seen of Indian officials — but then, he had seen very few. Nor had he any liking for the Chinese and it seemed that more and more of them would be coming to Western Tibet. They were likely to be more efficient than the Tibetan officials in suppressing the widescale robbery and theft which had made this area a happy hunting ground for outlaws like himself. Moreover, the Chinese leader, Major Shan-Tsin, obviously despised all Tibetans and took every opportunity to show Tombu that he regarded him as dirt beneath his feet.

But in any verbal exchange Tombu gave as good as he got, he had a very ready tongue and a gift for shrewdly calculated insolence. Near the border they passed some derelict huts. The Major said to Tombu:

'Your countrymen are good at hiding themselves, thief, maybe the occupants of these huts are watching us from some hiding place as dirty as themselves. I suppose you can distinguish a skulking Tibetan from a heap of ordure? Come, tell me if we have been observed?'

'Only by the birds, lord, and what do they know? — by the sun and what does he care? — by the wild goat, but he is too fastidious to enquire closely. These huts have been deserted for years,' and he spat carefully past his left foot.

The magnificent insolence of his reply and gesture, capped by a villainous grin, was not altogether lost on his captors. The Tibetan guarding him raised his rope's end to strike him but Major Shan-Tsin restrained him, saying it was unlucky to strike a buffoon. Then, turning on Tombu, he said, scowling fiercely:

'Keep a civil tongue in your head, insolent one, or I myself will split your gizzard with the greatest pleasure,' and drawing a knife he made a meaningful gesture.

Tombu grinned and said in his own dialect:

'When the belly is empty, the threat is also hollow, when the belly is full, the threat is forgotton.'

The Major asked the other Tibetans what he had said and, when they had told him, said:

'Take him out of my sight, or I will be tempted to violence.'

The other Tibetans secretly enjoyed Tombu's scurrilous remarks and refusal to be cowed by the domineering Chinese officer.

They took a week to reach Niti, making snow igloos in which to shelter at night. The Chinese had brought snow-shoes for the whole party which was a great help. At first the Tibetans were scornful of their use, preferring their own long woollen felt boots called 'Baukch', but they soon changed their minds. Tombu resolved that, when the expedition was over, if they did not let him keep his snow shoes, he would contrive to steal a pair. Tombu, too, was weather-wise and timed the crossing of the most exposed parts of the route so that they were able to avoid the wind at its worst. He had thought of the Chinese as plainsmen but they were much tougher than he had expected and earned his respect, if not his liking.

When they had reached Niti village, the Tibetans, instructed by Tombu, found and drank some of the fermented barley brew which the Bhotias call 'Jan' and the Tibetans call 'Rakshi'. Major Shan-Tsin heard the sound of revelry and interrupted the party. The other Tibetans were baiting Tombu, who was already dead drunk. The Major snatched the earthen vessel out of Tombu's hand and poured its contents into the snow. He then tripped the thief who fell face downwards in the drink-stained patch of snow, where the providence which protects drunkards saved him from suffocation. He then turned on the others:

'No strong drink until our mission is accomplished,' he said sharply.

One of the Tibetans murmured sullenly. The Major picked up the empty pitcher and smashed it across his mouth. There was no more trouble after that.

In every village notes were made of the number of houses, the road distances were carefully measured and topographical details likely to be of interest to a soldier were noted down. The Chinese had even worked out from their maps a detour via the Kuari pass, Ramni, Ghat and Nandaprayag, which would enable them to approach Chamoli from the south, and therefore be less likely to rouse any suspicion than if they worked south from the Dhauli valley. They could say, if questioned, that they were taking Tombu to Joshimath to hand him over to the authorities there as the nearest important administrative centre to the Niti valley villages which he was supposed to have looted. After taking notes all the way up from Chamoli they could continue up the Alaknanda valley to Mana and so back into Tibet over the Mana pass, with or without Tombu. By the time they reached Jhelam, eighteen miles below Niti, Tombu had a pretty shrewd idea as to the real object of this expedition. Though he was entirely uneducated, he was no fool.

Two miles below Jhelam the Dhauli river entered a narrow and impressive gorge. Their path traversed on the right bank of the river, sheer precipices rose above the opposite bank. As they emerged from the gorge their path was cut by a mountain torrent, the Juma Gad, coming in to join the Dhauli from their right. On the far side of this torrent, now in high spate, lay the deserted village of Juma Gwar. There was a rope suspension bridge across the torrent but, to their dismay, it was in a completely derelict condition. The four main ropes, two below close together for the foot-walk, and two above, more widely spaced and carried over stone towers at each end of the bridge, which supported the weight of the bridge, were still in position, though they sagged alarmingly and appeared to be old, dry and possibly rotten. But most of the bamboo cross slats of the footwalk were broken or missing. None of the thinner rope side-lacing between the upper and lower suspension ropes was left. The upper ropes were so wide apart that it was impossible to grasp both of them, even with both arms fully extended. The pulley wheels on both sides, used for hauling loads across by line, were still in position, though the line and sling were missing. There was, however, some spare line, in good condition, lying by the abutment on their own side. The torrent was too swift and deep to ford or swim and too wide in its present condition to span with a tree, even if there had been a tree in the vicinity to fell. They climbed a little way up their side of the torrent but found no feasible crossing place and soon the route became impassable.

They returned to the bridge and sat down to consider the problem which faced them. There was enough spare rope, they judged, to make a double line across the bridge. If someone could get across

to thread it through the pulley on the far side and they could im-
provise a wooden sling, they might be able to pull each other across
in that. Major Shan-Tsin called for a volunteer to climb across and
fix the pulley line. There was no response, this was something outside their experience. The torrent foamed past below the unsafe
looking and sagging suspension ropes, and far out into the main current of the Dhauli river, rolling great boulders as if they had been
pebbles with a dull grinding thunder like distant drums heard
through the roar of monsoon rain.

Tombu had listened impassively to the discussions. So far as he
was concerned, he had done his job. Obviously, the sensible thing
to do was to turn back. But, on the other hand, there was the
chance of an extra reward, even the possibility of escape. He
studied the ground on both sides of the bridge carefully and then
said, jeeringly shouting so that all could hear:

'Let the monkey show the leopard!'

They looked at him angrily, but their anger was soon forgotten
in new hope:

'Let Tombu go,' said the other Tibetans. 'His carcase is worthless,
he is already more than half a monkey.'

Major Shan-Tsin considered the suggestion carefully. Could they
trust the thief? he doubted it. All they could do was to keep him
covered with their rifles until he had fixed the line and they had
hauled him back in the sling. It would certainly be useful to test the
line and sling before they crossed themselves. He was a thief, he
might also be induced to behave by the offer of a reward. He decided to risk it:

'Very well,' he said, 'let Tombu go,' and calling Tombu up to
him, he showed him ten rupees:

'I will give you this when you have returned safely to this side.'

Tombu looked greedily at the money, rubbed his tummy and
mimicked a man drinking heavily, so that they all had to laugh.

'May I have a smoke before I go?' he asked. 'A smoke will steady
my nerves.'

Grudgingly the Major agreed. Tombu produced a villainous clay
pipe which he filled and lit. The ends of the suspension ropes, two
on each side of the stone archway piers, were tied to clusters of iron
stakes. A large boulder had been placed in front of each cluster of
stakes to prevent them being pulled out. Tombu went and sat on
one of these boulders. While he was smoking the other Tibetans
found some driftwood and started to whittle and notch it with their
knives and then tied three pieces together in a rough triangle to
form an improvised sling. The plan of operations was discussed

and settled. Tombu listened carefully. After he had been hauled back, the others would cross, one by one, and he would then be hauled across, last but one, the last man being the Tibetan who would be detailed to guard Tombu while the others were crossing. Tombu studied the ground on their own side with great care. He had noticed the Tibetan guarding him put his knife down by the boulder when he had finished whittling his section of the sling. Very carefully, while the others were still discussing their plans and completing the sling, he put his foot on the knife, worked it along towards him and, bending down to knock out his pipe behind the boulder, buried the knife under a small heap of flints. Then he got up and joined the others. They put the line through the pulley and gave him the two ends which he tied round his waist after they had removed the guard rope. He was just about to start across when the Tibetan missed his knife. There was a thorough search and then the man came up to Tombu and searched him. When he found Tombu had not got it he started to accuse the other Tibetans of taking it. The Major cut him short:

'You are holding us up,' he said. 'Don't bother about your knife now — you can look for it later.'

Turning to Tombu he said:

'Now go — and remember, no reward until you come back and you will remain in full view the whole time, we shall have you covered with our rifles.'

Tombu grinned:

'I don't propose to die yet,' he said.

They watched him start out, curious to know how he would manage with only one hand. Tombu grasped one of the upper ropes and, turning on his back to face them, swung his legs over it. Then, drawing his knees towards his chin and locking his ankles and knees round the rope, he shot his hand forward behind his head and took a fresh hold, he drew his legs toward him again and repeated the rest of his movement, and in this fashion he crossed over safely. It was obviously very hard work and at one moment he was in great danger. This was when he reached the middle. The rope sagged so badly that he was dipped in the swirling waters below and very nearly pulled off. They marvelled at his agility and strength.

When he reached the other side he lay exhausted for a few minutes, then he rose and threaded one end of the spare line through the pulley wheel, knotted it to the other end and signalled to the others to pull it back. When the knot reached them, they untied it, fixed the home-made sling on the line and then re-tied it.

They pulled the sling over to Tombu, but it had yet to be tested with a human load. He climbed in and was hauled back singing cheerfully. As he jumped out the other Tibetans clapped him on the back. He went up to the Chinese leader and held out his hand. The Major counted out ten rupees from the bag of Indian money he had brought to support the fiction that they were traders. As he gave the money to him he said:

'You can get drunk when you get back to Tibet.'

They tied the guard rope on him again and gave the spare end to the Tibetan who had lost his knife. He had searched without success and now gave up looking for it. The others started to cross. Tombu went back to his boulder, put his foot over the little pile of flints and had another smoke. When four of them had crossed, Major Shan-Tsin asked the Tibetan guarding Tombu to help steady the sling while he got into it, burdened with a satchel containing all his maps and notes. Tombu bent down swiftly and retrieving the knife from its hiding place, adroitly slipped it up his sleeve unobserved. As the burly Chinese officer was hauled across, Tombu stood beside his guard, close to the pulley wheel. He waited until Shan-Tsin had nearly reached half-way and then suddenly whipping out the knife, before the other Tibetan realised what he was up to, he severed the pulley line with one fierce slash. As the rope went slack and started to race through the pulley wheel, the sling dipped sickeningly. Shan-Tsin made a desperate lunge to reach the lower suspension rope of the footwalk nearest to him, he just managed to get one hand to it as he fell out of the sling. His reprieve was short-lived. Under his weight and the impetus of his fall the rope sagged to its limit and the Major was completely immersed in the raging stream below. Just for a moment he was able to cling on and then he was swept off the rope and away. The water was freezing cold, he hadn't a chance of survival.

As Tombu turned after cutting the line, the other Tibetan leapt at him, using the loose end of the guard rope as a flail. Tombu parried the blow with his sound arm and, as the other man grappled him, drove the stump of his other arm with all his strength into his opponent's solar plexus. The Tibetan folded up, completely winded. Tombu ran up to him and drove his own knife fiercely in the Tibetan's back — once, twice, three times. Then he severed the rope which held them together.

By this time the two Chinese soldiers on the far side of the bridge had recovered from their surprise. They had rifles but could not fire while the two men were locked in combat. So far, Tombu's plan had worked perfectly, but now he made a fatal mistake. Instead of dodging at once behind the stone archway pier of the bridge where he could have waited safely until dark and then slipped away unseen, he started to run for the nearest natural cover away from the bridge abutment. This was because he had noted earlier what he thought was a good line of escape, also he had no idea of the accuracy of a modern rifle. This cover was fifty yards away, to reach it he had to scramble up a steep slope overhanging the stream. There were a few sparse bushes on this slope which he thought would give him some protection on his way.

The first shot was low, if Tombu heard it at all, he certainly paid no heed, his ungainly body was covering the ground with remarkable speed and agility. The second and third shots were almost simultaneous. Tombu stopped abruptly. The impact of the heavy bullet spun him round, so that the little group across the stream could all see the ludicrous expression of surprise on his face, then he slumped sideways. Slowly he started to roll down the slope till, with gathering momentum, his body shot into the water, came up once, was rolled over and then torn away in a surge of grey foaming waters. For a minute after he had gone a small shower of stones continued to mark the passage of his body and the piece of rope which had still been loose round his waist when he started to run, but which had come away during his fall, slipped snake-like down the slope after him.

THE HERMIT OF HEMKUND

High in a secret cup, hung five thousand feet above one of the most beautiful valleys in the Himalaya and fifteen thousand feet above sea-level, is a little mountain lake. To reach it involves a journey of many days by pony, or on foot, from the plains. The valley itself can only be entered on foot and it is an arduous climb to the lake. There is nothing at first sight to distinguish this lake from hundreds of similar lakelets that hang like burnished jewels round the snowy shoulders of the mountain giants. Waters of the same indefinable green, suggesting unfathomable depths, reflect the light from sky, rock and snow, on certain days and at certain times throwing back the colours of the spectrum in a ripple of wind, like the flash of a fisherman's net cast against the sun.

But Hemkund, sometimes known as Lokhpal, is different and the difference is man-made. There is little to show for it, just a rude stone hut beside the lake, on its roof a solitary pennant flying, once white, now stained and ragged. But to this place, so it is alleged, came Guru Govind Singh, the great Sikh reformer. According to a local legend, he lived, though possibly in another incarnation, by the side of Hemkund and wrote those compositions which historians, more cautious than the common people, say were probably compiled after his death from his teachings and added to the original or Adi-Granth, the Bible of the Sikhs.

Neglected for many years, the story was never wholly forgotten. A stone hut was built at Gangria, on the edge of the forest in the valley below, where the path to Hemkund started. There were long periods when no-one lived there, or in the other hut beside the lake, but at intervals a Sikh *sadhu* would arrive out of the blue and stay for months, sometimes for years, and claim to be the guardian of the shrine which, in the manner of the East, was gradually established by the lake.

These *sadhus* were, for the most part, genuine holy men. The people of Punn, the only village in the valley, brought them food and milk. There was no friction although, since time immemorial, the villagers had set up their own Hindu images beside the lake. A dozen Sikh pilgrims would come every year and an occasional

38

mountaineer would go out of his way to see the beautiful lake on his way down the valley from the high peaks above. For this was the Bhyundar valley, the famous 'Valley of Flowers'.

This state of affairs continued until an energetic and pious ex-soldier founded a society in Amritsar with the object of bringing the shrine to the notice of all good Sikhs.

Year by year the number of pilgrims grew and the type of *sadhu* changed. Hemkund was claimed as a shrine of the Sikhs exclusively. Once all the Hindu images were thrown into the lake. But the villagers were still more angered when a *sadhu* claimed the site at Gangria as of right and demanded a government grant for the building of a pilgrim rest-house there. He began to cultivate one and a half acres in the open forest without the permission of the government or, what was more important, the leave of the village headman, who complained to the Deputy Commissioner. The ex-soldier wrote a very polite letter of apology from Amritsar and the *sadhu* was replaced, but the encroachments went on.

Such was the position when, in 1941, the Japanese invaded Malaya and, in 1942, overran Burma.

One day in September 1943 a handsome young Sikh arrived in Badrinath. There he made enquiries about Hemkund, some twelve miles distant, and spent a lot of money. He filled one tin trunk entirely with foodstuffs, another with books of a kind suitable for deep religious study and meditation. When questioned, he said that he intended to spend the winter at Hemkund. There were plenty of people ready to point out that this was impossible as he would be frozen to death, but in this unworldly town it did not occur to anyone to question why he was carrying a large army pack and wearing an army greatcoat from whose shoulder flaps all insignia had been removed. It happened, too, that no official heard of his intention before he left Badrinath. In this matter Santan Singh was lucky. Before he left Badrinath he wrote to his Regimental Depot, informing the Commandant that he was taking the punishment for desertion into his own hands — he was going up into the mountains and would not return, it would be no use looking for him.

Santan Singh duly arrived at Punn at the end of October. The days were drawing in and the sheep were being driven down from the higher grazing grounds. At Punn he engaged local coolies and gave a feast. Two days later he set out for Hemkund. The villagers had reason to remember his tin trunks as they toiled up the steep and narrow path, changing loads frequently and stopping to smoke as often as they changed loads. The path climbed through a tangle of raw red limbs of creeping rhododendron bushes, through stunted silver birch and giant balsam, over boggy patches of black peat, up natural staircases of rock whose steps were irregularly and tiresomely spaced, through warm sweet-smelling *mamun* grass as slippery as a dance floor.

At thirteen thousand feet they emerged well above the treeline onto the fine *bugi* grass of the sheep grazing Alps. Here there was no true Alp but the gradient eased a little. Santan Singh, coming silently from behind a rock buttress, on the outer edge of which was a little sun-kissed shelf, put up three *monial*, handsomest and shyest of all the Himalayan pheasants. Whistling in alarm, they rocketted in all their peacock finery down to the trees two thousand feet below. Soon the grass gave way to loose scree and that, in turn, to boiler-plate slabs of rock, seamed with cracks in which grew a profusion of alpine plants, now tracing a pattern of autumn rust, which must have made a carpet of colour in the summer. They disturbed snow partridge and once Santan Singh saw a sturdy snowcock on the skyline. As he paused for breath, he looked north across the valley. A wall of red and white thrust up out of woolly white clouds against a sky of dazzling, burning blue. The snow clung at fantastic angles to the rock, whose strata were folded in almost unbelievable contortions. Fifteen miles away the perfect white cone of Nilkhanta rose clear above the intervening ridges. It was the most beautiful and awesome view he had ever seen.

When they reached the lake, Santan Singh performed some devotions: then, before paying off the men, he ostentatiously opened the trunk containing food and emptied it into the lake. As he had hoped, the villagers were more impressed by this gesture than by any number of assurances that he intended to stay up all winter in a state of *samadhi* or suspended animation. They took leave of him with every mark of respect.

When they had gone he sat down and considered again his plan. He would wait here perhaps for a week — he had enough food for about twelve days in his pack — to satisfy the possible curiosity of the villagers. Then, after throwing all his books, cooking pots and brazier into the lake, he would slip down past the village at night and so out into the world again, a free man. It was a good scheme, he could see no flaw in it. He had no qualms in using the knowledge gained quite by chance from that religious society in Amritsar, for his action would probably add merit and certainly add interest to the pilgrimage.

A week went by pleasantly. The sun was so warm by day and shone in a sky and atmosphere so clear and sharp that Santan Singh almost regretted that he would not be staying here for ever. The nights in the hut were cold but bearable, he had taken the precaution of having some charcoal carried up. When his coolies had asked him what he would do when this was exhausted, he had replied sternly that in a state of *samadhi* the body required no heat. From the smoke of their fires, which rose every evening from the valley far below, so far that he could not see any part of the valley floor, he could mark the progress of the shepherds driving their flocks down towards their permanent winter quarters.

When he could detect no sign of life in the valley, he decided it was time to put his plan into operation. His week had stretched to ten days — ten days of peaceful relaxation. He had not imagined that solitude could bring such balm. How different from the terrifying loneliness of the jungle from which he had just come. There men had been pressed into the wet and steaming earth all round him but their proximity had brought no comfort. The jungle was all very well for small men like Gurkhas and Japs, but it made a fool of a big man like himself. Santan Singh was not a coward. He had deserted for a number of reasons but fear of the enemy or of death was not one of them. It was the jungle warfare which had got him down — a kind of claustrophobia — that and the unsympathetic attitude to his weakness of a hard-boiled company commander. The British had been beaten; they might still win, though he doubted it. If the Japs reached the plains of India, he would stand with his brothers to defend his native land; that would be different.

Well, it was time to go; the weather, too, showed some signs of deteriorating. That evening a wind sprang up and the sky became overcast. He would leave the next day. The night was warmer than usual.

Next morning he woke with a sense of disquiet, it was 9 a.m., he had overslept for the first time. Everything was deathly still. When he went to open the door of the hut he realised there was something wrong. By using all his strength he succeeded in pushing it open a few inches. But he pulled it shut again in a hurry for a slurry of snow drove into his face. In a panic he lit the brazier and tried to recollect what he had heard about snow and its dangers. he remembered that the villagers had said that it never snowed for more than a week at a time and normally for only three or four days. If he husbanded his food carefully it would just last for another four days. The charcoal would not last that long but luckily he had thought of bringing a small spirit stove. At least he would be able to cook. How he was going to keep warm was another matter, but he did not have to think about that — yet — except to put out the brazier at once which he had lit without thinking. When he realised there was nothing he could do until it stopped snowing, he felt better. He set about getting himself a meal.

On the third night it stopped snowing and the sky glittered with the brilliance of the stars. It was bitterly cold. He had eked out his charcoal by burning it only at night. He had used up the last of his stove spirit. He must get away the next morning. Now he heaped up the last of his charcoal on the brazier.

Next morning he woke late with a headache brought on by the charcoal fumes. Frantically he set to work to complete his plans. The snow made his task more difficult but by 10 a.m. he had thrown all his possessions into the lake, breaking the ice to do so. As he hurled the books in, the title of one of them caught his eye, a copy of the Granth. He hesitated and then carefully set it aside on top of a flat boulder at the edge of the lake. Then he set out for the valley. He had only the iron rations he had saved for this journey.

In ten minutes he was lost. Wherever he struck out a fresh line of descent he came on a precipitous drop. Under the snow there were no familiar features; wearily he struggled upwards again. It was now after midday and the sun had thawed the new snow. At each step he sank up to his waist. The strips of sacking he had wound round his boots and ankles were soaked and clogging; he pulled them off. He had long since thrown aside his khaki greatcoat and with it his army pack. His hands were raw and painful. He had to rest for a long time now in each hole to recover his breath and the strength to struggle out again. Soon, he knew, he would not have the strength to get out at all. He had no idea where he was; the mountainside and sky swarm before his eyes. Suddenly, as he toiled, the hut rose up before him. With gasping sobs he floundered the last few feet and collapsed inside. By the time he recovered he was already cold and stiff. He crawled into the doorway and sat in the sun. he had no food left, the rations he had saved for the journey lay in his pack, somewhere down the mountainside.

That night he was too cold to sleep. Somehow he forced his weary legs to obey his will and keep him moving until the early morning when out of sheer exhaustion he fell into an uneasy doze. He woke as soon as the sun reached the hut. The morning was fine and incredibly beautiful, but it hurt him to look at it. The snow was hard and crisp but he could not step out onto it. He had taken off his boots as they were wet through; now they were hard and stiff. he worked on them desperately with his hands, cursing the sun as it leapt high in the heavens.

He realised, if not with the clarity of a mountaineer, that he was facing the final crisis. He looked at the sky which glared back at him but revealed nothing, not a cloud, not a sign. Away, over the valley the sentinel peaks stook guard over him, the shoulders of the mountains above pressed down on him on both sides of the lake. His eye fell on the little book he had put aside; he picked it up and sat down on the granite boulder by the edge of the lake. Idly he started to turn the pages but it hurt his eyes to read. He put the book down and tried to concentrate on his own dilemma. He must start at once or he would never start at all. But he had no food and his eyes were throbbing painfully. The snow dazzled him and he had no glasses. Only the little lake was restful. The ice had gone and a light breeze was rippling the surface. If he turned away from it the glare hurt. Better, then, to wait till the evening. Suddenly he felt very tired, the quiet and peace laid its spell on him and he slept.

When he awoke the sun seemed just as high, the glare, if anything, more painful. When he looked away from the lake it was as if a thousand red hot needles were pricking his eyeballs. He turned back at once to look at the lake and started. Fifty yards away by the edge of the water sat a man cross-legged, naked save for a loincloth. He was reading from a book. His beard and the black hair swept up into a knot on top of his head proclaimed him a Sikh For a long time he gazed but the figure never stirred. He rose uncertainly and walked towards the holy man. When he was ten yards away from him he stopped and brushed the back of his hand across his eyes. When he looked again the stranger was looking directly at him. His eyes burnt like two fiery coals. Santan Singh could not look at them, neither could he turn away. Everything else grew dim but out of those two glowing coals a voice spoke:

'Why have you come here?'

'I have come to find god and peace,' muttered Santan Singh.

There was a pause, Santan Singh covered his face with his hands:

'It is good; thou shalt find both,' the voice replied.

Santan Singh advanced towards the *guru*, arms outstretched. There was no longer any pain behind his eyes, nor any sight within them.

Next morning the sun rose again in a cloudless sky, the snow sparkled as brilliantly, the snowy peaks dreamed over the valley. The ragged pennant fluttered over the little hut and the wavelets lapped against the foot of the big granite boulder as they had done for thousands of years.

Down below in the village the headman sat down with a very

ancient pen to write a report to the *patwari* of the birth of a son
to Chandan Singh — if it had been a daughter he would not have
bothered. His son helped him spell the words letter by letter. When
he had done he cleaned the nib in his hair. Slowly he looked up
towards Hemkund. High above the lake a snow banner was
streaming off the jagged tip of a rock pinnacle.

'Should we go and see, father?'

The old man shook his head:

'No man can reach Lokhpal now till the spring. He is dead or has
joined the gods. I must report this too.' And he turned again to the
paper before him and wrote laboriously.

When the spring came a party of villagers went up with the headman's son. They found his greatcoat and beside it his pack, but no
sign of Santan Singh. The hut was empty; also the tin trunk which
had held his books. Near the edge of the lake on a flat boulder, they
found a book placed carefully with a marker in it, as if someone
had just put it down after reading. The headman's son opened the
book at the marker and read. There was a sentence underlined; it
read as follows: —

'When thy stewardship is ended, thou must render an account.'

When they returned the headman called a meeting of the whole
village to hear the search party's report. After a lengthy and serious
discussion they reached their unanimous conclusion. The headman's further report to the *patwari* summed it up: —

'We have had our disputes in the past with these Sikhs but now
it is my duty to report that great honour has befallen our village
and our lake on their account. None other than the great saint,
Guru Govind Singh himself, has been amongst us. He returned to
spend the winter at Hemkund, but now he has vanished again. I
have proof. Kesar Singh, Chandan Singh and other villagers carried his food and his books up in October — but now nothing remains. The food he threw away before their eyes. We have found
a greatcoat and a pack containing food — untouched — and
besides these only a book which the *pandit* says is a copy of the
Sikh Granth. The Saint himself never came down — he has just
disappeared — a great mystery and a great honour . . . .'.

The legend of Lokhpal had been enriched even more dramatically than Santan Singh had intended.

SNOW TIGER

Havildar Bir Singh was a pensioner of the Royal Garhwal Rifles and one of the most important men in his own village. Lying at 8,500 ft. in a remote side valley of upper Garhwal, Binaik was one of the highest inhabited villages on the frontiers of the uninhabitable snows. Directly above the village rose the 13,000 ft. Rudradhar and beyond this a complex of still higher ridges running up to the Great Himalayan Range and the massive bastion of the four-square mountain Chaukhamba, 23,420 ft. above sea-level. Thick forests ran down the southern slopes of the Rudradhar to within a hundred yards of the village.

When Bir Singh came home in October 1943 after a visit to the sub-divisional headquarters where he had gone to draw his pension, he was informed that two women had been killed in the last week while out cutting grass in the forest. Both had been alone and their remains had not been discovered until the day following their disappearance. This was the season when the grass was ripening; it was also a busy season in the fields and the village women often started out late in the afternoon to cut grass and did not return till after dark. A part of each body had been eaten which seemed to rule out the possibility of their having been attacked by a bear. It was rare for a bear to touch the flesh of any human it had killed; when it did, it would not leave a morsel for any scavenger, for a bear is a jealous and greedy animal.

The village headman issued an order that no-one should stay out late and that no woman should go to the forest alone. In the week following Bir Singh's return a third woman was killed in broad daylight. She had ignored the order and gone alone. Some men, who were working near, heard her screams. Armed only with light lopping axes they ran to the spot but were not in time to see the killer, the noise they made having scared him off his kill. They found the dead women in the rocky bed of a ravine. Bir Singh, recognised by all as the best *shikari* in the village, had given orders that, if anyone else was killed, the body was not to be moved until he had seen it. So, while the rest guarded the corpse, two men were sent back to inform the woman's husband and Bir Singh.

45

As soon as the news was known, consternation reigned in the village and the panic soon spread to neighbouring villages. Word quickly went round that there was a man-eating leopard in the valley. Memories of the dread man-eater of Rudraprayag revived, of the dusk curfew and barred doors and windows. But now was an added terror, for who had ever heard of a leopard attacking human beings without provocation by day? Yet who questioned it was a leopard which was responsible? They knew of no other carnivore in the high hills which could turn man-eater.

Only Bir Singh had doubts. He remembered something that had happened ten years before. A tigress had come into the valley with two cubs. She had been sick but this did not seem to be a sufficient reason for her straying so far from normal tiger country. It had been a ten days' wonder for she died soon after while the cubs were still small. It was found she had been almost stone blind of cataract in both eyes. One cub had been killed almost at once, the other disappeared and was never seen or heard of again.

Bir Singh began to form a theory. He thought that the cub which had disappeared might have become injured or diseased in its old age and have returned to the area where it had first learnt to find its own food. Animals had very strong memories. It had, perhaps remembered the hunting as easy, for the local forests had then been full of game and had not known any tigers till they came. But its memory would have played it false, for now there was very little game left in the valley, thanks to indiscriminate slaughter by too many licence-holders in the period before the war. At this season, too, what few cattle there were had been brought in from the forest steadings because of the increasing cold, while the sheep had not yet descended from the higher grazing grounds above the tree-line. It would be too cold up there and, besides, there was no cover for a tiger. An old, perhaps an injured tiger, little game and difficult ground − the combination could perhaps explain a man-eater.

It had already been decided, after a hasty conference, that the whole village should turn out next day to drive the man-eater out of their valley and messages had been sent to other villages for assistance. This step had been agreed before Bir Singh had remembered about the tigress and her two cubs. If he was right about this, it would be as well that everyone should know that it was a tiger they had to deal with, not a leopard. He called the husband of the latest victim and asked him to leave the body where it was until he had made a reconnaissance. Bir Singh was trusted; the man reluctantly agreed.

Bir Singh took down his old single barrel hammer gun and

looked it over. It was a prized and faithful servant. He had bought it in Moradabad ten years ago from a local gunsmith. Unless you examined it very carefully indeed, you would have taken it for an imported English weapon, so closely had it been copied. When he had cleaned it and tested the action, he ate a light meal and then set out, taking, besides his gun, only a small leather bag of cartridges, a long shawl, a small deerskin mat and a *kukri*. The cartridges were precious lethal ball, his last three, jealously hoarded.

On his way he met the men, who had been guarding the woman's body, returning to the village. Although they had heard and seen nothing during their vigil, they had become afraid to stay any longer. They tried to persuade Bir Singh to return to the village with them, but he refused. He was relieved to find that they had obeyed his general instruction and the husband's agreement, conveyed to them by a special messenger, and had left the woman's body where she had been killed.

It was late afternoon when he reached the site of the kill. He approached cautiously up-wind and waited and listened for a long time before emerging from the cover of the trees out onto the edge of the ravine. The woman's body was lying at the junction of two ravines, the larger on which he was now standing, and a much narrower and very much steeper one which entered the other opposite him. This small ravine was like a dark funnel thrusting up towards the ridge. After a few yards the forest closed completely over it. He decided at once that this was the way by which the killer would return.

Everything was still. he measured the distance to the body by eye and then moved quietly to the rock he had selected to sit against for his lonely vigil. This was on his own or lower side of the main ravine, directly opposite the junction with the smaller ravine and 30 yards from the corpse. He had taken this exposed position by deliberate choice. His one experience of sitting up all night in the fork of a tree had taught him not to repeat it. There was no time, single-handed, to build a platform in the nearest suitable tree and the noise might scare the killer away or — more frightening thought — attract it before he was ready.

He sat on the ground on his mat with his back to the rock. In front of him at about knee height was a boulder which formed a convenient rest for the muzzle of his gun. From where he sat and without moving his position he could cover all the open ground between him and the body and between the body and the tree-shaded mouth of the smaller ravine. He placed the *kukri* beside him; his gun was already loaded. He placed another lethal ball

handy and wished fervently that he had a second barrel in which
to load it. If he missed with his first shot he would be lucky if he
had time to re-load. Wrapped in his dark oatmeal coloured shawl,
his khaki balacalava pulled over most of his face, he would be
hardly distinguishable from the rock against which he was sitting.
There he awaited the fall of dusk. He had a feeling that, if he was
right and it was a tiger, it would come before the last daylight had
gone. It had not had time to eat any of its victim, it would be
hungry, it might arrive any moment.

Two hours passed. At first there were sounds. Some men were
felling trees across the valley, the sound of the axe blows came ring-
ing dully. Now and again he heard the men's voices though he
could not make out what they were saying. After half an hour they
moved off. There were birds chattering in the undergrowth; a scold
of *seven sisters* dropped out of the forest behind him onto the soft
dust at the edge of the ravine, a babbling catherine wheel of grey.
Their antics were meaningless to him but he was glad to note that
they ignored his presence. Presently a long-spurred Kalij pheasant
came skulking by, so intent on turning over the leaves that it never
noticed him. Scufflings in the forest behind him betrayed the
presence of others. A troop of langur monkeys came crashing
through the tree tops like a sudden squall.

Gradually all sounds ceased, until he was aware only of the
sound of silence. The whole jungle was holding its breath, waiting
tense and expectant. The noise of his own heart beats pounded in
his ears, sounding a tocsin of fear. The sound of a single leaf falling
onto the stones of the ravine startled him; it was as loud as the noise
of a body landing on the rounded surface of a boulder, as sinister
as a stealthy footfall betrayed by a dry twig breaking.

He felt fear. What was he doing here? he had heard that man-
eaters chose human flesh because they wee not ordinary animals at
all but human beings transformed during the hours of darkness. He
had also heard that man-eaters circled their kills before returning
to them; the tiger might come out behind him. He fought these fears
resolutely as the evening started to close in. Towards dusk the chill
began to strike up from below into his bones despite the mat. Worse
still, a sudden storm blew up, in a moment he was soaked. All he
could protect was the breech of his gun and the precious cartridges.
The storm blew over as quickly as it had come. Bir Singh prayed that
he would not have to wait much longer. The ravine opposite him was
now a dark cavern and, though the main ravine crossing his front
seemed lighter again after the storm, he judged it would only be light
enough to see for about another quarter of an hour.

The quarter of an hour passed. Bir Singh was debating as to whether it would be possible to identify the animal if it came now — the main object of his reconnaissance — and, if it did not come soon, whether he would be taking an unreasonable risk to go home in the dark, when he heard the sound of a single stone dislodged some way up the ravine opposite.

The killer was coming — it could only be a matter of minutes. He leant forward slowly and took a sight along his gun. To his consternation he could no longer pick out the woman's body; he should have taken the precaution of placing a whitened stone beside it. One or two more stones were displaced — then silence. Bir Singh knew this moment, knew that it was no use straining the eyes because that only made one imagine a living shape out of the pattern of undergrowth or the mosaic of rocks. The moment of suspense was agonisingly prolonged and then, suddenly, rather as he suspected would happen, he was aware that an animal had arrived in front of him and was standing on the far edge of the main ravine. He sensed only that it was a large animal, he could not see it clearly, far less identify it.

What was he to do? After all his trouble he had no proof. If it had come by daylight, he had intended to kill it. Now it was too dark to shoot; only a lucky shot would kill or cripple and without that luck he might be killed himself. He thought of the dead woman's husband who had trusted him. Though no word had been said between them, he recognised his obligation to deny her body to the scavengers of the night, to the killer too, if he could stop him. He had arranged, with the headman's approval, that six men should stand by with a string cot. If they head a single shot, that would be the signal, either that he had killed the man-eater, or that it had not put in an appearance and they were to come at once. If they heard two shots in quick succession, it would mean that he had missed or only wounded the animal and were not to come; he would have to find his own way back with only one cartridge for his protection, a hazard he would deserve for his poor marksmanship. But, the situation was different to any he had envisaged. If he stayed, he would be helpless in the dark, a blind witness of a nocturnal feast he could not prevent and in very great danger himself. But, if he moved now, he would betray his presence and the man-eater's reaction was unpredictable; he would be entirely at its mercy. He thought of the men waiting for his signal. As he had not returned by dark, they might think he had met with an accident or had been killed himself by the man-eater and might come to look for him despite his instructions. And then came another thought —

would he be able to sit still there while the man-eater ate his fill of
the pitiful remains? And he knew that he would not be able, that
he would soon be paralysed by cramps, that he was already nearing
the limits of his endurance. He was an elderly man sitting in wet
clothes. The temptation came to him to fire a shot merely to scare
away the man-eater. His hand crept up the stock.

It was at this moment that he realised that the moon, now in its
third quarter, was coming up; already it subtle irridescence was
flooding the ridge above him. A few seconds more and it would be
shining full on the tiger — if it was a tiger and if it would wait.
Hardly had he realised this when the moon cleared the canopy of
trees behind him and shone full on the ravine in front. What the
moonlight revealed left him more frightened and perplexed than
what the darkness had concealed. It shone full on an animal too
large to be a leopard and yet like no tiger he had ever seen in the
life or in representations. He beat back his fear of the supernatural
and started to study the animal carefully. He thought it was a male
and full grown, possibly old. It had a very pale coat, it looked
almost white, but that may have been a trick of the moonlight. It
turned its head in his direction and there was a gleam of ice-cold
green from one of the great cat's eyes. His own side of the ravine
was still in deep shadow, the beast seemed quite unaware of his
presence. Yet, it seemed odd to him that it should stand there motionless for so long, in such a conspicuous position, right out in the
moonlight. His doubts returned — was it an animal at all?

One thing was certain — it made a tempting target. Bir Singh
was a sensible level-headed man; he had also been a crack shot in
his day. There ensued within him a battle between fear and ambition, between commonsense, which he thought of as cowardice,
and an old expert's conceit. Bir Singh's mind grappled with these
niceties only in the sub-conscious; when recounting how he solved
his dilemma, he used the direct words and simple language one
would expect of a fighting soldier.

All that he had ever heard of man-eaters disturbed on their kills,
of their behaviour when surprised or wounded, especially tigers,
spelt danger. And danger, not only for himself, but for others as
well if he only wounded the animal. But war, too, was dangerous
and one did not run away from that. Here was a new enemy; it was
his duty, then, to destroy him. The enemy target also presented a
challenge to his skill. This animal's destruction would provide a
story on which he could dine out, so to speak, for years. With a
tremendous effort of will he put out of his mind the thought that,
if he failed, it would be the tiger which would dine out.

Although it had seemed so long, only a few seconds had passed since the moon had taken a hand in the game. The animal took a step forward. Bir Singh sensed that it was about to spring on its kill. He had perhaps only a few seconds left in which to act. His left hand was already in position, cushioning the barrel on its rock rest; his finger started to close on the trigger, but now he no longer intended to fire a shot in the air. Round the muzzle of his gun as he aimed, the white marking round one eye made a clear and tempting target. With a silent prayer to his family god he pulled the trigger. The whole mountainside seemed to be falling on him in a shattering avalanche of sound; the man-eater dropped in its tracks, shot through the eye and brain.

He re-loaded and waited, reluctant to use another of his precious ball cartridges. The animal never moved. Cautiously he rose and approached nearer. When he was near enough he threw a stone at the animal's body; it never stirred. Satisfied now, he went up to it, his gun still at the ready. When he was sure it was dead he started to examine it. It was a tiger and a big one too. But its coat was so pale that he could understand why he had thought it to be white in the moonlight.

He heard men approaching and called to them. When they reached him and saw the dead tiger they started to talk excitedly:

'It is a snow leopard,' said one of them.

The others poured scorn on his suggestion but were cautious about proposing an alternative.

'It is a tiger,' said Bir Singh, 'the cub that escaped ten years ago.' he spoke with assurance:

'How are you so certain?' they asked.

Bir Singh unloaded his gun and then prodded the tiger with the butt:

'Because it has come back here, one hundred and seventy miles from tiger country, where no other tiger had come since it came with its brother cub and blind mother. Also I believe it was blind in one eye, the eye that was turned towards me. But I have no proof because my shot has destroyed that eye.'

THE BLOOD FEUD OF THE BISHTS

Naik Govind Singh Bisht stood stiffly to attention before his Commandant in the Military Police Barracks in Rangoon. Govind Singh was a hill Rajput from the district of Garhwal in India. Like many of his fellow hillmen there had been only a poor prospect of a decent livelihood for him at home. He had joined the Burma Military Police at the age of twenty six. Now, in June 1941, after seven years' service, he had applied for voluntary discharge for 'private and family reasons'.

The Commandant, sizing up the man in front of him, ruled out the likelihood of any service grievance. Govind Singh was a good policeman, he must try to dissuade him, though he had no great hopes of success:

'Well, Govind Singh, some trouble at home, eh?'

Yes, Sahib.'

There was a slight pause but Govind Singh offered no further information. The Commandant, trying not to sound persuasive, said in a matter of fact voice:

'I see you are due for promotion next month and should have a fine career before you in the Police. If I gave you long leave couldn't you settle matters at home and then return to us?'

Though the news of imminent promotion was a surprise, Govind Singh's face betrayed no sign of any emotion. The Commandant had not expected any. He knew that this was not only the drill of discipline and tradition, but also a protective pose, a silent declaration that the applicant was not to be diverted from his purpose by flattery or temptation.

'Thank you, Sahib, but I have no choice; things are such that I must go home for good.'

The Commandant did not press him further:

'Very well, Govind Singh, I suppose I must let you go. But, remember, if you would care to send a suitable young man from your village or, better still, your own son, I shall be glad to accept him in the Police.'

'Very good, Sahib — thank you, Sahib.'

The Commandant got up, came round the table and shook hands

with Govind Singh, who smiled for the first time. Then, springing to attention again, he took two paces to the rear, saluted smartly, turned about and marched resolutely out of the life and service which he had no real desire to leave. He was answering a call stronger than any ties of service or temptation of promotion.

As he watched him go the Commandant thought: 'Poor devil, I bet he is going back to a packet of trouble in some miserable dirty village. But no doubt his priorities are right by his own standards. I only hope he will be able to retain some of his self-respect and of the standards he has learnt in the Police.'

As he travelled home Govind Singh thought bitterly about the trouble at home which had forced him to give up his career in the police. It was scarcity of land which had led him to seek his livelihood away from home and it was this same scarcity which had been the cause of all the bad feelings and violence between the Padyar Bishts — his own sub-clan — and the Dosadh Bishts in his village, Deosari. The quarrel had started eight years ago when his father, Pancham Singh, had cultivated some waste land but Partab Singh Dosadh had managed to get it recorded in his own name in the land settlement. He still remembered vividly his father's black anger and how his elder brother, Lal Singh, had sought out Partab Singh and given him a good thrashing. After he had left the village the Dosadhs alleged, though it was never proved and he did not believe it, that Partab Singh's mother was killed, tied up in a sack and thrown into the river Pindar below Deosari. Later he heard that his own father, Pancham Singh, had been burnt to death in his cowshed. He was told that the Dosadhs had done this in revenge. In April 1941 his elder brother, Lal Singh, was killed. It was said that he had been inveigled to join a gang of lawless men in Deosari and then betrayed to the villagers of Sawar across the river who caught him red-handed in an attempted burglary and beat him to death with *lalthis*. He had been fond of his brother but had to admit, at least to himself, that he had not been the right sort of person to succeed their father as leader of the Padyars — he was far too headstrong and unpredictable. What they needed was a man of authority and good sense. His own family had held the leadership since the time of his great grandfather. Lal Singh's death had left Govind with the best claim to take over and he had accepted the responsibility on appeals from his relatives and friends. His aim was to try and stop the feud between the Padyars and the Dosadhs.

He realised it would not be easy. The Padyars were angry and had a score to settle; the Dosadhs were completely under the sway of their acknowledged leader, Partab Singh, a man some ten years older than himself. Partab was rather an unpleasant character, unscrupulous, vindictive, clever and a born intriguer. He was very influential and had the support of the local officials; the combination made him a dangerous enemy.

Govind himself was a much simpler and more straight-forward man, rather strong-willed and overbearing, who feared no-one. He was related by marriage to a retired Subedar-Major who was the doyen of all the military pensioners of the Royal Garhwal Rifles who had been given grants of land in reward for their services and who were settled in considerable numbers on what had once been the Talwari and Gwaldam tea estates near Deosari. This connection was a useful counter-weight to Partab's pull with the *patwari* and the headman. On his retirement Govind brought with him a certificate of exemplary conduct in the Burma Military Police, a shotgun for which he had not yet acquired a licence and familiarity with the use of weapons.

At first, when he got home, he was fully occupied with domestic affairs. His house and one cowshed needed repairs and, by the time these were completed, the harvest season had arrived. By then he had fully established himself as the leader of the Padyars and had persuaded them to avoid any further provocation of the Dosadhs. It was not till October that he applied for a licence to regularise his possession of a shotgun. This was refused on an adverse report from the *patwari*, the headman and the local forest guard that he had been poaching regularly in the Government Reserve Forest to supply all his relatives and friends with game. He had done so only once, for a special occasion, the feast to celebrate the marriage of a niece and was furious at this misrepresentation of the truth. He considered he had a better claim than many of the existing licence holders, including Partab himself. He was not the man to take this rebuff lying down; he continued to use his gun openly while his petition to the Deputy Commissioner for reconsideration of his claim was still under enquiry. The Dosadhs feared him and made a series of complaints alleging his high-handedness, his continued use of an unlicensed gun and his intimidation of families other than Padyars in that part of the village where he lived.

His training in the police influenced him to reply to these charges by petitioning the higher authorities to intervene and make local enquiries. But his representations were ignored and his appeal for a gun licence was refused. From that moment his laudable ambition to stop the feuding was replaced by a resolve to get even with Partab. He relaxed his strict control over the Padyars and persuaded some of his influential friends to lodge complaints against the *patwari* and ask for his transfer.

The bickering continued for three years without anything more serious happening than a few brawls arising out of deliberate grazing of cattle on each other's fields. The lay-out of Deosari lent itself to such hostilities. The village was built on four levels, the houses on each level being strung out in a line following the contours of the mountainside. Down below, five hundred feet above the Pindar river, was the main village where the headman and the *patwari* lived; above that was a cluster of mean huts where the artisans and menials lived; then came Seragad Tok, the stronghold of the Dosadhs. Highest of all, at 6,000 ft., on the edge of the Reserve Forest was Giwain Bhur Tok, dominated by the Padyars, where Govind lived. The cultivated terraces above Seragad Tok were owned by the Dosadhs, those below Giwain Bhur Tok by the Padyars. There was no physical boundary between them except for the terrace walls and two paths running up from the main village gave access to all the fields.

In March 1945, Govind came to know that Partab had recently bought an unlicensed shotgun for nineteen rupees from a widow in Talaur village through the services of Netra Singh, Jemadar forest guard, who was married to Partab's niece, and that Partab intended to plant this gun in one of Govind's cowsheds. When his appeal for a licence had been finally turned down, Govind had hidden his own gun. He reported Partab's plan at once to the Sub-Divisional Magistrate and alerted his own friends and relatives to keep a close watch on all his property.

Four days after sending this very circumstantial report, Govind was called out of his house by the *patwari* and headman, who were accompanied by a small party including Partab and his cousin Bahadur and two of the most respectable landowners of the nearby village of Sarkot. They took him to one of his cowsheds and there recovered a gun hidden in the roof. He protested to the two independent witnesses that this was a plot arranged by Partab Dosadh, but they said it was not their business to decide who was telling the truth. Govind was deeply mortified at the success of his enemy despite his precautions. The fact was that the gun had already been planted before he came to know of the plot and the delay in framing him was only due to the inability of the two neutral witnesses selected to attend the recovery any earlier.

Two days later, following a tip-off, Govind's brother-in-law, Man Singh, was stopped and searched as he crossed the border from Almora district. He was found in possession of twenty shotgun cartridges which he had just bought illegally in Almora

bazaar. He had no gun himself. It was immediately assumed by his
enemies that the cartridges were for use in Govind's gun. Govind
and Man Singh were hurriedly prosecuted under section 19 of the
Arms Act. Govind was faced with a dilemma. It was fairly common knowledge that he had owned a gun, though he was confident
that no-one would be able to prove he still possessed or used it. If
he produced his own gun, this would support his contention that
the one recovered had been planted, for no-one in his senses would
acquire a second gun if he had been unable to obtain a licence even
for one. But if he produced his own gun he was certain to be prosecuted for still possessing an unlicensed weapon. He decided to rely on being able to prove that he had been framed. In the event it
was the wrong decision.

Before the case came up for hearing, Man Singh said to Govind:

'We shall get no justice in the Sub-Divisional Magistrate's court;
I suggest we take direct action ourselves to teach these Dosadhs a
lesson.'

But Govind was not yet prepared to take the law into his own
hands, his training in the police still counted for something. Govind
had no particular liking for Man Singh who had married his sister
while he was away in Burma. If he had been at home he would have
tried to prevent the marriage. Man Singh was a very powerful
young man, a bully and possessed an ungovernable temper.

At the first hearing of the case in Chamoli, the Sub-Divisional
headquarters, Govind referred the magistrate to the report he had
sent him before the gun was recovered. But the magistrate made it
plain that he placed no reliance in Govind's report, holding it to be
an attempt to explain away in advance the fact pretty widely
known that he did possess an unauthorised gun. It was further
represented by the prosecution that he was a dangerous character.
He was only released on bail after great delay. Man Singh was given
the same treatment. By this time Govind was thoroughly embit-
tered, which probably explained his next and very rash action. As
soon as he was released on bail he sought out the *patwari* and said
pointedly:

'I shall not forget your part in this conspiracy. If you continue
to support Partab Singh in his intrigue, remember that I have a gun
which you have not yet recovered.'

The *patwari* immediately reported that Govind had threatened
his life. Govind was called back to the court, his bail cancelled and
he spent another twenty-two days in the lock-up before he could
produce sureties to the satisfaction of the Sub-Divisional
Magistrate.

So far, events had followed a fairly common pattern with the odds heavily loaded against the man who had incurred the emnity of the local officials. But now events took a violent and dramatic turn.

Govind was consumed with a burning sense of grievance. On the 2nd of May, just before the second hearing of the case, fixed for the 4th of May at Chamoli, Man Singh came to Govind's house in the morning and said:

'Listen, I have discovered that the Dosadhs are planning, as soon as the case is called, to complain that we have turned our cattle loose again on their fields. Is it not clear that they hope that the magistrate will cancel our bail and send us back to the lock-up? Partab and Bahadur have gone ahead to arrange all this with a lawyer.'

'We must find a way to prevent them,' said Govind angrily. 'I have a plan' said Man Singh. 'I have learnt from a *Pasi* who is employed to cut grass for his pony, that Netra Singh, Jemadar forest guard, and his wife are going this evening to stay with Partab's wife and daughter in Seragad Tok while he is away in Chamoli. We can go down to Partab's house under cover of darkness, lure Netra Singh outside on pretext of a message from Partab and dispose of him without the women knowing anything about it. We could kill and throw him down the first terrace below Partab's house in such a way that it would appear at first sight that he had fallen over the edge in the dark and broken his neck. Then we can start out with our sureties very early tomorrow, as already arranged, and join the *patwari's* party before the news of the Jemadar's death can reach Chamoli. If we attend in court, no-one will suspect us of having killed Netra Singh. Moreover, when the news does reach Chamoli, it is likely that Partab and Bahadur, alarmed for the safety of their womenfolk, will hasten back to Deosari, abandoning their plot to get our bail cancelled. If so, the case itself may have to be adjourned as they are key witnesses to the recovery of the planted gun.'

Govind had a particular grudge against the forest guard. His report that Govind was poaching in the Reserve Forest was largely responsible for his having been refused an arms licence. If this had been granted, his enemies would have been deprived of the opportunity of framing him under the Arms Act. The temptation to avenge himself and at the same time defeat Partab's latest alleged intrigue tipped the scales already evenly balanced in his mind between reason and emotion. Without bothering to question Man Singh further on the source of his information, he agreed to the proposal.

On the evening of 2nd May Chandri *tamta*, a blacksmith who lived in the *shilpkar* hamlet of Deosari, went up to Seragad Tok to return four *kurpis* (hoes with short handles) and three *darantis* (sickles), which he had mended and sharpened for Partab Singh Dosadh. The reason why he chose to do this at night was because he had learnt by experience that if he called at night he was given a good meal. He was not disappointed this time either. Partab's wife, Shrimati Guzri, gave him some of the meal she had prepared for Netra Singh Jemadar and his wife and grumbled that they had not come though expected long before dark. As it transpired later, Netra Singh had been unexpectedly delayed and planned to go to Deosari the next day instead.

When he had finished his meal, Chandri left Partab's house. He had almost crossed the courtyard when a voice called out of the dark in a friendly tone:

'Is that you Jemadar Sahib?'

'No,' he replied, 'it is I, Chandri *tamta*.'

'What are you doing here?' The voice was now hostile and suspicious.

Chandri was frightened and, as lying came to him more naturally than telling the truth, he said:

'I am just on my way to Bahadur Singh's house to collect some *darantis* to sharpen.'

'You are lying; this is not the way you would come to Bahadur's house from your home; also this is not a reasonable time to be on such an errand. You are up to some mischief — thieving no doubt while the menfolk are away.'

The voice was now quite close and he could see the shadow of a man. He made a move to run away, upon which a second voice said:

'Stay where yuou are, or I shoot.'

Chandri stood terrified. The two men came up. He was seized by an arm and the man who had first spoken said in a fierce harsh voice:

'Do as I order you and you will come to no harm. Now — listen carefully. You will go up to Partab's house and call to Netra Singh Jemadar to come out. You will say that you have an urgent message for him from Partab and that the womenfolk are not to be disturbed.'

'But the Jemadar is not there,' Chandri blurted out and at once regretted his indiscretion:

'How do you know? You are lying again; we know he is there.'

Chandri did not dare to argue the point further.

'Now, do as I have ordered you; I will be behind you with this, so try no tricks. Now, move,' and Chandri felt a steel point prick his back. Petrified with fear he moved towards Partab's door. He had not recognised the two men yet but he thought he knew the voice of the man behind him. If he was right and it was Man Singh Padyar, he had every reason to be frightened. Man Singh had the reputation of being violent and ruthless. If he had told the truth in the first instance they might have believed him when he said the Jemadar was not there. Arrived outside the door, he called out as bidden but his voice was weak and quavering with fear. He felt a sharp jab in his back and the voice behind him hissed:

'Louder — and speak with confidence.'

He called again — they must have heard that inside. There was a pause and then someone came to the door and a woman's voice called:

'Who is it — is it you Jemadar-ji?'

Chandri felt the man holding his arm stiffen; he heard the other man come up and start to pull his companion away from the door. But Man Singh, if it was he — and he was now almost certain it was — resisted. He heard the other man whisper angrily:

'You fool, we must get away at once, we cannot risk being recognised by the woman.'

There was no answer and in that moment the door opened and Shrimati Guzri stood in the doorway with a lantern. She recognised Chandri but probably not the man hiding behind him. Before he could get out of the light she recognised the other man:

'Govind Singh,' she screamed and turned to run inside and slam the door. But Man Singh was too quick for her. Pushing Chandri aside, he sprang into the doorway and, before she could put the bar across, pushed the door open. She threw the lantern in his face. He warded it off with his left arm and leapt at her brandishing his *kukri*.

Ignoring Chandri, Govind ran into the house after Man Singh, shouting. Chandri did not stop to see more. He ran all the way home but did not stop there. He was so terrified that he hid all night in a remote sheep shed. Next morning he left hurriedly with his family to stay with a cousin in Almora, where he remained until the end of June.

There was no eye witness of what happened inside Partab Singh's house.

Earlier that evening, Bahadur Singh's wife asked Lachchman Singh, a boy of sixteen, to call Kharak Singh, Partab's brother-in-law to help him make some butter. She gave the boy the *rora* (butter churning stick). Kharak lived in the main village so he went down there to give the message and together they went to Lachchman's house where Kharak made the butter while Lachchman made himself a meal and some tea for Kharak. After dark they set out for Bahadur's house in Seragad Tok. Kharak went in front carrying the *rora* in one hand, a lighted pine torch in the other. Lachchman followed behind carrying the butter. Their path lay through Partab's courtyard. Kharak had just reached the courtyard which was above Partab's house when there was a loud report. The pellets hit him in the chest but luckily he was only superficially wounded. He lifted his torch up high and shouted his own name to identify himself, thinking that someone had fired out of nervousness, taking him to be a thief.

Meanwhile Lachchman had come up and by the light of the torch they both recognised Govind and Man Singh, the former holding a gun and the latter a naked *kukri*. Instead of attacking them the two men ran away. Kharak started to chase them but, perhaps luckily for him, he tripped and fell, dropping the torch which went out and the two men escaped in the dark.

When he rejoined the boy Kharak said his wounds were becoming very painful and his chest was covered with blood. Before they went on to Bahadur's house he must re-light his torch and also, if possible, stop the bleeding. Then he found he had forgotten to bring any matches. Partab's house was directly opposite them. They went up to it and found, to their surprise, that the door was open. There was no light inside but they could see some dying embers in the fire. They called from the doorway but there was no reply. So they went inside, Kharak first while Lachchman put the butter down in the yard and covered it with the cotton sheet he had been wearing as a shawl round his shoulders. Lachchman was carrying his shoes, he preferred to walk barefoot at all times but more especially in the dark as he could feel the irregularities in the path better with his bare feet than in clumsy shoes. As he crossed the threshold his bare foot slipped on something wet and sticky. he rubbed his finger on the spot and cautiously put it on the end of his tongue. He tasted blood and spat it out: Kharak must be more seriously wounded than he made out. Kharak told him to close and bar the door and put the heavy door stone against it. While he was doing this, Kharak blew on the embers to coax them back into life so that he could re-light his torch. As he found blowing painful with his wounds, Lachchman took it over while Kharak discussed the mystery of the empty house. He came to the conclusion that the womenfolk must have gone to Bahadur's wife for company, or perhaps at her request as she was alone in her house. But no-one in their senses left their door open when they went out at night and this still remained unexplained. Kharak instructed the boy, as soon as he had got a light going, to try and find some water and a suitable piece of cloth, so that they could wash and bandage his wounds. As he lifted his torch higher to show the boy his way further into the room Kharak cried out in horror:

'They have been killed.'

Quickly he opened the door and taking the torch ran out into the night. Lachchman was so frightened he ran and hid behind a big straw bin in a corner of the room. There he stayed all night, too terrified to leave or to sleep. Once or twice he heard noises but kept quite still and quiet. The rats had come out to investigate.

By first light he saw Partab's wife, Shrimati Guzru and his daughter Mahadevi, a girl of his own age, lying in the room with their throats cut. Mahadevi's head had almost been severed; in one hand she still grasped a blood-stained *daranti*. He ran out of the room. There were bloody footprints all over the courtyard and bloody handmarks on the mud plaster round the doorway of the house. It appeared that the mother had been killed at once as she had only the one deep wound in her neck. But the girl's body and arms were covered with deep cuts — it seems she had put up a terrific fight for her life after her mother had been killed inside the house.

Lachchman ran down to Kharak's house and found him eventually lying in his cowshed. His wounds had stiffened and he was in great pain. he asked for some fresh water but Lachchman was too frightened to go to the spring. Instead he gave him some stale water from his own house. Eventually the boy summoned up enough courage to go back to Seragad Tok. He called first at Bahadur's house expecting to find that his wife had also been murdered. Great was his relief to find her still alive. He told her what had happened. During the night she had heard nothing. Later it transpired that no-one in Seragad Tok had heard anything unusual. Perhaps this was not so surprising as it might seem, as people went to bed early and closed and barred their heavy wooden doors and the wooden leaves of their few windows to keep out panthers who were bold enough to enter houses and carry off dogs or goats tethered inside. And they might not remember a single shot after dark as it was not uncommon for someone to loose off a round occasionally to scare away wild beasts.

Lachchman ran down to the main village to give the news. The headman of Deosari had gone to Chamoli in the Arms Act case. It was only when a large party had been collected and the headman of Sarkot, the nearest village, had been called, that they went up to the scene of the double murder. There, on a stone on the upper edge of Partab's courtyard, they found a clear footprint in blood and, not far away, a blood-stained shoe. This valuable evidence was almost certainly due to Kharak Singh's courageous, if foolhardy, action in chasing the murderers, whom he must have surprised almost immediately after they had completed their despicable deed.

Govind and Man Singh absconded and hid in the forest above Deosari, where they were supplied with food and up-to-date information by their relatives and friends on both sides of the border. Govind was horrified by Man Singh's action in killing the two women. He had tried to stop him killing the girl — he had already killed her mother before Govind could get into the house — but he had been unable to save Mahadevi. Man Singh had been like a wild beast, he could only have stopped him by shooting him. His intervention had only delayed the girl's death and given her the chance to inflict some grievous wounds on her attacker with her sickle before she was killed. Now he was saddled with this man, badly wounded and needing care till his wounds healed, because of their common involvement in the Arms Act case. Man Singh showed his true character by refusing to give himself up for these murders. He was quite content to allow Govind to share the blame. Govind accepted the position. He was unmarried and had many friends. There was just a chance that they might be able to prevent his arrest. Moreover, as an ex-policeman, he knew that he would be liable to be charged jointly with Man Singh and liable to the same punishment. He realised it would be difficult to convince any court that he was an unwilling party to the crime. His predicament aroused considerable sympathy on the ground that he had received sufficient provocation to explain, if not to justify the murders. The *patwari*, whose avarice and dishonesty had contributed more than anything else to bring about this tragedy, no longer commanded the respect of more than a handful of people in the locality. It was no secret that he had accepted a bribe of two hundred rupees to connive at the framing of Govind in the Arms Act case.

It was at this stage that George Mitchell, the Deputy Commissioner of Garhwal, arrived on the scene in the middle of May on his summer tour in upper Garhwal. Owing to other engagements he had no time to do more than record the evidence available up to that date and to obtain solemn assurances from leading local men that they would give full assistance to bringing the criminals

to book. It was only later that he came to know that most of these
assurances were worthless.

Given the circumstances, it was, perhaps, not surprising that Govind Singh decided that he might as well be hung for a sheep as for
a goat. From that date began a reign of terror for his enemies. His
first act of revenge was directed against his own cousin, Dewan
Singh Padyar. Some time before, Dewan's brother, Keshar Singh
Padyar, had betrothed his daughter to one Khem Singh Dosadh.
Govind resented this alliance on the ground that *biradari*
(brotherhood) had been broken. However, he agreed it could be
restored if Keshar did penance. A Brahmin was called and penance
was done to Govind's satisfaction. But Dewan refused to be reconciled — he considered his family had been unjustly humiliated. He
had previously been a close friend of Govind, but now turned
against him and supported the Dosadhs. At the end of May Govind
shot and severely wounded Dewan Singh. The same evening twelve
of his goats were found decapitated in his cowshed.

Man Singh had friends in Almora. In June he went there to consult a lawyer and several reputed murderers who had escaped
justice, as to how to prepare against a charge of murder. But he was
not the only person with friends in Almora; his arrival there was
reported to Partab and on his way back he was ambushed and arrested. He refused to make any statement. Unlike Govind he was
not held in respect by anyone and his arrest was widely welcomed.
Govind's friends and even some of the Dosadhs believed it was he
who had actually murdered both women.

In August Keshar Singh Dosadh, Partab's brother, was shot dead
in broad daylight while herding cattle in the forest. Partab himself
went everywhere armed with an escort of relations or friends. The
patwari was terrified and asked for a transfer. Mitchell had already
decided that he must be moved and the delay had only been due
to hitches in the chain of transfers which were necessary before he
could post the particular man he wanted to the Pindarwar circle.
Govind was officially outlawed and a price of two hundred and fifty rupees placed on his head. But this failed to produce his arrest
or any useful information that might lead to his arrest. His reputation now was such that no-one dared to go in search of him or even
to spy out his hiding place, which was only known to one or two
of his most trusted friends. His defiance of authority and the non-
co-operation of his sympathisers had reached a point where they
could no longer be ignored. Arrangements were made for twelve
armed police to be sent from Almora and Mitchell altered his
autumn tour programme in order to visit the area and work out a

plan for Govind's arrest. The armed police arrived on the 18th of September; Mitchell reached the Gwaldam forest rest-house on the 19th. Plans were discussed and settled. Plan A was to arrest all Govind's close relatives and friends in both districts on a charge of obstructing his arrest and to call on Govind to surrender within a time limit. Plan B, in case Plan A failed, was to impose a punitive police tax on all landholders in the area to pay for the cost of the armed police until Govind was arrested or surrendered.

In the afternoon, three British Officers of the Royal Garhwal Rifles arrived at the rest-house from a recruiting tour in Upper Garhwal and sat talking with Mitchell until after 11 p.m. when they went to bed. The armed police had gone down to the school a mile away, where they were to be billeted for as long as they were wanted. Mitchell went outside for a breath of fresh air before turning in. As he stood drinking in the cool night air and the breathtaking view of Trisul by moonlight, he heard someone calling over and over again 'Sircar-ji. Sircar-ji'. The voice appeared to be coming across the re-entrant of the Gwaldam pass. He called an orderly and they both listened:

'Shout back and ask him what he wants,' Mitchell told the orderly.

When he did so the reply was clear and startling:

'O you *bungalow-wallahs*, bring a light quickly and see what has happened.'

It was not only inside the bungalow that the story of Govind Singh had been discussed that evening. In a moment the British Officers' Garhwali orderlies appeared, eager for action. Mitchell left their masters to sleep, collected his shotgun, a torch and a trembling *patwari*. The little party took, most unwisely, a short cut down the re-entrant and up the other side. They made an awful noise. Not knowing the terrain they tripped over the stumps of old tea bushes and fell in and out of boggy pot-holes. When they reached the shop on the pass they saw there was a light and people still inside. But when Mitchell went inside, the company there all denied having seen or heard anyone or anything unusual. However, sitting on a bench outside the shop was the most scared looking man Mitchell had ever seen. Beyond discovering that he was a soldier on leave, no-one could get a word out of him. They waited quietly for some time, completely puzzled. After making a somewhat superficial search all round the shop and road, Mitchell was convinced that they had been hoaxed by someone with a misguided sense of humour. So they returned by the road which runs along the ridge and then drops down to the rest-house. It had been raining heavily earlier that evening — a last flourish of the dying monsoon — and at one point the path was a bog and they were preparing to make a detour to get round this when they saw, right in the middle of the track in front of the bog, a bamboo pole stuck in the ground and a roll of paper fixed in its split tip.

Back in the rest-house Mitchell unrolled the paper and found two notes from Govind, written in English and signed by him, one admitting and justifying all the murders and attempted murder and the other offering to surrender to the Deputy Commissioner if he would arrest and prosecute the persons responsible for implicating him falsely in the Arms Act case. There followed a long list of names.

At this point up came the armed police, eager to pursue the ingenious Govind immediately. Mitchell congratulated them on their enthusiasm and had some difficulty in persuading them that the chase would be futile. At midnight he sat down and re-cast the plan of campaign. Plan A now was to take Govind Singh at his word; the former Plan A became Plan B and the former Plan B became Plan C.

The *patwari* who had accompanied Mitchell so reluctantly on this nocturnal investigation was still the man who had taken an active part in prosecuting Govind Singh. Although under orders of transfer he had not yet left as his successor had not yet arrived. He had died many deaths between May and September. Some people had been taking malicious delight in assuring him that Govind would certainly kill him, the only question being how and when. Mitchell had excluded him from their discussion of plans. Luckily his relief arrived next day and was instructed to arrest all Govind's principal enemies and then to invite Govind to surrender to the Deputy Commissioner on his way back in early October.

Mitchell then left to complete his tour. Partab followed him to his next camp at Wan. He was obviously puzzled and suspected something. He was assured that active steps were being taken to end Govind's career of crime and was sent back with a note in English, which he did not understand, to the new *patwari*, instructing the latter to arrest him as soon as he delivered the note. He was duly arrested and within a week all the rest of the Dosadhs named by Govind were also arrested. Netra Singh, and the ex-*patwari* were suspended, also the headman of Deosari. To a puzzled public this seemed an odd way to employ the special police force sent to arrest Govind Singh. But it made sense to the retired Subedar-Major, whom Mitchell had to take into his confidence as he wanted him to convey his reply to the outlaw's message. At

Chamoli Mitchell received a telegram from the *patwari* to say that
Govind had agreed to surrender and has asked what date would be
convenient. He wired back to say 4th October at the Gwaldam
forest rest-house. When he arrived there on the 4th, there was a
polite note from Govind awaiting him to say he was slightly indisposed but would surrender at twelve noon on the 5th. Mitchell
hoped he would be punctual as he had arranged to catch a bus at
Garur, the road-head for Ranikhet, the same afternoon. It was a
twelve mile march on foot.

Meanwhile he recorded all the further evidence available about
the various incidents, including the statement of Chandri *tamta*
who claimed that he had stayed to watch what happened after
Man Singh and Govind entered Partab's house on the 2nd May. He
said he saw the two men drag the girl Mahadevi across the
threshold where Man Singh, holding her by the hair, pulled her
head back while Govind, kneeling on her body, chopped at her
throat with the *kukri*. It was only then, he said, that he ran away.
He told all this with the greatest assurance, illustrated with
dramatic gestures. He could not explain how it was that Govind
now held the *kukri* and Man Singh the gun. Mitchell had no hesitation in assessing this part of his evidence as pure fabrication. It was
so unlikely as to be unbelievable that he would have waited, at the
risk of his life, one second longer than necessary after he found
himself free to run away. Chandri was a tenant, indeed practically
a bond servant of Partab Singh Dosadh, whose hand was seen in
this embellishment — he wanted to make sure that his main enemy,
Govind Singh, would be accused of the actual murders of his wife
and daughter.

Mitchell had a strong sense of occasion. But, even if he had none,
he could hardly have ignored the all pervasive local atmosphere of
curiosity and tense anticipation. Towards noon the next day he
placed a table and chair in the middle of the lawn and sat down
behind the table facing the path which led down to the rest-house.
Behind him on each side was assembled a large crowd, including
many of the military pensioners in uniform and stiff with medals
and ribbons. The atmosphere was as solemn as that at a Durbar but
considerably tenser. The armed police had taken up position
directly behind Mitchell but they looked too much like a firing
squad with Mitchell himself in the line of fire and he ordered them
to conceal themselves behind a convenient hedge. He sensed that
Govind might be too offended or alarmed to come nearer if they
were paraded blatantly before him.

Punctually at noon a voice was heard shouting:

'I am Govind Singh: let no man lay hands on me till I have come before the Deputy Commissioner Sahib and stated my case.'

Two minutes after his call a well set up wiry man, wearing a rough doubled brown blanket, the ordinary dress of a hillman of upper Garhwal, and carrying only a small bundle, walked in slowly with impressive dignity and stood before the table, on which he placed his bundle.

Govind started an impassioned recitation of all his wrongs and of the persecution of the Padyar Bishts. He went back twelve years and led events up to May 1945. The audience pressed forward to hear his confession. he described their plan to kill Netra Singh, but at the last moment, seemingly, he lost his nerve or, as Mitchell preferred to believe, could not bring himself to admit publicly that he had assisted or failed to prevent Man Singh's insensate action. Instead, he denied the actual murders, lamely suggesting that his enemies murdered each other in order to place the blame on him. Confronted with his own signed notices of the 19th September, he admitted that he had written them but explained that he had only acknowledged responsibility because he thought that without some dramatic gesture of this kind no-one would have paid any attention to his request for justice against his enemies. Mitchell asked him who had killed the two women. he said he did not know. He also denied possession of any illicit firearm (but next day he took the police to his secret hide-out and handed over a gun.)

After his statement had been recorded by Mitchell in English and by his court clerk in Hindi, Govind picked up his bundle, came round the table and laid it at Mitchell's feet:

'I have two last requests, Sahib,' he said. 'Please give these things to my son — they are the only possessions which I would like him to have from his father.'

He opened the bundle. Prominent amongst the few personal articles were a cheap coloured print of a photograph of King George the Sixth, Govind Singh's good conduct certificate and the Burma Police Medal. A list of the contents was made and the bundle handed over to the Subedar-Major to give to Govind's son.

'And your other request?' Mitchell asked.

Govind stood to attention and said:

'Please also tell my son that it was his father's wish that he should leave our accursed village and join the Burma Military Police. The Commandant has promised to accept him if he applies.'

'That too will be done.'

Govind held out his arms; the *patwari* fastened the handcuffs round his wrists and he was led away. Mitchell left at once and was just in time to catch his bus at Garur.

At their trial before the District Judge in Almora both Govind Singh and Man Singh pleaded 'Not Guilty' but refused to make any statements or to call any evidence. In addition to the witnesses whose stories have already been told, the prosecution were able to produce evidence that Govind's footprint tallied exactly with the bloody footprint found on the stone parapet of Partab's courtyard and that the blood-stained shoe and also a small bag found inside Partab's house on the morning after the murders, belonged to Man Singh. The shoe was stained with blood of two groups, one the same as that of Mahadevi and the other the same as Man Singh's.

They were both convicted and hanged.

So ended the personal tragedy of Govind Singh. It had the saving grace that with it also ended the blood feud of the Bishts in Deosari.

It is fitting to be able to record, as a footnote to this story, that Partab Singh Dosadh and some of his party were tried and convicted of conspiring to make a false charge against Govind Singh under the Arms Act, for which they served various terms of imprisonment, and that the *patwari* and Jemadar forest guard involved in that case were both dismissed from service.

Govind's son was unable to join the Burma Military Police as the future recruitment policy of that force after the war was not yet decided. Instead, he was persuaded to enlist in the Royal Garhwal Rifles.

The
Law of their Fathers

MAP OF UPPER GARHWAL
Showing the Location of Story 'The Land of Their Fathers'

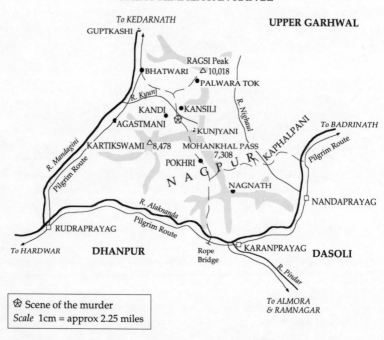

GREAT HIMALAYAN RANGE

UPPER GARHWAL

To KEDARNATH

GUPTKASHI

•BHATWARI

RAGSI Peak
△ 10,018
•PALWARA TOK

R. Kyun

KANDI •KANSILI

•AGASTMANI

KARTIKSWAMI △8,478

•KUNJYANI

R. Nighaul

MOHANKHAL PASS
7,308

POKHRI•

NAGPUR

KAPHALPANI

To BADRINATH

Pilgrim Route

R. Mandagini

Pilgrim Route

NAGNATH

NANDAPRAYAG

R. Alaknanda

Pilgrim Route

□ RUDRAPRAYAG

To HARDWAR   **DHANPUR**

Rope
Bridge

□ KARANPRAYAG

R. Pindar

DASOLI

To ALMORA
& RAMNAGAR

✿ Scene of the murder
Scale 1cm = approx 2.25 miles

THE LAW OF THEIR FATHERS

1. THE COPPER PLOT

Fateh Singh could not remember afterwards what had caused him to take the wrong path in the forest. He often passed that way and had never made this mistake before. He had hardly gone a hundred yards when he realised his error, but by that time his curiosity was aroused. He had never been along this path and had no idea where it led. As he was in no hurry he decided to follow the path to its end. After climbing gradually for nearly three miles, he came to a small, nearly level but derelict clearing on the edge of the forest. It was the beginning of April and late-fallen snow still lay in places. Though man-made — there were still traces of the original terracing for cultivation — nature had all but reclaimed the little holding. The place was utterly remote and forsaken. He judged it to be about one and a half acres in extent and its height 9,000 ft. above sea-level. Directly above it the mountainside rose steeply, covered only with the coarse yellow sweet-scented *Mamun* grass, which was used for bedding in the high hills. The path went no further. Wondering idly why anyone had troubled to come so far for so little reward, he was about to leave when something caught his eye.

Fateh Singh was a small elderly man, wiry and active. There was a short greying stubble round his chin; his eyes were that particular soft and cold blue, almost grey, which sometimes gives the impression of a hard calculating mind; at other times merely of watery short-sight. Fateh Singh was certainly a hard man but there was nothing weak about his eyesight. He had noted at once something unusual about the stone lying in his path.

He was still in the cleairng half an hour later and now there was no question of merely idle interest as he thrust this way and that, examining every stone of the low terrace walls and the natural rock

71

outcrop in or near the clearing. By the time he was satisfied and turned to go, his pockets were heavy with small pieces of stone finely veined with copper.

On his way down he met a woodcutter who told him that the clearing was called Palwara Tok and belonged to Kesar Singh, headman of Kandi. He confirmed that no-one had cultivated or even come near it for years, except for Kesar Singh's son, Dhan Singh, who sometimes came up to shoot bears. It was the bears which had ruined the crops and this had led to the abandonment of the holding.

Fateh Singh was in thoughtful mood on his way home. He had discovered what he believed might turn out to be a valuable strike of copper — anyway worth further investigation. This would not have been surprising in the area round Pokhri in the next valley to the south, which was famous for its copper mines, but he knew of none discovered this side of the Mohankhal pass and determined to keep the knowledge to himself.

There were three courses open to him. He could, gambling on the remoteness and neglect of the site, simply appropriate it without anyone's leave. Alternatively, he might explore and try to determine the direction in which the richest veins of copper ran and then stake a claim to a fresh plot of forest in that direction, close to Palwara, either without permission or, if he was prepared to risk the publicity, by applying to the authorities for a grant of waste land. Or, he could try to buy Palwara from its present owner, which would give him the right to exploit the holding and, in time, the adjacent land — a right he could expect to be able to interpret liberally in such a remote spot without any publicity and with little risk of antagonising anyone.

One feature was common to all three choices — he must conceal his real purpose. All mineral rights in the soil now belonged to the State; mining required the taking out of a licence and the payment of royalties to the government. He would grudge these. But the deciding factor was the unlikelihood of securing a licence, even if he did apply, since the government had decided, a few years ago, to discourage the mining of copper in new areas.

He decided that the first course was rather risky; without some title he might lose all the fruits of his enterprise. He rejected both alternatives of the second choice, because the vein might peter out or he might become embroiled with the owner of Palwara over their respective rights of extension. To apply for a grant would also involve too much publicity.

Fateh Singh decided to try and buy Palwara. Some publicity was unavoidable, but the transaction need only be known to three persons, the buyer, the seller and the *patwari*, who was required to register the sale. He had already thought of a plausible excuse for his interest in an apparently worthless and troublesome holding.

2. A BARGAIN LOST

Kesar Singh sat on the balcony of his house. It was a fine vantage point which commanded a view of the river, the traffic on the only road which passed through the valley and over the pass at its head and the Ragsi peak to the north. But Kesar Singh had no eyes for the view. He was gloomy and ill at ease, as anyone who knew him well would have recognised from the mere fact of his sitting doing nothing.

He was troubled about his son and this was the worst sort of trouble a man could have. A Hindu father had some claim on his son's piety; a Rajput headman had a right to expect his only son to follow in his steps and so maintain a family tradition which was as old as their family memory. But Dhan Singh did not seem to be aware of these obligations. In spite of all the entreaties of his parents and their friends, he was set on leaving the village to join the Sepoy Army of Bengal. The most sinister and disturbing stories were current about this service. Even if they were exaggerated, as Kesar Singh, being an honest and sensible man, was prepared to admit, it was common knowledge that few hillmen who joined the army ever returned. There were too many hazards and temptations. Even if these were survived, the leave earned was insufficient to cover the journey to the hills and back — at least twelve days each way from the nearest cantonment — with any time left over for visiting relations or friends. He had heard too that simple and illiterate boys from the hills who wanted to enlist in the army as soldiers were often taken for a ride and signed on merely as camp followers, a measure of the contempt with which they were regarded by the arrogant plainsmen.

Before the British occupation a man could have all the soldiering he wanted in the hills. There had been a constant border warfare with Almora as the petty hill chieftains pursued their dynastic feuds with almost predictable regularity and fluctuating fortune. But now all that had been stopped. Kesar Singh began to think that peace and security had been obtained at too high a price if it meant that life had become so dull for a high-spirited boy that he had to seek adventure in the plains. Worse almost than the thought of separation and loss was the knowledge that hillmen who went to seek employment in the plains were regarded there as a sort of menial, even in the Sepoy Army. This matter touched his pride. He resented the commiseration he read in the eyes of his friends; it was nearly true to say he had no enemies.

He heard someone coming up the steps behind the house and the creak of the floor boards on the wooden balcony. He rose quietly and passed into the room which opened off the front balcony. Through a half open window he saw that his visitor was Fateh Singh, the Thokdar and wondered what he could be wanting. Fateh Singh was neatly dressed in a well-fitting pair of homespun woollen jodhpur-style breeches and a long loose-fitting jacket of the same material with a fine kashmere shawl round his shoulders.

'Are you there, Kesar Singh?' he called.

Kesar Singh picked up a short *hookah*, the bowl was of brass in the shape of a large elongated egg about the size of a melon. It was chased with fine pinpoint engraving, known as *bidri* work — an old favourite. He made certain it was ready for use and then came out onto the balcony:

'Hallo, Fateh Singh — won't you sit down and join me in a smoke?'

He did not ask him his business.

'I'll join you with pleasure', said Fateh Singh.

Between these two there was a barrier which no amount of mutual smoking could conceal. It was not a social barrier, they were both of good Khassiya Rajput stock and respected each other's position. Kesar Singh as headman controlled the daily administration and dealt with the petty crime of two villages and a hamlet. The Thokdar was responsible for the payment of government revenue by forty villages. Each had his recognised place in the order of society. No — the barrier between them was deeper than any difference in status, it was one of character. Kesar Singh was a simple man, obstinate but generous, very deliberate in making his decisions, rather blunt in voicing them. He was absolutely honest and not at all inquisitive of his neighbour's affairs; he was not very intelligent but a man of great commonsense. Fateh Singh was crafty, quick-witted and ambitious. In spite of his nimble mind he was tactless and rude; he was also notoriously mean and quite unscrupulous. As a result he was rich but had made many enemies. Kesar Singh was universally trusted, Fateh Singh feared. Yet some people had not forgotten that, as a young man, Fateh Singh had opposed the Gurkha oppressors at great personal risk; he had worked against them cunningly, in his own fashion, and kept alive the flame of resistance long after more forthright methods had failed.

They sat down on the brown sheepskin rug with their backs to the wall. The hookah passed from Kesar Singh to Fateh Singh and back before any word was spoken. A leopard skin was hanging over the balcony railing; it was one of several trophies but it served Fateh Singh as an opening for the conversation:

'That's a fine skin,' he said admiringly.

Kesar Singh only grunted; it was not his best skin and no further comment seemed to him to be called for on this insincere tribute. There was a pause and then Fateh Singh continued:

'Didn't you have some trouble this year with a panther?'

Kesar Singh considered carefully before replying. He had no particular trouble with any panther this year. Of course, there were always some casualties, Fateh Singh knew as much about these as he did himself, such matters were the common exchange of village gossip. Why couldn't he come to the point of his visit?

'No,' he replied, 'Not panther — bear — two she-bears to be precise.'

'Well, bears then,' Fateh Singh took him up, 'they are worse, for they ruin the crops as well and when one is getting old it is not so easy to kill them.'

Kesar Singh looked at him squarely. In his younger days he had been a famous bear hunter; now he left it to the younger men.

'Well, what of it?' he said in a tone which should have warned Fateh Singh to be careful what he said next. Unfortunately he read the warning wrongly. He saw that the headman was in a bad mood and thought the occasion called for a little flattery. So he said:

'Oh nothing — but we are getting on, you and I; it's a pity the young men nowadays haven't your spirit and your patience.'

Now it was a fact that his son Dhan Singh had sat up several times for bears during the past year without success. Kesar Singh did not know if Fateh Singh had heard of this, but his recent thoughts were still rankling as he replied abruptly:

'I can see nothing wrong with most of the young men and I imagine it is not true, as some say, that a large family must be content to share their inheritance of courage.'

Fateh Singh, a widower, had three grown-up sons, he did not mistake Kesar Singh's meaning; yet he appeared to have missed the implication, which surprised the headman for usually Fateh Singh missed nothing and was quick to take offence. His retaliation was more subtle:

'Is it true that Dhan Singh wants to leave Kandi?'

Kesar Singh's eyes narrowed; he thought he began to understand where this apparently casual conversation was leading. He nodded but said nothing.

'What will you do?' said the Thokdar.

Kesar Singh shrugged his shoulders:

'I have tried my best to persuade him to stay, but he is determined to go. What is it to you, anyway?'

'A pity', said Fateh Singh, 'for as long as any of our families can remember, your family has provided headmen for Kandi — a pity,' and he sighed.

'And what is wrong with Dhan Singh that he should not succeed me as headman in due course? I am not senile yet, am I?' demanded Kesar Singh, stung at last out of the even tone of old men's gossip.

'Oh, nothing, nothing,' said Fateh Singh hastily, 'but you must be aware of what people are saying,' and he shot one quick malicious glance at his host: 'But that is not what I came to talk about; I have trouble enough of my own to know better than to interfere in that of others.'

Kesar Singh acknowledged this audacious mis-statement with another grunt; he was controlling himself with difficulty. But Fateh Singh pursued the line of conversation he had started, ignoring the headman's obvious irritation:

'Children nowadays are so self-willed and insistent,' he said imperturbably, giving up all attempt to mollify the ruffled headman; — 'take my own sons for instance — only the eldest can become Thokdar after me, but they all want equal shares of land; I am at a loss how to provide them all.'

'Why try?' said Kesar Singh sarcastically.

Fateh Singh ignored the interruption:

'I have tried to buy land everywhere but no-one will sell.'

'If you offered more, they might,' said Kesar Singh bluntly.

For the first time Fateh Singh was nettled:

'People seem to think I am wealthy,' he said warmly.

'Well, aren't you?'

'Of course not! Even if my ancestors had been, there is no chance for a Thokdar to keep his wealth now. First the Gurkhas, then the British! The former squeezed us dry, the latter have taken away all our perquisites and so prevented us building up again; now we are only figureheads.'

Kesar Singh already felt better now that he had scored a point or two off Fateh Singh. So he nodded politely, though he did not really believe the Thokdar. The latter resolved to come to the point at once as he saw that at last the headman was in a better mood:

'What do you think people are asking me for land to-day?'

'I have no idea,' said Kesar Singh, though he knew very well.

Fateh Singh sighed:

'A hundred rupees an acre! − can you believe it − sheer robbery.'

Kesar Singh had completely recovered his good temper; there was some satisfaction, too, in getting more than his fair share of the hookah since Fateh Singh was doing most of the talking.

'Oh, I don't know,' he said. 'I think that is a reasonable price to-day for good land.'

Fateh Singh looked at him with feigned surprise:

'It wasn't particularly good land they were offering me. Nobody offers good land if they think they can sell inferior. But you are an honest man − haven't you any land you would be prepared to sell for less? I only want something suitable for growing potatoes.'

Kesar Singh considered the matter:

'Very little,' he said. 'No, none that I could really spare, certainly nothing under seventy-five rupees an acre.'

'Nothing cheaper than that − what about Palwara?'

It was Kesar Singh's turn to look surprised:

'How did you come to know about that useless piece of land? I didn't think you could possibly be interested in that, even for growing potatoes. Yes, of course, there is Palwara − let's see − it cannot be more than one and a half acres, it is over 9,000 feet up and isolated. One crop in three never ripened and, when there was a good crop, it was flattened by hail or by bears, rootled up by wild pig or eaten by deer. We have given up all cultivation there for some years. I expect we would have been prepared to sell it for fifty rupees an acre or even less.'

'Would have been?' queried Fateh Singh.

'Yes, you see my son is opposed to any sale, he's very keen on hunting and that's about all it is any use for. So, though in effect we have abandoned the holding, it is still recorded in the name of our joint family and will, I suppose, remain so until Dhan Singh changes his mind.'

Fateh Singh concealed his disappointment. Already the germ of a new idea, which promised an even cheaper bargain, was beginning to form in his mind. It should be easier to do business with the son than with the father, more than easy in the circumstances,

though riskier. He thanked Kesar Singh for his hospitality and got
up to go. As he reached the corner of the balcony he paused and
said:

'Ah well, I knew it was only an outside chance. You are lucky
to have a son who is so easily contented with such a useless piece
of land.' And with this parting shot he took his leave.

As he heard the Thokdar clumping down his steps, Kesar Singh
reflected with curiosity on his visit. There was something odd
about his interest in Palwara. He was sure it would be of no interest
to Fateh Singh's sons and his parting remark had confirmed this.
Perhaps he had been rather hasty in refusing it. If he had waited,
he might have discovered why Fateh Singh had taken all this trouble to enquire about it after such an elaborate approach. Kesar
Singh was too simple, for all his shrewdness, to realise that by his
honesty he had provided Fateh Singh with just the opportunity he
wanted. Instead he simply put the matter out of his head.

As soon as he was off the steps of Kesar Singh's house, Fateh
Singh turned into the narrow lane that ran behind the house. He
had gone about ten yards when, out of a still narrower foot passage
enclosed between the blank walls of two other houses, a man came
out suddenly and almost ran into him. Their eyes met in instant
recognition for a matter of seconds only before they had passed
each other. Fateh Singh was accustomed to black looks but he had
never read such a brief and naked message of hatred. He half turned, expecting the other man to do the same, and braced himself for
an outburst. But Kundan Singh kept straight on without looking
back until he was out of sight.

Fateh Singh shrugged his shoulders — Kundan Singh was his
nephew by marriage — to be precise, his dead wife's brother's son.
He was not surprised at the look he had received. These relations!
Nine times out of ten they were useless or worse, so much dead
wood that ought to be lopped off. This Kundan Singh for instance
— the man was still heavily in debt to him and unable or unwilling
to pay even the interest. He was an inveterate gambler, an
obstinate debtor, like his father before him. Fateh Singh would
have broken him long since, but his own family had pleaded with
him, successfully in the end, to leave Kundan Singh alone, because
of the disgrace they would all suffer if the feud was carried to its
bitter conclusion. Naturally Kundan Singh disliked him; he, in
turn, despised Kundan Singh. He was a miserable creature; it was
said that he was squeamish and could not stand the sight of blood.
A man of spirit would have done something long since. Fateh Singh
had given him enough provocation, though, mind you, he had

been careful to do nothing that was not recognised to be his due by custom — yet none the less, provocation. Bah! — the man was chicken-hearted and he was about to dismiss him from his thoughts when an idea suddenly came to him that he could use Kundan Singh to further his present object. This idea gave him lively satisfaction and he set off with a brisker step to look for Dhan Singh.

3.   THIRTY PIECES OF SILVER

He found him down by the river where he had been making a fish trap. Fateh Singh did not really know Dhan Singh and studied the young man carefully. 'I have just been seeing your father,' he said.

Dhan Singh eyed him warily, ready to take offence if this was another ambassador come to reason with him. Fateh Singh came straight to the point:

'I thought you had left to join the army in the plains; perhaps you have given up the idea?'

Dhan Singh did not know what to make of the Thokdar's interest. He knew him only slightly and what he had heard about him did not dispose him to be friendly.

'What does it matter to you', he said, 'whether I join the army or not?'

'It matters this to me', said Fateh Singh, 'that there are many young men in the Hills who have no means of livelihood because there is not enough land to support them. Their best remedy is to join the army. Yet, because of traditional prejudice and the opposition of their parents, they are dissuaded from taking this sensible action. Now, if a young man of good family like yourself, with no problems about land, were to enlist, others, I am sure, would be encouraged to follow your example.'

Dhan Singh looked at him in astonishment, he had not expected to find an ally in the Thokdar, the most influential man in the neighbourhood.

'I have not yet enough money for the journey', he said, despondently.

'Will your father not let you have money for these expenses?'

Dhan Singh shook his head. 'He does not approve of my intention; I can expect no help from any of my family.'

Fateh Singh was silent, apparently absorbed in thought. Then he said:

'I told you that I have just been seeing your father. My reason for seeing him was to find out if he and the other family co-sharers would be willing to sell Palwara to a friend of mine. Your father said he would be agreeable and that he was sure that the other co-sharers would also agree, all, that is, save you, Dhan Singh, as you wanted to keep your share in it. Is that so?'

'That's true, it is a favourite place of mine for hunting.'

Fateh Singh nodded and smiled:

'I see — but you don't have to own land to hunt over it.'

'Perhaps not, Thokdar-ji, but the owner has a better right than anyone else to be there at any time for any purpose.'

Fateh Singh nodded understandingly, the point particularly appealed to him.

'Besides,' said Dhan Singh, 'I hope to build myself a hut there sometime. This would be of great help for my hunting.'

'It is a pity you are so fond of Palwara, Dhan Singh, for I know of someone who is prepared to make you an offer for your share and to pay cash for it — to you separately.'

Dhan Singh's eyes opened wide with astonishment and then became suspicious again. Nevertheless, his heart began to beat faster.

'Whatever does he want to buy it for?'

'I am not certain, but I believe he wants some land which is not much good for any other crop, in which to grow potatoes.'

'Why does this man not come forward himself?'

'He is a relation of mine who has been very helpful to me and this is why I am now trying to help him.'

Dhan Singh frowned and fell silent. He knew that he ought to report this approach to his father, but he sensed that, if he did so, Fateh Singh would almost certainly withdraw his offer. Fateh Singh waited patiently — he did not expect his ruse to fail. After a few minutes' thought, the temptation to accept the offer and probably his last chance to enlist in the Sepoy army was too strong to be denied. Dhan Singh said:

'What would this man give me for my share?'

Fateh Singh smiled to himself: 'It is too easy,' he thought. 'He told me to offer you twenty rupees', he said.

Dhan Singh looked disappointed:

'That's not enough' he said.

'Thirty rupees, then?'

Dhan Singh brightened:

'That's better, make it fifty.'

'No', said Fateh Singh, sure now of his vistim, 'my instructions were to offer not more than thirty rupees. Your share is not really worth that, but as you want the money so badly,' and he winked openly at Dhan Singh, 'I'll pay you thirty rupees on behalf of the purchaser, but not an anna more.'

'Done!' said Dhan Singh, but added 'You won't tell my father that I am accepting money separately for my share?' Dhan Singh could not hide his anciety.

'Of course not! But in case he should discover and to avoid any awkwardness I suggest it would be a good idea if you left as soon as possible. Here is the money.'

He counted out from a bag what seemed to the boy an endless pile of silver. When Dhan Singh looked a little embarrassed, Fateh Singh said drily, 'Here is the bag too.' And threw him the empty bag — he had thought of everything.

'I will leave tomorrow,' said Dhan Singh, hastily throwing the money back into the bag.

'That's good,' said Fateh Singh, 'but first we must draw up and you must sign a document agreeing to the sale of your share of Palwara. I will write it out on this stamped paper, you can then sign it, or make your mark and I will witness it. No mention will be made of the money. Then the purchaser can take it to the *patwari* for registration after you are safely away and out of your father's reach.'

It all sounded so easy, but Dhan Singh had to confess:

'I do not know how to sign my name and I have no mark as yet. I have never had to do with any writing.'

Fateh Singh was not to be defeated. He had known that the boy was illiterate — indeed, his whole plan was based on that fact.

'Well, never mind,' he said 'we'll take your thumb impression instead — I'll show you how to do it. Luckily I have brought some of the special ink required.'

For some minutes Fateh Singh was busy writing out the document. Then he took Dhan Singh's thumb impression, read the document out aloud, including what he said was his own signature as witness. He put the paper in his pocket and left Dhan Singh still wondering at the stroke of luck that had come his way. Next day he slipped away unknown to his parents. He felt bad about this and resolved that when he was earning good pay he would return the money to his family.

When he reached Bareilly twelve days later, he found the recruiting depot and enlisted at once. He gave his correct name but

a false address, just in case there was some regulation which required the army authorities to notify his father of his enlistment
and posting. This was to the 18th Native Infantry Regiment in
Bareilly itself. The date was the 16th April 1857, an unfortunate
time to have chosen to join the Sepoy Army. But Dhan Singh knew
nothing of its grievances and unrest. There we must leave him for
the moment and return to events in Nagpur.

4. THE TANGLED WEB

The day after he had concluded his business with Dhan Singh,
Fateh Singh went to see Kundan Singh in his village, Kansili.

'It is no use my pretending,' he said, 'that the proposition which
I am going to put to you is due to any friendly feelings on my part.
You must understand that this is entirely a business matter —
nevertheless, one in your own interest too. The position is this. I
have been looking out for a suitable plot of land in which to try
an experiment of growing the new improved seed potatoes introduced by the English foreigners. I have found a site, Palwara,
above your village. It belongs to Kesar Singh, headman of Kandi
and his family. They have abandoned cultivation there, but are still
recorded as owners. Kesar Singh told me that they were unable to
sell because his son, Dhan Singh, was unwilling to part with his
share. I have persuaded Dhan Singh to change his mind. I have here
his thumb impression on an agreement to sell his share. I do not
wish to offend Kesar Singh — he is very touchy about his son, and
I am sure he would resent the fact if he came to know that I was
able to persuade him to sell, when his family had failed to do so.
So I want you to buy Palwara — it is not far from Kansili, you
know Dhan Singh, it would be quite natural for you to buy it.'

'If I had any interest in it, or money', Kundan Singh said
sarcastically.

Fateh Singh ignored the interruption:

'If you will agree, I will write off two hundred and fifty rupees
of your debts. I will, of course, also pay for the land.'

'It is too good of you, to be sure!' said Kundan Singh mockingly;
he was full of the deepest suspicion.

'You have not heard all yet', said Fateh Singh drily:

'There will be three conditions. I shall require you to execute, privately, of course, a deed transferring full ownership and possession of this plot to me and my sons as soon as you have bought it. This will be some return, at least, for my generosity — though Palwara is almost worthless — and ownership, as you say, could have no interest for you who are penniless and childless.'

Kundan Singh clenched and unclenched his fists and scowled darkly. Fateh Singh noted but ignored the gesture:

'The other conditions,' he continued, 'are that you do not mention the re-sale to anyone and that you do not come near Palwara yourself, or take any interest in it, on pain of forfeiting the remission of your debts.'

'And what if I refuse your offer and conditions?'

'It will not be fatal to my plans — but it may prove awkward for you. I would remind you that it was only due to special pleading by my own family that I agreed to forbear from selling you up for your debts. My previous decision can easily be reversed. The matter lies in your own hands.'

Kundan Singh thought swiftly. He shrank from the consequences of defying the Thokdar. He had done so once before with disastrous results; he was puzzled and suspicious but full of curiosity. Why was Fateh Singh so anxious to avoid the direct purchase of this plot? And, if it was worthless, why was he prepared to pay so much for it in one way or another? But he could not see how he himself stood to lose anything by accepting. The good will of Kesar Singh meant nothing to him. Of course, knowing Fateh Singh, there might be some trap, but he sensed that Fateh Singh's interest was in this land, not in harming him. Perhaps he could use this to bargain for better terms.

'Very well,' he said. 'I accept your proposal and conditions, if you will agree to write off five hundred instead of only two hundred and fifty rupees of my debts.'

'I am glad you have chosen to be sensible', said Fateh Singh, 'but I could never consent to let you off as much as five hundred rupees,' — he thought for a moment — 'Look; I will make it three hundred and fifty.'

Kundan Singh did not think it would be wise to bargain any further; he was well enough pleased to obtain a remission of three hundred and fifty rupees for acting as agent, signing his name and minding his own business to humour Fateh Singh. He agreed to the terms. Fateh Singh gave him detailed instructions:

'You will wait one month; then you will go to Kesar Singh with Dhan Singh's agreement to sell and offer the family not more than seventy five rupees for Palwara. If they will not agree to sell, you must inform me at once. In that case, I am afraid I will not be able to remit any of your debts — so you had better not fail.'

As they parted Fateh Singh warned him once again:

'In your own interest, remember — you had better not come anywhere near Palwara from now on, or tell anyone how you came to buy it. If Kesar Singh, or anyone else asks you why you are buying it, you will say to grow potatoes there.'

When he was alone, Kundan Singh examined the document Fateh Singh had given him. He saw it was undated; he also noted one Murari Singh's signature as a witness to Dhan Singh's thumb impression. He was one of the few people who knew that Murari Singh was dying; he was too ill to have made the journey to Kandi. His suspicions returned. Was the paper a forgery and was this the reason why the Thokdar wanted to keep his own name out of the transaction? In one month's time Murari Singh might be dead and with Dhan Singh well out of the way, it would be difficult to prove a forgery. But, if it was a forgery and the gamble was good enough for Fateh Singh, it was good enough for him too. He would keep the suspicion to himself, who knows it might be useful sometime.

Fateh Singh had his own but rather different reasons for postponing legal action for a month. He hoped, indeed, to conceal, not forgery, for he had taken the precaution of obtaining Murari Singh's signature on a blank piece of stamped paper before he set out to see Kesar Singh, in case it was needed, but misrepresentation and deceit. He also had to make certain that there was likely to be enough good copper accessible in Palwara to make it worth his while mining with all the trouble and risk attached.

In the next week, with the help of his three sons, Fateh Singh cleaned and ploughed Palwara. This done, they set to work to locate the richest vein of copper and to break it out. It was hard work. They were handicapped by their inability to use gunpowder; also, to avoid arousing curiosity, they went to Palwara only four days a week and never all set out together in that direction. Work, therefore, progressed slowly.

For over three weeks no-one came near or discovered their activities. But at the very end of April, the *patwari*, Guman Singh, happened to be passing fairly close to Palwara on his way to the scene of an accident, which might have been 'arranged' or, as he thought more likely, a case of suicide. It was curious how the death rate from 'accidents' amongst young married women and widows always went up in the spring.

His investigation involved a pathless climb through the forest.

As he halted to recover his breath, he heard sounds of activity from the direction of Palwara. This struck him as curious because he knew the holding had been abandoned for some years. He decided to go and see what was going on, if possible without revealing his presence. A quarter of an hour later, after a most careful approach, he crouched in the undergrowth on the edge of the clearing. He was astonished when he peered out cautiously to see the transformation wrought since he had last been there. More particularly he wondered why anyone should think it worthwhile to try and remove the rock outcrop. Normally men only bothered to do this on valuable home fields. But the greatest surprise of all was to find that the men working in the clearing were Fateh Singh Thokdar and his sons. They might have bought it, though no-one had yet reported the sale. But whatever could have induced them to buy it? Only a closer examination would have revealed this.

Guman Singh left as unobtrusively as he had come without discovering the real object of the Thokdar's interest. After some discreet enquiries and intelligent observation, he was able to meet, as if by accident, Fateh Singh's eldest son, Trilok Singh, on his way towards the ridge below which Palwara lay. On being asked where he was going, Trilok Singh said he was going to arrange for some charcoal — this being the explanation the family had agreed to give if anyone showed any curiosity to know where they kept going.

'Ah, then', said Guman Singh 'perhaps you will be able to tell me if there is any truth in the rumour that someone has bought Palwara?'

He sensed at once the sudden tenseness in Trilok Singh as he replied:

'Why should I know anything about it? I don't even know where Palwara is. Why do you want to know anyway?'

'Oh, I heard a rumour that it was being cultivated, and I only thought that if you have business with the charcoal burners above Kansili, you might have heard about it. I believe it is the only clearing in that area.'

'I'm sorry,' said Trilok Singh, 'but I know nothing about it.'

Guman Singh next approached Kesar Singh:

'Is there any truth in the rumour that your have sold Palwara?' he asked.

'No. Fateh Singh did come to see me some weeks ago, but I told him that we were unable to sell because my son, Dhan Singh was unwilling to sell his share. I have heard no more. Now Dhan Singh has run away it is impossible to sell.'

For a day or two Guman Singh puzzled over this matter and con-

sidered what action he should take. There was obviously
something going on which Fateh Singh wanted to keep dark. Fun-
damentally Guman Singh was an honest man. But it was very difficult for a *patwari* to be entirely honest and disinterested in every
matter that came to his notice. He was well aware that Fateh Singh
had more enemies than friends. Privately, he considered his un-
popularity to be well deserved. He knew that he would be well paid
by some of the Thokdar's enemies for any information which they
might be able to use against him. He would not do that. Moreover,
he hesitated to take any step, even in the apparent course of duty,
that was likely to be interpreted as unfriendly by the powerful
Thokdar. Sometimes he envied Fateh Singh his independence of
public and private opinion. A *patwari* could never afford to be like
that; he had to think twice and then again before taking any
positive action and then wait anxiously for weeks in case his judgement had been at fault. When in doubt it was generally safest to
do nothing. This was, after all, a very petty matter; perhaps there
was some valid explanation. Guman Singh decided to do nothing.

Trilok Singh hastened to tell his father of his conversation with
the *patwari*. Fateh Singh suspended work in Palwara and waited
for a little, but, as nothing further happened, he concluded that
Guman Singh had enquired out of idle curiosity rather than real interest or duty. These *patwaris* were a meddlesome and inquisitive
lot, taking advantage of their official position to become
busybodies and intruders. Though they had taken every possible
precaution, it was obvious that their activities in Palwara had not
altogether escaped notice. He could not rely on the *patwari* not
coming to verify the rumours. To offer him some inducement now
to keep his mouth shut, would turn his curiosity into open suspicion. From that moment Fateh Singh began to think how he could
contrive to get Guman Singh transferred to another circle. They
had done enough exploratory work to satisfy him that it would be
worthwhile proceeding with his plans.

On the 5th of May Kundan Singh went to see Kesar Singh in
Kandi. He offered to buy Palwara for fifty rupees and showed him
the agreement deed with Dhan Singh's thumb impression. The
headman examined the document slowly and looked up puzzled:

'Why did you see Dhan Singh separately before coming to see
me? When he agreed, why did you not bring him to me to confirm
his agreement? Why have you waited so long to see me after getting
his consent?'

Kundan Singh was prepared for such questions. He knew that
Dhan Singh had run away from home the day before Fateh Singh

had come to see him in Kansili with his proposals. So he said:

'I knew that Dhan Singh wanted to keep Palwara in the family — he told me so one day when I met him in Kansili on his way to sit up for a bear. I thought it best to see first if he was willing to change his mind before troubling you. I was coming to see you but when Dhan Singh ran away from home I thought you would not want to discuss this business just then.'

Kesar Singh was partly mollified, but still suspicious:

'How did you persuade him? Did you pay him money?'

'No,' said Kundan Singh truthfully, though he was pretty certain Fateh Singh had done so. 'I told him I only wanted to buy the land to see if potatoes would grow there and that, if later, he really wanted to build a hut there, I was sure this could easily be arranged. . .'

Kesar Singh grunted:

'Hum! It seems that Palwara has suddenly come into demand for the growing of potatoes. Fateh Singh Thokdar came to see me with a similar request only a month ago. He has not approached me again, so I suppose he is no longer interested.'

'Did he make you an offer?'

'Well, not exactly, because I had already told him of Dhan Singh's objection to the sale of his share. But I did mention seventy five rupees as the price we would want for it, if we could sell it. It would be reasonable to raise that, now that so much interest is being shown. But I said seventy five and I will stick to that if you can pay cash.'

Kundan Singh did not miss the headman's meaningful look as he said this. He was hardened to this now; with his reputation it was only to be expected. He laughed with good humour and said:

'You will get cash — tomorrow, or the day after, when I bring the sale deed back for our signatures.'

'Very well, make it the day after tomorrow, in the evening, and I will have the other members of my family here to agree and sign.'

Next day Kundan Singh called to see Fateh Singh in Kunjyani. The Thokdar gave him the money. Kundan Singh completed the purchase the day after and brought the deed to show Fateh Singh. When the re-sale deed had been signed and Kundan Singh had been given a note of hand remitting his debts, Fateh Singh said:

'You will have to report your purchase to the *patwari* and show him the deed — but there is no particular hurry for that, it is only a formality. But don't forget it — I shall expect a report of your having done so in, shall we say, one month's time?'

Kundan Singh agreed, but forgot to ask for a copy of the

re-sale deed — he was no longer interested in the business.

Fateh Singh was pleased with the progress of his strategem. He needed more time now to complete his survey in Palwara and to obtain a trial assay of the quality of the copper. He hoped that, when Kundan Singh did report, the *patwari* would be satisfied that this was the explanation of the rumour he had heard, without bothering to inspect the plot. Of course there was a risk that he might come to inspect before Kundan Singh reported, but he thought this was now unlikely. He had come to know that the head of the District, the Assistant Commissioner, would be arriving on the 13th May for a week's stay at Karanprayag, only twelve miles away, and then coming on to Nagpur. The *patwari* would be fully occupied preparing arrangements for his visit and for the inspection of his own records in connection with the land settlement. The arrival of the Assistant Commissioner also presented him with the opportunity of opening his campaign for the transfer of the *patwari* by boldly approaching the highest authority in the District. If he had the opportunity he would also put in a word to discredit the character of Dhan Singh in case that young man changed his mind and came home sooner than expected. He set his fertile mind to work on what he would say to poison the mind of the Assistant Commissioner against both men.

5.   AN INTERVIEW

John Nevill had been Assistant Commissioner in Garhwal for nearly three years, though he had served elsewhere in the Kumaon Division for two years before that. He had been posted to this remote district, which others avoided, where there was no social life, no promotion to be expected, at his own wish and on the recommendation of his godfather, the almost legendary Commissioner of Kumaon. In spite of his title, which might seem to relegate him to some position of subordinate authority, he was in effective charge of the whole district, his main task at the moment being to carry out a new land settlement. This meant that he had to tour extensively; he was now on his summer tour of Upper Garhwal. Nevill had been attracted to this remote and beautiful region by a healthy curiosity about the people — well perhaps — but more decidedly about the geology and physical structure of these stupendous mountain masses. The geology of the Himalaya was a truly fascinating study. Here were strewn, in rich profusion, text book examples of the most violent convulsions of Nature, tectonic windows into an exciting world quite independent of the world of man. He was no trained geologist. Perhaps it was just as well, for, by remaining only an amateur, he was saved from total absorption in a subject which could turn a man into a burrowing worm or a tapping troglodyte. He was now as interested in the reactions of the people living in these delectable highlands to their physical environment and spiritual heritage, as he was in the rocks beneath their feet, or threatening their precarious homes and cultivation. Moreover, he had come to realise that man himself was an important agent in the process of erosion, his own worst enemy in the struggle against the forces of nature.

Fateh Singh did not make the mistake of arriving too early for his interview at Karanprayag. This would have shown undue eagerness; he wished to avoid giving any cause for comment. He wanted to give the impression that he was only paying his first duty call on the head of the District. He was also confident that he would not be kept waiting. When the orderly learnt who he was, he showed him in before other humbler visitors who had arrived before him. This was the custom of the country, which no-one would have thought of questioning. Some day this might be altered, though Nevill could not envisage that day. For the time being it worked well. The small man came with a request, petty, but all important to him, or with a grievance which was often real enough. He was prepared to wait all day, if necessary, and the important thing was to see him and hear him out patiently. The local notable, though he might also want something for himself, called in any case because of his own position, and out of respect for the representative of the government. Who else could properly inform him of everything that was going on in his locality? Thus, though he might make no clear distinction himself between his private interests and his public business, it was considered that he had a good claim to be shown in first, quite apart from the fact that he would be mortally offended if he were to be kept waiting. Another category of visitor, probably common to every district in India, was the vain man, who sought an interview mainly to be able to boast to his friends that he was on intimate visiting terms with the head of the District. It was unwise perhaps to disappoint him altogether, but, with experience, one grew cunning in devising means to shorten such interviews.

Fateh Singh went out of his way to be informative. Nevill found him an intelligent and interesting visitor. The conversation, starting with the usual polite exchanges about the weather and the crops, local demands and grievances, progressed eventually to a discussion of personalities with a freedom which Nevill usually expected only from familiar and frequent visitors. He had never met Fateh Singh before. The latter's comments were, on the whole, fair and reasonable, though he did not fail to give an adverse opinion on some of his worst enemies with whom he had no particular quarrel at the moment. He judged, rightly, that Nevill would be more likely to rely on his opinions where they were moderate, if he were frank about his dislikes.

He gave a shrewd appreciation of the *patwaris* then serving in the northern circles of the District whom he knew but omitted any mention of Guman Singh, the *patwari* of his own circle. Nevill naturally interpreted this, as Fateh Singh intended he should, as being due to proper delicacy and only requiring some prompting from him to rectify the omission. Fateh Singh also calculated that his deliberate omission would have prepared the Assistant Commissioner for some adverse comment and this too was the effect he wanted.

'And what of your own *patwari* then?' Nevill asked.

'Guman Singh is a good *patwari* — I was one of those who asked that he should be sent to our circle — but that does not mean that we really want him for ever'.

'How long has he been in it?'

'Eight years, Sahib'.

Nevill thought to himself — 'he is right, eight years is too long; and yet, if a *patwari* is well thought of, the people generally plead that he should be allowed to stay on, no matter how long he has been in the circle' — so he asked:

'Why do you think he has been long enough?'

'Sahib after two years even a stupid man must know his circle; at three years a *patwari* is at his best and on his best behaviour in order to earn another two years. After five years he thinks he is safe for another five and he begins to show his confidence in many little ways that are not always pleasing.'

'And in what ways has Guman Singh demonstrated the truth of your shrewd analysis, Thokdar Sahib?'

Fateh Singh shifted a little in his chair. Nevill wondered if he had ever sat in one before. It was difficult, he had noted, for his visitors to sit at ease in a chair if they had anything on their minds. At last Fateh Singh said reluctantly — like a schoolboy who knows it is wrong to sneak:

'He has married a second wife, last year, in Pokhri; his new wife is daughter to one of the lealding landowners.'

Nevill understand at once. Guman Singh would be identified now with the interests of one or more local families; their enemies would no longer consider or allow him to be impartial. It was also fair to assume that Fateh Singh himself was not on good terms with this particular landowner.

'I see', he said 'anything else?'

Fateh Singh shook his head:

'I have nothing against him myself, Sahib'.

Nevill was impressed by his moderation, in spite of a doubt that persisted — such disinterested advice was a little unusual. Was Fateh Singh an honest man, or a very astute intriguer? He asked him many more questions on a variety of subjects and his answers convinced Nevill that he was, at least, a very shrewd and intelligent man. Almost inevitably, so it seemed, the subject of village headmen came up, for they were a vital link in the administration. Fateh Singh was quite ready to talk about them too. When he came to speak of Kesar Singh of Kandi, he warmly praised him as a good headman but added with a sigh that unfortunately he was getting old and would soon be past his job.

'He has a son to succeed him, I suppose?' asked Nevill.

'He has a son, Sahib, an only son, who gives him great trouble and anxiety, for he is a good-for-nothing. I fear great difficulty will arise over the succession.'

'What is wrong with the boy?'

'Sahib, have you ever heard of the expression "Son of the cow-dust hour"?'

Nevill nodded: he had heard the expression but he was surprised to hear it in the mouth of a hillman. This was the name given in the plains of northern India to those born in that magical hour of the twilight when the cattle are newly returned to byre down all the village lanes, leaving their dust, mixed with the smoke of evening fires, hanging still and ghostly in the chilling air; when the shapes of men and animals become elusive and insubstantial. In that hour the scent of flowering shrubs is overpoweringly sweet and heavy, the acrid smell of burning cow-dung, so sharp and pleasant to the nostril, is mixed with something more — an indefinable exhalation from earth and trees released from the scorching seal of the day's heat.

Nevill told Fateh Singh he had only associated this expression with the plains.

'We have the same hour in the hills at certain seasons,' said

Fateh Singh. 'It does not last long but children born in that hour
are said to be touched by a spell. Some, when they are older, disappear and are found later wandering by the burning ghats; others
consort with soothsayers and magicians; a few', and here Fateh
Singh's voice sank to a dramatic whisper, 'are said to turn at that
hour into were-wolves and, while they are absent, strange and
terrible things happen on lonely paths and at remote and isolated
homesteads. In any case, children of the cow-dust hour do not
make reliable companions or useful citizens. If they remain at home
they are a burden to their parents; if they wander abroad they often
become beggars or criminals.

'Alas! — Dhan Singh, the only son of Kesar Singh, is one of these
unfortunate persons. Everyone knows how he used to spend days
and weeks wandering about the mountains hunting instead of helping his father. And now he has run away, so it is said, to join the
sepoy army, sure proof of his treacherous and unstable nature.'

'Why do you say that?' asked Nevill, interested in his last
remark.

'I have no opinion of the Bengal Sepoys', said Fateh Singh stiffly.
'They are either too proud and arrogant to notice lesser beings or
nothing more than uniformed dacoits.'

In Nevill's pocket was a confidential report from Almora, just
received, of the Sepoy discontent in various cantonments of the
North Western Province. Did this man know something about the
trouble or was he merely voicing the mistrust and dislike felt by
many hillmen for all foreigners from the plains? On the whole he
thought it must be the latter but he considered carefully before he
replied:

'Of course there are bad as well as good Sepoys. But the army
provides an honourable and useful career for a boy — you should
not think worse of this boy for joining it.' He paused for a moment
and then continued: 'What I do regret, myself, is that we have no
Hill Regiment for such lads to join; they are like fish out of water
in the sepoy battalions of the plains.'

For a moment the scheming hillman forgot his immediate purpose and the better side of Fateh Singh was revealed. Nevill saw his
blue eyes light with fire and heard the swiftly indrawn breath which
preceded his prompt reply:

'Sahib, you are right — how very right — it would make all the
difference. If we had had such a regiment we should never have
allowed the Gurkhas to occupy our land so easily.'

Though the glimpse was brief, it increased Nevill's respect for
Fateh Singh — somehow he could not admit to liking the man.

'Well, thank you Thokdar Sahib, for all the information you have given me,' he said. 'I will bear it in mind and, in particular, I will look further into the case of your *patwari* — and this boy, Dhan Singh too, if I find an opportunity.'

Fateh Singh left well satisfied, Nevill seemed to have been interested and impressed. But, if he had been able to read and understand Nevill's thoughts, he would have derived considerably less satisfaction. For, as he listened, Nevill experienced a curious double reaction. One part of his mind, the romantic, sensitive part, was quite ready to accept the reasonableness of Fateh Singh's explanation for what he considered the unsatisfactory behaviour of the boy, Dhan Singh. The other, the practical, well-disciplined part, dismissed this as pure rigmarole and superstition and was more impressed by what he had said about the *patwari*. It was this part of his mind which prompted him to wonder why the Thokdar had gone to the trouble of coming and telling him all this against the boy. He felt there must be some hidden motive — no doubt he would discover in time. An opportunity might soon present itself as he was moving in the direction of Nagpur *parganah* on his way to Kedarnath. It also happened that there was a small matter which required his attention in Kandi village itself.

Fateh Singh did not know this but he decided it would be prudent to suspend further activity in Palwara until the Assistant Commissioner had left the immediate vicinity.

6.   A VILLAGE ENQUIRY

Nevill left Pokrhi, Nagpur, at the beginning of the last week of May. He had arranged to visit Kandi to try and settle a dispute which had been dragging on for some time over the village water supply. He hoped at the same time to find out something more definite about the headman's son and to gather more opinions about the *patwari* to check against his own impressions and Fateh Singh's information. Kandi was on the way to his next halt at Guptkashi and the dispute about the water supply gave him a good excuse to linger a little longer on one of the most beautiful marches in Upper Garhwal — one of the most interesting as well, as this was one of the few areas still to provide evidence of the once widespread worship of the Snake-God, Nag, in the District.

He stopped to have his picnic breakfast on the Mohankhal Pass. To the north, through a frieze of mountain oaks festooned with silver lichen, the ridges climbed in steps, each veiled in mist of a different blue, to a serried mass of snow peaks, stretching like an endless sea of waves frozen into motionless breakers beneath a burning blue sky. The shadow of the forest-clad ridge on which he sat, fell in knife sharp definition on the slopes of the next ridge facing him. He ate almost without looking at his food, reluctant to lower his eyes for a moment from the transient feast before him. He could eat the same food, drink the same coffee for breakfast every day, if he so wished, but must starve for at least a year before he could devour this vision again, with no certainty that he would ever see it again. So he concentrated his gaze in the hope that the view would be burnt indelibly into his memory. He got out paper and pencil and drew the outlines, noting in the colours and contrasts of light and shade as an aide-memoire. Below, he wrote 'Vision of Nirvana' May 1857! On the whole he was glad he was not an artist, for he guessed that an artist would never be satisfied that he had been able to do justice to what he saw.

In Kandi, which he reached before noon, the headman's house was distinguishable from the other better built houses only because of its position in the centre of the village, commanding the junction of three main paths. The *patwari*, Guman Singh, went ahead up the steps to the first floor. Nevill heard him warn the womenfolk; there was a swift patter of naked feet and the swish of full skirts as they disappeared into an inner room. This was not because they had any inhibitions about being seen by an Englishman and a stranger — in the villages of the Hill Rajputs strict purdah was uncommon — but because it was not proper for women to hang around at an official and business interview.

Inside, when his eyes had become accustomed to the dark, Nevill found himself in the general living, working room. On the floor were a large brown sheep-skin rug and two old and stained Tibetan saddle-cloths. A heap of uncleaned raw wool lay in one corner and some clean and carded wool in another pile. There was one small window with two wooden shutters, both tightly closed. The Balcony outside the room was quickly filled by the curious, thereby making the room still darker. There was, rather incredibly, an old high-backed rocking-chair, upholstered in Turkey carpeting.

Kesar Singh was sitting on a string bed with carved and painted wooden legs. Round him was drawn a sheep-skin rug which had once been white. He seemed unwell and made profuse and embarrassing apologies for not being able to rise and receive his guest fittingly. Nevill accepted the offer of the rocking chair. He was conscious of being observed through the crack of the inner door. There was some heavy breathing and then a giggle followed by a sharp reprimand and next minute a good looking middle-aged woman came in. She gave Nevill a shy bob and handed Kesar Singh a brass cup full of steaming milk. The old man put a huge spoonful of dirty sugar into it, stirred it, to Nevill's relief, with the spoon and not with his finger, and then offered it to him. The woman brought bananas, oranges and nuts and Kesar Singh duly set them before Nevill and pressed him to eat.

That must be his wife, thought Nevill, and the bright eyes behind the crack of the door his daughter. He drank the milk slowly, it was so hot. Kesar Singh looked at him anxiously:

'Is the milk not to your liking — some more sugar perhaps?'

Nevill assured him it was perfect and, indeed, it was most refreshing. He would be having his own tea soon but he ate some of the fruit to oblige his host. His wife brought a boiled egg and Kesar Singh peeled the shell with his gnarled fingers. Nevill ate this as well, hoping that nothing else would be produced.

As Kesar Singh dispensed the timeless hospitality of the East, the other landowners crowded politely into the room and were made welcome. When Nevill had finished eating and drinking, he came straight to the point with the briefest of formalities.

'I have come about your village water supply dispute. I was going to ask your headman to take me to the alternative sites suggested for a second water tank but, as he is unwell, I will ask someone else to show me the sites.'

'I will come with you, Sahib, my indisposition is of no account. It is really old age that is troubling me and for that there is no remedy, neither *mantri* nor medicine.'

Nevill was firm and would not let him come. His illness, however, provided an opportunity to broach the other matter he had in mind, the subject of his son and the succession to the post of headman.

'Old age comes to us all, Padhan-ji', he said. 'It is time, perhaps, we thought about appointing your son to succeed you — you have a son I believe?'

The old man was visibly distressed:

'I would nominate my son, Dhan Singh', he said, 'but Siva has chosen another task for him; it is too much, perhaps, to ask the god to change his mind.'

There was a respectful but rather awkward silence, the other shareholders were all watching Nevill.

'I am willing to help,' he said, 'but if Siva has spoken. . .'

'You can help,' said Kesar Singh eagerly,' it is not too late. He will come back if you arrange; he is in every way suitable to succeed me.'

Nevill looked round the room:

'Who beside his father will vouch for Dhan Singh?' he asked.

There was no reply: Kesar Singh looked round slowly:

'Come,' he said, 'if you have anything against him, speak up before the Sahib.'

No-one spoke: Kesar Singh turned to Nevill:

'Listen, Sahib, I will tell you why they remain silent. They think my son is a wastrel because he has run away to join the Sepoy army. It is not their fault, they only understand and approve what they know. Let them choose Harendra Singh or Sher Singh, either will do well enough. But if you want a really good headman, then choose my son.'

'Where is your son?'

'I do not know, Sahib; he ran away to join the Sepoy army. If I knew where he was, I would send for him. As you say, it is time I made way for my successor.'

'Are you sure he has joined the army?'

'I am certain of nothing, Sahib, save that he will make a good headman', and the old man relapsed into an aggrieved silence.

Nevill had no wish to distress him further:

'Never mind,' he said 'we will talk about this again, later . . . now, about this water tank. . .'

Kesar Singh was obviously relieved at the change of subject:

'As for the water tank, Sahib, there are two parties, each pressing for the site of its own choice — it is the curse of our village. I have given my opinion, which is known to the *patwari* here. But you will hear all the arguments and decide — otherwise it will never be decided.'

With the *patwari* leading the way and a long procession tailing behind him, Nevill was taken to the two sites. As soon as they reached the first a wordy battle was joined between the rival parties, who crowded over the site in their eagerness to out-argue and shout each other down. With difficulty Nevill got them to keep quiet while he heard the spokesman first of one and then of the other group. The same performance was repeated at the other site. The reason for the difference of opinion was simple.

Kandi was a long straggling village, built, as usual, along the contour of the hillside. There was one small spring at one end and a little, almost vertical rivulet at the other end. The former was already feeding a water tank but this was above and some way from the village. The rivulet, on the other hand, flowed right past the other end of the village and those who lived at that end wanted another water tank at the level of their houses. Those who lived at the other end wanted a bigger tank by the spring. It was common ground that the present tank was not large enough and that the village could only afford one new tank.

When he had heard them all, Nevill asked the *patwari* for the headman's views.

'Kesar Singh says the spring is already used. If anything should happen to it, there would be no store of water for the village — therefore it would be wiser to use the stream.'

'And what is your own opinion?'

'Sahib, it is very difficult to decide. In principle I think I agree with Kesar Singh; but, on the other hand, the rivulet is very slight, it is not, perhaps, very suitable for a tank of the size required and some years it almost dries up in the summer.'

At this babel broke out again. Nevill looked up patiently into the sky; gradually the hubbub subsided. They all looked expectantly at him, as if he could provide some magic solution — and so he did:

'If you will agree on a site about halfway between the two in dispute,' he said 'the government will give you iron pipes and the water can be taken from both sources into a new tank.'

There was a puzzled, almost suspicious silence. They only knew of bamboo pipes, but these would not be suitable here, for there were many bends through the village and the pipes would be vulnerable to accidents and mischief-makers. But iron pipes, who had ever heard of them? No-one dared say it, but might they be unclean? The British rulers had many strange and unorthodox ideas and habits. The situation was saved by an old man who said diffidently:

'I have seen iron pipes — in the palace of the Nawab of Oudh. Sometimes they made strange noises but the water was good.'

That was enough to satisfy his fellow villagers. So a neutral and central site was chosen and Nevill promosed to send iron pipes. They came after many months, long after the new tank was ready and were pointed out proudly to all visitors, the first pipes of their kind, until piped water supplies were no longer a novelty in the hills.

Nevill had noted the *patwari's* reply. He was not so inexperienced as to accept this as proof of Guman Singh's impartiality. But, at least, if it did not prove his impartiality, it showed that he was shrewd. So far no-one in Nagpur had made any specific complaint against him. He decided, on principle to transfer him to some other circle, but only when a suitable opportunity occurred.

As for Dhan Singh, he could reach no decision without seeing the boy. There was no doubt he had gained some kind of bad reputation, but he found it difficult to believe that a son of such parents could really be a criminal or wastrel. What, then, of Fateh Singh's insinuations? Were they the product of some private or family quarrel, or the prelude to some purposeful intrigue? He made a note to see him again — but fate decreed otherwise.

7.   A MOONLIGHT RECONNAISSANCE

At the beginning of June Kundan Singh decided to go to the main Pilgrim Route market at Nandaprayag to order some wool. While emptying the pockets of his blanket coat in preparation for the journey he came across the Palwara sale deed and remembered that he had not yet reported the transaction to the *patwari*. He looked at it with disgust and was tempted to throw it away. It would serve Fateh Singh right if he was double-crossed. On second thoughts, however, he decided this would only react on his own head; Fateh Singh would certainly find some way to repudiate the remission of his debts. He read the document carefully and his previous suspicions were revived. Why had he been forbidden to come anywhere near Palwara? What was Fateh Singh up to? He decided to see the *patwari*; he would report the purchase if he thought it advisable to do so after talking to him.

He opened the subject warily with Guman Singh:

'Do you think these new seed potatoes from the plains a good thing to go in for?' he asked.

'I have heard so,' Guman Singh said, 'but I have no personal knowledge; no-one has grown them yet in my circle. But I hear they are already well established in Patti Nandak.'

'I thought of trying them,' said Kundan Singh. 'I hear they grow well in poor ground at almost any height.'

'So they say,' agreed Guman Singh and, surprised to hear that the improvident Kundan Singh should be considering the matter at all, he looked meaningly at him and added:

'I believe it is difficult to get the seed and rather expensive.'

'Maybe — anyway I have bought some land cheap, but I am not sure whether the sale is in order. One of the co-sharers has only given his thumb impression; now he has gone away, so it is not possible to obtain personal confirmation of his agreement.'

'Well, his thumb impression may be good enough — it depends on the circumstances. Have you paid for this land?'

'Yes, in cash.'

'Quite a reformed character! — but it was perhaps rash to pay before you were certain the sale was in order. Where is this land? Have you the deed?'

Kundan Singh did not see how he could obtain any further reassurance without producing the deeds:

'Here are the papers,' he said and passed them to the *patwari*. Guman Singh read the documents slowly. he was aware that Kundan Singh was watching him closely. The contents certainly interested him but he disguised his feelings:

'Well,' he said, 'it seems to be in order, though, of course, I shall have to check it with Kesar Singh and his family. You were clever — or lucky? — to get Dhan Singh's agreement before he ran away from home. But why have you taken so long to report to me?'

'I was not certain that I wanted to go through with the sale,' said Kundan Singh lightly.

'Although you have already paid the sale price?'

'I could sell it again.'

'I see. Are you sure you have not sold it again already — at a profit?' Guman Singh asked banteringly.

'Why do you say that?' — Kundan Singh looked at him sharply.

'Oh, it was just a joke!' said Guman Singh, 'you're such a gambler!'

Kundan Singh laughed wryly: 'You think the title is quite sound?'

The *patwari* thought swiftly. The whole thing was very odd, but really none of his business. He did not believe Kundan Singh had the means to buy any land, or that, if he had, he would have spent it on such a doubtful proposition, calling for hard work with very little, if any, return. It was quite out of character.

'Why, yes,' he said: 'I have said so already — subject of course, to a formal check.'

When Kundan Singh rose to leave, Guman Singh said casually:

'I suppose you have ploughed the land already?'

'No, not yet — why do you ask that?'

'Because someone has', said the *patwari*, his turn now to watch the other man closely. He saw Kundan Singh start slightly. Aware of his bad relations with the Thokdar, Guman Singh decided to risk telling him more.

'As a matter of fact, I know who it was,' he added.

Kundan Singh thought he knew too, but was full of curiosity:
'You seem to know more than I do about Palwara; why didn't
you tell me this before?'

The *patwari* looked at him knowingly:

'I keep my eyes open but my mouth shut,' he said.

Kundan Singh ignored the danger signal, his curiosity was too
demanding. 'Did this person register any sort of title with you?' he
asked.

'No,' said Guman Singh, 'he is not that sort of person,' and he
winked broadly.

Kundan Singh was now almost certain that the *patwari* was
aware of Fateh Singh's manoeuvres — perhaps he was in league
with him. He felt angry and humiliated, but he concealed his feelings and decided to put a bold front on it. If the *patwari* already
knew about the re-sale condition there was no point in trying to
conceal it. His conscience was now quite clear about disobeying
Fateh Singh's instructions.

'I did not know you were on such intimate terms with the
Thokdar', he said sarcastically: yes, I have sold this plot to him.
You didn't really suppose I would want to keep it, or to go to all
the trouble of trying to grow any crop up there?'

'Somehow, I did not think so either,' said Guman Singh with a
chuckle, and then added:

'When did you sell it to him?'

'Oh, about a month ago.'

'I see,' said Guman Singh. 'You are well rid of it. I can't understand why you ever bought it. Have you a copy of the sale deed?'

Kundan Singh felt uneasy: 'No, not on me,' he said. 'Oh, well,
never mind,' said Guman Singh, 'no doubt the Thokdar will
register his title in his own good time.'

Guman Singh was now still more certain that there was
something fishy about the whole business. Why had Fateh Singh
ploughed the land even before Kundan Singh had bought it? . . .
Why had he not bought it direct from Kesar Singh? . . . Why had
Trilok Singh denied all knowledge of Palwara?

Kundan Singh was due to set out for Nandaprayag the next day,
but the more he thought over his conversation with the *patwari*,
the more curious he grew. Who in their senses would plough land
so early for potatoes which could not now be planted till next
spring? Why had Fateh Singh warned him to keep away? . . . What
were they up to? He decided he must go and see Palwara for
himself, in spite of Fateh Singh's warning. He would go that very

night; there would be a moon, and he could expect to be able to investigate safely without fear of interruption.

Kundan Singh was superstitious like all hillmen. This night journey was an ordeal he would never forget; only his curiosity and his hatred for Fateh Singh kept him going. The ordeal was enhanced by the night being uncannily still. Only the sound of his own progress seemed to be loud, enormously magnified by the silence of the forest.

When, at last, he reached Palwara, he was amazed, as the *patwari* had been before him, by the work already done by Fateh Singh. He had not realised that the holding was so high and so isolated; it would be most vulnerable to damage from hail, frost and wild animals. he doubted whether even potatoes could be successfully grown there. No wonder the *patwari* had been so sceptical. He started to explore more closely. After a while he came to a large rock outcrop on the upper side of the clearing. The turf and topsoil had been dug away on one side, exposing the line of dip of the rock and the roots of a large rhododendron bush. The bush itself had been spared, it was growing close against the rock face and seemed to have been left deliberately to conceal something. He parted the lower branches and looked through. There was quite a large pit behind the bush, extending also into the hillside. He climbed through. It was dark save for a single shaft of moonlight which lit a corner of the floor of the pit and revealed a heap of spoil. It also revealed part of the chipped face of the rock; he examined this with mounting interest. When he got closer, he saw that the heap of spoil in the corner of the pit was carefully covered with turf. He removed some of this and found a heap of small pieces of rock. He picked up one and took it into the moonlight. As he turned it over in his hands there was a glint of metal. He whistled softly and put the stone in his pocket. When he had covered up the heap again he climbed out and went home. Next morning he examined the piece of rock; it was finely veined with copper lodes. So that was it! Now he understood the Thokdar's little game and his anger was mixed with fear, as he realised he had been fooled and trapped. He had had a fortune in his hands, only to lose it again to that old fox. And if the copper mining was discovered, Fateh Singh would saddle him with the responsibility as the new owner of Palwara. Despair filled his heart, despair and fury. Somehow he must recover the re-sale deed. But how? Or, he might play for safety and go to Kesar Singh and persuade him to cancel the original sale, whether he got the money back or not. If he did get it back, he would keep it for himself —

perhaps he could extract more from Fateh Singh by way of
blackmail to compensate for the almost certain cancellation of the
remission of his debts.

Meanwhile he had arranged to go to Nandaprayag to meet a
Bhotia trader he knew to order wool for the autumn; perhaps he
would be able to think out some plan of action during the journey.

8.   AND A MURDER

Fateh Singh was out early; he had left his home in Kunjyani at five-
thirty in the morning before anyone was about in the village and
none had seen him go. He climbed a rough path which soon took
him above the fields and into the forest. Despite his age — he was
just short of seventy — his slightly bow-legged but still springy hill
gait carried him along at a good pace. When he reached Palwara,
a six mile walk, he sat down and rested. The sun was just touching
the crest of the ridge across the valley with a golden brush; a
delicate blue haze coated the valley itself. Here and there the
tops of trees thrust through the mist. It was very still. In the
undergrowth he could hear the growing activity of anonymous
birds, pheasants he guessed by the sounds and locality. He rose
and, after looking round carefully, went over to the copper workings. Like Kundan Singh the night before, he pulled the foliage of
the rhododendron bush aside, slipped through and disappeared
from view. Inside, he examined several small samples of rock. They
were a dull yellow and rust red, veined with thin bands of verdigris
green. He picked up another piece and examined it carefully. He
had not been there when his sons had broken out these latest
samples two days ago, but he knew they must be near the richest
vein. There was no need to delay any longer. He whistled with
satisfaction and visions rose before him of a mountain full of copper as rich as that of the famous Dhanpur mines.

As for the rule which reserved all mineral rights in the soil to the
ruler, the shadow of any overlord in Garhwal had been fitful and
dim in the past and even now the foreigners who had turned out
the Gurkhas did not claim to rule on behalf of any lawful king.

No doubt his activities would be reported in time, and he might
be made to pay royalties, even to stop mining, but before that he

hoped to recover enough copper to make him the richest man in Upper Garhwal. Partly because of the reasons given by the Assistant Commissioner for the government's objection to new mining of ore, but more cogently because it would be impossible to keep the smelting secret, even in the cave behind the Ragsi peak, he had decided that it would be safer to bribe one of the licenced coppersmiths in Pokhri to accept his ore and smelt it along with the ore obtained from the authorised mines. He would contrive to have the ore from Palwara carried down in panniers topped up with charcoal on the ponies of the charcoal burners who worked in the Ragsi forest.

He lit a small fire and cooked himself a meal. It would be his only meal till the evening and he had a long journey before him. He heard someone coming and presently saw his sons approaching. He slipped the three richest samples of copper ore into the fold of his blanket coat and rose to greet them.

'I have taken three samples,' he said. 'They will suffice. I am going down now to Ramnagar to get the samples assessed and valued against the best hill copper — you remember the pieces I showed you which I obtained from that coppersmith in Pokhri. I am going home to get them on my way; also a change of clothes as it will be hot down in the plains. Meanwhile, no more digging now; instead, cover up as much of our work as possible until we can start mining in earnest. It will be safer to wait until Guman Singh is transferred from this circle. As you know, I have taken steps to safeguard our legal title to this land. But, if our possession and the mining become too hot to hold, we can father both onto Kundan Singh.'

Fateh Singh joined in his sons' laughter at the trick he had played on their indigent cousin.

Three-quarters of an hour later he was back on the road three miles from and heading towards his own village, Kunjyani. The time was about 9 o'clock and he had already walked over nine miles that morning. He sat down to have a rest and a smoke and it was the smoke from his *biri* which Kundan Singh noticed first as he came round a bend in the road. Fateh Singh was sitting on a rock on the outer edge of the road with his back to him but Kundan Singh recognised him at once.

He was overcome with dizziness. He had to go and lean against the roadside bank, pressing his temples against the cool rock to calm the throbbing pulses which raced in swift waves from his heart to his head and back. The opportunity he had prayed for and awaited for years had suddenly presented itself, without warning, as so often happens in life. He had resigned himself to the belief that it could never happen to him; he had never sought it deliberately and even now shrank from it.

The scene was set, the stage empty save for his enemy. A gentle steady breeze stirred the leaves of the trees and bushes beside the road, the sound would cover that of his own movements. Far below, the river flowed swiftly in its rocky bed; its voice too was another ally. Nothing save the breeze stirred on the hillside, the road and the valley were deserted. At last the gods had listened to him and assuredly because of this final wrong that had been done him. His childlessness had been a bitter grief and shame to him: everyone knew this, Fateh Singh above all. Yet the Thokdar had traded on this to use him casually, cynically, for his own purpose, to make his recent contemptuous, humiliating offer, the last he should ever make! He knew he had only a few moments for what he had to do but no more of these were wasted in coming to a decision, for suddenly he was filled with resolution.

He put down his shoes, which he had been carrying, and the small cloth bundle which contained all that he needed for his four day trip to Nandaprayag. In his belt was a small woodcutter's axe; he took it in his hand. Bare-footed he crept up behind Fateh Singh, he never took his eyes off him. Now he was there. He could see that Fateh Singh was examining something in his hand, his whole attention was concentrated on it. Kundan Singh just had time to see that it was a piece of copper ore before he swung the axe down, blade reversed, on the back of Fateh Singh's head. The thin pill-box cap provided no protection; Fateh Singh crumpled forward without a sound. Kundan Singh thrust the axe into his belt and seizing the Thokdar dragged him into the re-entrant twenty yards further on and then, with great difficulty, up a twisting path which led deeper up the gully. When he reached a small, almost level shelf above and out of sight of the road, he rested for a moment or two. Had Fateh Singh not been old and spare he could never have dragged his body so far. He ran back and fetched his shoes and bundle. He was trembling all over: this would never do, he had by far the most difficult part of his task to complete. He opened the bundle and started to eat but the food choked him. He took a swig out of a small bottle of home brewed barley liquor — that was better — he took another and then drained the bottle and threw it aside.

Suddenly, to his horror, Fateh Singh started groaning. He went to the edge of the shelf and looked over. There was no-one in sight on the road. He stepped back. He had a horror of blood; besides it was a dangerous witness. So, with his bare hands he started to throttle the still insensible man. The sounds would haunt him till his death, but they did not last long. Sweating and panting he regarded the corpse. Now it was done. No chance now if someone should come on them, to say that he found the Thokdar lying on the road, injured, it might be supposed, by some casual falling stone dislodged from the hillside above by a browsing goat or a foraging monkey.

He cast all discretion to the winds and started feverishly to strip the doubled blanket coat off the body. When he opened it out, two lumps of ore, like the one he had seen Fateh Singh examining, rolled out. Besides these were only tobacco, tobacco bowl, tinder and flint and fifty rupees in silver in a small leather bag. He pocketed the tobacco and money. Quickly he felt all over the dead man's shirt and his hands closed convulsively on the papers that crackled in an inside pocket. They were sewn in and must be valuable. He tore out the stitches and found the re-sale deed. He had not time to examine this and stuffed it in his pocket. He could decide later whether to keep or destroy it. He spread out the blanket and dragged the Thokdar's body onto it. With great difficulty he succeeded, after several attempts, in doubling the legs back and tying the ankles to the wrists with bark fibre twine. He threw Fateh Singh's cap, tobacco bowl, tinder and flint beside the body and then pulled half the blanket over it. As he had hoped, it was just long enough and wide enough to cover the body except for the head and neck. He rummaged in his own pocket and found a piece of rope, slipped it round and trussed the corpse roughly but effectively in the blanket. He started to bind the open end firmly round the Thokdar's neck with some more of the bark fibre twine — luckily he had a good supply as he had intended to cut some *ringal* bamboo on his way back from Nandaprayag at a place he knew a little way off the road. Just before he finished the job, he noticed the two pieces of copper ore. As an after-thought he pushed them inside before he finally tied up the neck of his improvised sack. They were heavy and would help to sink the body. There was a kind of poetic justice, too, in sending them with his enemy to a watery grave.

Seizing the grim bundle, he dragged it down the slope, onto the road and along it for twenty yards, till he came to the bend directly opposite and facing the point where Fateh Singh had been sitting. This bend rounded a bluff where there was a sheer drop to the river two hundred feet below. The sandstone face ran smoothly for its whole height without a break, there was nothing that could catch a falling body on the way. it was an ideal launching slip for an unwanted corpse. As soon as he got it there he pushed it over and

watched it till it hit the water with a great splash. That put paid to
a feud which had lasted for twenty years of his own life and forty
years of his father's, for Kundan Singh had inherited many
liabilities from a father as improvident as himself.

Kundan Singh straightened up. For the first time since he had
strangled Fateh Singh he bethought himself of his own safety. He
looked round, there was no-one, not a sound; he looked across the
river but could see no sign of life. He looked up behind him and
immediately saw something that gave him a nasty turn. How
stupid to have forgotten where he was. Straight above the shelf
where he had killed the Thokdar was a small cave dwelling built
into the side of the hill, a nunnery. He should have remembered,
the path up which he had dragged the body led up to it. For minutes
he scanned the building. Was it occupied? They would certainly
have seen if they had come out, but the odds were they would not
have come out unless they had heard something. The building was
often empty, it was not really a nunnery in the proper sense, merely
a temporary resting place for these shy old women with their grey
shaven heads and wrinkled leathery faces. He knew he ought to go up
and see. But, supposing there were some nuns there and they had
witnessed the murder, what could he do about it? If he had been
a real murderer there could only have been one answer. But Kundan Singh was not made of that stuff; already he was terrified by
what he had done. The madness and the strength sent him by Siva
had evaporated. All he wanted now was to get away from the place
as quickly as possible. Without thinking of anything now save this,
he ran on his way until he was forced to stop from sheer
exhaustion.

9.   THE INVESTIGATION

Fateh Singh had let it be known in the village that he was going to
Ramnagar to make enquiries into the prospects of marketing
potatoes next year. The return journey would have taken him at
least four weeks. He was a widower and lived in a separate wing
of the house, the rest of which was occupied by his eldest son,
Trilok Singh, whose wife also looked after Fateh Singh. His only
servants were a cowherd and a shepherd, who continued with

their routine duties without bothering about the Thokdar's
whereabouts, and a half-wit boy, said to be some relation, who
acted as personal servant and pony boy on his journeys. He had
been given leave to go to his home on this occasion but Fateh Singh
had not informed anyone else of this and it was assumed that the
boy had gone with him to Ramnagar. Fateh Singh's three sons were
all away from home. This was certainly curious but was not con-
nected in any way with the Thokdar's absence in the minds of his
neighbours. The sons had taken considerable pains to conceal the
fact that they were living in the forest near Palwara in a grass hut
abandoned some years ago by wandering Gujar graziers, to which
they returned at night after working all day to cover up the traces
of their excavations at Palwara and in buying and transporting
charcoal to the cave on Ragsi peak above Palwara where they intended to store the ore. They bought charcoal separately from a
number of woodcutters to conceal the extent of their purchases.

It was quite likely that Fateh Singh's disappearance would not
have led to any enquiries for at least six weeks if it had not been
for an extraordinary coincidence by which his youngest son, Dalip,
on the first occasion of his returning home to fetch some more food
and to see that everything was in order at home, sat down to rest
on the very rock on which his father had sat only a week before,
when he was attacked by Kundan Singh. Dalip was thinking about
the copper and wondering how they would be able to conceal their
transport operations later, when his attention was caught by a
piece of copper ore lying just below the level of the road where he
sat. It looked so utterly foreign there that he thought he must be
the subject of a practical joke at the hands of some ill-disposed
demon. He hesitated for some time, keeping his eyes on the piece
of copper ore in case it should suddenly disappear and then, sum-
moning up courage, he went down to pick it up and immediately
noticed something else — his father's pocket knife — lying close
beside it, the blade open. There was no mistaking that, for it was
not one of the rough and ready country-made knives fashioned by
the local blacksmiths from the iron quarried at Mokh in Dasoli, but
an English one which his father had greatly treasured. Nor was it
likely that it had fallen out of his pocket, for he would never have
put it there with the blade open. He retrieved both stone and knife
and hurried home. There he obtained confirmation that his father
was thought to have gone to Ramnagar. But, at his father's house,
no-one had seen him come back to fetch a change of clothes. He
went to a certain stone in the inner wall of his father's room. It
looked like the other stones save that the mud plaster round it

was slightly cracked. He removed the stone carefully and put his hand into the cavity behind. He hoped it would contain nothing save a small black box in which his father kept certain documents — he did not let even his sons know where he kept his money — but, as he felt round, his hand closed on a small cloth bundle. Quickly he took it to the light and opened it. His heart sank, for inside he found three small pieces of almost pure copper. They were the samples which his father had obtained from the coppersmith in Pokhri. It was inconceivable that he would have left without these, for his last words, when he parted from them on the path below Palwara, were that he was going straight home to fetch them and a change of clothing. Dalip searched the room thoroughly, his father's wardrobe was not extensive, he knew every item of it and the only thin outfit suitable for the plains was still in the cedar chest. He was sure now that his father had met with some accident. He hurried back to Palwara to warn his brothers. Together they returned to Kunjyani and gave the alarm. They had to conceal the clue provided by the piece of copper ore, but they made the most of the finding of the knife and of their father's failure to call at home for thin clothes.

A search party was organised and went straight down to the river, for it seemed that, if their fears were justified, it must be somewhere down there that they would find him.

On the 10th June, on his way back from Kedarnath, Nevill was stopped by a party of villagers at the point on the road near Kandi where Fateh Singh's knife had been found. He was informed that the Thokdar was missing and that a search party had just started to drag the river for him. In view of this news he halted by the roadside.

An hour and a half later the search party found Fateh Singh's body caught above a large boulder in some rapids half a mile further down the river. Shouts were exchanged and his orderly told Nevill excitedly that Fateh Singh had been murdered and thrown in the river in a sack. The blanket, rather, with its grim contents was soon lying on a string cot by the side of the road. The considerable cavalcade, which accompanied Nevill on tour and which had now caught him up, came to a halt, obstructing the whole road and soon the lazier coolies who had dawdled behind came up at the double. Before a large crowd, which grew as the news spread, Nevill personally supervised the unpleasant business of the inquest on the spot.

When he reached the point of recording how Fateh Singh came to be missed, he realised they must be close to the scene of the murder. This gave him a convenient excuse to clear the road. He was also relieved on personal grounds to see the last of his camp staff and their transport moving off reluctantly. There would be some chance now of his tents and a meal being ready for him when he reached his next camp at Nagnath after concluding this business. Only Fateh Singh's three sons, the rest of the search party, the *patwari*, Nevill's own court clerk and one orderly remained, but after some time the headman of Kunjyani and some other relations of the dead man arrived.

When the blanket was opened out, it was all Nevill could do to look at what lay within, and he was astonished again, as he had often been before, at the matter of fact, almost callous, composure with which the *patwari*, friends and relations, yes, and even the murdered man's eldest son, examined and identified the bloated human remains that lay before them.

For Trilok Singh the examination brought also an unpleasant surprise in that he quickly noticed that the re-sale deed for Palwara executed by Kundan Singh, which he knew had been securely sewn in the inner pocket of his father's shirt, was missing. No-one else noticed the torn stitching. In the circumstances he dared not say a word about this.

Guman Singh was an experienced officer and discovered marks of discolouration, very faint because the whole body was discoloured, but still recognisable as a strangler's handiwork. He also found a dark patch at the back of the dead man's head due to suffusion of blood under the skin and this was almost certainly to be explained by a blow delivered probably from behind. If it had been caused during his fall into the river, the scalp would have been torn or, at least, very much more abraised than it was. No money was found though the Thokdar would have needed money for his journey to Ramnagar. But Trilok Singh thought it possible that his father intended to pick up money at his home at the same time as his thinner clothes.

As soon as the body had been examined, it was covered up again under the blanket and it was while they were doing this that two small pieces of rock rolled out onto the road. One rolled right up to Nevill's feet; he picked it up and was surprised at its weight and colour. He had seen something like this before and turned it over several times to examine it. The other piece had been picked up by Trilok Singh. He pocketed it without examination and Nevill noticed that he was looking very queerly at him:

'H'm, ballast', said Nevill aloud and put the lump of stone in his pocket. Both pieces together were still very inadequate as ballast, as had been proved by the distance the corpse had been carried down the river. There was something odd here which he would have to look into later.

As soon as he had completed his notes and obtained the necessary signature, the *patwari* took Nevill aside:

'Sahib, a decision must be taken at once about the trial of this case.'

'The trial?' said Nevill 'aren't you going a little fast? We have to find evidence and a suspect first.'

'We shall find the murderer assuredly,' said Guman Singh with confidence, 'but if you send the body for post-mortem, that will be the only evidence you will get.'

It was put tactfully but Nevill understood what he meant. Time and again he had been faced with this dilemma but never in such a remote spot as the present. The problem was this. The rules of evidence under the English system of criminal justice required not only expert evidence, if available, of the cause of death, but also concrete, or at least very strong circumstantial evidence that a particular person could have been, and was the most likely person to have been responsible for causing the death of the victim by that means before he could be charged and tried as an accused. To establish the cause of death beyond question, even though the dead man was obviously the victim of foul play, a post-mortem was considered desirable, if not absolutely essential, if only to narrow the field of possible suspects. Where it was established beyond doubt that a man was murdered and killed in a particular way but no further evidence was available as to who actually committed the crime, English justice washed its hands of the case.

To the Indian, on the other hand, the body of a human being was still the sacred temple of the soul until the latter had been ritually released and the body burnt by the nearest male relative of the deceased. If Hindu sentiment in this matter was offended, no further evidence was likely to be produced. Moreover, the native code did not accept the impropriety of finding and punishing the murderer, although there might be no evidence against him as understood by western terms of reference. Its justice continued, where the westerner's ended, by resort to more primitive methods long since renounced by the western world. Though these methods often produced spectacular results, they relied too much on chance and superstition to ensure that the innocent should escape unjust condemnation.

Nevill compromised:

'We can probably do without a post-mortem; in fact, I don't

think a post-mortem will be necessary, even if it were possible, in this case. But we must have some evidence, Guman Singh, enough to satisfy the courts, even if you can divine the murderer by some other means.'

The *patwari* said resignedly: 'Very well, I will do my best.'

'I will discuss this with you further,' said Nevill. 'Meanwhile, you can tell these people to take and burn the Thokdar's body.'

'Your Honour, I will tell them at once; they will be grateful.'

In a few minutes they were alone:

'Now, Guman Singh, let us see if we can find any clues on the spot, for it seems likely that the murder took place here as well as the disposal of the corpse.'

They examined the road carefully for some distance on either side; there was nothing to show, for the surface was either hard rock, flints or grit. Nevill had already examined the rocks at the edge of the road, just above the place where the pen-knife had been found, but this had provided no clue. He took the piece of stone out of his pocket and examined it closely. He knew enough of geology to recognise it now for a piece of copper ore and that he was unlikely to find any more in the immediate locality. This piece and the other which had rolled out of Fateh Singh's blanket must have been brought here either by the murderer or by his victim. The road for miles abounded in loose pieces of rock, their descent was a constant hazard of the hill roads. The murderer would hardly have troubled to bring these particular pieces with him, either as weapons or as ballast. They must have been brought then by Fateh Singh — or, of course, they might have been deliberately planted by the murderer. But why? This was interesting but baffling; he could not see for the moment what it could have to do with the murder.

'Guman Singh, do you know of any copper mine or outcrop round here?' he asked.

'Copper, your Honour? No, I know of no copper on this side of the Mohankhal pass. There is plenty, of course, over at Nagnath and round Pokhri.'

'This is a piece of copper ore, look — it is one of the stones which rolled out of Fateh Singh's blanket', and Nevill gave it to the *patwari* to examine.

Guman Singh shook his head, he was as perplexed as Nevill.

They were standing just in front of the re-entrant close to which Fateh Singh had apparently been attacked. While the *patwari* was examining the ore curiously, Nevill tried to reconstruct the crime. He could not help thinking that if Fateh Singh had been attacked

and then strangled, the murderer must have taken a grave risk if
he accomplished all this on the public road. It might have happened
at night but somehow he did not think so. His sons had said he had
parted from them early in the morning and never reached his home.
The penknife with its blade open suggested that Fateh Singh was
occupied in doing something with it when he was attacked and, for
this, he would have needed daylight. If the actual murder had not
been completed on the road, unless the murderer had had at least
one accomplice, he could hardly have brought the corpse from very
far to throw it in the river. Following his train of thought, he looked up the re-entrant directly in front of him.

'Guman Singh, what is that building up there?'

The *patwari* followed the direction of Nevill's eyes:

'It is a sadhu's hut but deserted now for many years; sometimes
nuns stay there. Let us go and see — this is the path.'

They had gone only a few yards when Guman Singh, who was
leading, pointed excitedly:

'Look, something heavy has been dragged up or down this path!'

They reached the small shelf and both saw the bottle. it was lying
in one corner, an ordinary gourd bottle of the type used by
travellers. Guman Singh picked it up and smelt the neck; then passed it to Nevill:

'Jan,' he said, 'the bottle is empty but it has contained the liquor
not so very long ago.'

They found nothing else. From here the rock dwelling was out
of sight but, a few yards further, it came into sight again. As Nevill
looked up he thought he saw a figure draw back into the doorway
— it was an impression of movement, he could not be quite sure
he had actually seen anyone and told himself that it was because
he was keyed up and hoping to find someone there. He told the *patwari* in a low voice.

'Well, we shall soon find out,' said Guman Singh. 'There is only
one entrance.'

When they got there, the *patwari* called out re-assuringly:

'It is I, Guman Singh, *patwari* of Nagpur Talla and with me is
the Assistant Commissioner Sahib. We would speak to thee; we
will wait outside.'

There was no reply. They looked at each other; the *patwari*
nodded towards the doorway and said aloud:

'We will go in, there is no-one there.'

He took a step towards the entrance but almost at once there was a
flutter deep within the doorway and next moment a slight figure
emerged, hands folded in supplication, and fell at their feet — a

nun. Nevill could not tell her age but her hair was close shaved and greying. She must be over fifty he thought. Guman Singh gave her respectful salutations and then questioned her. In an almost incoherent babble she told them of the murder of Fateh Singh. When he was being throttled, she had heard the sounds and run out to see what it was. When she realised a man was being murdered, she hid in fear but saw the corpse being dragged along the road and thrown over the cliff. She had been too terrified to report the matter to anyone; she had been living here ever since. No-one had come to see her. No, she could not remember the exact date, but it was about a week ago. Yes, the murderer was alone; no, she did not know him and did not think she would be able to recognise him again, but she would try to describe him. She did so and the *patwari* made some notes and then, turning to Nevill, said:

'Sahib, here is your only eye-witness, but you will never get her into any court.'

'I suppose and fear you are right,' said Nevill. 'Do you recognise anyone from her description?'

The *patwari* nodded:

'I am not absolutely certain but I believe it must be Kundan Singh, a relation of Fateh Singh. He is a reckless gambler and was heavily indebted to the Thokdar, there is an old feud between them. But I am a little puzzled because he is a timid man, apart from his gambling, and afraid of physical force; he is not the stuff of which murderers are made.'

'We have a proverb — "Even a worm will turn" ', said Nevill.

The *patwari* nodded:

'It could be possible,' he said. 'There has been great provocation in the past and something odd has been going on recently between them over some land, but so useless that no-one would bother to fight about it.'

Turning to the woman, Guman Singh said kindly but firmly:

'Your knowledge is now our knowledge; you are relieved of any further responsibility. Stay here and, if anyone asks you anything, you know nothing — see? I will come back in a few days' time; when I send you a message, come down on the road. You will draw water at the spring until I pass by with a man. As we pass look carefully at this man. When we have passed, you will go back to your dwelling and stay there until I come to you. You will tell me if that was the murderer; if so, your business will be done and you will be free to leave at once — if not, you will wait until I do find the right man.'

She agreed meekly. Nevill was astonished. When they were back on the road, he asked the *patwari* how he could be certain that she would obey his instructions. Guman Singh was confident:

'Until the murdered man is avenged, his ghost is liable to haunt this spot and then the nuns would be frightened to come back here,' he explained.

'But the funeral obsequies can now be performed by his son — won't that suffice to lay his ghost?' asked Nevill.

'The ceremonies will take some time longer, she will not leave until they are concluded and it will take a few days before she learns of the funeral. Meanwhile she will do as I bid and that should give me enough time to test my theory about the culprit. But you will see — she will not come into any court to give evidence, not even before the village elders, and we cannot compel her, for it is written in the ancient laws of Manu that anchorites secluded from wordly affairs cannot be called as witnesses.'

Nevill considered for a while: then he said:

'What do you want me to do?'

Guman Singh looked at him doubtfully and then at the ground; he seemed to find some difficulty in replying.

'I won't mind what you say,' Nevill added.

'Sahib, couldn't we hold the trial before a village court?' Guman Singh seemed greatly relieved now that he had dared to speak out what was in his mind. Something stirred inside the young Assistant Commissioner, a sense of excitement and anticipation. But he remembered his position:

'I will think about it,' he said, 'Perhaps we could call it an enquiry.'

'Call it what you will, Sahib, but first see and hear what happens before the village court.'

'Well, perhaps. I'll leave you now to continue your investigation. I must get on to my camp. Let me have a report as soon as you can. I shall be at Nagnath for another week. . . By the way, don't forget the copper ore, I'm convinced it has something to do with the crime.'

'Very good, your honour.'

10. THE IDENTIFICATION

Guman Singh did not expect to find Kundan Singh at home. He was told that the latter had gone to Nandaprayag over a week ago to order wool, it was not understood why he had not already returned. Guman Singh thought he knew why — his delay confirmed his suspicions. But Kundan Singh might return any moment, there was no time to be lost.

The *patwari* reached Pokhri the same evening and set out early on 11th June for Kaphalpani. There he arranged for two reliable men to watch the bridge across the Nighaul river below the village. Kundan Singh was almost certain to return by this route, if he returned at all, as it was the most direct. Somehow, the *patwari* thought he would, as he had taken steps at once to stop the news of the murder being carried to Nandaprayag.

One man was to loiter on or near the bridge and the other on the third hairpin bend of the road which climbed steeply from the river crossing. The man below, who knew Kundan Singh, would signal to the man above as soon as Kundan Singh crossed the river and the second man would warn the *patwari*, who would be waiting on the road above him. This man would go on ahead to Pokhri and would be available to go ahead to call the nun down to the roadside spring either the same day, or, if Kundan Singh stopped the night in Pokhri, the next day. His plan worked perfectly.

Kundan Singh had spun out his visit to Nandaprayag for as long as he dared. But eight days had already passed since he left home and people might be beginning to wonder why he had not returned. Reluctantly he started back the day after Fateh Singh's body had been recovered. During his enforced idleness he had begun to think about his future. If he was lucky enough to get away with this murder, he would use Palwara to his advantage. When there was no longer any chance of a case being brought against him, he would go to Trilok Singh and do a deal — he would promise to keep his mouth shut about the copper in exchange for the remission of all his debts, and some cash to set him up independently for the first time in his life. But these bright hopes could not altogether lay the spectre of fear which dogged his steps as he set out for home.

On his way he turned aside to cut the ringal bamboo as he had originally planned; he would make this the excuse for his delay in returning, should anyone question him about this. He had done the journey from Kansili to Nandaprayag, twenty four miles, in one day; now with a heavy load of bamboo he would stop a night at

Pokhri on the way. When he reached the Nighaul river there was
a man repairing the near buttress of the bridge. He knew him slightly and gave him a nod as he passed. The bridge was narrow and
the surface none too good; Kundan Singh was also carrying sixty
pounds of ringal bamboo on his back, so he kept his eyes on the log
planks and thus had no opportunity of seeing a man on the cliff
road ahead receive a signal from the man behind him on the bridge.

The *patwari* was waiting round a corner almost at the top of the
hill. He had found his vigil very boring and was glad it was over.
He sent the messenger on to Pokhri. When Kundan Singh came
round the corner he almost ran into Guman Singh who was just
getting up from the side of the road, as if he had been resting on
his way up the steep climb. Kundan Singh's fears returned with a
rush. The *patwari* — what did it mean? However, there was
nothing he could do about it. He halted and eased his load, hoping
that the *patwari* would go on — but no, he was in a sociable and
talkative mood.

'Hello, Kundan Singh, where have you been?' he asked.

'Nandaprayag,' said Kundan Singh. 'I have been ordering wool
for next winter.'

'Very provident of you; what was the price?'

'Two and a half seers to the rupee.'

'That's reasonable enough if the quality is good; that looks good
cane too,' and Guman Singh came up close and started to examine
the ringal bamboo. He noticed the small axe tucked into Kundan
Singh's waist rope.

'H'm, not bad — a tidy load to carry though.'

Kundan Singh said nothing, he was on the alert and uneasy.

'From whom did you order the wool, by the way?' the *patwari*
asked:

'Shib Singh of Malari,' said Kundan Singh.

'I know him, he is fairly honest,' said the *parwari*. 'As a matter
of fact most of the Bhotias are honest enough in the matters of trade
though now and again you come across a real bad'un.'

Guman Singh proceeded to enlarge upon the subject and Kundan
Singh breathed again more freely; perhaps this was, after all, a
chance encounter — it must be, for how could Guman Singh have
known he was coming just at that time. His confidence returned.

'Shall we go together?' said the *patwari* affably; Kundan Singh
could not very well refuse. They stopped at Pokhri for a meal. The
patwari said casually:

'Are you stopping here for the night?'

'No,' said Kundan Singh. 'I must get home, I am already late.'

He had intended to stop at Pokhri but had changed his mind. He was overcome by an urge to get home at once and find out in his own way, discreetly, how Fateh Singh's failure to return home was being accounted for. He felt confident that foul play was not yet suspected, for in that case the *patwari* would know about it and would hardly have failed to mention it to him — a relative known to be on bad terms with Fateh Singh — either as news or, as a police officer to check up on his recent movements. He had not even asked him how long he had been away. He hoped the *patwari* would have to stop in Pokhri himself but to his annoyance Guman Singh said:

'Oh well, we can go on together then: I am on my way home too; I can come with you as far as the turning to your village. Hadn't you better engage a man to carry your load? You must be tired and there is still a long way to go.'

'I can't afford to hire porters, I'll manage', said Kundan Singh, 'but don't let me keep you back — I'll take my own time.'

'I am in no hurry', said Guman Singh, 'and I'd like company.'

They went on, the *patwari* chatting easily and Kundan Singh answering mostly in monosyllables. On the Mohankhal pass Kundan Singh sat down to rest. The *patwari* went on a few yards before stopping; he had seen a man coming up the hill towards them — the man he had sent to warn the nun. When he reached them Kundan Singh saw him stop and talk briefly to the *patwari* but he was too far away to hear their conversation. He had completed nineteen miles of his twenty-four mile journey with a heavy load and was feeling very tired.

When they started off again the *patwari* said:

'By the way, when I saw you last, if you remember, I asked you if you knew who had been cultivating Palwara. You said you did not know. Well, I have found out — it was Fateh Singh, Thokdar and that his intention was to plant potatoes there. He told me he was going down to Ramnagar to order seed potatoes for the autumn.'

Kundan Singh listened with interest, but his mind fastened only on one piece of information — that Fateh Singh was going to Ramnagar. So that was it! They thought he had gone to Ramnagar — he had not yet been missed. There was a pause, the significance of which Guman Singh did not miss, before he replied:

'I shouldn't have thought Palwara was any good for any kind of crop; Fateh Singh must have taken leave of his senses to waste his time and money on it.'

'I don't know about that,' said Guman Singh. 'They say the

new variety of potatoes does very well in high and exposed sites.'

Kundan Singh had forgotten his physical tiredness in the relief he experienced from the news about Fateh Singh. But the relief was short-lived. As they neared the scene of the murder a new anxiety overwhelmed him. It had been his intention to take a field path just after leaving the pass, which, though longer and more strenuous than the road, especially for a man with a heavy load, would have enabled him to avoid passing the fatal spot. With the complication of the *patwari's* unwanted company he could think of no convincing excuse to make the detour. If he had been alone and for some reason obliged to keep to the road, he would have run past the spot. But now he had to brace himself to act normally.

They reached the spot. Kundan Singh avoided looking at anything in particular, his feet followed each other automatically and he tried to make his mind a blank. But it was no good, he couldn't do it. He tried to concentrate on thinking out what he would say when he got home to explain to his friends the delay in his return. Suddenly, he heard the *patwari* say:

'This is where they found the body of Fateh Singh.'

He stopped abruptly and slewed round towards the *patwari*:

'What's that?' he said. 'What did you say?'

'Haven't you heard? Fateh Singh has been murdered; his body was found in the river just below here, tied up in his own blanket. Look, here is the piece of rock which we believe may have been used to kill him with', and Guman Singh produced the piece of copper ore which Nevill had given him. By using shock tactics he had hoped to trap Kundan Singh and also to obtain some clue to the significance of the copper ore, as instructed by Nevill.

Kundan Singh hardly looked at it; he wanted to say something, anything, in a casual, matter of fact way, but no words came. He clutched at the strings which passed each side of his neck and by which he held his load of cane, as if by pulling them tighter he could constrain the guilty secret which sought to burst from his perspiring body. With a great effort he controlled himself. The reaction left him weak and feeling rather faint. He found a convenient rock and, leaning back, eased his load onto it:

'I feel a little overcome', he finally managed to say. 'He was my uncle by marriage.'

Guman Singh looked at him curiously, with some inward satisfaction — he had not missed the signs of panic:

'I did not think there was any love lost between you two', he said.

Kundan Singh felt trapped. He was certain now that this had not been a chance encounter, though he could not understand how they had found the body so soon and why suspicion should have rested on him. To his relief Guman Singh did not pursue the matter any further. He picked up his load and they went on.

They came to the spring, there was a figure bending over the trough. As they came up he saw it was a woman — a nun.

'Ah!' said the *patwari*. 'I could do with a drink myself — and I expect you need one even more than I do.'

At last Kundan Singh saw an opportunity to get away — if he was going to be allowed to get away at all:

'If you'll excuse me', he said. 'I must get on', and he made to pass on.

The *patwari* did not try to stop him. As Kundan Singh passed the trough, the nun turned and looked at him. He looked away at once, but it was too late; in that instant he read the truth in her eyes — she had recognised him. A terrible conviction gripped him. Oblivious of the *patwari's* presence, he looked up at the rock dwelling and then back at the nun. So there had been a witness after all! From the visions of untold future wealth which had beguiled him his mind descended painfully to grapple with the more immediate problem of saving his own skin. There was just a chance that this meeting with the nun had been accidental, as also his encounter with the *patwari*, and that the two were unconnected; but it would be more prudent to assume that he was, at least suspected — as a known enemy of Fateh Singh. That emnity would be inherited by Trilok Singh, his eldest son. It would be unsafe now to reveal his possession of the re-sale deed of Palwara as his son might know it had been stolen from his father by the murderer and he would suspect Kundan Singh. These thoughts troubled him as he toiled up the last clumb to Kansili, too exhausted to think out any plan to counter such suspicions.

When Kundan Singh had gone, Guman Singh turned to the woman:

'Your confirmation — was that the man?'

She nodded.

'Good, now go in peace — no need to wait any longer. The due obsequies have been completed, the body has been burnt, the soul has been released.'

She joined her palms before her face and made a slight obeisance. Giman Singh acknowledged it respectfully. She picked up her pitcher and left.

Guman Singh was well satisfied with his day's work. When he got home he wrote out his report for Nevill. He had no doubts —

he had found the murderer; in due course he would discover the motive.

11. THE MAY MADNESS

Throughout May tension had been mounting in Bareilly since the news of the uprisings in Meerut and Delhi. As a raw recruit of only two months' standing Dhan Singh could hardly be expected to know what it was all about. He had not yet taken the oath or been enrolled. As a hillman, too, he was considered an outsider and not to be trusted with any confidences on such delicate matters. But from the very date he joined the regiment he heard a great deal of loose talk about grievances and fears. In his ignorance he thought this must be the natural behaviour and talk of soldiers, especially as the words were not accompanied by any action. Discipline was strict and pride in the regiment high.

On 21 May, however, a general parade of all troops was held, at which the Brigadier-General commanding the Station, a stout old warrior who was held in general esteem, re-assured the Sepoys as to the intentions of the government and called on them to remain steadfast and not to listen to wild rumours and suspicions. Dhan Singh turned out with the rest of the 18th Infantry; even he realised that there must be something wrong to call for such an unusual address. After the parade he overheard some of the native officers expressing satisfaction at these assurances and their determination to put their fears and suspicions behind them. Some of them, he gathered, had done so publicly before the General at the parade; from the back of the parade he had not been able to see this. Dhan Singh thought no more about the matter.

But, on 29 and 30 May, large numbers of mutineers from Ferozepore passed through Bareilly and spread the wildest alarms. A large European force with artillery was on its way, so they said, to destroy all the native regiments. On the night of the thirtieth, instead of retiring to their hutments, large numbers of the men stayed in the lines and the night passed amidst scenes of the utmost confusion. Dhan Singh sought out three hillmen with whom he had struck up a slight acquaintance — one a recruit like himself, the others men of two to three years' service — and they discussed the situation.

One of the older men said he would do as his native under-officers decided; the others were afraid to discuss the matter further in his presence. But Dhan Singh could tell that they agreed with him that this trouble was none of their business and they should not become involved. Nothing was agreed save to await the morning's events.

Sunday morning was quiet as usual. But at 11.00 a.m. on this day, 31 May 1857, a gun was fired in the artillery lines — just a single shot and, as if at a signal, pandemonium broke loose. Sepoys poured out of the lines, armed and in a highly excitable state. In a short time firing could be heard from the direction of the European officers' bungalows.

Dhan Singh rushed out, like many others, to see what was happening but without any clear idea what they intended to do. He had not taken his rifle. He found himself, along with the other hill recruit, Ram Singh — a Kumaoni — in a party of the 18th infantry advancing in anything but military formation towards the Indian cavalry lines. This was not an accident. The ringleaders knew that the attitude of the native cavalry might prove decisive and their object was to win them over before their officers did so.

Dhan Singh heard a horseman approaching at a sharp canter from a side road; the junction was already blocked by the Sepoys. He could see nothing for the press of bodies in front but he heard the sharp command and recognised the voice of the old General. The men were shouting, the words of command were drowned and then two shots rang out. The Sepoys split as the horseman charged into their midst and Dhan Singh just caught a glimpse of the General, his face pale, his gloved hand stained crimson from the wound in his chest, as he swept by on his maddened charger.

Dhan Singh understood now what was happening and took a sudden decision. The army as a career seemed to be finished for the moment. In any case it had not been particularly attractive to date during his brief apprenticeship. The whole of his time off parade had been occupied in performing fatigue duties and various menial tasks for particular under-officers.

While the dust of the stricken Brigadier's exit still enveloped the group of infantrymen, he nudged Ram Singh and they both slipped through a hedge and dropped into a ditch on the far side. They waited until the others were out of sight and then made off across country towards the hills. Their first care was to avoid recognition as Sepoys by either side; so they stripped off their uniforms until they stood only in their loincloths and undershirts. They made for an outlying bazaar with the idea of buying some civilian clothes. But they found, when they got there, that the only cloth shop had already been looted. There was no sign of the owner. But they found some rough peasant clothes lying discarded behind a box at the back of the shop. Putting these on, they made across country avoiding the main road. They saw many signs of lawlessness which they knew must have been committed long before the fateful gunshot in Bareilly. In one village, which they had found deserted they helped themselves to two stout *lathis* (staves) lying in a burnt out house. They saw other men in the distance also moving across country away from Bareilly, some still in their Sepoy uniforms, but made no attempt to join them as they were uncertain of their reception.

When night fell they had made about twenty miles. Hunger drove them onto the road to find a wayside food shop. There were five men already inside eating, two of them obviously Sepoys. The proprietor eyed the newcomers with disfavour but said nothing when he saw they had money and were prepared to pay for their meal. No-one spoke while they were eating, but as soon as they went outside to have a smoke and a breath of fresh air, the conversation started again inside.

After a while a man came out and sat down beside them. he puffed at his *chelum* (clay pipe) for some minutes and then said in a guarded tone:

'What news, brothers, do you also travel by night or sleep?'

Dhan Singh had been studying him carefully and decided he was not a Sepoy and not a local villager either. he had also decided that it would be useless to pretend that they themselves were villagers of the district. So he said:

'We are pilgrims bound for Hardwar.'

'Ah!' said the other, eyeing their clothes, 'you have been robbed on the road perhaps?'

'No,' said Dhan Singh, 'we thought it safer to travel off the roads and in these clothes.'

'Very wise', said the other, 'very sensible — and may I know how far you have come?'

'We don't rightly know how far we have come today', said Dhan Singh, evading giving the information wanted. 'We are strangers to these parts. What place is this?'

The stranger took a long pull at his pipe before replying. Dhan Singh could see he was sizing them up carefully as he smoked and he grew uneasy. But their inquisitor seemed to make up his mind suddenly to be friendly. Ignoring Dhan Singh's last question, he said:

'I know of a place where we can sleep safely; come with me.'

Dhan Singh looked at Ram Singh doubtfully; neither of them made any move. The man came up closer and said in a low voice:

'It is unhealthy to rest for the night on the roadside — too many decoits, in uniform and out. There are some in there now', and he jerked his head in the direction of the shop. 'Come, I know a village close to here where we shall be safer.'

When he saw that Dhan Singh still hesitated, he said ingratiatingly:

'You are two young strong-looking fellows. God knows if you are really pilgrims but you look honest to me. I too would travel to Hardwar; let us go together; three pairs of arms are better than one.'

So that was it — he was afraid. Dhan Singh nodded his assent and signed to Ram Singh. They all three got up and left unobtrusively. In a village a mile further on and about the same distance from the road their new companion knocked confidently on the door of one of the humbler mud-brick houses. After a few moments a man came to the door, unlocked it and let them in. He looked questioningly at the two hillmen. Their new-found friend introduced them:

'My road companions, Dhan Singh and Ram Singh.'

'They are welcome; is it a meal?'

'No, friend, we have fed — but we would rest here for the night. Four pairs of arms are still better than three,' and he nudged Dhan Singh meaningly. The other man laughed nervously:

'At your service, Bikram.'

He showed them into an inner courtyard where there were four string cots.

The night passed without incident. Once, just before he dropped to sleep, Dhan Singh thought he heard a commotion from the direction of the road and he saw his host sit up quickly on his cot and listen. But the noise died away and he slept.

They travelled in this manner for five more days. In every village where they stopped for the night Bikram seemed to know someone, for he was a barber and, as he explained to Dhan Singh and Ram Singh, all barbers were brothers.

'Murderous company', said Dhan Singh with a grim. 'We are lucky to have survived so far.'

Bikram laughed:

'We barbers are a timid race, but we know the value of a whole skin — like some of you soldiers!'

Dhan Singh looked at him sharply:

'How did you know we were soldiers?'

'Oh, I guessed that night we met. But I kept quiet because I could see that the better policy. As the saying goes — "Between the blind soldier and the wall-eyed man providence has created friendship" — Anyway, it doesn't matter now, does it?'

'No, I suppose not. We would prefer, however, that you kept the knowledge to yourself — if a barber can do such a thing.'

'Of course, of course; are we not the confidants of kings and concubines?'

'In my country', said Dhan Singh, 'we have a saying — "If you want to keep a secret, shave yourself".'

The next day they felt safe enough to return to the road and were lucky enough to be able to hire an *ekka*, which took them in two more days to Hardwar. The heat was intolerable. Dhan Singh looked longingly at the dim outline of the hills, so near now, so desirable that he wondered how he could ever have wanted to leave them.

On 9 June, after taking farewell of Bikram at Hardwar with many expressions of gratitude, Dhan Singh and Ram Singh resumed their journey but no longer in the guise of pilgrims as they were able to buy suitable clothes in Hardwar.

At Lachmanjhula, fifteen miles north of Hardwar, they were stopped by a patrol of specially enrolled Garhwali militiamen guarding this gateway into the hills. They were closely questioned but, being hillmen themselves and knowing the object of these enquiries, they had little difficulty in satisfying the patrol that they were not lawless men seeking to enter the district to create trouble.

They reached Karnaprayag on the fourteenth, where their paths parted. Ram Singh turned east up the Pindar valley which would take him to Almora by the Gairsen route. On the fifteenth of June Dhan Singh returned four miles on his road and crossed the Alaknanda river by a rope bridge to enter Nagpur.

His brief exile had taught him much and cured him of his infatuation for a career in the Sepoy Army. Now he was returning gladly to his own land and home, but a little fearfully as he was doubtful of his reception.

He stopped that night at Pokhri, the informal capital of Nagpur Parganah.

When he reached his home in Kandi village next day his father was out; his mother was too overjoyed to ask any questions. His father came home in the late afternoon, he was delighted to see his son. After two hours came the questions as Dhan Singh had expected. He was asked about his life in the army, his duties and his treatment, his pay and his holidays. Dhan Singh had decided that he would not conceal anything from his father, but it was not going to be easy.

'After how many days will you have to start back to rejoin your regiment?' Kesar Singh's voice betrayed his anxiety. Dhan Singh drew a deep breath:

'I am not going back to my regiment — it is being disbanded.' Dhan Singh was only anticipating the inevitable. He was relieved to find that his father accepted his answer without further question. Kesar Singh was doubly pleased — pleased that his son was not going back to the army and pleased that it had only taken him two months to discover for himself the truth of his father's advice, which he previously ignored. He had only one more question and that now only out of curiosity.

'How were you able, son, to afford the cost of your journey to enlist in the army?'

Dhan Singh had hoped that his father might have forgotten about this.

'Father, the answer to this question will not please you. I am deeply ashamed of my part in this affair. Fateh Singh, Thokdar gave me thirty rupees for my share of the joint family ownership of Palwara. He told me he was acting for a friend who wanted to grow potatoes there. I realise now . . .' His father interrupted:

'The old devil! He came to see me on the day before you ran away and offered to buy Palwara. He said he wanted to grow potatoes there himself. I told him we could not sell because, although the other co-sharers might be willing, you were not prepared to part with your share. I heard no more from Fateh Singh, but, about a month later, Kundan Singh, a poor relation of the Thokdar, came to see me and said he wanted to buy Palwara. He showed me a document which contained your agreement to sell your share to him. I called all the other co-sharers and showed them the deed. After some discussion we agreed to sell but doubted whether Kundan Singh could afford our price of seventy five rupees. To our surprise he brought the money in cash the next day. This man is a spendthrift and a pauper. Where did he get the money? Why all this devious and secretive manoeuvring by the Thokdar? And why is this worthless piece of land involved?'

'Father, I know nothing of all this. But my conscience has troubled me ever since I accepted the money and I should like to make amends by repaying the thirty rupees. . .' Kesar Singh broke in:

'That you will not do, my boy, and why?' he spoke grimly: 'Because Fateh Singh paid this money illegally as part of a deceit and, therefore, forfeited all right to it, and, still more to the point, he was murdered on the third of June. Kundan Singh is suspected to be the murderer and his trial is to take place at Nagnath on the eighteenth of June, the day after tomorrow. I did not propose to attend, but, in view of our involvement over Palwara, I have changed my mind. You had better come with me, son.'

'What about the money, Father?'

'Justice will be done if you keep the thirty rupees but renounce your share of the sale price we got for Palwara.'

'It is too generous, Father.'

'Not at all. The thirty rupees was tainted money; no-one else will touch it. You were lucky not to have suffered some harm by spending it.'

12.   THE TEMPLE TRIAL

The Charge

Kundan Singh was arrested on the 13th June. Nevill had agreed that the Inquiry should be held by a special *panchayat* at Nagnath. He proposed to attend the Inquiry himself. He had made up his mind that he would not intervene at all unless it was absolutely necessary in the interests of justice. He would be a spectator, privileged, so he felt, to attend the ceremony revived out of a past that was already growing dim. Alas for good resolutions! He had determined not to intervene, yet he found himself doing so more than once for reasons which surprised himself. He called it an Inquiry, but everyone else there regarded it as the trial of Fateh Singh's murderer.

The joint *panchayats* of Pokhri and Nagnath selected five elders, with the *Sarpanch* of Pokhri as president of the court. On the morning of the trial, the 18th of June, such a large crowd gathered that it was decided to hold the proceedings in the temple courtyard.

This courtyard was of a type occasionally found in the hills. Its rectangle of terraced steps enclosed a bathing tank fed by a hot spring. The steps were broken at only one place which formed the entrance passage from the road, sloping down gently to the level of the water in the tank. On each side of this passage the steps ran up to give access to a covered arcade or cloister which was balanced by a similar but continuous colonnade opposite on the other long side of the pool. On the third side the steps ran up to a high stone wall. A little way in front of this wall and growing out of the steps themselves was a fine peepul tree, some of its branches overhanging the pool. The bole springing from the partly exposed roots, gave an impression of great muscular strength like the neck of a strong man lifting an enormous weight. In the deeply sculptured hollows between these sinews stood stone images of Hanuman and Ganesh, painted a bright scarlet, and many little lingam stones of Siva. It was a beautiful and satisfying tree; even on the most airless summer day its leaves were hardly ever still.

On the fourth side was the temple. This and the wall opposite it were built of green granite; the colonnade was of red sandstone, the capitals of its sturdy pillars projected boldly and were deeply carved. The steps were of grey granite and worn smooth by countless generations of worshippers. The hot and slightly sulphurous water gushed into the tank through a massive stone spout carved in the shape of a hooded cobra's head. Over the main entrance into the temple was carved another, a truly giant cobra's head in whose shadow clustered many smaller snakes' heads, for the temple was dedicated to the Snake-God Nag. The Pagoda roof, common to many Hill Temples, was a striking testimony to the cultural interchange with Tibet.

When, at the beginning of the ninth century A.D. that astonishing young reformer and proselytizer, Shankaracharya — he died at the age of thirty-two — forced the hillmen to accept the greater gods of the Brahmanic pantheon, they found comfort in the fact that most of these all-powerful and universal deities assumed at one time or another, the form of one or more animals, birds or reptiles. The simple hillmen were able, therefore, to continue worshipping some of their old animistic godlings under a cloak of respectability and with the connivance of almost equally ignorant priests.

The snake occupied an ambivalent position in Brahmanic mythology. He was usually depicted as a hydra-headed demon, warring endlessly against the gods who trampled him underfoot. But, sometimes he was a beneficient ally, whose intelligence made him a valuable and watchful guardian. Vishnu, the Preserver, laid himself down to rest on Ananta or Sesha, the serpent, whose hood was raised protectively over the head of the sleeping god. The Naginis, the female snakes of Hindu mythology, were snake charmers in their own right and form — half woman and half snake — who came to tempt men with their seductive charm, a rational extension of the Garden of Eden story. Ignorant man is inclined to

placate what he fears by worshipping it. It is significant that the
snake worshipped in India is always the deadly cobra. Though
many people die every year of snake bite, the Indian will not go
out of his way to kill a snake, especially those living in or near
houses. Instead he will put out a bowl of milk.

With a limited grasp of theology and with native loyalty, the
hillmen endowed their own older and more intelligible godlings
with the attributes of the greater deities. The Nagas worshipped
their Snake God as the fount of wisdom and justice, where the orthodox Brahmanic theology assigned him no more than intelligence
and invisibility and banished him to the underworld, where he
guarded earth's treasures, jewels and gold, with sleepless eye.

Into this amphitheatre poured the largest crowd Nagnath had
seen for years. They filled every inch of it save for the stone-flagged
terrace in front of the temple where the village court and its
Brahmin advisers sat behind a trestle table. Nevill and the *patwari*
sat together at right angles to the court and two steps higher. The
accused stood before the *panchayats*. The atmosphere was that of
high festival. While the crowd was still flowing in, vendors of
sweetmeats, refreshments and coloured drinks hawked their goods
round the steps together with pedlars of pottery cups, toys and
caps. There was even a clown with a performing monkey dressed
as a dancing girl and a talking mynah in a cage. Anything more
unlike the public gallery of the Old Bailey it would be difficult to
imagine.

When the courtyard was full, the temple servants drove the
clown and the hawkers away. Nevill estimated that there were not
less than seven hundred people assembled, possibly up to a thousand as they were so tightly packed.

Kesar Singh and Dhan Singh had arrived early to get good seats
at the top of the steps which climbed up to the long red sandstone
colonnade on the long side of the courtyard nearest to the road.
They sat on the top step on the temple side of one of the large red
sandstone pillars of the colonnade which gave them a good view
and excellent hearing of the judges, the accused, the prosecutor and
witnesses. But the pillar hid them from the greater part of the audience to their right.

The proceedings started with prayers, followed by a long disser-
tation in Sanskrit by one of the priests on the merits and rules of
guidance of the ancient criminal code of Manu, illustrated with
copious extracts and examples. Once started he found it hard to
stop: such an opportunity was obviously rare and not to be
neglected. He reminded his audience gravely, without a spark of

humour from beginning to end to relieve the tedium of his lecture, that the evidence of various kinds of witnesses was worthless, that of others unreliable. No trust could be placed in persons with a pecuniary interest in the dispute, who were familiar friends or confessed enemies of the parties, who were entirely dependent, former perjurers, convicted thieves or heinous offenders. Of little value was the evidence of menial servants, cooks, mean artificers, public dancers or singers, persons of ill-fame or cruel occupation. The evidence of persons who were hungry, thirsty, tired, intoxicated, excited by lust or influenced by wrath, or who had lost any of the organs of sense was no more acceptable than that of priests of deep learning in scripture, of students of theology, or of recluses engaged in unworldly meditation.

And here he paused, as if to emphasise the admirable reasonableness and impartiality of the great lawgiver. But, instead of ending on this eminently practical note, he was off again, warning them to accept only with the greatest caution the evidence of single witnesses unless of impeccable virtue, of persons suffering under the strain of grief, from grievous disease, or who were merely mad, the evidence of decrepit old men or of small children. Finally, he reminded them that the evidence of one reliable man was worth that of many women because their understanding was inclined to waver. Though final, this was by no means the end of his advice. It was plain common sense not to examine too closely the competence or veracity of witnesses to violence, should their evidence be contradictory. Decision should be according to the plurality of credible witnesses of equal virtue. If the issue was delicately balanced in this respect, the evidence of a twice-born Brahmin who had performed public duties would be decisive.

The crowd started to fidget with boredom; less than one per cent understood a word of what he said. Some time after he could no longer be heard effectively he came to an end and sat down.

After this learned homily it was a relief when the *Sarpanch* rose and said in the familiar patois of their own hills:

'In the name of Pushkara Nag, god of wisdom and justice, I call on all concerned to speak the truth before this court after taking oath, the farmer on his cattle, the husband and father on the heads of his wife and children, the twice-born by the names of the seven great *rishis*. Remember that he who gives false evidence endangers his future life — no Ganges pilgrimage will avail him. Who utters falsehood against another kills a thousand kinsmen — he shall be like a man who eats fish greedily and swallows the bones. If anyone is accused let him answer, or he will be adjudged guilty. In the

name of Nag let justice be done in the matter of the murder of Fateh
Singh Thokdar.'

At last the trial could start. The *patwari*, Guman Singh, was called and related the known and undisputed facts. From this he passed
to the suggestion that Fateh Singh had had many enemies, several
of whom might have had sufficient motive to murder him but not,
apparently, the opportunity. He would, therefore, name only one,
the actual murderer, who also seemed to have had the opportunity.
Nevertheless, he reminded the court that the victim's next-of-kin
was also entitled, by immemorial custom, to name an accused and
a sentence and these would also have to be taken into
consideration.

'Now,' said Guman Singh, 'I have told you that Fateh Singh left
his home early on the 3rd of June with the intention of going to
Ramnagar. No-one actually saw him start and he went alone. But
it seems that, before leaving for the plains, he went up the road
towards Kandi by arrangement to meet his son Dalip to discuss
some business and that he told him that he was going to call in at
his home on the way to fetch a change of thin clothes for the plains.
Dalip will give evidence that he parted from his father at about 8.30
a.m. Fateh Singh never reached his house. On the same morning,
Kundan Singh, son of Dhum Singh, of Kansili, who, as you know,
is a relation of Fateh Singh by marriage, left his home, by his own
admission, some time before 9.00 a.m. to go to Nandaprayag to
order twenty-five seers of Tibetan wool from Shib Singh Bhotia of
Malari. From his home to the scene of the murder is about one mile.
He would have reached this spot, which he had to pass, at about
the same time as the Thokdar. It would appear that Fateh Singh
stopped on the roadside and took out his penknife for some purpose. If Kundan Singh overtook him while he was seated and occupied in some way with his knife — perhaps he had stopped to
eat — he could well have had an opportunity to come on him
unawares.'

Up to this point there had been some shuffling and coughing
amongst the audience; but now there was dead silence as they
waited expectantly for further details. The *patwari* continued:

'Kundan Singh had not more than one day's business in Nandaprayag and I have verified that it took him, in fact, only one day
to complete his business there. It would take him in all only three
or four to do his business and get there and back. But he did not
start back until nine days after he had left his home. Why this
delay? Was it, perhaps, because he was afraid to return or reluctant
to repass the scene of his crime?'

Everyone was now looking or trying to look at Kundan Singh. He returned their stares rather truculently, nursing his courage on a secret hope. The *patwari* continued:

'I met Kundan Singh on his way back from Nandaprayag and before he reached his home. As we passed the scene of the crime, I told him that Fateh Singh had been killed and his body recovered from the river below. He acted like a guilty man and almost fainted though he had no love for the Thokdar. He was carrying a light lopping axe, which he had taken to cut ringal bamboo on his way home. It was the sort of weapon which a man could easily have used to knock out or kill Fateh Singh. Here it is,' and Guman Singh suddenly produced the axe and held it up for all to see.

At this the tension in his audience broke and he waited for a minute to regain silence before resuming:

'But he did not kill him with this axe — it seems he only stunned him with it or with a stone — otherwise he could have thrown him in the river there and then. Evidence on the spot and on Fateh Singh's body shows that he was dragged up the slope above the road and there, out of sight of possible travellers on the road, he was finally strangled to death. This reconstruction is consistent with the accused's well-known fear of the sight of blood. This explanation is supported, too, by the only eye-witness of the actual murder, who had never seen the accused before but described him to me and later identified him . . . unfortunately she is a nun and unwilling to give evidence before any court, and, as you know, she cannot be compelled. . .'

The *patwari* paused as a long murmur rippled through his audience. Guman Singh continued, he had nearly finished making out his case.

'As for motive, Kundan Singh was heavily in debt to Fateh Singh and living on his charity — if that is really the right word — shall I say, rather, existing at his mercy. "Debt, indeed, was his wife", as the saying is. I have here the accounts produced by the Thokdar's eldest son; they show that Kundan Singh owes nearly three thousand rupees. He has no hope of paying off such a large debt.

'I do not know what drove Kundan Singh to this final desperate act — perhaps it was something trivial — who can look into the human heart save the gods? It is certainly not my business; let Kundan Singh answer for himself!'

The *patwari* sat down. Dalip Singh was then called and gave evidence of the time and place of his last meeting with his father. He explained that he and his other two brothers were all away from

home on that day in connection with various forest contracts. His
father had sent him a message asking one of them to meet him. At
this meeting Fateh Singh told him he was going to Ramnagar and
would be away for some weeks. In reply to a question from the *Sar-*
panch he said his father had told him he was going to Ramnagar
puzzled 'it is a very long way to go just for potatoes; there are
puzzles 'it is a very long way to go just for potatoes; there are
plenty available locally.'

'I think it was some very special kind of potato,' said Dalip, glancing nervously at his brothers. Nevill suddenly recalled his conversation with Fateh Singh at Karanprayag. He conferred rapidly with
the *patwari* who rose and said: 'Fateh Singh may have intended to
experiment with the new variety of potatoes introduced by the
English.'

'Ah! — another costly experiment, I suppose, introduced by the
Government — like the Chinese Tea-gardens we have heard so
much about in Badhan.' said the *Sarpanch* drily.

Nevill smiled to himself. This old boy was no exception to the
general rule — that hillmen regarded all innovations with the
deepest suspicion, always had good reasons for opposing them and
so ensured that their successful introduction would be unlikely.

Dalip Singh went back to his seat, thankful to escape any further
questioning. The *Sarpanch* called Trilok Singh and asked him if he
wanted to accuse anyone of the murder.

At first, after his father's death, Trilok Singh had felt only anger
and the desire to avenge himself on the murderer. Later, he also
began to feel some concern for his own and his brothers' position
in the matter of the copper. Because of the theft of the re-sale deed
he suspected Kundan Singh from the first, but found it difficult to
believe Kundan Singh capable of such a murder. He certainly did
not believe Kundan Singh would have killed his father because of
his debts, as suggested by the *patwari*. But, if he had found out
about the copper, that might possibly have driven him to such a
violent deed. If so, surely, in his own interest, he would keep quiet
about the copper, for, if he revealed his knowledge, it would also
supply a motive for the crime. Could he rely on Kundan Singh's
silence? He was not sure; he decided he must be cautious in his reply
to the *Sarpanch's* question.

'I do not know who killed my father,' he said, 'but the evidence
you have heard about Kundan Singh is at least worthy of your
serious consideration. I would like to reserve my accusation until
I have heard all the evidence and Kundan Singh's reply' and he
looked meaningly at Kundan Singh. The latter understood that

look perfectly and took a sudden resolution. All his life he had been
subjected to pressure of one kind or another from this family; he
would break free now, whatever the risk — at whatever cost.

The *Sarpanch* turned to the *patwari*:

'Any further evidence?'

Guman Singh shook his head. The *Sarpanch* turned to Kundan
Singh:

'You have been accused of murdering Fateh Singh; what have
you to say?'

'Why should I have wanted to kill Fateh Singh, my uncle-in-law?
I could not rid myself of my debts by killing him. How do I know
when he was murdered or where! I was at Nandaprayag; I was
delayed returning because I went in search of ringal bamboo. I have
been named because I am poor and have no influence. Fateh Singh
treated me badly and I was in debt to him; this is well known and
makes it easy to accuse me. But there is no evidence; the alleged
identification by a nun was just a put up show, the *patwari* cannot
substantiate it. he chose a nun as witness because he knew she
could not be produced as a witness before you. I am not a man of
violence, everyone knows that. But I think I know who did murder
the Thokdar.

He paused dramatically, he had the full attention now of the
crowd as he continued:

The Counter-Charge

'Two months before he died, Fateh Singh practised a trick on the
family of Kesar Singh, headman of Kandi, and in particular on his
son Dhan Singh. The family owned a remote holding, called
Palwara, in the forest above my village of Kansili. It is useless for
cultivation and the family were ready to sell it to Fateh Singh, all,
that is, save Dhan Singh who objects to the sale of his share.
Unknown to Kesar Singh, Fateh Singh persuaded Dhan Singh to
agree to the sale of his share of Palwara and to put his thumb impression on a document to that effect. Instead of taking it in a
straightforward way to Kesar Singh to complete the purchase of
Palwara in his own name, he tried to keep his action secret by forcing me, under threats, to pose as the purchaser of Palwara, which
I was to pretend I wanted for growing potatoes. For this service he
magnanimously agreed to remit three hundred and fifty rupees of
my debts. But he took good care to see that I should obtain no
other benefit from this bogus purchase. He made me sign a deed

transferring ownership and possession of this plot to him and his
sons. Why was he so interested in this land? Not for growing
potatoes — that was just a blind — Why did he want to conceal
his interest? I will tell you — I found out by accident. He had
discovered copper there. He wanted to dig for it secretly as the
government has banned further mining of copper. When I found
out I told Dhan Singh, who was furious at the trick played on him.
I knew he was the only member of his family who was interested
in Palwara, or ever visited it. If you are looking for a motive and
a murderer, — there is your man!'

This accusation caused a considerable sensation. Dhan Singh
started to stand up in order to protest at this false accusation. But
his father put his hand on his son's arm and pulled him down.

'Not yet,' he said in a low voice, 'He does not know you are here
and may commit himself to further lies in the belief that you are
not here to rebut them. They should do you no harm and will react
on his own head in the end. But listen very carefully now to the rest
of the proceedings as you may be called to give evidence.'

Nevill was probably the only person present who was not taken
completely by surprise by Kundan Singh's accusation. He recalled
Fateh Singh's visit, the hint that Dhan Singh was in some way ab-
normal, perhaps possessed, or a criminal. He began to think that
the case was not so simple as made out by the *patwari*. The latter
had made no mention before the court of the copper ore found with
Fateh Singh's body — he had admitted to Nevill that he had failed
to find any clue linking it to the murder. But now Kundan Singh
had supplied the link. He was very bold and certain about it but
Nevill was by no means convinced that he was telling the whole
truth. He felt that the accusation against Fateh Singh could be true;
it would explain the presence of the copper ore samples in Fateh
Singh's blanket coat and the curious look Trilok Singh had given
him when he picked up one of those samples and he himself had
picked up the other. The accusation against Dhan Singh was more
puzzling. There was some mystery here still to be solved. He recalled, too, Fateh Singh's subtle insinuations against the *patwari*.
These were intelligible in the context that he had made a secret purchase, and had indulged in illegal mining and wished to conceal
these activities. Guman Singh knew too many people and too much
about his circle; a new *patwari* would take longer to discover
details of this kind — if he ever discovered them.

As for Guman Singh, he could have kicked himself for failing to
discover what Fateh Singh had been up to in Palwara. Of course,
this must be the true explanation of his interest; he was far too

astute to waste his money and time on the cultivation of such
marginal land. But he was deeply suspicious of Kundan Singh's accusation against Dhan Singh. His own belief in Kundan Singh's
guilt was now stronger than ever.

The first vocal reaction, however, came from Trilok Singh. He
no longer doubted that Kundan Singh was the murderer. He had
done his worst; now he must make sure of destroying him.

'It's a lie!' he shouted. 'Now I understand and I will tell you how
Kundan Singh has twisted the truth. Yes, my father was looking for
a piece of land where he could try the experiment of growing the
new kind of potato. At the beginning of April he asked Kesar Singh
if his family would sell us Palwara for this experiment. He was told
that this was impossible because Dhan Singh was unwilling to part
with his share. To our great surprise Kundan Singh came to my
father a few days later and said he had persuaded Dhan Singh to
agree to sell his share. He said he had a document to prove this and
that he was proposing to buy this plot and might be willing to re-
sell it to us later, if we made it worth his while. My father suspected
some trick, but, as he was keen to get hold of a suitable plot of
land, and Palwara seemed to be ideal for his purpose, he agreed
that if Kundan Singh succeeded in completing the purchase in a
lawful manner, he might consider buying it off him, the consideration being the cancellation of some of his debts. Towards the end
of May we discovered that Kundan Singh had been digging for copper in Palwara. Before we could do anything about it, my father
was murdered. Now I am certain that Kundan Singh was the
murderer. He has accused Dhan Singh to save himself and because
he knows that Dhan Singh cannot be here to defend himself.'

Dhan Singh nudged his father but Kesar Singh shook his head
and said: 'Trust me, son, and wait a little longer.'

The *patwari* was on his feet again and asked permission to put
further questions to Trilok Singh and Kundan Singh. When he had
received the consent of the court, he asked Trilok Singh:

'You told me and Dalip has also told the court that your father
was on his way to Ramnagar to order seed potatoes when he was
killed. Where was he intending to plant these potatoes? What was
the urgency to order them in June when they could not be planted
till the following spring?'

'I do not know and I have no knowledge of when these potatoes
have to be planted. My father did not tell us all the details of his
plans.'

'Can you deny that he intended to plant them in Palwara Tok?'

'I can neither deny nor admit — I do not know.'

'Did your father buy Palwara from Kundan Singh before he was killed?'

'No.'

'How and when did he discover about the copper?'

'When he went up to see if the plot was worth buying for his potato experiment.'

'Very well. I put it to you that after his startling discovery, your father was likely to have been even more interested in buying this plot — if, in fact, he had not already bought it — but not for potatoes, and that he was on his way to Ramnagar, not to order seed potatoes, but to have two samples of copper from Palwara tested for quality.'

Trilok Singh gave the *patwari* a sharp look:

'You may say so,' he replied, 'but where is the evidence?'

'Two pieces of copper ore were found in your father's coat when his body was recovered.'

At this point the *Sarpanch* interrupted:

'Enough about this copper — we are not concerned with that, but only with the murder of Fateh Singh, Thokdar.'

Guman Singh pleaded:

'It is not possible to arrive at the truth about this murder, unless the truth about this copper is cleared up. It is possible that the copper, in some way or another, will provide the motive for the murder. But I will restrict my questions to those which are necessary to prove who is telling the truth about this matter and what light, if any, it may throw on the motive for the murder.'

'Very well,' said the *Sarpanch*, 'you can continue, but do not forget your undertaking.'

Guman Singh turned back to Trilok Singh:

'You say your father only discovered that copper was being dug at Palwara towards the end of May. How was it, then, that you did not discover this in April, when you, your brothers and your father cleared and ploughed Palwara?'

'Who says so?'

'I do. I saw you myself one day at the end of April — and you had almost completed your task — very thoroughly too.'

A murmur ran from those of the audience who had followed this exchange. Trilok Singh did not turn a hair; he decided that the *patwari* was only bluffing and that he would call his bluff:

'You must have been mistaken,' he said firmly. 'We never went near Palwara till the end of May.'

Guman Singh had no witness to support him; he left it at that and turned to Kundan Singh and asked:

'When did you discover that Fateh Singh was digging for copper in Palwara?'

'About a week before he was killed.'

'Before, then, you came to me to register your own title to this land?'

Kundan Singh thought desperately; he was becoming more and more enmeshed in lies. After a slight pause he said sullenly:

'I was only doing what Fateh Singh had ordered me to do; I did not want to lose the remission of my debts. I knew my title would be worthless unless the re-sale deed was cancelled.'

'Or were you planning to double-cross both Fateh Singh and Dhan Singh?'

'It never occurred to me; how could I afford to mine the copper?'

Guman Singh went on relentlessly:

'When and where did you meet Dhan Singh? What was he doing? Where was he going?'

Kundan Singh threw all discretion to the winds; each lie was more preposterous than the one before. He was a desperate man, fighting for his life. Dhan Singh realised this and also how right his father had been to counsel patience. Kundan Singh said in reply to the *patwari's* questions:

'I met him quite by chance, near Agastmani, two days after I had discovered Fateh Singh's deception. I assumed he was going home.'

'Where is he now?'

'I do not know where he is. Perhaps he has heard that Fateh Singh's body has been recovered and is in hiding.'

'Did you tell him you were going to register your own title to Palwara? Did you tell him that you had re-sold it to Fateh Singh?'

Committed to a series of lies in order to try to maintain a consistent line, Kundan Singh's mind was working remarkably nimbly:

'Yes, I told him everything. We agreed that the best course was not to let Fateh Singh suspect anything until we were ready to deal with him.'

'And how did you propose to deal with him?'

'Dhan Singh was doubtful whether his family would be prepared to cancel the sale to me. He was even more doubtful whether they would be interested in the copper or prepared to apply for a licence to mine it and to let me have a share in the profits to compensate for the loss of the remission of my debts which I was sure Fateh Singh would cancel. So we planned to get a proper price for Palwara from Fateh Singh on the threat of exposing his fraudulent intrigues and his illegal digging of the copper.'

'A proper pair of villains! It would seem that there was not much to choose between you and the late Thokdar.'

'It was the only kind of language he would understand,' said Kundan Singh bitingly.

If the details of this intrigue, as represented by Kundan Singh, were true, it seemed that neither he nor Dhan Singh had any sufficient motive to kill Fateh Singh, for that would be like killing the goose that laid the golden eggs. But, if they were false, and particularly the implication of Dhan Singh, then it followed that Kundan Singh would have had sufficient motive to kill Fateh Singh before the latter came to know that his own intrigues had been discovered and before anyone else discovered either. Guman Singh's next question showed that he was aware of this:

'If you and Dhan Singh were planning to blackmail the Thokdar, why should Dhan Singh have wanted to kill him?'

For the first time Kundan Singh seemed to be confused:

'I do not know,' he said. 'He is a soldier and a man of violence, but not very intelligent. I had some difficulty in persuading him to accept my plan. Perhaps, on second thoughts, he was afraid that Fateh Singh might get the better of us.'

'How do you know that Dhan Singh is a soldier? Did he tell you so?'

'No — but I heard — everyone knows that he ran away from home to join the Sepoy Army.'

'And yet you met him at Agastmani within two months of his leaving to join the army — very strange that you did not think to question him.'

Kundan Singh was at a loss for any explanation.

'Did he tell you of his change of plan and intention to kill Fateh Singh?'

'No — he should have met me again to discuss our plans, but he failed to turn up.'

'Where was that to be?'

Kundan Singh had an inspiration:

'At Nandaprayag; I waited for several days, but he never came.'

Guman Singh made no comment on this new explanation for Kundan Singh's delay in returning home; he felt more certain than ever that he was lying. Instead he asked Kundan Singh:

'Have you got copies of the various documents which you allege were drawn up in connection with Palwara?'

'Yes, I have them all and in some cases the originals.'

Kundan Singh looked straight into the eyes of Trilok Singh and a flicker of triumph came into his own. He had played Trilok Singh at his own game, called his bluff and still had the ace of trumps up his sleeve.

'Finally, Kundan Singh, do you wish to call any witnesses?'

'No — my documents are my witnesses.'

The *patwari* resumed his seat and the *panches* conferred together. After a few minutes, the *Sarpanch* held up his hand for silence. When he had obtained this, he said:

'In this case, the *patwari* has accused Kundan Singh with good reason; Trilok Singh also accuses Kundan but for different reasons, while Kundan Singh accuses Dhan Singh. We cannot complete this trial until Dhan Singh is called and given an opportunity to answer his accuser. The Court will, therefore, — the rest of his sentence was drowned by a commotion amongst his audience. Two men had stood up: Kesar Singh was well-known and recognised at once; a few people who knew him also recognised Dhan Singh.

'Dhan Singh. It is Dhan Singh!' they shouted.

When all was quiet again, Kesar Singh addressed the Court:

'I and my son, Dhan Singh, have attended this trial from the beginning. Never have I heard so many lies. By all means question my son — he will tell you the truth and only the truth. I have brought him up very strictly.' Kesar Singh sat down and Dhan Singh was called before the Court.

The Prodigal Son

Nevill saw a sturdy, well-proportioned young man, who stood easily, the focus of all eyes. Nevill studied him with interest. So this was Kesar Singh's only son, son of the cow-dust hour, he recognised the likeness now. He seemed the very opposite of a criminal type. Nevill looked quickly at Kundan Singh. He had turned like everyone else to see the newcomer; he stood as if petrified, unable to disguise the alarm written all over his face.

'Now for the fun!' thought Nevill.

The *Sarpanch*, addressing Dhan Singh, said:

'You have already heard that Kundan Singh son of Dhum Singh of Kansili, has accused you of murdering Fateh Singh Thokdar on the 3rd of June this year, about three miles from Kunjyani and near Kandi on the road from Bhatwari. But it is now my duty to restate the accusation in full with the reasons given for it by Kundan Singh.

Nevill, on a sudden impulse, felt there was something he had to do before the full accusation was re-stated. He felt swiftly in his knapsack — yes — it was still there — rose and strode forward till he stood before Dhan Singh and the *panches*. The *Sarpanch* looked questioningly at him:

'Have I your permission to ask Dhan Singh two questions before the whole accusation is repeated?'

The *Sarpanch* nodded, though he was as puzzled as everyone else by this interruption. Nevill held out the piece of copper ore which he had picked up when it rolled out of the dead man's blanket:

'Do you know what kind of stone this is?' he asked Dhan Singh.

The boy looked at it carefully:

'No,' he said 'it is very unusual,' and then, looking up enquiringly straight into Nevill's eyes, he added:

'Where did you find it?'

Afterwards, when trying to recapture first impressions, Nevill always came back to that question, direct and guileless. Measured against that all suspicions seemed unworthy. From that moment he was convinced of Dhan Singh's innocence.

'It was found with the body of Fateh Singh,' he said and asked his second question:

'Have you seen any stone like it anywhere and, if so, where?'

Dhan Singh examined the stone again, taking and turning it over in his hand:

'I have seen others like it, somewhere,' he said and stood frowning as he tried to recall where. Everyone watched Dhan Singh as if he was an oracle. Suddenly his face cleared:

'I have it,' he said. 'Palwara, that's where I saw such stones — some years ago, when I was helping my father terrace the clearing.'

With that the tension was broken; there were some murmurs of astonishment. Nevill went back to his seat conscious that he was followed by puzzled but respectful glances. Now that he had done it he felt a little guilty at his intervention, remembering his resolution and realising further that he had acted as an advocate rather than as an impartial observing magistrate.

The *Sarpanch* took up the interrupted proceedings. He re-stated Kundan Singh's accusation and asked Dhan Singh what he had to say in reply.

'What can I say?' said Dhan Singh. 'The whole accusation is absurd. In the last week of May I was with my regiment in Bareilly how then could I have met Kundan Singh near Agastmani? On that day, the third of June, as I can prove, I was on my way from Bareilly; to Hardwar to return home. Did I fly, then, from the plains to Nagpur in one day like one of the ancient Rishis?'

'Where did you go when you ran away from home?' the *Sarpanch* asked:

'To Bareilly, where I joined the 18th Native Infantry Regiment.'

'And you have been there ever since?'

Dhan Singh hesitated and Nevill saw, or thought he saw him glance towards him, half in appeal, half in fear, before he answered:

'Until the end of May.'

'And after that?'

'I came away to the hills.'

The *Sarpanch* looked at him in surprise:

'You only joined the army in the middle of April and they gave you sufficient leave to visit your home so soon afterwards? Very odd indeed that they should have been so generous!'

There was rather a long pause and then Dhan Singh said in a low voice:

'I ran away from the army.'

Trilok Singh, sitting near enough to hear him, leapt to his feet; he had, from the beginning, doubted the accuracy of the *patwari's* version of the actual murder — how could Kundan Singh have dragged his father up the hillside single-handed? He must have had an accomplice. It was Dhan Singh he had named as the murderer, it was part of the truth:

'Both these men are lying!' he shouted. 'Dhan Singh ran away from the army — perhaps, or he may have been dismissed — but earlier than the thirtieth of May. It is my belief that both these men were concerned in my father's murder; that they planned and carried it out together.'

The *Sarpanch* told him angrily to sit down and keep quiet and then, turning to Dhan Singh, said:

'Son, you are concealing something. Why did you run away from the army? Speak out and have no fear.'

Again Nevill caught that quick glance in his direction as Dhan Singh repeated sullenly:

'I tell you I ran away from the army and decided to come home.'

'Very well,' said the *Sarpanch* in a distinctly less sympathetic tone of voice 'since you refuse to answer my question, have you anything further to say?'

Dhan Singh looked relieved and Nevill wondered why. He should have realised that he had antagonised the court and raised very reasonable suspicions against himself. Why had Dhan Singh run away from the army? The end of May . . . a light suddenly dawned; his latest confidential report, brought by runner from

Srinagar, his headquarters, mentioned the Sepoy rising in Meerut on 10 May and that further trouble was expected in other Cantonments. So that was it! He looked with fresh interest and understanding at the young man who was now speaking.

'I have only this to add,' said Dhan Singh. 'I do not know who murdered Fateh Singh, or why he was killed. I do not know what the copper at Palwara has to do with the crime. But you may be interested to know that Fateh Singh came to see me one morning late in March, the day before I left my home to join the army, and paid me thirty rupees for my journey expenses in return for my agreement to sell my share of Palwara. I was very glad at the time to get the money and never gave a thought to the possibility of my having been tricked; I understand now for the first time that this may have been so. I never saw Kundan Singh at all, nor did he meet me later at or near Agastmani or anywhere else.'

'At last,' thought Nevill, 'the truth is beginning to emerge.'

A murmur from the crowd seemed to show that others, too, were aware of this.

'Have you any witnesses to prove your alibis?', the *Sarpanch* asked Dhan Singh.

'As for my whereabouts and movements at the time of the murder I could try to find and produce some of my Sepoy friends and a barber with whom I travelled from Bareilly to Hardwar, but it will be difficult.'

The *Sarpanch* shook his head:

'In the heart of the fruit lies the worm; who knows if there is an honest man in the plains, let alone in the Sepoy Army?'

There was a general laugh. Dhan Singh spoke up boldly:

'I do — there are at least three.'

The audience rocked with delight. The *Sarpanch* regarded him with indulgence — he seemed to have forgotten his earlier displeasure — but he was not disposed to take him seriously:

'There is a quicker and a better way, my son.'

The *Sarpanch* turned to confer with the other four elders and their Brahmin advisers.

Nevill stretched his legs and relaxed. He had had to concentrate severely to follow the proceedings, most of which had been conducted in the local dialect which bore some, but very little, resemblance to the parent Hindi language and was full of bewildering and meaningless pre-fixes and suffixes, a broad lazy patois which was hypnotic in its effect and fascination. One or two points had eluded him but he grasped the gist of what had passed. He considered the problem which faced the village court — no medical evidence, but that did not matter much, no witnesses and, so far, no evidence directly related to the actual crime. There were two suspects, some circumstantial evidence, mostly of a negative character, and plenty of accusations and counter-accusations, most of which sounded to be false. He was intrigued to know how the elders would proceed next. He had no doubt in his own mind that Dhan Singh was innocent of this crime, but could he honestly say he was yet convinced that Kundan Singh was guilty? True, his enmity with Fateh Singh and his curious involvement in the matter of Palwara made the case against him rather black. But the charge of actual murder, as it would be viewed by an English court, so far rested on the nun's identification, which had not been proved. The case was altogether too flimsy.

He saw that the consultations were finished. The *Sarpanch* rose and, when he had obtained silence, said:

'We are agreed that the matter should be decided by ordeal, the ordeal of Nyaya — swimming.'

For a moment there was silence and then a burst of applause. But Kundan Singh, when he could make himself heard, protested:

'I have no use for magic; I wish to be tried by the government court and rules of evidence.'

Everyone save Nevill heard him with astonishment. Such a statement, in popular estimation, was almost tantamount to an admission of guilt. What could a remote court know of the truth of a matter like this? Of course, lawyers could prove anything, if you paid them enough, but everyone knew that Kundan Singh was penniless. As for Nevill, though he knew he would have been hard put to justify his attitude to an English lawyer or judge, he felt sure from that moment that Kundan Singh was the murderer. This man had grasped, his wits no doubt sharpened by his danger, that he was unlikely to be convicted by a regular court.

The *Sarpanch* answered Kundan Singh sharply:

'If you are dissatisfied with the verdict of this *panchayat*, you will still have the government court.'

Nevill thought:

'This is where I should intervene to stop the proceedings.' But he knew he was not going to do so. He could not help feeling excited at the prospect of actually witnessing one of these traditional ordeals of which he had read and heard but which he had never expected to see for himself. He justified his silence by the same argument which had been used by the *Sarpanch*, though for rather different reasons — namely, that this was only an inquiry, not a trial. It was a convenient subterfuge for all concerned.

Ordeal by Water

Two pieces of paper were brought, strong shiny parchment hand-made from the local oleander plant which grew wild in the woods. Dhan Singh's name was written on one, Kundan Singh's on the other. The papers were then sprinkled with perfume and the five sacred products of the cow and invoked with prayers. Finally they were rolled up inside small balls of stiff clay which were fixed to the ends of two tall staffs of reed. These were placed under a cloth and turned round each other several times, so that no-one could tell which name was attached to which reed. The reeds were then given to two temple servants who waded into the tank from opposite ends, each carrying a reed which he stuck upright in the mud coating the floor of the tank at his own end. Next, two tanners were summoned and given their instructions. After an invocation to Varuna, god of water, and to Nag, the presiding deity of the temple, a Brahmin priest gave both tanners *tilak* by affixing a circular spot of red lead in the middle of their foreheads. The tanners then entered the water clad only in loin-cloths and took up their positions, standing in the water, one at each end of the pool. The *Sarpanch* explained that at a given signal both men would immerse simultaneously. The ordeal would be decided according to whichever tanner came up first. The reed nearest to him would immediately be destroyed along with its ball of clay and paper. The other reed would then be taken out and the name of the winner of the ordeal, or in other words, of the innocent man, would be read out from the paper attached to that reed.

There was a tense silence as everyone watched the *Sarpanch's* hand. Suddenly it fell and the two tanners dived under the surface together. A few bubbles came to the surface and then all trace of the swimmers vanished. The water by this time was thoroughly stirred up and muddy.

Nevill thought that, as a pure test by chance, this would be hard to beat and he was still wondering which was the more astonishing, the ingenuity or the credulity of man, when the first tanner broke surface. He stood still just where he emerged, only his head above water, somewhere in the middle of the tank. A few seconds later the other tanner came up, well at the other end from where he had started. The *Sarpanch* called him out. Now a rope was brought and the two temple servants measured the distance from each reed to the tanner still standing in the tank. The difference appeared to be only about five feet. The reed closest to the tanner was taken out and destroyed; the other was carried to the *Sarpanch* who detached the ball of clay and opened it out carefully. When he had recovered the paper, he washed it carefully in a bowl of water and then held it up so that all could see the paper though they could not read the name written on it. He called two witnesses at random from the crowd to verify that he called out the name actually on the paper.

Nevill's excitement was shared by everyone present. It was all wrong, of course; he should have disapproved of all this tom-foolery, but nothing would have induced him to do so now. He looked quickly at Dhan Singh and Kundan Singh. The former was staring at the *Sarpanch* like everyone else — save Kundan Singh who was looking at the ground, his face a pallid mask.

'Dhan Singh,' — the two words floated clear through the still air and immediately the tension was broken. There was a long sigh from the crowd. Nevill looked at Kundan Singh; he had not moved his position or changed his expression. He is guilty, thought Nevill, he knew what the result would be even before it was announced:

'Kundan Singh,' said the *Sarpanch*,' 'the gods have spoken; have you anything further to say?'

Kundan Singh stood silent, his position and expression had not varied even under the direct question. The *Sarpanch* repeated his question and waited. All eyes were on Kundan Singh. At last he raised his head. He seemed quite composed and when he spoke his words were firm and confident, but his audience were shocked by the intensity of hate in his voice.

'Yes, I will speak. Fateh Singh was my uncle-in-law, my father was his wife's elder brother. While she was alive I was not treated badly. But, as soon as she died, seventeen years ago — my father had died three years before that — Fateh Singh began to treat me as less than dirt beneath his feet. And why? Because he had decided that I was as bad a risk as my father had been before me, because he feared he would never get his money back. He was so mean that this hurt him more than anything a man could deliberately devise to hurt another man. Before the gods, I had no deliberate intention to wrong him; it was just my weakness as many of you know. Yes, I am a gambler, like my father before me — I cannot help it — but, the gods help me, I would rather be a gambler and a murderer than Fateh Singh. Everything I won through gambling went to him; whenever I lost I became further indebted to him. He never restrained me but traded on my weakness.

'Some of you know part of the story, none of you know it all. The amount of each debt was never very large, but in the end the sum of my debts ruined me. Five years ago I arranged to marry a second wife. My first wife had died three years before that without

giving me any children. Fateh Singh did not want me to have any
children by a second wife, for by law they would have to be given
some provision out of my estate before he could foreclose on it. He
demanded immediate repayment of my debts. When I pleaded my
inability, he cut off all my so-called allowances and started to fast
on my doorstep. Think of it — he a Thokdar and I his poor relation! While my house lay under this curse, naturally my new
parents-in-law would not allow my marriage. I was shunned by
everyone. But I decided to call his bluff. Some of you know the
story, but you do not know why I decided to risk my soul. He told
me he knew that I could never repay my debts, but that, if I agreed
to repudiate this second marriage, he would be content and give up
his fast. I refused and stuck to my refusal: eventually he gave up
his fast. From that time he hated me; it was the only time I got the
better of him during his life. But my triumph was hollow and short-
lived. My father-in-law-to-be informed me that he could not approve a son-in-law so godless and so much in debt and that he had
thought better of marrying his daughter to me. I had no money or
heart to fight for my rights. I could get no other wife; that devil had
achieved his object after all.

'I already loathed hiim, but I would never have laid a hand on
him — you know I am not a man of blood — had it not been for
his final action shortly before he died. Two and a half months ago,
he came to me with a proposition. He said he had found a plot of
land near Kansili in which he wanted to grow potatoes. This plot,
Palwara, belonged to Kesar Singh, headman of Kandi and his
family who could not sell it because Dhan Singh, only son of Kesar
Singh, was unwilling to sell his share. However, Fateh Singh told
me that he had persuaded Dhan Singh to agree to sell his share. As
he did not like to offend Kesar Singh, he wanted me to buy Palwara
on his behalf. For this service he agreed to remit three hundred and
fifty rupees of my debts. He made three conditions — that I was
to execute a re-sale deed, conveying ownership and possession of
this plot to him and his sons, as soon as I had completed its purchase — that I was to tell no-one of this re-sale, and that I was not
to visit Palwara or go anywhere near it, on pain of forfeiting the
remission of my debts. I thought the last two conditions were very
odd, but did not see how they could do me any harm. So at first
I just put them down to Fateh Singh's well-known preference for
secretive and devious methods of doing business. And I did not
want to lose the chance of a reduction of my debts. Moreover, I
sensed that if I refused his request he would have no compunction
in foreclosing. And so I agreed to his terms. When he had gone,

I examined the document he had left with me. I noted that it was undated and that the witness to Dhan Singh's thumb impression was not Fateh Singh, as one would have expected, but one Murari Singh. I knew this man was dying and too frail to leave his bed. However, if Fateh Singh wanted to practice forgery and deceit, it was no concern of mine, as I only had a passing interest in this transaction. A month later, as instructed by Fateh Singh, I saw Kesar Singh, showed him Dhan Singh's alleged agreement to sell his share, and offered to buy Palwara. The sale was completed two days later. I reported this to Fateh Singh, executed the re-sale deed and was given a conditional promissory note in respect of the remission of my debts. The Thokdar told me there was no great hurry to register my purchase of Palwara with the *patwari* and suggested that a month's delay would be quite reasonable. On 2nd June I went to see the *patwari*; he said my purchase of Palwara seemed to be in order, subject to a formal check. He went on to tell me, though not in so many words, that Fateh Singh and his sons had cleared and ploughed Palwara even before I had bought it. My suspicions were aroused. This operation could have no connection with the planting of seed potatoes next spring. Why this indecent haste? Why was the re-sale to be kept so secret? Why was I forbidden to go near Palwara? What were they up to? I decided to go and see for myself, despite the Thokdar's warning, and that very night, as I had already arranged to start for Nandaprayag the next morning, 3rd June. I found the copper workings. I knew then why he really wanted this miserable parcel of land, that he had planned to frame me as the legal owner and therefore presumably responsible for the illegal mining if their activities were discovered.

'That was the crowning insult — to use me with such contemptuous audacity as his stooge! And to mock me again on account of my childlessness! Next day I came on him by chance on my way to Nandaprayag. A devil entered my heart — so I killed him; but I am not guilty of murder. He deserved to be killed! And there sits another of the same brood, and there, and there, the viper's brood!' And Kundan Singh pointed a quivering finger at Trilok Singh and his brothers, while his voice rose to a note of hysteria as he continued:

'They have tried to conceal their own offence by giving false evidence against me. Let them be punished along with me! Call on Nag who saved me from the crime of causing an innocent man to be condemned for murder, and on Siva, the all-seeing, to judge them!'

As Kundan Singh finished, he mouthed horribly with incoherent animal sounds and had to be restrained forcibly from flinging himself at Trilok Singh.

'So', thought Nevill, 'it is over; they have reached the truth in their own way, now what will they do with it?'

This dramatic confession had caused a mild tumult amongst the audience. Here and there men were arguing hotly for or against belief in the truth of Kundan Singh's statement. There was a whispered consultation between the elders. The *Sarpanch* turned to Trilok Singh:

'What penalty do you demand?'

Trilok Singh looked round slowly: he saw faces interested, hostile, stupid, and some scornful and his anger flared up:

'You have heard this liar: he falsely accused Dhan Singh of murdering my father; next, he has accused my father, my brothers and myself of digging copper when all along he was digging it himself. No doubt my father went to see him; I do not know what passed between them, where or when they met.

'You ask me what penalty I demand? A life for a life — I demand his life!'

Kundan Singh thrust a hand into the inner pocket of his shirt. His guards struggled with him, thinking he intended violence, but he managed at last to throw down the documents which he had nursed throughout the trial — his last cards. They could do him no harm, or good, save to confound his enemy:

'See for yourselves whose allegations are false', he cried. 'Here are the true documents: the re-sale deed which they forced me to execute to give them ownership and possession of Palwara; Dhan Singh's agreement to sell his share, my purchase of Palwara and Fateh Singh's promissory note for the remission of my debts. Now let Trilok Singh deny!'

Nevill saw Trilok Singh's face for a second: it was pale and tense. He had reckoned on the murderer destroying the re-sale deed which he had stolen and which might incriminate him. He had not reckoned on the still stronger instinct of a life-long gambler.

Nevill looked round to see how Trilok Singh's call for the death penalty and Kundan Singh's retort had been received. It was clear that many, considering only the crime of murder, agreed with Trilok Singh. The *Sarpanch* looked at the documents and then showed them to the other *panches*, but it was obvious that they could not make much sense of them. They consulted together again and with their Brahmin advisers and then the *Sarpanch* commanded silence:

'The trial is concluded in respect of the facts of murder,' he said.

'The sentence will now be considered by the court,' and he looked questioningly at Nevill.

By the terms of their agreement with him the *Panchayats'* task was completed. But Nevill realised that the agreement was really worthless, for he could not bring Kundan Singh before an official court on a charge of murder on the evidence which had established his guilt before the village court — unless he maintained his confession, which experience warned him would be most unlikely. He ought to have foreseen this but had hoped then for some evidence which could be used in a properly constituted court. Let them pass sentence too; he could still take the matter out of their hands, if it became necessary. So he told the *Sarpanch* to continue.

While the village court deliberated, Nevill asked that Dhan Singh be called to talk to him. As soon as he came up, Dhan Singh started to thank him with a boy's sincerity and awkwardness.

'What are you thanking me for?' asked Nevill.

'Sahib, you proved my innocence at the very beginning, there was no need for the ordeal.'

'Oh yes, there was,' said Nevill, surprised himself at the definiteness of his own views. 'It was necessary to convince everyone, publicly, of your innocence and of Kundan Singh's guilt.'

Dhan Singh replied earnestly:

'As for Kundan Singh's guilt, Sahib, does it matter? He did right to kill Fateh Singh.'

Nevill wanted to laugh but controlled himself:

'Well, if that's how you feel,' he said, 'and your views are shared by others, perhaps I ought to take the case out of the *Panchayats'* hands and try it in my own court.'

Dhan Singh wrinkled his brow, he felt that the discussion was getting rather beyond him and said nothing. To his relief, Nevill changed the subject and began to question him about his adventures since he left home. They were still talking when the chatter of the crowd began to die away and they saw the *Sarpanch* on his feet.

When he had obtained complete silence, he said:

'The gods have revealed that Kundan Singh killed Fateh Singh and he has also confessed. The ancient laws recognised two crimes in murder, an offence against the state and an offence against the person. The punishment for the former was death, unless there were sufficient mitigating circumstances. As for the personal offence, the price of a *Kashattriya* in blood money used to be one hundred cows, the equivalent to-day of about fifty cows. If he can pay the price of fifty cows, Kundan Singh will expiate the personal blood guilt; if he cannot, then we recommend that he should forfeit his life to Trilok Singh.'

There were some murmurs, but they soon died away. Trilok Singh looked well enough pleased, he was confident that Kundan Singh could not pay. The *Sarpanch* turned to Kundan Singh:

'Can you pay the blood money?'

Kundan Sisngh shook his head.

'Will anyone pay his fine?' asked the *Sarpanch*. There was no response; whoever paid the fine would be considered to share the guilt.

'Kundan Singh, are you content to accept the verdict of this court?'

'I accept; what have I to do with further courts or trials? There are many here who should be grateful that I have rid them of this mean and arrogant Thokdar; but, if they are not prepared to come forward to help me, I am content to pay the penalty for my deed.'

An old man rose in his place; Nevill saw it was Kesar Singh. He addressed the Court:

'We cannot approve Kundan Singh's deed, but my family have some sympathy for him. As apparently he now owns Palwara since his purchase has been held to be valid by the *patwari*, while the so-called re-sale deed seems to be the subject of controversy, perhaps the government would be willing to allow enough copper to be mined to meet the cost of fifty cows — the blood money — after which the mining would be stopped? The Assistant Commissioner Sahib is present; let us obtain his approval and the matter is as good as settled.'

There were murmurs from the crowd, Nevill could not make out whether of agreement or otherwise. But before anyone else could speak, Trilok Singh leapt to his feet and shouted:

'No! I demand justice according to the ancient laws — at once and according to the sentence already passed!'

An uproar followed his outburst which the *Sarpanch* quelled with difficulty.

'Not so fast,' he said. 'The ancient laws have been invoked. Very well, but we have not yet finished dispensing justice in this case. In the matter of this murder there is still to be considered Kundan Singh's offence against the community and whether there were such mitigating circumstances as would justify witholding a capital sentence on this charge. To decide this it is necessary to find out who is speaking the truth about the digging of copper in Palwara and who is making the false accusation, Trilok Singh or Kundan Singh. My first question is to Trilok Singh:

'Do you still maintain that Kundan Singh was responsible for digging the copper in Palwara?'

Trilok Singh thought swiftly. He had accused Kundan Singh; if he retracted, proof or no proof, everyone would believe that he, his brothers and his father had dug the copper themselves. If he maintained the accusation he could never prove it. But could anyone disprove it? What did it matter anyway — the *Panchayat* had ignored Kesar Singh's suggestion — Kundan Singh would have to forfeit his life on the personal charge, the false accusation could do him no further harm.

'I do,' he said, scowling at Kundan Singh.

Turning to Kundan Singh, the Sarpanch asked him:

'Do you still maintain that it was Fateh Singh and his sons who were mining this copper?'

'Who else?' said Kundan Singh. 'Is it likely that I could have done all this work single-handed? But, if you require proof, then I do not know what to say.'

'But the gods know,' interrupted the *Sarpanch* 'we have had enough of lies on all sides; we will let the gods decide.'

The *Sarpanch* consulted his Brahmin advisers and rose again almost at once. To an audience beginning to lose interest and tire of the proceedings he announced:

'This time the ordeal shall be by fire. Copper is the metal in dispute, it shall be used for this trial. Whichever of these two men shall not be able to carry a piece of heated copper in the palm of his hand for fourteen paces unscathed, shall be held guilty, both of false accusation and also of mining the copper. If both succeed, both shall be held guiltless. If both fail, it will be proof of the truth of the old saying that thieves often fall out. Moreover, if both succeed or fail, there will be no mitigating circumstances in this murder. Do Trilok Singh and Kundan Singh accept this ordeal?'

Kundan Singh accepted without emotion or interest. Trilok Singh was dismayed but he knew it was useless to protest. The crowd would not be cheated of their second thrill. Public opinion would condemn him if he refused. The only alternative was to confess the truth, but he could not bring himself to do that, he would never live it down. Better to take the chance offered by the ordeal than to eat the dust of disgrace and drain the cup of cowardice. His dominant thought now was to get the death sentence on Kundan Singh confirmed in such a way that he could not escape the verdict. Sullenly he said:

'I accept.'

Nevill half rose — really this was overdoing it! But even as he sought words to protest he realised the falseness of his position. He had accepted the first ordeal without protest, how could he object to the second? The *Sarpanch* had noticed him rising and caught his eye. Instead of protesting, Nevill produced the piece of copper ore for the second time that day:

'This piece of copper ore was found with the murdered man — I offer it for the ordeal.'

He had a most curious feeling as he said this — as if he was being prompted by some power outside himself. Certainly he had not meant to say this when he started to rise. Somehow, too, it seemed most important that his offer be accepted. The crowd was looking at him, a sea of faces, curious and uncomprehending at first, and then, as they began to appreciate the significance of his offer, smiling and nodding their approval. It was the kind of dramatic touch they loved.

'It will do very well,' said the *Sarpanch*. 'What could be more fitting? Now we only require one more similar piece of copper ore.'

And then happened perhaps the most extraordinary occurrence of all in this singular trial. Walking as if in a trance, Trilok Singh came up until he was in front of the *Sarpanch*, bent down and placed a second piece of copper ore beside the other, which was lying on the stone platform in front of the village court where Nevill had placed it.

'This is the other piece of copper found with my father,' he said in a strange thick voice, amidst a silence more intense than any that had gone before. As he walked back to his place a long murmur of astonishment rippled back to the farthest seats in the courtyard.

The *Sarpanch* picked up the two pieces and examined them closely, weighing them in his hands. He was apparently satisfied that they were approximately the same size and weight. Then, he called up the temple servants and said:

'Let the preparations be made.'

Ordeal by Fire

A brazier was brought and the two pieces of copper ore were placed on top of the glowing coals. A priest invoked them with prayers, calling on the god of fire to inspire them to justice. He poured in sandalwood, musk and camphor; the heavily perfumed smoke rose straight upwards, for there was not a breath of wind.

A space of fourteen paces, about thirty feet, was measured out in front of the elders; Trilok Singh was placed at one end and Kundan Singh, facing him, at the other end. When the two pieces of copper ore were heated sufficiently to scorch a peepul leaf and reduce it to ashes, two temple attendants, armed with iron tongs, each picked up one piece and went and stood, one by each contestant. Trilok Singh and Kundan Singh were instructed to hold out their right hands, palm uppermost. At a signal from the *Sarpanch*, each attendant placed a peepul leaf on the palm outstretched in front of him and, at a second signal, the hot copper stone on the leaf. Both contestants moved forward at once.

Kundan Singh walked steadily, his head up, keeping his palm taut and his fingers bent back. Trilok Singh walked hurriedly and kept his eyes on his hand. Some of the old men, who had seen this kind of ordeal before, shook their heads — he was making a mistake to look at his hand, he should have kept his eyes fixed on the attendant at the other end of his course, waiting with his pair of tongs.

There was not a sound from the huge crowd which watched fascinated; there was not a sound of any kind. It was one of those still breathless days that burn themselves out in the golden glory of a Himalayan summer. The two men passed each other, Trilok Singh had only four paces to go, when suddenly the leaves of the great peepul tree started to shiver gently in some breeze which never reached the courtyard below. Trilok Singh started violently. He had been conscious of pain, yes, but he had forced himself to think of it in the abstract, as being somewhere outside his body, not localised in the hand which drew him forward like a magnet. But his fortitude suddenly crumbled; he thought he could hear as well as feel his hand burning. With a sob he tried to drop the copper ore. But he had no control over his hand; instead of dropping, he clutched the copper convulsively. As his cupped and curling fingers closed over it with an involuntary cramp, he felt an excruciating pain and screamed in agony. At last he flung the hot copper from him and nursed his burnt hand. The piece of copper ore bounded down the steps and into the tank with a sharp hiss which was echoed by hundreds of human mouths. Trilik Singh sank moaning to the ground while Kundan Singh strode confidently to his mark. The *panches* came and examined Trilok Singh's hand and held it up forcibly so that others could see the livid weals. They then held up Kundan Singh's hand to show it unmarked. Everyone was talking at once; this was a day that would not easily be forgotten.

After a while the *Sarpanch* called for order:

'We must now conclude our business,' he said. 'We have no concern with Trilok Singh's offence, if any, in mining copper without a licence — the Assistant Commissioner Sahib is present himself and will decide what to do about this. But Trilok Singh has made a false accusation with the deliberate intention of aggravating the enormity of Kundan Singh's crime. That is a serious offence of which we must take cognisance. I have consulted with my fellow *panches*. We consider this crime merits a heavy fine and have, therefore, decided that Trilok Singh be fined the value of fifty cows, to be paid as compensation to Kundan Singh. I imagine there can be no question in the circumstances now of ability to pay.'

A titter spread through the audience as they began to realise the significance of this sentence. The *Sarpanch* continued:

'Having disposed, therefore, of Kundan Singh's personal offence, we come finally to consideration of his offence against the community. The result of the second ordeal leads naturally to the conclusion that Kundan Singh suffered extreme provocation. Though a feckless gambler, he is not otherwise a man of criminal tendencies. We, therefore, find that there were sufficient mitigating circumstances to justify our waiving the death sentence. Instead we recommend Kundan Singh's banishment for life from his home and village. As he has no family, this is a merciful sentence.'

He looked enquiringly at Nevill who recognised his cue and rose at once. He had already decided what to say:

'First, I would like to congratulate the village court on the wisdom and justice of its decisions and final recommendation. As for the wisdom and justice of the gods — you have all been witness. Next is the question of Kundan Singh's sentence. I accept the recommendation made by the village court. Kundan Singh will not be tried again. Finally, you have left me four problems to decide — what action to take about the irregular mining of copper, whether the copper in Palwara should now be mined under licence and proper control, whether Palwara should be returned to its lawful owners, the family of Kesar Singh, to cultivate, now that it has been cleared and ploughed and, finally, what to do with Kundan Singh now that he had been banished from his home.

'Fateh Singh has already been punished for his sins. Though we have a saying in my own country that one should not speak ill of the dead, it cannot be denied that events have proved that Fateh Singh was not really worthy to remain a Thokdar, had he lived. We cannot punish Fateh Singh who was the chief offender; we can and must, therefore, punish his sons, whom he led astray and who were willing accessories to his plans. I shall recommend to my Directors, through the Commissioner, that the post of Thokdar, which they promised to maintain as hereditary in Fateh Singh's family, subject to good behaviour, be suspended indefinitely. Not until the honour is earned again by signal public services and upright behaviour will its restoration to any member of Fateh Singh's family be considered.

'As for the copper, let it stay where it is. I will take the responsibility in case it is a rich and easily accessible vein. I do not think it likely. I have seen many of your copper mines in Garhwal and the veins are all thin and troublesome to exploit. I have also seen your forests and what happens to them when they are used for smelting the ore. What would you do without your forests? Either you keep your land and flocks and homes or the copper will eat them up. So, I say — let the copper remain undisturbed in the earth.

'As to the future of Palwara, if the rightful owners insist on keeping and cultivating it, that is their right. But for as long as it remains accessible there will always be the temptation to extract copper against the Government's wishes and your own interests. I recommend that this land be returned to the forest from which it was reclaimed.

'About Kundan Singh — he is banished and penniless. He is not a hardened offender. What is to become of him? How are we to avoid his becoming a real and habitual criminal?', and, turning to Kundan Singh, Nevill said:

'What say you, Kundan Singh?'

Kundan Singh shrugged his shoulders:

'What do I care? Hang me if you will.'

'I cannot hang you, for we have no proof acceptable to our courts. I am sorry I cannot oblige you.'

Kundan Singh stared at him incredulously:

'If you cannot hang me, can your give me a job?'

Nevill joined in the general laughter that greeted this very sensible question:

'A shrewd question, Kundan Singh! I am sorry but it will be very difficult to find employment for a confessed murderer.'

Kundan Singh flung himself at Nevill's feet:

'Take me as a groom, a watchman, even as a *patwari's* assistant!'

There was more general laughter. To cap it all, the performing monkey, reminded perhaps, of some trick taught it by its master, raced up and prostrated itself beside Kundan Singh, holding out its master's cap for alms: what had been high drama threatened to turn into low comedy. Nevill decided to bring matters to an end:

'Enough,' he said firmly. 'I will consider your request', and he told his orderlies to take charge of Kundan Singh and bring him to his camp for orders.

Nevill had spoken in Hindustani and only the literate amongst
his audience followed him. The *Sarpanch* now repeated what he
had said slowly in their own dialect, while Nevill listened and watched its effect on the crowd. It was clear that they considered the
punishment proposed for Trilok Singh and his brothers to be
heavier than any that had gone before, heavier than their so-called
offence called for. This part of the *Sarpanch's* translation was heard
in dead silence. Nevill had rather expected this reaction but he had
been resolved to impress on these people his determination to stop
such evasion of restrictions imposed in their own interest. If they
could not appreciate the ends he would see that they understood
clearly the means he intended to use to educate them. It was not
the best way, but if it was the only one they could understand at
the moment, he would not hesitate to use it forcefully.

His remarks about leaving the copper in the ground were better
appreciated, the *Sarpanch* venturing to add, as his own comment,
that it was well since the holding was surely accursed. This was
something they could understand and Nevill saw many heads nodding in agreement.

For the same reasons perhaps, Dhan Singh and Kesar Singh rose
to say they did not want to retain ownership of Palwara, Kesar
Singh said he had not yet consulted the other members of his joint
family but he was sure they would agree. No-one disputed his decision — the holding was accursed, let it go back to the forest.

As for Nevill's solicitude for Kundan Singh's future, this was
something they could not understand at all. He had been lucky to
escape with his life; what he did with it after that was his own
concern.

Nevill watched the people stream out of the courtyard, told
Dhan Singh and Kesar Singh to report to him the next day for consideration of Dhan Singh's suitability to succeed his father as headman of Kandi, and bid farewell to the *Sarpanch* and his fellow *panches*, until there were only three men left besides himself and the
patwari — Trilok Singh and his two brothers. They were binding
up his hand. Nevill walked up to them and said:

'Come to my camp and I will give you some proper ointment for
your hurt.'

Trilok Singh looked up at him and said bitterly:

'I have tasted your justice — how do I know that your medicine
will be any better?' and he turned away without another word.

EPILOGUE

Nevill signed, dried and sealed the official report he had just written on the cholera situation and on the steps he had taken to isolate the District from the revolutionary infection sweeping the plains. The crisis had forced him to postpone the completion of the Settlement and to hurry back to his headquarters. He handed the cover to the mail runner waiting outside in the verandah.

The house was intolerably stuffy; even the verandah was airless and uninviting. He walked out to the low parapet wall which ran in front of the house. The latter was built on a cliff overlooking a great sweep of the Alaknanda river and the town of Srinagar sprawling along its banks. Srinagar was the capital town of Garhwal, not to be confused with the other and better known Srinagar, capital of Kashmir. This Srinagar was only 1,800 ft. above sea-level, hot and malarious, a place to be avoided between April and October.

He had walked all day, this last day of his summer tour, through a valley which had been like an oven, the rock walls storing and reflecting the heat of the sun, the parched foothills on either side crouching nakedly in their rags of scrub under a sultry and dust-charged sky. This belt of dust, in summer, hung over the lower foothills, often to a depth of thirty miles from the plains and only cleared off with the monsoon rains. It extended several miles into the air and its upper limit could sometimes be seen as a hard line stretching right across the arc of heaven. But, more often, it melted in imperceptible gradations of haze into the faint steely blue of the hot weather sky.

To the south-west he could see the outline of the hills, dark against the evening sky, the two prominent peaks of Nar and Narayan standing guard over the valley, which was hidden in a heavy white mist. These peaks stood, one on each side of the valley. It was popularly believed that one day they would fall into each other's arms, bringing flood and disaster to the valley. Some thought that this fall would also mark the end of the British Raj. They looked stable enough at the moment in spite of the news from Delhi.

He leant on the wall to enjoy the cool breeze which had sprung up. The sound of a temple bell floated up from below; it might almost have been the five-minute bell for an English church service until it was suddenly and harshly drowned in a jangling cacophony of bells and conch horns which broke out simultaneously from every temple in the valley.

As he listened, the mood of questioning but hopeful assurance in which he had reflected on the trial at Nagnath only a week before, left him. How could he have been so presumptuous as to imagine that a mere hundred years would suffice to change all this. The fortress of popular Hinduism had stood for centuries, it was little impaired as yet — a fortress dark and grim, guarding its secrets and its people jealously from the rest of the world.

Opposite him an orange glow flared up through the mist, and, after one or two false starts, burned steadily — a funeral pyre most probably — on the far bank of the river. By its light he could make out the line of the river and a gleam of dark hurrying waters sweeping round the great bend below him. Many of these waters never reached their natural destination, the sea. Engineers, he supposed, would some day dam and divert them further for the benefit of man. But the destiny of the people themselves — who could predict that?

Tales
of a Tahsildar

TALES OF A TAHSILDAR

INTRODUCTION

The name and office of Tahsildar will be familiar to all those who have served in northern India. For others, a brief description will have to suffice.

A Tahsildar was, and so far as I know, still is a subordinate official in charge of a revenue and civil area of administration called a Tahsil. In the United Provinces (now Uttar Pradesh) where the scene of most of these stories is set, a Tahsil varied in size from four hundred to six hundred square miles, with a rural population of anything from one hundred and fifty thousand to three hundred thousand, living in some one hundred and fifty to three hundred villages. There were, on average, four Tahsils to a District, six Districts to a Division, and eight Divisions or forty-eight Districts in the Province. An average District in the U.P. was from about one third to one half the size of all three Ridings of Yorkshire combined.

The British adopted the Tahsil from the Moghuls, who, in turn, inherited the unit, if not the name, from the system of village and district administration which they found in existence when they started to devise their own system of administration in India.

It would not be a great exaggeration to say that the whole revenue and civil administration of the British Raj in northern India hinged on the Tahsildar — the man who actually saw that the order was carried out. To give some idea of the variety of task required of him, he had, for instance, to measure the rainfall on the roof of the Tahsil building, the political temper of a dozen of the largest villages in his area, the damage done to crops by severe frost, storm or flood; he might have to arrange for the extermination of locusts, a duck shoot for the Governor, or for fuel and hay for a brigade on their way through his Tahsil.

It was sometimes best not to enquire too closely through how many mouths the order passed before it reached someone so humble that he could pass it no further and so had to carry it out himself. The important thing was that the job was done and that everyone, including the Tahsildar himself, knew that he was the

161

man responsible. I doubt if things have changed much in this respect since the British left the country. Of course, there were incompetent and dishonest Tahsildars. But, on the whole, they were a worthy and resourceful body of men, the nuts and bolts of the so-called steel frame.

It gives me great pleasure, therefore, to pay a tribute in these tales to the memory of a most remarkable Tahsildar, who served under me in the district of, shall we call it Mustypore, in the early 1930s. He was a political refugee from Afghanistan, one of several who were given sanctuary and employment in British India. He was a square peg in a round hole if ever there was one. But by sheer strength of character he had got right on top of his job with the minimum of exertion, to the exasperation of his more orthodox and hard-working contemporaries.

Without more ado, therefore, let me introduce you to Rahat Ali Shah, Tahsildar of Islamabad and the story of: —

1. The Failed Racehorse

One day in the hot weather of Mustypore was very like another; one was grateful, therefore, for any break in the monotony.

One morning, about 10.00 a.m., while I was in my office seeing visitors, I heard a commotion in the drive outside my bungalow, punctuated by stentorian imprecations. I recognised the voice of my friend, Sardar Rahat Ali Shah. Shortly afterwards the orderly came into my office and said:

'The Tahsildar Sahib of Islamabad — am I to show him in?'

He spoke with due deference but I sensed the antipathy in his voice, conveyed with all the subtlety and resignation of the East. I pretended not to have noticed the meaningful inflexion and merely nodded. The orderly went out. As he passed through the doorway, letting the 'chick' fall behind him, he sighed, loudly enough for both me and my visitor to hear, but in such a way that he could explain it away, if necessary, as due to the flatulence to which he was a chronic victim.

It was Saturday. On Wednesdays and Saturdays official visitors had precedence. On other days of the week, if they wanted to call during visiting hours, they had, ordinarily, to make an appointment by telephone or letter and in any case to convince me that their business was urgent. It was past 10 a.m. now; a number of officials had already called during the cool of the morning. The orderly reflected that the visiting hours were nearly over . . . and there was still a certain contractor . . . but he would have to go and put him off again.

The oriental visitors room or, as often as not, verandah, provides an incomparable school of psychology, infinitely superior, in this respect, to our own impersonal if more impartial arrangements. In the long lazy hours the *peon*, reclining against the wall of the cool verandah, seldom wastes his time merely minding his own business. He is the direct medium between visitor and visited, interpreting the one to the other with all the embellishments of imaginative artistry; applying to one visitor the respectful innuendo, to another the soft answer, to a third the contemptuous aside. To read the mind of every visitor like an open book, to know the likes and dislikes of his employer and to calculate to a nicety his reactions and their value to an impatient suitor — this was a fascinating study and a profitable business.

When Rahat Ali entered the room it appeared, suddenly, to be full, but at the same time brighter. He was a vast man with a heavy but soldierly figure, a big head, prominent beaked nose, full high-coloured cheeks and fierce pointed and waxed moustaches. He carried himself in public with a natural and somewhat aggressive swagger, reserving for informal moments and for his friends a disarming ingenuousness and a boisterous sense of humour of the school boy variety. His huge gusts of laughter exposed devastating visions of stained and broken teeth as inescapable as the infection of his mood. He was very shrewd and incurably lazy.

The dress he was wearing now was of his own devising — his 'Revenue-Collecting' he called it. Above elegant pointed light yellow boots he wore red leather gaiters the colour of raw liver, tight khaki twill breeches and coat with enormous concertina side pockets. At his hip was a service revolver, a .45 Colt, and across his swelling chest a leather bandolier containing three cartridges, all of different bores and none of them fitting his weapon. I had asked him about these once. He had explained with a grin that they impressed the ignorant and deceived the knowing, and snapping open the Colt, he had shown me that it was fully loaded save for the one empty chamber at the top. In his belt was stuffed a heavy riding crop; he twisted in his hands a vulgar check tweed cap of the style then known as Apache. It was appallingly greasy.

Some might smile in private but none, even of the local notables, would have dared to take any further liberty at the expense of Sardar Rahat Ali Shah, Afghan political refugee by the will of Allah and Tahsildar of Islamabad by the grace of the British Government.

As he sat down we both smiled, as it might be at the opening round of a school boxing match. I had not summoned Rahat Ali and he was not in the habit of calling frequently and unnecessarily over trivialities like some officials. The odds were, therefore, that he had come to ask some special favour.

We talked shop for some time — a necessary but tiresome preliminary. The Sardar, I knew, considered it distasteful for gentlemen to have to refer to such matters at all. That these formal discussions sometimes included items which proved awkward to explain did not, however, unduly depress him; nor the fact that promotion to the rank of Deputy Collector did not come his way, was not likely to come his way and was no longer a subject to which he referred. He was satisfied if his superiors appreciated a gentleman, something that no amount of promotion could create. He had an efficient assistant and led, on the whole, an easy life, clouded only at intervals by the prospect of the civil lock-up, for the shadow of his debts, like that of his figure, never grew less. He was an incorrigible gambler.

After a while the conversation turned — I do not recall why — to gardening. The Sardar brightened; he knew something about gardens. I mentioned a project for turning a disused camping ground near his *tahsil* into a fruit and vegetable garden. He listened politely and, at the proper moment, reeled off a catalogue of the salads he would grow there, ending with cucumber and a loud smack of his lips to show his appreciation of that succulent plant. I remember I expressed some doubts:

'I generally find it pretty tasteless in this country,' I said.

The Sardar considered the matter and then said:

'Sir, the growing of cucumber is not so easy — I mean the Kabuli cucumber, not the watery 'loki' of Hindostan which, as you say, is tasteless. First the seed must be obtained from Kabul and, if possible, a little of my native soil — but I weary your Honour with unnecessary details.'

'Go on,' I said.

There was a pause and then he said, speaking more slowly:

'Talking of my native soil reminds me of the object of my visit. I would request your Honour to grant me three months leave from April. I wish to prosecute my claim to our ancestral lands,' and he looked me straight in the eye as he always did when he lied most unblushingly.

I went to the cabinet and got out his file:

'Here,' I said, pulling a letter out of the file,' is the last and final word on your ancestral lands; you have seen it already. Mr White did his best for you — it would be a sheer waste of time and money to pursue the matter further.'

Rahat Ali did not even bother to look at the letter:

'Sahib,' he said,' we have have a proverb in our own country: —
"There are many ways of answering an awkward letter but only one
way of getting rid of an importunate beggar", — besides, the leave
is due to me.'

There was more than a hint in his eyes, though they were smiling. I thought it over. I ought to refuse, of course, or, at least, to
say I would think it over. But I smelt a story; if I refused there
would be no story. And all the time those sharp smiling eyes were
boring into me. I made up my mind to risk it. Things were quiet
and his assistant well able to look after the *tahsil* in his absence.

'Very well,' I said. 'I will grant your leave — on condition that
you keep out of debt and out of Afghanistan.'

'Sahib, the word of an Afghan Prince. . .'

'Is not worth one midday pull of a punkah coolie,' I finished the
sentence, perhaps rather rudely.

Rahat Ali looked hurt, nevertheless grinned broadly, revealing
some of his appalling teeth.

The interview was over. I walked out onto the verandah with my
visitor. There was a scraping of chairs and some rather too
elaborate salutations, hand to brow. I noticed a fat contractor,
whose name, I remembered, had already been announced three
times by the orderly — that, of course, explained the sigh: a seedy
looking Anglo-Indian whose trousers were so short that they did
not even cover the top of his boots, and a veiled woman with three
very dirty children. I would have to see them all, even the contractor, though I was tempted to put him off in the hope that he would
demand his consideration back from the orderly who was still sulk-
ing. But first there must take place the Sardar's ceremonious
leave-taking.

In the drive stood the most fearsome looking horse I had ever
seen. In the first place it was too long in the body, but let that pass
— the same could be said of many a good horse. The Indians have
a saying for it: — 'The moon has struck him'. A quick appraisal of
its neck told a tale of unbending obstinacy; it stood over at the
knees and one hock was enlarged, permanently I had no doubt.
The shoulders were a bit better, though too narrow. But it was the
head and, in the head, the mouth which claimed foremost attention. It was the ugliest head and the hardest mouth I had ever seen.
The bit matched the beast — a wicked affair covered with spikes.
The saddle and harness were definitely provincial. The animal was
dozing on three legs, a thin brown liquid drooling occasionally
from one corner of its mouth. A small boy, who looked sus-

piciously like one of the Club tennis boys, stood at its head with a self-conscious smirk on his face.

The Sardar was watching me closely. When I turned to him he broke into one of his most disarming smiles:

'My new charger,' he explained proudly. 'A failed racehorse, B.Sc.'

He looked anxiously at me to see if I would play the game.

'B.Sc?' I queried obediently.

'Bombay Steeple-chaser, your Honour,' — Rahat Ali stood to attention and saluted. We both laughed and I looked again at the animal incredulously.

'I can prove it, your Honour — I have his pedigree somewhere,' and the Sardar started to search his voluminous pockets. Watching him with amusement, I saw his expression change; some awkward afterthought must have presented itself. It had: he confessed to me later that the pedigree was in a letter of recent date addressed to him at the Taj Mahal hotel. He had never obtained leave to go to Bombay. The search diminished in tempo and died. Rahat Ali shrugged his shoulders:

'I cannot find it, but no matter; my wife's uncle bought him in Bombay after his career had finished.'

'And gave him to you, I suppose?'

'Yes, your Honour, a family arrangement. He is a long distance stayer, slightly unsound, but a horse of great heart.'

'He looks stronger in the head than in the heart. But it is better sometimes, as the saying goes, not to look a gift horse too closely in the mouth,' I said rather fatuously.

Rahat Ali bowed slightly from the waist — I felt I had deserved the gesture.

'And have you brought him in specially to show me, Rahat?'

'Your Honour: I also had work on the way.'

'Do you mean to say you have ridden him all the way in this morning?'

'Your Honour — we walked.'

I calculated swiftly:

'Twenty seven miles in a day! I shall be losing a valuable officer. Anyway, mind you walk him home as well.'

'I will try my best to follow your Honour's advice but the decision does not rest with me entirely.'

I must have looked incredulous for he added earnestly:

'Sir, he raced under the name "Lord Nelson" — there is still a touch of the old devil left in him.'

Rahat Ali grinned and, putting on his Apache cap back to front with the peak pulled well down behind, saluted smartly once more and walked down the steps. The boy brought the horse over. Its seventeen hands towered above the Tahsildar: I was curious to see how he would mount.

There was quite an impressive gallery now — all my visitors, the orderlies, the mali and his small son with the basket of weeds still on his head; my wife's darzi removed his big toe from the handle of the sewing machine just in time to catch the spectacles which fell off his nose as he rose to watch the fun. Rahat Ali was enjoying himself. The steps were ornate and flanked by a wall in the shape of a curling scroll. The Sardar mounted the tail of the scroll and, from there, with surprising agility, transferred himself suddenly onto the correct section of equine anatomy before him. Ostentatiously he pulled out a rupee and, bending down, gave it to the small boy. I caught the words 'Telegraph office — at once.' It was only then that I noticed that the boy had a telegram form in one hand, already written out. As the Sardar straightened up he deliberately caught my eye and grinned:

'Just to tell my lawyer my leave is sanctioned,' he said and, after saluting me with his crop, he brought it down smartly across the relief map that was his charger's quarters. They moved off unhurriedly.

'Nothing,' I thought, 'will ever induce that animal to break out of a walk.' But I was wrong. Apparently the trouble started on the Mall, only three hundred yards from my gate. As they passed a stationary refuse cart (locally known as an 'iron-clad'), its lid wedged open with a stick, the racehorse snorted. It would be nice to believe and better still to be able to prove that the smell offended his well-bred sensitivity. It is, I fear, more likely that, in common with most horses, he disliked buffaloes. The buffalo standing within the shafts of the iron-clad shied and the lid of the cart fell with a monstrous clash. The buffalo bolted but only for a few yards; the racehorse also bolted but did not stop till it reached the *Tahsil* thirteen-and-a-half miles away and forty five minutes later, in circumstances of which I was myself a witness.

But, before that, the whole affair nearly came to an abrupt and fatal end at the main Cantonment cross-roads. The traffic constable was passing one of those large canvas frames on wheels which advertised the current programme at the local cinema. Hearing the thunder of flying hooves bearing down on them, the two men in charge abandoned the frame right across the road down which the runaway was approaching at what the Tahsildar afterwards assured me was thirty-eight miles an hour, for he had his stopwatch out to test his uncle-in-law's veracity, as he put it.

Rahat Ali just had time to note that the film was called *The Lover's Leap* before they rose at the obstacle and sailed through the top half, tearing the lovers apart and overturning the frame. At the canal bridge, where he should have turned off down the canal road, the most direct route, Rahat Ali was unable to turn his mount and shouted at the *tendal* standing by the gate. The man did not hear what he said but took in the situation and very sensibly rang up both the Tahsil and my bungalow which he knew the Tahsildar had been visiting. His message was brief and to the point: 'Tahsildar Sahib bolted on horse.'

I had seen the seedy Anglo-Indian in boots and was just about to see the fat contractor when the message came. I got my car out at once. I was a little anxious for Rahat Ali because of that harness. At the canal bridge the *tendal* told me the runaway had not gone by the canal road, so I followed the district board road in the hope of picking up some clues. Two miles out of the Cantonment I came on a *dhobi* still contemplating with despair the washing which he had spread out to dry along the verge of the road. A trail of dusty hoof-marks betrayed the passage of the fugitive. Five miles down the road I found the Apache cap and, two miles further on, fragments of harness — unidentifiable — which might have been there for twenty minutes or twenty years.

Here the district board road crossed the canal again and took a wide turn before eventually reaching the Tahsil, whereas the canal road ran straight there. I was confident that Lord Nelson would make for his home port and only hoped he was sensible enough to realise that this was no longer Bombay. I was no longer so anxious about Rahat Ali; if he had not fallen off up to this point the odds were that he was still aboard. But, having come so far, I was curious to know how the affair would end. The canal road was gated. After seven miles I doubted whether a retired steeple-chaser would face the gate, especially as there was an easier way cross-country, the normal approach to the Tahsil for anyone on horseback. I had a key so opened the gate onto the canal road and stepped on it. I was just in time to see the finish.

There was quite a good field out, thanks to the gate-keeper's timely message. The doctor was there with a stretcher, the litigants had left the court with their lawyers, all the clerks and orderlies. There was the usual miscellany of touts, beggars, *sadhus*, small boys and pi-dogs.

As I approached the Tahsil I saw, some three fields away, a great roll of yellow dust, billowing across the plain. It thinned and then dramatically parted to reveal the iron horse making very heavy weather of the fallow. In fact he was approaching at a slow trot which grew slower every minute — and no wonder. The saddle was empty but, slumped over the withers, hung the Tahsildar, fast as a leech, his arms round the horse's neck, his whole sixteen stone bearing through his knees on the unfortunate animal's forehand: 'Bolted on horse' was a very apt description. Gradually the disjointed trot dropped to a broken stumble. Half a field away I could distinguish the set jaw and clenched teeth of the rider, his hair, eyebrows and moustaches white with dust, his cheek pressed close against the lathered neck of his mount.

With a last agonised stumble the charger reached the Tahsil compound and sank to its knees. Rahat Ali slid forward gently onto his. For a moment horse and rider rested immobile, exhausted. The doctor rushed up with his stretcher: the Sardar released his vice-like grip and waved him away. Stiffly he disentangled himself and surveyed his distressed mount. There was a look of the utmost satisfaction on his face. A *syce* appeared unobtrusively, the horse heaved laboriously to its feet and was led off, dead lame.

'Water,' croaked the Sardar hoarsely; there was a rush to comply. When it came he swilled out his mouth generously and blew his nose. Then he turned to his audience. For the first time he noticed me: He drew himself up and saluted. Then he closed one eye and gave me a monstrous wink with the other:

'Your Honour, the Half-Nelson Touch!'

2. *The Car with the Silver Points*

Sardar Rahat Ali Shah sat smoking his hookah on the verandah of his quarters at Islamabad. He sat on an old rocking-chair and watched the rain. There was no novelty in this for it had been raining continuously for a week. But it was restful and soothing, especially after a heavy midday meal. Rain, too, kept applicants and litigants away. He had satisfied his conscience — if he could be said to have one — at an early moment by ordering his assistant to inspect the office; after all, that was what assistants were for.

Now he tried to make his mind a blank, an exercise which some of his superior officers seemed to think he overdid. But he could not rid himself of one small anxiety, which anchored his consciousness to earth and clouded his enjoyment of the present hour. Only a small cloud, mind you, yet none the less irritating.

Rain like this in September was bad; it always meant trouble somewhere and, if somewhere, then almost inevitably in

Islamabad. The soaked earth could not absorb any more moisture, the mile-wide river could not carry it away fast enough: there would be floods and, in the wake of floods, epidemics. All this would mean extra work for the Tahsildar.

Just as he had reached this dismal conclusion, he heard, above the sound of the rain and the bullfrogs, someone shouting. With a premonition of bad news he took the mouthpiece of his hookah out and hung it carefully on the rest. One slipper was off and he leant over to fish for it with one hand; with the other hand he did up the top three buttons of his breeches. Ready now for any emergency, he assumed a ferocious expression just in time for the benefit of the Irrigation Department *beldar*, who ran past the verandah shouting: —

'The canal is breached, the canal is breached!'

'Where?' demanded Rahat Ali, but the *beldar* paid no attention to him and ran on to the Canal Overseer's quarters, repeating parrot-wise his cry.

The Sardar shrugged his shoulders and relaxed again in his chair. Carefully he undid again the top three buttons of his breeches and picked up the mouthpiece of his hookah. This was the Overseer's business. He tried to concentrate on watching a lizard which had hardly moved for three days. It had grown so fat that it could now afford to pick its insect out of those which came within reach of its tongue. 'Very soon it will fall off the wall,' thought the Sardar with one half of his mind: with the other half he was thinking: —

'And suppose it is true, what then? What will the Overseer do?'

Flick! — the lizard had missed. From somewhere came a new sound 'tsuk, tsuk'. He craned around: there was the other lizard, the critic on the wall. Rahat Ali resumed his thoughts: 'And, if the Overseer does nothing, do I do nothing too?'

Flick! — ah, he got him that time, a large flying ant.

'Bravo!' said the Tahsildar aloud. He had got so used to the sound of the rain that he could hear, through it, the papery rustle of the ant's wings in the lizard's mouth.

'Tsuk, tsuk, tsuk,' — the other lizard ran forward towards the first which started to wave its tail very gently.

'Perhaps I ought to send a warning telegram at least; if there is any truth in the rumour the Overseer will let me know.'

His thoughts lacked the confidence requisite for action. For some time the only sounds on the verandah were the hubble-bubble from the hookah and an occasional 'tsuk, tsuk' from the lizards. The newcomer had ceased to dispute the other's territory and was busy establishing his own empire. The rain outside made a wall

shutting them off from all other living creatures. No word came
from the Overseer's quarters. The bloated lizard caught and
devoured three more winged ants. Rahat Ali compromised: 'When
he falls off, I will send the wire.'

Ten minutes passed; the lizard disposed of three more ants and
moved onto the ceiling. Rahat Ali watched him with fearful
fascination and shifted uneasily. Finally he called an orderly.

At eight-o-clock that night, with a roar and a final splutter, an
ancient model T Ford, its lights almost extinct, jerked to a stop in
the portico of the Collector's bungalow and Sardar Rahat Ali Shah
climbed stiffly out. He was plastered with mud and soaked to the
skin. Round his head was wound a dirty piece of cloth on top of
which sat his beloved Apache cap, the peak pulled down to one
side, so that, helped by a good cross wind, as he explained later,
most of the rain had run off outside the car instead of down his
neck. He was accompanied by an equally wet and mud soaked
driver. Before coming up the steps Rahat Ali wrung great handfuls
of muddy water out of his coat, shirt and cap. The clothes were wet
but the man inside them exuded a warm vitality; already a cloud
of steam spread round him, the heavily waxed moustaches still
bristled aggressively. He said something to his driver who disappeared towards the servants' quarters. On the top step of the verandah the Sardar came punctiliously to attention and saluted. I had
watched all this, fascinated, from behind the wire-gauze doors and
came forward now to greet him:

'Come into the office, Rahat, it does not matter how wet you
make that. Let me get you some dry clothes, some food and a
drink,' and I called for a strong whisky and soda.

But the Sardar waved aside offers of dry clothing and
refreshment:

'Later,' he said. 'First my duty. Your Honour, I have come to
report.'

He stood to attention and saluted.

'Proceed,' I said, 'but make it short or you will catch your death
of cold.'

'Your Honour, at 3.00 p.m. to-day the canal *beldar* came running past the Tahsil shouting that the canal is breached. I think, 'This
is the Overseer's job and, anyway, the *beldar* is a fool and no
reliance can be placed in his report.' Then I think, 'Perhaps, at
least, I should enquire further and even send a warning telegram.
If the canal is not yet breached, it soon will be.' Such rain! I see,
in my mind, the flooded fields and the ruined crops: I see the kind
Collector Sahib working out with much pain the figures of loss of

revenue: I picture the government giving remissions to these pig-dogs of landlords and tenants who are already taxed too low.

'So I send my orderly to enquire. I come to know that the telegraph line is down, the canal telephone line is down; presently I learn that the Overseer, too, is down — with a bellyache and that all the canal coolies have run away. I think, 'the *beldar* is a fool but the Overseer is a cunning man — the rumour must be true.' At six o'clock my orderly reports that the canal is indeed breached at Bansgaon, six miles south of the Tahsil — the village *chowkidar* has just arrived to confirm the rumour.

'I call my driver, Ahmad, to bring the car. I drive onto the canal road and turn north; the *beldar* run out to stop me, shouting something I cannot hear. Bah! I spit at him and drive on. The rain pour; I get wet, the car get wet, Ahmad get very wet as there is a hole in the hood just above his head. But what matter? I think: 'The Collector Sahib is waiting for me; he is trusting Rahat Ali will bring correct news, he knows he is not afraid of a little *pani*'.

'This is famous; we go like a horse on fire — but not too fast as the canal road is slippery — till presently it gets dark. The car lights are very dim. I think: 'Ahmad has lent my battery to the Tahsil lorry driver without my permission.' I do not argue the point with him but make him light a hurricane lantern and sit on the wing. The car skid from side to side of the canal road; Ahmad is very frightened and call on Allah, but I am firm. I count the miles carefully up to six and then, suddenly, there is no road. Too late I see the gap, Ahmad not see it at all. As I grip the wheel I imagine to myself it is the neck of that *beldar* or perhaps of another *chowkidar* who fail to report. It is too late to stop. I put my foot down on the accelerator and we fly. Ahmad jump off with the lantern. Something hit me in the belly, something hit me in the head. Ahmad come up miraculously unhurt, still holding the lantern. By its light I see that the canal bank has been undermined, it has caved in on the side of the canal and my car is lying in the hole.

'Then I see we are not alone — there are villagers gazing helplessly. I ask them politely to help me pull the car out. They gape at me. I ask them again politely.' The Tahsildar paused in his headlong narrative to grin in response to my involuntary smile, 'And then I jump out with my whip. It take an hour but we get the car out. I order the villagers to repair the road for my return. Ahmad is full of doubts about the car, he wants to take out most of the engine, but I am firm. I sit at the wheel, Ahmad wind the handle and the engine make water. When she is finished, Ahmad hit the carburettor with a spanner — nothing happen; he hit the plugs — nothing happen. Then he start winding again — this time she start. O bravo! She has never fail me for she has silver points.'

'Silver points!' I exclaimed. 'How did she come to have silver points and what good are they?'

'Ssshh!' Rahat Ali put his finger to his lips and then bellowed in a stage whisper:

'I bought her from a Catholic priest. He told me: "Every car have a devil; sometimes the devil creep into the engine." So I fix her silver points and the devil creep back again discomforted.'

'Your Honour, I have taken much of your valuable time — I await your Honour's orders.'

I telephoned the Executive Engineer, then turned back to Rahat Ali:

'He says he is going out himself with an assistant as soon as he can, but first he must make arrangements to have the canal telephone line repaired and for coolies and repair materials to be sent out if necessary.'

Rahat Ali snorted.

'What will they achieve between them? Nothing. If they start at all to-night, which I doubt, it will only be to shout directions to each other for the rest of the night. In the morning they will come to me for help. I will go back now to be ready for them.'

I looked at the puddle of water on the floor:

'You have not yet had your whisky and soda.'

The Sardar saluted. Before he lowered his arm again he had also lowered the whisky and soda. He gratefully accepted the loan of a khaki shirt, an old pair of plus-fours and a raincoat. One final salute and he was gone. From the porch came the splutter and roar of the car with the silver points. As he swept out of the drive his car lights threw a brilliant beam on the garden and gateposts. I sat down thoughtfully, wondering whose battery Ahmad had been able to borrow at this time of night.

I met the Executive Engineer at the Club three days later:

'Well, have you plugged your leaking canal yet?' I asked.

'We have, thanks mainly to your invaluable Tahsildar and his car.'

'The car with the silver points,' I murmured reminiscently. 'I'd like to hear the story. Come over to the bar and have a drink.'

'Thanks — a chhota peg: I'll tell you the whole story, it's quite an epic.'

The whole story? I wondered and inwardly reserved judgment. It was a mean suspicion, but I doubted whether the Executive

Engineer knew the whole story. After all, he could hardly know
Rahat Ali well enough.

'This is what happened,' said the Engineer:

'When I got out to the breach, with great difficulty, the morning
following your telephone message, I found my Overseer, recovered
of his indisposition, and the Tahsildar on the spot, directing a gang
of about fifty coolies. The real breach, by the way, was at Bansgaon, not at the spot where the Tahsildar had had his accident.
That was only a minor subsidence, already temporarily repaired.
The Overseer's excuse for not reporting the breach direct to me was
that, as both lines were down and he understood the Tahsildar was
going into headquarters himself by car, he had seen no point in sending a messenger on foot. Your friend, standing behind him, gave
me a fearful wink which won my heart at once.

'The breach was not as yet very large but potentially dangerous,
for we can't hold up much water during the rains. I have already
wired for the diversion of as much as possible to other branches,
but I knew it would take some time for these measures to bring any
relief down here. So it was important to fill the breach as quickly
as possible. The coolies did not appear to be our regular gang, I
pointed out, however, what must have already started to dawn on
them, that they were wasting their time dropping sandbags into the
breach. They were being swept away as fast as they threw them in.
Something larger and heavier was required to hold the smaller
stuff.

'I asked the Overseer why he had not brought any sleepers or
round piles from Islamabad. He avoided my eye but replied sullenly
that there were no coolies there — he has probably not paid them
their wages for weeks. 'Off you go,' I said to him, 'and take these
men with you. Bring back everything you can find.'

'The wretched man looked embarrassed but was saved further
humiliation by the Tahsildar, who let out a roar at the wet and
miserable villagers he had impressed. The Overseer left with most
of them, glad to escape further questioning.

'If only there had been a tree anywhere near we might have felled
and used that. But, of course, there was nothing for miles, not even
a sizeable thorn or mimosa.

'Anyway, there we were, standing about, looking rather foolish.
I noticed that some of the villagers had not gone with the Overseer
but I made no comment, it would hardly have been tactful in the
circumstances. It was obvious now that they had come at the bid-
ding of the Tahsildar and not of the Overseer.

'Your beefy friend stood by the edge of the breach, frowning ferociously, as if he thought he could stem the flood waters by the power of human expression. I took the opportunity to look at the famous car. It seemed rather the worse for wear and no wonder after its rough passage the night before. It had a marked list to port and two crumpled wings; the framework of the hood and fragments of its fabric were draped drunkenly round the back and in its place a tarpaulin sheet had been rigged up as a temporary cover. A derelict car in a desolate landscape. But I looked at it with respect. After all it was there, a feat beyond the capacity of a heavier modern car. I had had to leave my own at the Tahsil and come on by *ekka*.'

The Tahsildar suddenly gave up his meditation and came over to me:

'Sahib,' he said. 'I have an idea — is my car any good?'

'It doesn't look too good,' I replied, 'but appearances are obviously deceptive — in fact I have conceived a great admiration for your car.'

'He flushed a little at that and bowed in the most delicious fashion.'

'Wait a minute,' I interrupted, 'like this,' and I mimicked the well-remembered gesture. The Engineer laughed:

'That's it exactly! I envy you — his entertainment value must be enormous. Well, he then solemnly offered to have his car pushed into the breach. I said to him:

"It is a very good rule not to scrap anything until you are quite sure that you have something better to replace it. I don't think the occasion really justifies such a sacrifice."

He grinned — by the way, what a villainous grin he has — and said: 'That rule, Sir, of which you speak — in the case of my car it would be more honoured in the breach.'

'Neat, wasn't it? I should never have suspected him of the wit.'

I groaned and called for two more whiskies:

'You don't know Rahat Ali,' I said.

'What could I do?' went on the Engineer. 'He forced me to admit that his car would make an excellent block-ship — if we could get it into the breach.

'Then we shall use it!' he said and, despite my protests, he set to work at once. Seeing that he was determined, I joined him in a committee, so to speak, of ways and means. It wasn't so easy. Our problem was to deliver the car, adequately loaded, into the breach without losing the ballast on the way. We had the rest of the sandbags, filled with earth only, which they had been industriously filling up to the time of my arrival. They were better than nothing but would have to be tightly packed and secured in the car, if they were not to fall out and be washed away at once, in which case the car would probably be swept away as well. We discussed all the possibilities rather inconclusively. Even if we could load her securely, could we move the car, thus laden, over the soft and slippery surface of the canal road the short distance necessary to the edge of the breach? We decided we had better try that first. We moved the car as close to the edge as we dared. We packed the bags in and tied the old tarpaulin tight over them. But as soon as we started to push the car she showed unmistakable signs of bedding down in the road. Moreover, it now struck us that, even if we could move her, she would almost certainly dip over the edge slowly and turn turtle, the ballast would either fall out or take her straight down the edge of the bank instead of across the breach.

'Rahat Ali scratched his head:

"She must help herself,' he said. Remember she was a T Ford — no clutch pedal or gear lever. We could not induce her to commit suicide by leaving her in gear and starting the engine. There was silence while we ruminated. Then Rahat Ali said slowly and deliberately, ticking off the points as he made them with one enormous forefinger on the other: 'We cannot push her to the edge, she is too heavy; she must be heavy or she will wash away; even if we could push her over, she will fall on her nose. We must shoot her clear of the bank so that she will fall more or less upright. She will not drive herself — the matter is urgent. Very well then!' and he smashed his closed fist into the cup of his other palm. 'I will mount her myself, it is a master's privilege: I will drive her into the breach like goddam!'

'Once he had made up his mind nothing would deter him. I flatly refused to allow him to risk his life. But he said I was not his superior officer: if I cared to ring up the Collector Sahib, he would obey his orders but no-one else's. He knew perfectly well I could not ring anyone from there. Finally, as a concession, he agreed to allow a life-line to be tied round his waist.

'The sandbags were removed and the car pushed back some distance so that he could get a flying start. The bags were then repacked in the back of the car only and Rahat Ali climbed into the driving seat. But the old car, as if aware of the diabolical plot, refused to start. Rahat Ali winked at me:

'She no fool,' he said. He climbed out again and took a piece of paper from his pocket. Standing in front of the car bonnet, he appeared to be reading out the contents of the paper, his lips moving but no sound forthcoming. When he finished he gave the piece

of paper to his driver. Then he climbed back into the car.
"She go now," he said. Believe it or not, she started at once.

'I thought at first that he had gone through all this play-acting
to impress the villagers, but afterwards I decided he had done it
mainly for his own satisfaction. He is obviously a born actor and
must be dramatic in all he does — rather like an Italian.'

I nodded — it was very true, but I still doubted if it was the
whole truth.

He allowed us to put the rope round him; then he pressed the
accelerator down slowly. The wheels span, the whole car shuddered. Suddenly she was away! The coolies sprang back and car
and driver sailed over the crumbling edge of the bank. My heart
was in my mouth; would they overturn? But no, they sailed out
miraculously on an almost even keel long enough for all four
wheels to be clear before the pull of gravity asserted itself. The fact
that she was more heavily loaded behind than in front must have
helped.

The car started to settle as soon as it hit the water. Rahat Ali just
had time to climb onto his seat and jump clear. The coolies began
to hurl more bags onto and in front of the car as it sank. Rahat Ali's
driver and I had hold of the life-line. We started by paying it out
as we felt his bulk being swept down the race of flood waters and
then, as he reached shallower water, we checked him, the Apache
cap broke the surface and then a pair of moustaches. We pulled
him in to the bank — he looked just like a performing sea-lion. He
had the satisfaction of seeing a substantial barrier arising long
before the sleepers and piles arrived from Islamabad. It took us
three or four hours after that but, eventually, we closed the breach.

'I must say he is a grand chap, that Tahsildar of yours! I expected
him to mourn the old car, but not a bit of it, he seemed as pleased
as Punch. By the way, when he makes his claim for compensation,
I should like to put in a good word for him.'

'Thank you, I'll remember your kind offer, if it should be
necessary to take advantage of it. And thank you for the story —
well up to form. I must say I would like to have seen Rahat Ali
played like a big fish!'

When the floods had subsided, I rode out to inspect the damage
done to the crops. Rahat Ali accompanied me on his humbled
charger. He abused it horribly whenever it showed any sign of life.
Just before leaving I said to him:

'The Executive Engineer has told me about your car and your action in helping to close the breach in the canal. It will not be
forgotten.'

Rahat Ali looked at me innocently:

'Your Honour may be transferred next month, or next week, or even to-morrow. Who will then remember or care what I have done? I would prefer my reward now and at your hand.'

'Well?' I said, expecting an inflated claim for compensation.

'Your Honour, I request fourteen days leave on urgent private affairs.'

I pulled up in astonishment:

'But you had three months leave only last April! I fear to contemplate how many new debts that must mean. And, apart from any other consideration, you have never told me the story.'

'Ah, that . . . the story is not yet complete. But about this leave, I assure you, Sahib, it is for very urgent and important private affairs. As for debts, there may be one or two more, of course, but there is certainly one less,' and he dropped his voice as if to excite my curiosity.

'Going to Afghanistan again?' I asked.

'Sir, the word of an Afghan Prince. . .' he started indignantly but broke off and looked rather pained.

'I tell you what, Rahat Ali — I'll take one more chance. You can have your fourteen days leave, if you promise to tell me the whole story when your return.'

'It is a bargain, your Honour.'

'And, Rahat Ali. . .'

'Your Honour?'

'Before we part, I should like to know the real reason why you sacrificed your beloved car with the silver points so readily to save these pig-dogs of landowners and tenants, as you called them, any further losses — not to mention the Government.'

'Ah, your Honour is all-seeing and all-knowing! I will tell you. Let us dismount and sit by this grove and presently someone will bring us some fruit.'

When we were seated he said earnestly, but I noticed he avoided my eye:

'She was insured; now I shall be able to buy a modern car.'

So he was sensitive, after all — who would have thought it!

'I am disappointed in you, Rahat Ali: and, anyway, you could not possibly get very much for the old car.'

'Why not, Sahib? She was heavily insured. A friend of a friend negotiated the policy — there were no questions. I hope there will be none now that she is well and truly buried beyond reach of post-mortem.'

'You old villain,' I said. 'I don't believe you will get away with it.' (But he did — the company jibbed a bit but eventually he compromised with them, still very advantageously.) 'I think I had better be going; it is not good to remain in the company of so much corruption.'

Rahat Ali beamed with pride:

'Your Honour flatters me!'

'Before I go, though, there is just one more thing I should like to know. What was it you read out in front of the old car to make her start?'

To my surprise Rahat Ali looked sheepish and avoided my eye:

'That was the Insurance Policy' he said.

3. *The Fingers of Firdaus*

I was camping near Islamabad in the cold weather when Rahat Ali told me the story he had promised. After inspecting the new Tahsil garden, which was coming along nicely, he invited me to tea. It was a good tea with cakes obviously ordered from Delhi. Amongst other delicacies, were cucumber sandwiches, made as they should be with very thin wafers of bread and butter and plenty of pepper and salt.

'The cucumber was grown in the Tahsil garden,' he said proudly. 'The seed came from my own village.'

'You brought it back when you returned from your three months leave, I suppose?'

'Your Honour is all-seeing: you shall now hear the full story as I promised.'

The introduction was dramatic:

'Your Honour, you are taking tea with a murderer,' he said and his eyes twinkled. 'I really mean it, but, of course, we do not call it murder in our country. I killed to avenge our family honour — in Afghanistan — it was a duty,' and he sighed. 'The world is also rid of an accomplished villain,' he added more brightly.

I suppose my eyes must have rested instinctively, if only for a second, on his revolver, for he took me up at once, politely but firmly:

'No, Sahib, in Afghanistan there are only three weapons for this kind of affair, the rifle, the knife and . . . these,' and he spread his great hands on the table before me.

'Sahib, God gave me these. They are not good for writing letters or fortnightly confidential reports: some women have complained that they are not sufficiently skilful or gentle . . . but there is no need to ask Allah for what purpose he gave Rahat Ali a pair of hands.'

He was lost in meditation for awhile and then he told me the story:

'In the village of my wife's family in Afghanistan there lived a man called Mohammad Din, whose only distinction, and that an unenviable one, was to have brought into the world a handsome but dissolute son. He was called Firdaus. From an early age he excelled in the art of thieving — a vice which our mistaken people sometimes account a virtue. Firdaus even stole from his own relations and friends and shamelessly from his father's guests. He came to be known as Light-fingered Firdaus. He grew up attractive to look upon, skilful at games and, curse him, he had the gift of song. He soon added to his other accomplishments some fairly promiscuous philandering.

'My father-in-law had three sons and, besides my wife, another, unmarried, daughter, the youngest of the family, beautiful but wilful and a constant anxiety to her family. I will not bore you with the whole story. As you have probably already guessed, Firdaus seduced her. Her eldest brother, Rahim, wanted to kill her but his father would not allow it. Instead, she was sent in disgrace to an uncle and aunt who lived in Quetta. Firdaus had disappeared and Rahim went in search of him. He never came back; neither did Firdaus.

'After three months Rahim's younger brother, Mahmoud, grew restless and one night he slipped away, leaving a brief message that he had gone in search of his brother. When, after another three months, he also failed to return, my father-in-law called a family council. The matter had become extremely serious and he called all the male relatives, old and young. I also attended — I did not tell your Honour, for you might have refused me permission and that would have been awkward.'

Rahat Ali gave me a charming smile and went on:

'My youngest brother-in-law, Akbar, was only recently married and others of us offered to go in his place to avenge the family honour. Although Akbar insisted on his right, he was over-ruled. I also offered my services. At first my father-in-law demurred:

"There will be international complications if it comes to be known," he said. I was able to convince him he was wrong. I pointed out that secrecy was now the most important requirement for success; that I was no longer known or remembered in Afghanistan, having left when I was still only a boy; that if anyone recalled me by name, he would be most unlikely to recognise me by sight or expect to see me in my native land.

'So it was decided that I should seek out Firdaus to destroy him.

I explained that I could not expect to obtain more than three months leave and did not want to waste any of this chasing a shadow. It was agreed, therefore, that I should not obtain leave until there was some definite or fairly reliable news of the whereabouts of Firdaus. This might take a long time to obtain, so outwardly it was made to appear that the family conference had broken up inconclusively. Any suspicions that might have been aroused in the mind of Mohammad Din would be lulled by Akbar's continuing to stay at home and the discovery, if he cared to make it, that all his male relatives in Afghanistan had returned to their normal occupations. He knew I was in the service of the British Government in India, that I had gone back there and would never imagine that I could be a potential avenger. If no news came, my father-in-law would call another family council.

'Shortly after this Mohammad Din disappeared from the village. He was followed to the northern frontier of Afghanistan where he met a young man. If this was Firdaus, he was no longer the well-groomed lady killer; he had grown his hair long and wore old clothes. The spy was not certain of his identity but reported that this young man had joined the northern caravans as a strolling player. Of Rahim and Mahmoud he found no trace. This information was thought good enough to act upon.

'Your Honour was kind enough to grant me three months leave. I was disguised and furnished as a merchant and set out to join the summer caravan which leaves Kabul in May. Mohammad Din, who was back, has long ears, so all the preparations were made in the greatest secrecy at Peshawar and cost my father-in-law a lot of money. I promised to contribute part of my three months leave salary.

'When I joined the caravan I was disguised as an old man and I was rather careless, so the other merchants thought, of my goods. In particular, I often opened a big box in public view and displayed its contents, fingering the silks and brocades lovingly so that all who cared could see. It was such a large box that if it had been heavily loaded it would have been impossible to balance it on a pack camel. But below the finery, which was only on the surface, were bags filled with *neem* leaves. If anyone should obtain unlawful access to the box he would probably assume they contained tea. To have filled them with tea would have been an unnecessary expense. Only my servant knew of these bags and he was a trusted family retainer who came from a relative's house in Kabul.

'It was a large caravan. There were half a dozen minstrels, strolling players and jugglers amongst the camp followers. Any one of these, I thought, might be Firdaus, also in disguise, and I set myself to study them all closely. But none of them seemed to be the man I wanted. One evening, when we had halted at a large town — it was actually Herat — there was a competition organised between the camp followers. Each performed his best skill at juggling, fortune telling, knife throwing, story telling or singing. Some new performers had joined the caravan here. One of these exhibited amazing sleight of hand, more particularly in picking the pockets of his audience. He was the right age, height and build to be Firdaus, though I could not recognise him. I began to watch him narrowly. he also excelled at knife-throwing. He split a piece of straw at forty five feet; pierced the ace of spades on a playing card at thirty feet and finally, amidst the gasps of the spectators, he cut a human hair stretched across a board at twenty five feet distance. While he threw he crooned softly. I heard some of his words and my heart beat faster: "That for the shadow which comes from behind, and that for the lame man with the voice of a crow! Their kind I serve like this . . . and this!"

'Was it just a coincidence — Mahmoud had been slightly lame and had a notoriously harsh voice? I enquired discreetly about the newcomer. No-one seemed to know who he was or anything about him save that he had only followed the caravans since last year. I was still in doubt when it came to the final competition — in singing. The same man won this handsomely and someone asked him to sing one more song to celebrate his victory. He was only too ready to oblige. With a look of scorn towards his defeated rivals he sang in praise of that bard who had only to listen once to the song of his fellow competitor and then sang it better than the other could ever hope to do. It was a well known song but this time there was a new verse which no-one had ever heard before. In it the champion minstrel's skill was attributed to the thieving ability of his ancestors. By the way he sang this verse it was plain that the singer had made it up himself and was vastly pleased with his original conceit.

'And I was pleased too, for I no longer had any doubt of his identity. I hobbled to my big box and drew out a silk scarf and threw it to the winner: 'For the silver throat of the robber of our pence!' I cried.

'I watched the man and noted how swiftly his eye followed from the scarf in his hand to the silks and brocades gleaming in the open box.

'Next day it was given out that I was indisposed. All day I was carried in a litter. In the evening my servant grumbled amongst the other servants and followers that he was required to prepare a sleeping draught for which his master demanded certain rare herbs and would not be satisfied until he had enquired for them throughout the caravanserai. When my servant persisted in his enquiries, someone suggested amidst general laughter that, provided a strong enough drug were used, his master would never know what had been added. There was only one man who was really interested — the winner of the previous day's competitions. he helped my servant brew the concoction which I was to take. he asked a number of questions, casually, such as a stranger might ask out of idle curiosity — how old I was, where I came from, did I sleep alone, was I very rich and so forth. All this was duly reported to me by my servant and I smiled grimly.

'The stage was set: now, Sahib, imagine the scene. When all slept save the furtive carrion questers of the night, a shadow passed silently behind my tent. From within the only sound was of deep breathing. The thief felt with his hands round the outside of the tent until he identified the shape of the big box. Soundlessly he slit the canvas and slipped inside. A weak night-light was burning smokily. On his bed of heaped rugs lay the old merchant deep in drugged slumber. The intruder bent over him for a moment to assure himself that he would not be interrupted; then he turned back to the box. To his surprise it was unlocked. It was true, then, what they said in the camp, that the old man was too careless, or too wealthy, to bother about the security of his wares. Or, was it a trap? he hesitated and fingered his knife. But another glance at the sleeping figure reassured him. Besides, he could open the box and still keep an eye on its owner.

'He put the tools down which he had brought to force the lock and, holding the knife between his teeth, he lifted the lid cautiously. When it was fully open, he bent down swiftly and thrust his hands down to feel for what he wanted. Imagine his surprise when his hands were seized and a sharp pull unbalanced him so that his knees hit the box and his heels the air. The knife fell out of his mouth into the box. His natural reaction was to try and release his hands. They were released at once. Too late he realised that his only hope lay in keeping them engaged with his enemy's. His throat was seized in a grip of iron and a figure rose from the box.

'The drama was played out there in the dim light. Gradually the two figures reversed their positions till the man standing in the box was bending over the other outside it. The death rattle was

drowned by the stertorous breathing of the man lying on
the bed — my servant dressed in my disguise.

'When Firdaus was dead I stepped out of the box and lit my
torch. By its light I searched the features of the dead man till I
found what I had been looking for, a small mole concealed beneath
the hair above his right ear. My father-in-law had noticed it when
Firdaus had once been suffering from ringworm. If I had still had
any doubts they would have been set at rest when I found in an inner pocket a ring which had belonged to my brother-in-law,
Rahim.

'Working swiftly and as silently as I could, I hid the body of Firdaus in the box, covering it with some of the bags of *neem* leaves
and finally with a thin layer of silks and brocades. I closed and
locked the box and disarranged the contents of some of the other
panniers of merchandise. I removed the wig and false beard from
my drugged and still sleeping servant and rearranged them on
myself.

'As dawn came I woke him violently and loudly exclaimed that
we had both been heavily drugged and my boxes robbed. I called
Allah to witness that it was no longer safe to remain with this
caravan and declared that I was leaving as soon as my camels could
be loaded. By the time I was ready to go a small crowd had collected. Before further enquiries could be made by the camp police,
a lazy lot anyway, I departed full of laments and recriminations.
Those merchants who saw or heard me leave, no doubt shrugged
their shoulders and thought, "What else could the old fool expect
if he paraded his goods so ostentatiously and carelessly?"

'But I no longer did so. Now I allowed no-one save my own personal servant into my tent. Although we were still travelling in the
hills and the air was cool, at the end of the second day I deemed
it advisable to rid myself of the corpse. That evening we camped
on sand near a stream. With the help of my servant we buried the
body of Firdaus beneath the tent. We put sand in the box below the
neem leaves so that the camelmen would not notice any difference
in weight. Aha! he was a clever boy, that old merchant, he thought
of everything!

'Before I buried Firdaus I considered whether I should bring
anything more than my word and Rahim's ring home to my wife's
family. After a little thought I cut off the ends of the fingers and
thumbs of the dead man. Those light-fingereds members would go
still lighter to the grave!

'I sold off all the camels and goods and returned unobtrusively
to my father-in-law's house. As you can imagine he was delighted
with my success and decided to give a big feast in celebration. But

there was no time to make the necessary preparations before my
leave expired. So the feast was not held till October. it was for this
I requested your Honour for a further fourteen days leave.

'Although nothing had been said outside the family, the whole
village knew why my sister-in-law had been sent away and two of
her brothers and Firdaus had vanished. My father-in-law now gave
out publicly that the family had decided to give up the blood feud,
largely persuaded by his son-in-law, serving with the British
Government in India, who considered such feuds barbaric and
futile. That was a good jest between us!

'My father-in-law made a special point of inviting Mohammad
Din to the feast. He pointed out to him that they were both getting
on in years and now had only one son each; that if the feud continued he would never see Firdaus again. Mohammad Din was
suspicious at first, but in the end he agreed to let bygones be
bygones and to accept the invitation. He conveyed tactfully that he
did not expect Firdaus to be invited and his host agreed that that
perhaps would be going too far.

'Aha! — that was a great feast and talked of for months afterwards. Has your Honour ever tasted the dish called "Eye of the
mountain gazelle"? — No? Well, that is a dish! and Rahat Ali rolled
his eyes and smacked his lips.

'Imagine then, small pieces of raw liver inserted in the middle of
delicately split ripe Kabuli grapes, the whole lightly browned in
butter. At the very end of the meal, as was proper, my father-in-
law served cucumber sandwiches to clean the mouth.

'The relations all voiced their appreciation of the meal: my
father-in-law turned towards Mohammad Din, seated on his right:
"Capital! Capital!" exclaimed Mohammad Din, affable after the
best helpings of every dish.

'At this, my father-in-law let out such a roar that we thought all
the lamps would be extinguished. We others wept with laughter,
following his lead — all, that is, save Mohammad Din. He grew
quiet, sensing that he was the butt of this unexplained mirth. When
he had had his fill of laughter my father-in-law turned to Mohammad Din and said, his face and voice stern: "The eye of the mountain gazelle which we ate contained only raw liver — but the por-
tion which you ate contained, in addition, the finger-tips of Firdaus."

'Of course, they had to be thrown away long before, but
Mohammad Din was not to know that!'

There was a pause during which I tried to visualise what it must
be like to live in two such different worlds.

'And the end of the matter?' I asked, for I knew the story could not end at that after such a deadly insult.

Rahat Ali shrugged his shoulders.

'The story was through the whole village next day. Mohammad Din could not face the ridicule. He left the village two days later and has not been seen since. But, who knows? — he may yet seek his revenge.'

Politely I refused the last cucumber sandwich.

'I dare not take the risk of accepting it,' I said, 'not from the hands of an uncommon murderer!'

Rahat Ali grinned and his eyes twinkled mischievously.

'Your Honour! Perhaps you would care to try this *bhindi* or fried "lady's fingers" instead?'

1950

A GENTLEMAN'S AGREEMENT

In the days of the Raj a District Officer habitually made all sorts of decisions on the spot and on his own initiative. The field for this healthy exercise narrowed as communications improved and control from the centre tightened, but it was never entirely closed. In 1934 I had occasion myself to take a responsible decision on the spot in rather exceptional circumstances.

In the hot weather of that year, while still a very junior officer of under six years service, I was sent to Allahabad to officiate for the District Magistrate who had gone on short leave. On the morning of 12th August I received a telegram in code from the Chief Secretary of the United Provinces Government to say that Pandit Jawaharlal Nehru was on his way by train under police escort from Dehra Dun jail to Allahabad and that on arrival he was to be released temporarily on parole to be with his wife whose condition had deteriorated alarmingly. Kamala Nehru was suffering from tuberculosis — from which she eventually died — and the disease was already well advanced, otherwise she too would have been in jail like her husband and other political leaders.

She was a woman of indomitable spirit. In spite of her frail health she was if anything even more determined than her husband to continue the struggle against British rule in India. Nehru himself admits in his autobiography that there were times when he wavered and contemplated retiring from the conflict so that he could remove his sick wife to Switzerland for the conditions and treatment which she needed, but that Kamala would not hear of it. Nehru himself had now been in jail for about three years, with one small break, and had served six months of his latest sentence.

I was instructed in the telegram that the Government was most anxious that he should be released without delay and with the minimum of publicity but that they were not prepared to release him unless he gave an undertaking not to indulge in political activities or speeches while he was out of jail. Finally, I was warned that he might be 'difficult' and that I was to use my discretion as to how I put this offer and condition across to him.

The Government was afraid that large scale demonstrations

might occur at the larger stations of big cities on the more direct East Indian Railway main line if it came to be known that he was travelling through them. So he was being sent by a devious route through the northern districts which would land him eventually at Prayag, a small and out of the way station in the cantonment of Allahabad, in the middle of the night.

About 11.00 p.m. I went down to meet the train. Late at night Prayag station presented a dreary picture, dirty and ill-lit, with no shelter for the passengers and no suitable room for a private interview. Luckily it was not raining. Down the whole length of a very long platform the passengers lay, most of them asleep on the ground, wrapped in their white cotton sheets, waiting for the next train that night or the next day. In the dim light they looked like rows of corpses laid out ready for the funeral pyre.

When Nehru alighted from his train I could see he was tense and anxious. He had not been told, but he had guessed why he was being sent to Allahabad. He had no precise information of his wife's condition and was understandably worried. He was a man whose face was a true barometer of his mood. In repose his expression was aloof and enigmatic; when he was tired or feeling depressed it was grey and drawn; when he was annoyed it was sour and scornful, the lower lip pouting expressively — no attempt at camouflage. When he was angry, which was often, it was hard and suffused with a dark flush and his eyes flashed; when he smiled the charm was instant and magnetic. His was a fascinating face, handsome and eye-compelling, responsive to every mood of the vast crowds who flocked to hear his passionate vibrating speeches. It was the face and voice of a potential dictator who was saved from this fate by his intellectual honesty, his high standards of integrity and morality, the fastidiousness of a true aristocrat.

That evening he was sad and tired. he had endured a long, hot and uncomfortable journey of a whole day and a night, tortured by anxiety and painful thoughts. I gave him some detials of his wife's condition and then the Government's message, using the word parole which had occurred in the telegram. There was a short silence and then he said with considerable vehemence:

'You mean that I am required to give this undertaking as a pre-condition of my release?'

I agreed this was so and realised at once that he was going to be 'difficult'.

'I could never agree to give such an undertaking,' he said, 'It is repugnant to my conscience as a patriot. What is this offer of release on parole save an insult dressed up in polite language?'

In vain I protested that French had, for long ages, been the language of chivalry and release on parole the most honourable treatment one could offer a captive foe. He brushed my arguments aside. If it had ever had such a meaning, he said, it no longer applied, anyway not in India and I recalled then that a famous Punjab Nationalist leader had spurned an offer of release on parole on similar conditions to see his dying son. Nehru went on to explain that he had no intention or heart to indulge just then in political activities or speeches. He was out of touch anyway with current political events after six months in jail. He wanted to devote all the time he was allowed to nursing his ailing wife. But he could never give an undertaking.

However, if Nehru was obstinate in his refusal, I was equally obstinate in my determination that some way must be found to release him this very night. If I sent him back I was certain that news of the whole episode would leak and that tremendous capital would be made out of it by the Congress Party. It was obvious, too, that he was longing to see his wife. Up and down the platform we walked for over half an hour arguing the matter, picking our way in and out and over the recumbent bodies of the ghostly sleepers, while the silent group of policemen stood back in the shadows wondering what it was all about.

The situation seemed to me ridiculous if it had not been so serious. Here was a man desperately anxious to be released to see his wife and a Government genuinely desirous of releasing him for this purpose. Yet, because he was too sensitive and high-minded to give an undertaking, though he had no intention of doing what the Government feared, and because the Government, that collective impersonality, was too cautious and calculating to trust him without such an undertaking, we had reached an impasse.

The telegram had said that I was to use my discretion: how far could I stretch my terms of reference? I took a sudden decision without much hope of better success and said: 'Well, you won't give any undertaking — could we come to a gentleman's agreement and leave it at that?'

He stopped pacing, stood deep in thought for a moment and then his face broke into a charming smile.

'A gentleman's agreement between you and me?' he said slowly.

'Yes, I think I could accept that because it implies no undertaking to the Government.'

And so it was agreed and I released him. I am sure that what decided him to accept my formula was not only the use of the phrase 'Gentleman's agreement' instead of 'on parole' to provide a way out of giving any undertaking to the Government, but also the fact that I was prepared to trust him.

The Government accepted my action, I think with some misgivings, but I had really forced their hand. I believe their nervousness was due to a fear that if Nehru had indulged in any political activity or speeches they would have been obliged to re-arrest him in the full glare of publicity in the middle of visiting his sick wife, thereby inviting a great public outcry and a reprimand from the Government of India for their ineptitude.

One cannot help wondering further, whether they thought Nehru capable of doing this just to embarrass them!

They entirely misjudged him. Nehru remained out for a brief eleven days. During this period he was under constant pressure to make pronouncements on Congress policy but refused, mainly for the reasons he had already given me. But, in his autobiography he wrote:

I had also a feeling that in view of the courtesy shown by the Government in allowing me to come to my wife, it would not be proper for me to take advantage of this for political purposes. I had given no undertaking or assurance to avoid any such activity, nevertheless I was continually being pulled back by this idea.

This was the only time I met Pandit Jawaharlal in person. To the Government he was probably the most dangerous man in India. Obviously they were ready to agree that he was an honourable man, otherwise of what value was any undertaking. But, apparently they were not prepared to go any further than that. That a mere stripling should proceed to treat him as a human being must have been for them an alarming experience!

Anyway, to the relief of all concerned, the 'Gentleman's agreement' had worked — at least for those eleven days.

A SNAKE IN THE GRASS

I met the Khan Sahib first in 1933, when I was posted as Joint magistrate to Benares District. I was then a bachelor and staying with the British Superintendent of Police for Benares State. Khan Sahib Sheikh Mohammad Umar was a regular visitor, a patriarchal figure with long white beard in flowing robes which he wore with immense dignity. Though he was only seventy, one could be forgiven for thinking that he had survived from the 18th century. He came as an equal, outside official visiting hours, without requests for any favours. His talk was direct and amusing; he criticised the Government as freely as he did its enemies. He had a keen sense of humour and was a welcome visitor. He was landlord of Chandpur village about eight miles east of Benares city. His tenants were all Hindus whom he treated with paternal kindness, and who in turn treated him with great respect. In this matter Chandpur village was not unique. In pre-Independence India, at least, there were many instances of this kind of association, which worked quite harmoniously. I do not know what the position is now. He employed as his agent a Hindu called Markandey Singh, whom he trusted implicitly. I suppose that out in his village he lived very much the kind of life lived by his ancestors, with which he was entirely content.

I returned to Benares as District Magistrate at the end of 1936. In April 1937 the Indian Provinces became self-governing and the Congress took office in the U.P. All save one of the Ministers were Hindus, the exception being Rafi Ahmad Kidwai, a Congress Muslin, perhaps the shrewdest and certainly the most efficient administrator in the Cabinet. Acceptance of office by the Congress was the signal for increased activity by their followers. They went round looking for, or stirring up grievances. This was to be expected and had to be dealt with in more tactful ways than when they were in open or secret confrontation with the Government. Sometimes they exposed a genuine wrong; sometimes their enthusiasm went too far and became embarrassing even to their leaders. There were many professional agitators who had worked for the Congress in adversity who now expected to be rewarded.

Understandably it was difficult for the Ministers and other Congress leaders to deny them.

My marriage in November 1937 made no difference to the Khan Sahib's visiting habits. He told my wife in the most charming way that she must be very inexperienced, so he had appointed himself honorary supervisor of our servants in order to satisfy himself that they were looking after us properly. We all, including the Khan Sahib himself, regarded this as a great joke. I suspect the servants deliberately committed some sins of omission or commission to see if the old man would spot them. As a matter of fact he knew quite a lot about the menage of a European household in India and I think his greatest pleasure in playing this game was in showing off his knowledge. He never sent any fore-warning of his visits which took place at all hours, so that he was overtaken by one of his prayer times on more than one occasion, when he retreated to our front verandah to say his prayers and comb his beard.

One evening in February 1938 we had just reached the coffee stage after a small and very informal supper party when my bearer came in and leaning over me whispered, 'Khan Sahib has come.'

'Ask the Memsahib if he is to be invited in,' I said. But before he could reach my wife the old was in the doorway beaming at everyone.

'Come in Khan Sahib,' I said. The patriarchal figure was already in.

'Will you join us for coffee Khan Sahib,' said my wife. He bowed graciously towards her, pulled up a spare chair and sat down at the table.

'Allow me to introduce Khan Sahib Sheikh Mohammad Umar,' I said. 'The finest gentleman in the district.'

'He is insincere flatterer,' said the Khan Sahib, but he looked very pleased. He made himself agreeable to his neighbours, asking what they did, were they married, had they any children? His manners were impeccable and the sound effect of sucking his coffee through his beard was fascinating. When he had drunk his coffee he looked round with a mischievous twinkle in his eye:

'I am in the habit,' he said, 'of paying calls on my friends the Collector Sahib and Memsahib just to assure myself that their servants are behaving properly. But, as they have company to-night, I will forbear on this occasion. Moreover I am rather late as one wheel of my trotting bullock cart came off on my way in. When it is repaired,' and he made signs to my bearer to go out and enquire, 'I shall take my leave.' Turning to the *khidmatgars* he added with mock ferocity — 'But I shall be back soon to see what villainy you have been up to.' He joined heartily in the laughter that greeted this sally. My bearer came back to say his cart was mended and ready in the drive. As he rose to go and after thanking my wife for the coffee, he said to me in a hoarse whisper, 'I shall come back to see you in a few days to consult you about the affairs of my estate.'

I nodded but said nothing. I thought I knew better than the old man what was wrong but it was no use telling him that I suspected his agent was disloyal as he would hear nothing against him. Ironical that he should concern himself about the honesty and efficiency of our servants when he was so blind to the dishonesty of one of his own.

A few days after his nocturnal visit I received an invitation from the Khan Sahib to bring my pig-sticking friends out to Chandpur the next week-end and for all of us to spend the Saturday night at his house. Chandpur was one of the areas on the Tent Club map as there was Kadir country between the village and the Ganges. We had not hunted it yet and the invitation was accepted with alacrity. It was the most amusing, if not the most fruitful meet of my experience. Four of us went out, a Police officer, two Army officers and myself. The Khan Sahib followed the spears in his trotting bullock cart, i.e. across very rough country. Whenever a pig broke, he stood up in his cart and shouted his view halloo, or if he saw a pig breaking back he stood up and gesticulated wildly. One of us had to keep an eye on him, not only to mark his signals, but also to see that the old man did not fall out of his cart and need assistance. After a good day with a modest bag of two boar we returned to enjoy the Khan Sahib's generous hospitality. We had an enormous *pilao* washed down with beer. In the open courtyard where we had our meal there were four *charpoys* complete with mosquito nets, all ready for our nights rest. When he judged that we were replete the Kah Sahib said slyly:

'Would you like to finish with some English fruit cake — I have some in that cupboard.'

We went over to the glass-fronted cupboard standing in the verandah and there to our fascinated gaze was revealed two shelves full of McConachie's tinned foods. We gazed awestruck.

'When did you get these Khan Sahib?' I asked.

'In 1915,' he said and watched our faces. We hastily expressed our inability to eat any more after the enormous meal we had just eaten.

He roared with laughter:

'I show them to all my English friends when they come here but most surprisingly none of them are brave enough to sample my tinned food.' The day was rounded off by a marvellous night's sleep.

Next morning he invited me to see his fishing tank. This was a rectangular man-made pool. From the middle of one of the long sides a small wooden pier projected over the water. At the end of the pier there was a small bamboo and reed shelter where the Khan Sahib sat to fish, cross-legged and shaded from the sun. The tank was stocked with Rohu, an Indian relation of the Chubb, which grew to quite a good size. He showed me the bait he used, which advertised itself long before we reached the tin. It was the most disgusting stuff I have ever smelt. He told me the recipe with great relish but I have now forgotten it.

He chose this moment, when we were alone, to broach the subject of the difficulties he was having in his village.

'Some of my tenants are witholding payment of their rents and I have noticed a lack of respect which I have never experienced before. Markandey says it is the doing of the Congress agitators.'

'Have you seen any such person in the village?'

'No, Markandey says they come secretly at night.'

'You still believe and trust him?'

'Of course, he has been with me for years.'

'Well, Khan Sahib, nothing very much to go upon yet. Let me know if there are any further developments.'

I was sorry for the old man; he seemed to me very vulnerable. I had received hints from some of the district staff which made me deeply suspicious of his agent's honesty.

My fears were soon realised. The old man turned up at my house three weeks later almost speechless with anger:

'They have removed and hidden both wheels of my trotting bullock cart; they have spilt all the bullocks' *bhusa* over the yard. Worst of all, they have wrecked my fishing hut.'

'And what explanation had Markandey Singh to give for these actions?'

'He says it is the Congress men who are responsible. He says he dared not oppose them for fear they might do worse.'

'He did not give you any warning of their intentions?'

'No, Sahib, he said his own life was in danger.'

'What are you going to do, Khan Sahib?'

'I have decided to go and see the only Muslim Minister in the Congress Government. I am going to ask him to restrain his party workers and to punish those responsible for the acts of sabotage.'

'Rafi Ahmad Kidwai may find it difficult to do this, even if he sympathises with you.'

'He will listen to a brother Muslim, though he pretends to be a Congressman.'

I had my doubts but admired his spirit:

'I will wait till you have done this, to see what happens, and then I will come to your village and make an enquiry.'

'Thank you, Sahib; I am going to Lucknow to-morrow.'

'I will send the Kanung on some excuse to keep an eye on your house and affairs while you are away.'

'No need, Sahib, but thank you all the same. I have told Markandey to be alert.'

A week later I had a brief note from the Khan Sahib to say that the Minister had promised an enquiry and had asked the Chairman of the District Congress Committee to see me. This gentleman, Pandit Deonandan Dixit duly came to see me. He told me that when complaints were made against Congress workers, his Committee's usual practice was to conduct their own enquiry. But in this case there seemed to be no complaint against any specific person or persons and the Minister had asked that I should conduct an enquiry and that he should accompany me as an observer. This seemed to me an excellent suggestion. Pandit Dixit might consider that without his presence the enquiry might be one-sided, the Minister probably thought that without my presence the zemindar — a Muslim — might be prejudiced, and I was pleased that the Minister had chosen the correct authority, the District Officer, to conduct the enquiry.

We went out to Chandpur a few days later. The villagers were called and assembled in the Khan Sahib's large courtyard. The old man sat upright and very dignified facing the villagers with Markandey Singh standing beside him. I asked the headman to stand up:

'What is your grievance against the Khan Sahib?' I asked.

'I have no grievance myself,' he said. 'Let others speak for themselves.'

'Who has a grievance against the Khan Sahib?' I asked.

Five or six men got up. In each case the grievance was the same. Their rents had been raised without notice and contrary to the law. I asked for facts and figures and told the *patwari* to produce the record of rights. While I was doing the checking, eight more men stood up to make the same complaint. When I noted all the names and figures, I turned to the Khan Sahib:

'Have you raised their rents as claimed by these tenants?'

'Most certainly not. I would never do such a thing against the law, though many of their rents are lower than I could legally

charge on the basis of the last settlement. They know this well. I
have treated my tenants as my own children.'

'May I see your current rent roll please?'

He took it from Markandey Singh and handed it to me. On examination the rents recorded in the rent roll tallied with those
shown in the record of rights. I turned to Markandey Singh:

'Did you write up this rent roll?'

'Yes, Sahib.'

'And did you also collect the rents?'

'Yes, Sahib.'

'Did you collect only the rents recorded in the rent roll, or the
increased rents as stated by these fourteen tenants?'

'I collected the increased rents as ordered by the Khan Sahib. He
also ordered me to record the correct rents in the rent roll on threat
of dismissal.'

'I see; have you paid these increased rents to your master?'

'Yes, Sahib.'

'Can you prove this?'

'No, Khan Sahib never gives receipts.'

I looked at the old man; I thought he was about to have an
apoplectic fit. But controlling his fury he turned to the villagers and
said: 'I have treated you fairly all my life. Do you really believe I
would suddenly take leave of my senses? Do you really believe I
would impose and accept unlawful excess rents? Markandey Singh
tells me that all this is the doing of Congress agitators who have
been coming secretly to turn my tenants against me and also apparently to intimidate my own agent to make false statements
against me. Is this true? If so, speak up and tell the Collector Sahib.
If not, do you believe me or Markandey Singh?'

This was received with an uncomfortable silence and some shif-
ting of haunches amongst the squatting villagers, as if something
urged them to rise but caution bade them wait. The headman rose
slowly to his feet:

'My grandfather and my father were both headmen of Chandpur
and I succeeded them thanks to the recommendation of Khan
Sahib. I am an old man now and must soon relinquish the post. But
my conscience would not allow me to serve a day longer if I failed
now to tell the truth. There have been no Congress agitators coming openly or secretly to this village. It was Markandey Singh alone
who thought out this scheme to get Khan Sahib into trouble. He
claims to be a secret Congress worker well known at their District
headquarters. He said we should not get into any trouble as it was
the Congress Party's policy to get rid of all *zemindars*. When this

was achieved, he said the tenants would no longer have to pay any rents, only the government land revenue. He arranged that some tenants should pay the increased rents, while others should refuse to pay any rents, so that there would have to be an enquiry, which would be conducted by the Congress. He promised that all excess rents would be repaid after the scheme had succeeded. It was he also who suggested damaging Khan Sahib's bullock cart and destroying his fishing shelter, so as to provoke him to anger and harsh treatment of the whole village. I objected to such actions, but he must have persuaded someone to do these things. I did not report all this to Khan Sahib because I knew he would not listen to anything against Markandey Singh.'

The headman's speech was received in dead silence. The Khan Sahib was staring at him, mouth agape — he was speechless. On Markandey Singh's face I saw an insolent and sly smile. It appeared he was confident that no-one would support the headman with whom he was known to be on bad terms. I turned to the villagers:

'Come,' I said, 'do not be afraid to speak; no-one will be punished for speaking the truth.'

After some hesitation three men got up, to be followed by half a dozen more. 'What the headman says is true,' said one man and all the rest agreed.

'Is there anyone who will say that the headman's report is not true?'

Only Markandey Singh spoke:

'What he says is all lies. He has a grudge against me because I was not in favour of his appointment as headman. It is true I am a Congress worker and the Congress will support me. You will be punished for supporting your zemindar and for trying to win favour with the District Officer, who is a friend of the Khan Sahib.'

I ignored his outburst and asked:

'Is there anyone now who still has a complaint against the Khan Sahib?'

Three men got up and after conferring together, one was pushed forward to speak:

'We have no complaint against Khan Sahib; our complaint is against Markandey Singh. For years he has been unlawfully taking grain and other produce from us in the name of his master. Because we knew Khan Sahib would not believe us, we kept silent.'

There were many murmurs of agreement. Markandey Singh was quick to reply:

'I took what I did for my master, not for myself.'

At this point Pandit Deonandan Dixit intervened:

'It seems that accusations are now being made against a Congress worker rather than against the *zemindar*. I think that the District Congress Committee should now investigate these complaints.'

'Perhaps they should,' I replied,' but first it would be well to obtain confirmation of his own statement that he is a Congress worker. Have you a list, Pandit-ji, of authorised workers in the district?'

Luckily he had brought his list. I got the impression that he was rather apprehensive as he started to look through it. When he had finished, he said — again I thought with relief:

'He is not recorded as a Congress worker and I have never seen or heard of him before.'

'In that case,' I said, 'we can now finish this enquiry here.'

The Khan Sahib rose slowly to his feet, white faced and trembling with fury. He had been bottling up his emotions all through this interruption and I expected a tremendous explosion. I was not disappointed.

'So, I am a tyrant and an ogre am I? Only fit to be thrown to the wolves, am I? Or just a silly old man who was simple and stupid enough to trust his black-hearted and dishonest agent? I am sorry I have allowed myself to be deceived for so long.'

Then turning to Markandey Singh who was grovelling at his feet, he said fiercely:

'Do not look to me for mercy or forgiveness; you are dismissed, but before you leave you will repay to each of the tenants whom you have cheated the amount that is due to him. Fetch the money now.'

I sent an orderly with Markandey Singh just to see he did not try to decamp. He came back very soon and, sullen-faced, repaid the excess rents.

'Well,' I said,' that concludes the enquiry. It only remains to ask the Khan Sahib if he wishes further enquiry to find out who damaged his bullock cart and destroyed his fishing shelter.'

The Khan Sahib was obviously upset:

'No, Sahib, we will settle these matters between ourselves. I am confident that my tenants will repair the damage themselves and that is all I want.' There was a chorus of assurances.

'Then all is settled,' I said. 'No-one will be prosecuted as a result of this enquiry.'

As we left I said to Pandit Deonandan Dixit:

'I hope you are satisfied by the enquiry and that justice has been done?'

'Of course, the name of Congress has been cleared, none of our workers had any hand in this affair. As for Markandey Singh, he seems to be a rogue and has tried to bring the Congress into disrepute. Nevertheless, it does nothing to alter our Congress opinion that all *zemindari* should be abolished. His bad actions illustrate one of the evils of the system. Either the landlord oppresses the tenants or his servants do with or without his approval.'

I smiled: 'Pandit-ji, I think perhaps we should not enter upon discussion of politics just now. I have to obey existing rules and recognise existing institutions with all their faults, which I try my best to set right or mitigate. But you are free to dream dreams and make plans for a future India, which is much more exciting. Really I envy you!'

The Pandit laughed: 'You British officers are so charmingly frank, but so obstinate.'

As he got into his car, I made my parting shot:

'Anyhow, I trust you will not enrol Markandey Singh as a Congress worker now that he is unemployed.'

He looked indignant but his disreputable looking driver let the clutch in fiercely before he could reply.

Two days later the Khan Sahib came to see me. he seemed to be his old self again.

'I have come to thank you, Sahib, and also to apologise for ignoring your warnings about Markandey Singh.'

'Perhaps it was just as well Khan Sahib, that things should have been allowed to come to a head, like the proverbial boil. How will you manage without an agent?'

'I have appointed Bholu Ram, the headman. He is not very clever, but at least he is honest.'

'That is good: then you will need a new headman.'

'He has a son of thirty-five years, a good boy. I have brought him with me.'

'Will the village approve him?'

'They have proposed him for the post.'

'Then I will see him.' The old man called him in.

A neatly dressed and pleasant looking young man ran forward a few steps and then bending double with his hands clasped above his head and only just clear of the floor, took two more steps to rise to his feet in front of me, the traditional and universal obeisance of the Indian lower classes, an automatic act which they do not feel to be demeaning or subservient, though it may appear so to the onlooker.

'How much have you paid or promised the Khan Sahib to recommend you for the post of headman of Chandpur?' I asked severely, not daring to look at the Khan Sahib in case I should be unable to keep a straught face. The young man looked extremely startled and then at the Khan Sahib, who must have winked or smiled, because a broad grin spread over his face and he said: 'One lakh, Sahib.' We all burst out laughing.

'And your fishing shed, Khan Sahib?'

'It has been rebuilt. Now you must come as my guest and fish there.'

I thanked him but inwardly prayed that the shelter might be demolished again by a cyclone before I was obliged to accept the invitation.

'And what have you done with Markandey Singh?' I asked.

'I have shut him in a small room which he is sharing with three cobras. It is a punishment of which my grandfather was very fond.'

I looked unbelieving at the old man: 'You are joking Khan Sahib?'

'I am not joking, Sahib. It is a punishment to fit his crime.'

'But you can't do this sort of thing to-day. The trouble which you have just survived is as nothing compared to the trouble you will be in if this man is harmed. We must go to Chandpur at once to release him, if he is not already dead. I will tell your driver to follow in your cart with the headman-elect.'

We did not speak during the drive but as we got out of my car, the Khan Sahib said:

'He can come to no harm, Sahib, the poison fangs were removed before we put the snakes in the room.'

'That is almost worse, you old sinner. He will have died a hundred lingering deaths, instead of only one, sharp and short. He may be off his head by now — how long has he been in there?'

'About twenty-four hours, Sahib. He has been given food and drink, strong drink.'

When we opened the door slowly, we saw the three cobras coiled up together asleep in one corner. In another corner sat Markandey Singh, staring at the snakes, his eyes glazed with fear. He did not appear to have heard the opening of the door and he made no sign of recognition as we came in. His food was untouched but the drinking bowl was empty. It was too much to hope that the snakes had shared it and so remained too comatose to investigate the wretched agent. I went in quietly and led him out. His body was as stiff as a board, confirming my worst fears. One of the cobras raised its head and hissed but made no move.

I took Markandey Singh back to Benares and into hospital. I told them that he thought he had been bitten by a cobra and was suffering from shock, a symptom of which they were well aware, as it accounted for nearly as many deaths as actual snake-bite. After a week of heavy sedation, he recovered. I have no idea what became of him after.

When I next saw the Khan Sahib he was quite unrepentant.

'He has had his lesson, Sahib — I fancy he will not cheat again.'

Reluctant as I was to condone in any way the old man's 'short, sharp, shock' treatment, I had to admit to myself that it was probably more effective than a prison sentence. And it earned a further dividend. Word got round of what he had done and I suspect it was not just a matter of chance that Chandpur was one of the few villages in the District which escaped the attention of socialist enthusiasts preaching the new millennium.

For his sake I am glad that the Khan Sahib did not live to see the *zemindars* reduced in land, income, status and influence in the new independent India.

1972

FRAGRANCE OF CEDAR

1.

No-one knew what attraction the fertile but bare red plain of the Buka'a could have for a retired cavalry officer and aide-de-camp at the Imperial Court of the Emperor Franz Joseph. No-one knew but many were ready to hazard a guess as to why Count Otto had retired in 1903 into what was obviously not a voluntary exile from his native land. A political scandal was, of course, most commonly mentioned, though details remained scarce and varied considerably. Yuctan, the postman, maintained on a precarious and irregular salary by the most casual and dilatory of government departments, declared that the Count was really a secret service agent, sent to report on the activities of the French who had established a very strong influence in this part of the Middle East. In the course of fifteen years service there were few interesting looking letters which Yuctan had not opened; but the half-yearly letters that arrived for the Count, stamped with the Imperial seal, contained only bank orders — Yuctan had to rely on his imagination for the rest. Anisa, the wife of Mohammad Yasin the innkeeper at Ksara, was convinced that the scandal was of a more intimate and domestic nature — the Count had compromised a princess and killed her husband in a duel after denouncing him as a homosexual; the money was, of course, 'hush-hush' — but then Anisa was an incurable romantic. Yasin himself pooh-poohed his wife's ideas — such affairs were of common occurrence amongst the aristocracy in Europe and taken lightly; if it were not so the Lebanon would be flooded with banished paramours. No, for Yasin the Count was just another of the wealthy eccentrics who chose to live abroad, but doubly so for choosing to live in the Buka's.

Naturally, this gossip reached the ears of the Count and mildly amused him, but he did nothing to allay their curiosity. The peasants, in general, accepted him with as little question as the miraculous powers of the Virgin Mary, or the reality of the dragon slain by St. George. Moreover the Count was a good employer and paid wages punctually. He had bought the farm of Ali Muftar at Ksara for a price which caused that half-hearted yeoman to regret

203

publicly the hard work he had put into the land. This had been
negligible as the Count soon found to his cost. Though the soil was
unquestionably fertile, he soon grew tired of the limited choice of
local crops. The farm included a small vineyard, the grapes were
sweet but coarse. Perversely, in the face of local advice, he decided
to try and improve the indigenous vine by selective grafting. After
seven years of assiduous cultivation he had improved the local vine
to such an extent that a French connoisseur, whose palate had been
coated with fine dust after a day's partridge shooting, had declared
in an unguarded moment that the wine almost merited the title of
'Chateau Ksara du Grand Liban'. As such it was soon to pose in
a rather self-conscious publicity on the bar counters and tables of
a limited number of Hotels Splendide, Grand and St. Georges in
Beirut, Tripoli and other less well-known tourist resorts of the
region.

Count Otto lived simply and made few acquaintances. He rode
frequently but alone and, as often as not, his ride would take him
to the summer villa near Baalbek of His Excellency the German
Consul in Beirut. This was most charmingly situated in a tamarisk
grove beyond the town and overlooking the ruins of a temple to
Venus, which was reflected in the clear spring waters of a willow-
framed pool. It was a favourite resort of the Count, who found
here a gracious reminder of the life he had abandoned. Friendship
with the Consul, a kind but stolid Saxon, had followed Count Otto's infatuation with his villa — mainly as a matter of convenience.

His own farmhouse at Ksara was large but lacking any charm.
It had a certain bare dignity, supported by a few retainers in a faded
livery, who were also supposed to guard the estate against the
threat of unpredictable Druse raids. So far, these had never
materialised. The farm, bought on a passing whim, at first
disgusted him because it parodied so miserably the more fortunate
vineyards of his native land, Moravia, and ended by enslaving
him, body and soul, in an attempt to achieve the impossible, a real
vintage wine in the Lebanon. Vanity and pride, sometimes, but not
always, the enemies of reason and sanity, salvaged for him
something out of the wreck he imagined he had made of his life.
Destiny, which he reproached bitterly whenever he thought of the
past, saved this scion of the oldest and ripest hierarchy in Europe
from the idle decline of so many of his compeers and ordained instead a vigorous middle age of honest if not particularly rewarding
toil.

To break in on the age-old self-sufficiency of one of the world's
backwaters, even with such a mildly intoxicating innovation as

Chateau Ksara du Grand Liban, was not easy. The government taxed him reasonably but provided no services. Foreign-made goods were scarce and very expensive. Labour was bewilderingly irresponsible. Any day in the spring the foreman might come to announce that all the labourers had gone off for the day to a marriage in the mountains. There were days when even the foreman failed to turn up and explained afterwards that he had been ill, though there were no signs of illness. In the harvesting season, when every hour was precious, each family group in turn took time off to attend a different harvest festival. In the Buka'a were no roads, only rutted tracks. Transport of the increasing produce of the farm became a real problem which drove the Count, for the first time since he had settled in the country, to appeal to the provincial Governor.

In the history of the old Turkey which has vanished, there were few officials who combined the ambition to plan a progressive programme with the ability and energy necessary to carry it out. Djemal Pasha, Governor of the province of Damascus, Defender of the Faith and oppressor of the poor, must certainly be numbered amongst those few. To him, Turkey was still an Imperial Power but a Power which could not afford to ignore the march of progress if it was to survive. He understood the importance of good communications. Also, like a good Turk, he resented, while coveting the exorbitant profits being made by the French concessionaires from the railways which they had constructed and now managed in the Lebanon and in Syria. The British, with their usual hypocritical insolence, were objecting strongly to the construction of the Bagdad railway by the Germans, while extending their own line from Egypt up the coast of Palestine and across to Maan. Always it was the foreigners who obtained the biggest profits. Djemal persuaded his own government to initiate the most ambitious project of all, a railway line to link the existing Aleppo-Hama line to Damascus and then south through the desert to Medina and Mecca. The Hejaz line to serve the pilgrimage would bring great merit and eventually handsome profits. But Turkey, groaning under the expenses of punitive measures against the rebel Armenians and the Kurdish brigands, sucked dry by the twin leeches of foreign exploitation and domestic corruption, could ill afford the capital cost of a new railway running through hundreds of miles of unprofitable desert. It was launched on a series of unsound contracts, aided by an even more questionable series of state lotteries. As it crawled southwards it fed increasingly on the country through which it passed. Far from coal and before the age of oil, its only fuel was wood and, as it advanced, so the scanty forests disappeared. When he was told there was no more timber to fell Djemal pointed out that the peasants lived in wooden houses; they could use other materials or live in their cowsheds. He had their olive trees and vines cut down to feed the hungry engines of his construction gangs. He even threatened to cut down the few remaining cedars in the famous grove which had once supplied Solomon with timber for his new temple in Jerusalem. Only the Patriarch's intervention saved them.

Thus, when it came to his Excellency's knowledge that there was a wealthy foreigner — all foreigners in Turkey were wealthy — applying for better communications in the Buka'a he was only too willing to oblige — at a price. This particular foreigner's predilection for encouraging cultivation of the forbidden grape did not offend or worry Djemal Pasha as he observed with satisfaction a bottle of the choicest 'Pol Roger' on his own sideboard. The Prophet had never tasted vintage wine, far less champagne, or he would have realised that his denunciation had been over-hasty and undiscriminating — no doubt he had been motivated by the taste of sour grapes. However, such comfortable reflections were best kept to oneself; when it came to business the Prophet's error was a useful spanner with which to tighten the screw. For the trifling sum of £T 40,000 the Count was promised a single line track through the Buka'a. An unfortunate misunderstanding, by which the track was aligned to pass on the other side of the extensive valley from Ksara, was remedied by a further contribution of £T 10,000. As he did not possess so much capital the Count took a loan from the Ottoman Bank, repayable over ten years and mortgaged his farm to the Bank as security. As it happened he never obtained any benefit from this deal as the line was still under construction at the outbreak of the first World War. It was of considerable strategic value to the Turkish and German armies and the object of constant sabotage by the Arabs until the Turks destroyed it themselves as they fell back before Allenby's victorious advance.

2.

One day in the middle of October 1913 Count Otto rode over to Baalbek. He had been invited by his friend the German Consul for a couple of days partridge shooting in the hills. He shared with the Consul a love of open air sport and a hearty contempt for what constituted sport in the Lebanon. Any peasant farmer with a gun and a couple of dogs could roam the hillsides at will, which, had they been in Europe, would have been strictly preserved for the gentry. It was one of the few points on which exile had not modified his views. Such sturdy independence offended his sense of order and undoubtedly resulted in game becoming increasingly scarce. Nevertheless the hill partridge shooting offered fair sport.

As he approached the Villa de la Source Otto reflected again with the usual pang of regret how much pleasanter a retreat this would have been for a gentleman of taste than his austere and rather ugly farm at Ksara in the midst of its great red fields. The weeping willows swept low over the cool waters of the pool and the dust and heat seemed suddenly remote. He spent his evening in a state of mild melancholy and just before dusk wandered out, past the ruined temple of Venus, leaving his host discussing the next day's programme with a stocky peasant who looked just like a fat-tailed sheep as he bent over to follow the Consul's finger on a map. No-one had ever explained to the Count's satisfaction the local use of this extra fold of trouser seat which looked like a collapsed bustle. His own private opinion was that it had evolved to cushion the rider from some of the painful impact of travel on mule-back. The mules in these parts had the sharpest and boniest backbones of any four-legged beast of burden in the world.

As Otto breasted a slope, the six great columns of the temple of Jupiter thrust up out of the shadows in that cold light that precedes the swift fall of night. His eye did not linger on any other detail of the massive ruins below — he had seen them many times and in many lights — but swept across a belt of poplars and stony plain to the darkest purple of the horizon to rest on the noble shoulders of Jebel Sunnin. A faint rose reflection lingered on the summit ridge which stood out clearly against a band of yellow sky. To the north-west two patches of eternal snow gleamed from the upper slopes of the Jebel Arz — the Cedar Mountain. He turned. To the east the Anti-Lebanon burned like gigantic heaps of pink slag still glowing from the furnace. When he turned again, a thick line of black cloud hung over the whole sweep of the western horizon. It was as if some idle god had boldly drawn his charcoal across the whole frame of sky. In a moment it was dark and he was stumbling back through the stony fields and sand dunes.

The morning was fine with promise of heat later. They rode across the plain; when they reached the hills they sent the horses back and walked. When it became too steep to walk in comfort in the increasing heat they mounted mules and rode up a rough track, which soon degenerated into the rocky bed of a dry stream, till they met the picturesque party of peasants with the guns and dogs. Their luggage was sent direct with the mules to the inn at the foot of the pass where they were to spend the night. With a bag of 21 partridge and 3 hare they ended their morning shoot at the Col des Cédres, where they ate their lunch of unleavened bread, goat's milk cheese, black dates and grapes, washed down with a bottle of white wine. By common consent it was agreed to abandon the afternoon's shoot as planned as the beaters were anxious to return home in good time to prepare for the celebration of the harvest festival to be held that evening.

'If we agree,' said the Consul, 'they will probably all get drunk this evening and turn up late for our morning shoot to-morrow. But if we refuse they will get drunk all the same and fail to turn up at all. It is best to humour them. I am at fault and apologise for choosing this particular day, I had forgotten all about the harvest festival and that idiot of a muktar failed to remind me.'

'No need to apologise,' said Otto. 'It is extremely pleasant up here; by all means let us be lazy with a good excuse.'

From the Col, over 8,000 ft. high, there was a magnificent view in all directions except to the west and south-west. Looking back east over the red plain of the Buka'a the Anti-Lebanon ran away in folds of pink and violet to the gap leading to Damascus. Beyond that Mt Hermon was just visible on the south-east horizon. Far to the north-east the desert stretched away beyond Homs. Directly north over the pass lay a vast amphitheatre of bare hills. Below that the ground fell in steep terraces to the Kadischa valley which dropped down towards Tripoli, north-west, in a jagged dark ravine. Further to the north-west, over a gap marking the line of another deep gorge, lay the sea but it was hidden in the heat haze.

The Consul drew Otto's attention to a small dark patch near the bottom of the limestone cirque below them:

'The Cedars of Lebanon,' he said.

It was the first time that Otto had seen the famous grove and he voiced his disappointment aloud, for at that distance it showed no bigger than a man's clenched fist.

'Ah — but you would be enchanted if you saw it at close quarters' said the Consul, who proceeded to give statistics of the girth, spread and age of the largest trees.

'Besides, my dear Count, it is still a place of pilgrimage to men of imagination and that means something in this materialistic age.'

'Bah! Trippers,' Otto replied.

'No, not only trippers.'

'Then sentimentalists, poets and the like — almost as bad!'

The Consul laughed:

'Have it your own way since there is obviously no pleasing you.

But seriously, the cedars really are fine. Now we are so close you ought to go down and see them. As we have finished our sport we have some time on our hands. I will send for the mules so that we can ride back before dark.'

'Very well — as you wish; I will compose a suitable ode on the way down.'

Otto's sarcasm was lost on the worthy Saxon.

They went down through the bright afternoon sunlight into that great bare bowl which had once been clothed by the noblest forest in Phoenicia. Not a tree, not a shrub or flower to relieve the glare reflected from the pale rock and dust. Far below, the houses of Besharre, clinging to the rocky lip of the Kadischa gorge, stood out in the sun like matchbox dolls-houses against the deep shadow marking the opposite side of the chasm.

When they reached the grove Otto had to admit he was impressed. The individual trees were magnificent but the real magic of the place was the sudden transformation from naked barrenness to enchanting green. Under the huge low-spreading branches there was a rusty carpet of pine needles through which the rough grass thrust its tiny spears; in the glades between the trees the grass spread invitingly short and springy. Above, the wind gently rustled the upper branches and brought them heady draughts of frangrance. Apart from themselves the grove was empty. Otto noticed a small inn at the lower edge of the grove but no sign of life there. He would have liked to linger but the Consul was thirsty and suggested descending to Besharre for a drink before returning over the Col. Otto reluctantly agreed.

The Palace Hotel at Besharre was a modest enough hostel. The floor of the main hall was covered with marble slabs — Otto thought they were probably imitation marble; on the walls hung stuffed trophies of the chase, the heads of wolf, gazelle, wild ass and boar, all very real. Occupying the full width of the wall opposite the front door was a complete section of a giant cedar on which were carved hundreds of initials. Below it was a small notice to say that the proprietor, Babar Bey, was licensed to sell small slivers of cedar as souvenirs. The room was generously supplied with brass spittoons.

While the Consul was engaged in some argument with the muleteers outside, Otto idly turned the pages of the visitors book. It went back to 1898, a date he was not likely to forget, though he had often tried to banish it from his mind. In that year, at the age of twenty-one with the prospect of a brilliant career before him, he had, with great foolhardiness, not only formed a liaison with a young

Czech actress of humble origin, but also dared to introduce her to
Viennese Society. In other circumstances he would probably have
got away with his youthful indiscretion; but in this case, unfortunately, the Archduke Leopold Ferdinand, eldest son of the last
Grand Duke of Tuscany, was infatuated with the same girl. Indeed,
he had been the first to discover her in a remote garrison town in
Galicia and had discreetly arranged for her to come to Vienna. The
Emperor despised and disliked Leopold, a man of vain and unstable
character. The dislike was mutual, Leopold holding the Emperor
responsible, in particular, for thwarting his marriage to a young
girl of good family with whom he had fallen in love. But Franz
Joseph ruled the House of Habsburg with a rod of iron and
Leopold, it seemed, stood in too much awe of him to rebel. But in
1903 Leopold, who had previously been shut away in a private
lunatic asylum for three months by the vindictive Emperor, suddenly decided to defy him by marrying the Czech actress. Franz
Joseph was furious and disinherited him. Although he had nothing
to do with Leopold's act of defiance, Otto was held responsible for
introducing her to Viennese Society and guilty, therefore, of pro-
viding the temptation which led to Leopold's disgrace. There were
other Royal princes to protect. The Emperor decided to make an example of Otto as a deterrent to other young rakes. He was banished
from the Empire and all his houses and estates were confiscated.
The only saving grace in this disaster was that the Emperor made
arrangements that he should receive in exile part of the income
from his confiscated estates. His friends told him that this had been
done because he had been a great favourite at Court and had many
sympathisers. Otto thought it more likely that the old dictator was
shrewd enough to make certain that the exile would have the means
to stay away.

These painful memories ran through his mind unbidden as he idly turned the pages of the book and noted the names of many well-
known visitors since the turn of the century. He closed the book
with a grimace. On the wall above the book he noticed a signed
photographic portrait, sadly faded. He did not recognise the man
portrayed but the signature was reasonably legible as one he had
already seen in the visitors book — 'Alphonse, Marie, Louis de Prat
de Lamartine' Of course, he was the great romantic traveller, he
could not have missed this pilgrimage! Moreover, his beloved
daughter, Julia, had died in Beirut and he had sought distraction
from his grief, not only in copious outpourings of the muse, but
also in many journeys in the Lebanon, Syria and Palestine. There
had been a revival of interest in his poetry and writing in the last

years of the century. Otto himself had no use for its content or style — the sticky sentiment, the morbid pre-occupation with death, the excessive refinement of thought, the sheer bulk of repetition.

But she had adored his poems, this young woman who had wrecked his life. She would stride across the room declaiming the lush sonorous lines in adulation of nature and its divine origin, more particularly when she discovered how he detested them and wanted to tease him. Though irritated, he remembered that, at the time, he did not take the matter too seriously — he took nothing very seriously in those days. Her enthusiasms were also ephemeral, no doubt she would grow out of this one too. He had found that the only way he could stop her when she was in one of these moods was to learn some of the dull stuff himself and recite it to her with grave mockery. She would fly into a rage and throw one of the poet's books at him.

For some years he had continued to receive news of her from his friends in Vienna; how she grew tired of Leopold and left him; of her divorce and Leopold's generous settlement which enabled her to return to Vienna and resume her former gay life. But after the scandals which led to her being banished from Vienna, he heard less and less about her. She had gone to Paris, Berlin, Milan; she had not changed her mode of life. He had shut her out of his mind and heart. Friends wrote to suggest that he should approach the Emperor for a pardon; they felt confident of success. The House Law of the Habsburgs had to be upheld but even the Emperor himself kept an aging ex-actress as his companion confidante and comforter in the little house with yellow shutters tucked away discreetly in the Schoenbrunn Palace gardens. Otto had considered the temptation carefully and had rejected it. He might be pardoned but it would now be difficult to recover his estates; he could hardly expect to be given new ones. His pension would not be sufficient to support him at Court or in Viennese society, hardly sufficient to support him in any self-respecting role in Western society. His only skill was in estate management and he now preferred independence at Ksara to working for someone else for a living.

As Otto turned away from the portrait a door opened, admitting a strong odour of garlic from the kitchen and the smell of coarse strong tobacco from the saloon. The proprietor bustled up to him exuding bonhomie. Babar Bey was fat, genial and a good host.

'My good friend, a thousand pardons — I hope you have not been waiting long. I have been attending to a very important order — very important' and he rolled his eyes expressively.

'You will stay, monsieur, one night, two nights, as long as

you wish. I have excellent rooms and food. You will want to visit
the Cedars and witness the harvest festivities? — all can be
arranged.'

When he learnt that the Count could not stay he was not
deterred:

'But you will stay for dinner at least; you must see the harvest
moon and the dancers — it is to-night they perform. A party of my
guests will be going up to the Grove.'

'Thank you, but we must return to the village over the Col des
Cédres before dark. Besides, we have left all our luggage at the inn
there. I regret I must deny myself these pleasures.'

'But it will not be dark, monsieur; the moon will light you
magnificently over the pass. Or you stay in my hotel, I will lend
you a nightgown.'

'Your own?' asked Otto, amused by the rascal's persistence.

Babar Bey roared with laughter:

'My own, my own, if you so wish — there is room for two inside
it; otherwise, if you prefer, you can have the Duke of Ragusa's
ancestral nightgown — he left it in settlement of his account.'

Otto felt he could be tempted but explained that he was sure his
friend, the German Consul, would not approve the suggestion.
Babar Bey was quick to note his shift of ground and pressed home
his attack:

'Let your friend return then, but you will stay, eh? I will arrange
congenial company — a beautiful lady perhaps?' 'And he cocked his
head on one side and winked.

Otto smiled:

'You are more than kind, my friend, but I must decline — even
the offer of a beautiful lady.'

'A thousand pities, then — forgive me if I misjudged you,
monsieur.'

With this parting shot the Consul came in, hot and irritated, and
Babar Bey transferred his blandishments to that stolid and worthy
man but without success. Otto noticed that he made no mention of
a beautiful lady, he was clearly a shrewd judge of character. it was
rather disturbing, however, that this jovial innkeeper had quickly
sized him up so differently. He had fondly believed that ten years
of his new life had obliterated all traces of the young Viennese rake
as well as all desire to return to that old life.

The Consul was in a bad temper. After rebuffing Babar Bey he
came over to Otto and said:

'The muleteers are grumbling, they want to get back in time for
some festivity in their own village to-night. They threatened to

leave without us. I think they suspected we intended to stay the night here; apparently there is some special attraction here as well, as no doubt that old gas-bag has already informed you. To-day everyone seems to be moonstruck. Well — I have given the muleteers some money to get themselves drinks and promised that we will leave in half an hour.'

They went into the saloon for their own drinks. When they left Babar Bey saw them to the door, still the courteous host despite their brief patronage. As Otto passed him he winked extravagantly and whispered:

'You come again, monsieur — remember — a beautiful lady!'

All the way up to the Cedars Otto was ill at ease. He despised sentimentality, yet, on the merest caprice of imagination, the flimsiest association with the long dead past, he had been stirred by feelings he could not suppress. He decided there was a way he could fight this more satisfactorily than by running away. He must put himself to the test. He would stay and watch the harvest moon rise and flood through the enchanted grove; he would expose himself to the sensuous pleasures which he mocked and to which he fancied himself immune.

They reached the Grove. Despising himself for the subterfuge he said to the Consul:

'Frederick, my good friend, I find I am very tired; I do not think I am up to crossing over the Col to-night. I have decided to stop at the inn here for the night. But I would not dream of asking you to change your plans or suffer any inconvenience. You go on and I will rejoin you in the morning, early, in time for the shoot.'

The Consul expressed his concern:

'But you have no clothes for the night; it is too late to send your bag down now, even if I could find a man willing to bring it.'

'No matter, I can manage for one night if you will pardon me arriving unshaven tomorrow.'

'At least spend the night at the Palace Hotel. This is a very rough inn here and the food, if there is any, will be execrable. Also, you will not be able to hire a mule from here for your journey to-morrow.'

'Thank you, but I will chance it here; there is bound to be some food for tonight's festivities. I do not fancy walking back to Besharre — and I do not think I could face all those trophies of the chase again or our fat host's welcome. I will arrange to send for a mule from the village in the morning. Please do not worry. You said the beaters might be late tomorrow; if I do not turn up in time for the start of the shoot, do not wait for me.'

The Consul saw that he was determined. He was a diplomat, trained to note changes in mood though not always imaginative or sensitive enough to diagnose the causes. He did not believe the Count's excuse or understand why he did not tell him the real reason — his wish to witness the harvest festival. But he was too polite to press the matter further. The Count was a man with a closed past, nothing criminal or dishonest of course — he had made it his business to enquire discreetly through semi-official channels when they first met and struck up their somewhat incongruous friendship. But it was a past alien to the German's whole way of life and upbringing. So, suppressing his curiosity, he agreed to Otto's proposals and left with the muleteers.

When he had gone, Otto strolled over to the inn on the edge of the Grove. A plump pleasant-spoken woman answered his call and showed him up the stairs into a simply furnished but clean little room at the back of the inn. The window looked out onto the trees. Across the landing, opposite, was a larger room; the door was open and Otto caught a glimpse through the window of the magnificent view over the valley.

'I would prefer the front room,' he said politely.

'Alas! — it is already booked, Effendi. But I have two more rooms if you would care to choose.'

'Oh no — this will do me very well, I am quite content,' and then he added, curious: 'Who is to be my fellow guest?'

'A lady, Effendi. I do not know her name, the message did not say, but she is rich, she has a maid.'

'And has also paid for her rooms in advance, I suppose?'

The woman smiled:

'I did not ask for payment in advance.'

'Then I will not be outdone. Tell me the charge and I will pay you now.'

'Oh no, Effendi! — that would not be proper at all.'

'How do you know I am proper myself, arriving alone, a stranger and unannounced?'

'I flatter myself I can recognise a gentleman,' she said, and gave a little bob.

He smiled:

'Nevertheless, I would like to pay now — I shall be leaving early in the morning.'

'As you wish. I rise early myself; it will be no trouble to prepare you a meal before you leave. You will take supper this evening?'

'Will the lady be arriving for supper?'

'Oh yes — she has ordered something special and wine; it has already been sent up here.'

Then I will wait and have supper with the lady.'

She looked doubtful and then laughed with him. He paid the room charge, told her he was going out to sit under the cedars and was turning to go out when she remembered something:

'Where is your bag, Effendi? I will carry it up to your room.'

'Ah — that is coming up later, please do not bother, I will carry it up myself.'

He was a gentleman and to sup with a lady — he must not confess the truth to the good woman.

'Let me at least lend you a rug,' she said.' It can be cold sitting under the trees at this time.'

She ran off and came back with a black goat-wool rug, soft and fleecy — home-made he had no doubt. He accepted it gratefully, even if he did not really need it now, it would be invaluable later in the evening.

3.

Otto spent the rest of the late afternoon lying at the edge of the grove, watching the light and colours changing over the valley. he enjoyed the relaxation and idleness, he had not done anything like this for years.

He was roused by the sound of a party arriving. They were some way off and made for the inn. He watched them idly; there were men and women, presumably tourists — perhaps the party Babar Bey had spoken of. They made a great deal of noise and were obviously in high spirits. They disappeared into the inn. After a while he followed them and went up to his room to tidy himself as best he could. He was still in rough shooting clothes and suddenly had doubts about forcing himself on the company of a female stranger, not to mention a lady with a maid. He looked in the mirror and straightened his jacket. Of course, he was only playing a part and this was the dress rehearsal — he would enjoy explaining that. He had no idea how the play would go and whether he would enjoy that or not. He had a curious feeling of exhilaration, like a schoolboy playing truant and not caring to think what would happen if he were caught.

He came out onto the small landing and was about to go down the stairs when the door of the room opposite, the room with a view, opened and a woman came out. For a few seconds they stood looking at each other without a word and then she said:

'Pardon me for staring — I thought you were someone I once knew — the resemblance is remarkable.'

'On the contrary, Vilma, it is I who should apologise for having changed so much that you can only detect a resemblance. To me it is your reality which is so remarkable.'

She put her hands on the rail of the balustrade and leant forward to observe him more closely — or was it to steady herself?

'You — Otto? — but, of course, your voice has not changed. What are you doing here and in fancy dress?' and she started to giggle helplessly.

Otto tried to look severe:

'You have not changed at all; how often have I warned you not to giggle like that in front of strange gentlemen!'

She drew herself up:

'You forget; I am now a matron and a woman of the world.'

'What world, may I ask?'

'Not our old world, not your world, Otto. I am only interested now in the world of culture, the world of Egypt and Carthage, of Greece and Rome, the world of artists, of poets and philosophers, Dante's Italy, Goethe's Germany, Shelley's and Byron's Greece, the slums of Verlaine.'

'Holy Saints,' he thought. 'I believe she is serious. I ought to have expected something like this, I suppose, if I had ever expected to see her again.'

'And which of your luminaries has lured you here?" he asked with a light irony. He saw in her face the look of low peasant cunning which had once so delighted him:

'Surely it is now your turn to answer some of my questions?'

He refused to be drawn. Instead he said banteringly;

'Anyway, it seems you had some education from your Archduke.'

'No,' she said amused but with a glint of anger in her eyes,' not from that madman!'

'Not even a touch of madness? I hear you became a vegetarian and joined a nudist colony.'

She looked dismayed:

'So you too heard of that "scandal"? I tell you I did it only to expose that insufferable hypocrite. He posed as a radical and denounced his own order, conveniently forgetting the thirty thousand ducats a year which he drew from that connection. I took advantage of a chance encounter with another madman. At first Leopold pretended to be interested but, when it came to the point, it was too much for him. He was only saved from a howling mob of naked men and women by revealing that he was an ex-Archduke, whereupon they started fawning round him like puppies instead of stripping him of all his clothes as they had intended.'

She grimaced: 'It was too much for me as well — such dreadful people!'

They both laughed and then Otto, becoming serious for the first time, asked:

'Did you ever love him?'

'Like asking a lady her age, it is a question a gentleman should not ask,' she said sourly.

'Nevertheless, I ask it again — did you ever really love him?'

'No!'

'Did he love you?'

'Never! He only married me to escape from the clutches of that old tyrant the Emperor. I saw through that but I was not a fool — I only married him for his money.'

'But you left him?' He was about to add, 'as you left me,' but thought better of it. She looked at him, eyes wide with wonder but devoid of innocence:

'Did you not know? You seem to know all about me,' and then, looking down disconcerted, she added:

'Let us not discuss it further, the subject is distasteful to me, it was all a disaster. I'm sorry, I forgot — you must hate me.'

'No, Wilhelmine, I do not hate you — I could never hate you. I do not know what you have been doing all these years but you did wrong to leave me. I would have married you, if that had been your wish. I was not as wealthy as the Archduke but we might have managed. Does that sound very arrogant or unconvincing?'

'Neither — I believe you would have married me — but you would never have made me respectable and, if you had tried too hard, I would have left you too.'

'Yes, I can well believe it, but there is no telling now where we might have gone together — to the dogs I guess.'

She shrugged her shoulders and sighed:

'All I know is that you have suffered greatly because of me — I was not worth it.'

'I would not be so hypocritical as to deny it,' he said bluntly. 'But no more recriminations. For me there has been gain as well as loss. I am quite content now with my lot, I am happy in my exile. Are you happy in yours?'

She looked at him curiously and, after a moment's hesitation, said:

'Of course, I am rich, I can travel, I have amusing friends.'

'But no home?'

'The world is my home.'

'H'm — rather too large for comfort I should say.'

'But very exciting!'

She had recovered from her temporary mood of depression and her eyes sparkled:

'No more catechism, Otto! It is my turn now. Where do you live and what are you doing?'

He told her briefly. He was afraid she was bored. She considered for a moment and then asked again:

'And what are you doing here and in those dreadful clothes?'

Now he must dissemble; she must not know the truth, she would be too amused for his comfort; it would spoil the make-believe of the moment.

'I have never seen the Cedars — I came out of curiosity. They told me it would be a good occasion because of the harvest festival. As for these clothes, I came on from a shooting trip; I thought this might be more exciting. By a piece of luck it is.'

'Then we think alike,' she said gaily and took his arm:

'Come, we will celebrate this meeting. You will dine with me and meet my friends and then we will go to worship Saturn's daughter and the sister of Apollo!'

'For myself,' he said mockingly,' Sylvanus and the Great God Pan.'

As they descended to the public rooms below Otto tried to analyse the situation and his feelings. This incredible meeting — had he not been forewarned? The visitors' book and memories of the past, the photo of Lamartine, the 'beautiful lady'? Was it his test? And the test itself — was it any longer important? He was not sure. What was certain was that, if he had gone back with the Consul, he would have remembered only a passing mood, evoked by the beauty of the grove and the date in a visitors' book. As it was he was now committed to the stage and would have to see the play through. And Wilhelmine — what of his feelings towards her? That was still an enigma, like her presence which still somehow seemed unreal, though he felt the firmness of her arm on his and the subtle thrill of her perfumed body. She was a little plumper but bore no marks, so far as he could detect, of the unending chase after pleasure in which he believed she had indulged. She was wearing a simple high-waisted Empire style dress, cut low in front and behind and nearly reaching the ground. But what Empire? He looked again surreptitiously and decided that if it was the Roman Empire, it must be the so-called decadent period. How ridiculous they would look coming in together, like a Music-Hall turn!

But he need not have worried. The company seemed very un-orthodox — indeed, as he soon discovered, actors and poets, all young and vociferous. Their entry was greeted with shouts of delight and cheers. One young man raised his glass and called out: 'Tableau vivant! Drink to Diane and Actaeon, modern style!' She introduced him all round. his name obviously meant nothing to them. They were not at all curious as to the reason of his presence and he had a feeling that they were accustomed to the engineering by Wilhelmine of such unexpected stage entrances.

After a few drinks they all trooped into another room to dine. Wilhelmine sat at the head of the table; Otto sat on her right. She talked gaily, mostly to her young companions but not forgetting to draw him into her conversation from time to time. On his right was a young French actress, who referred to Wilhelmine as her 'patronne'. He soon discovered that her life ambition was to take the lead in *Antony and Cleopatra* at the Odeon in Paris.

'In that case,' he said, 'you have come to the right part of the world but too late.'

'How so?'

'The wild asses are now extinct.'

'But you are wrong, monsieur! There are still wild asses in Pamphylia, I have seen them myself — and the bath where Cleopatra is said to have bathed in their milk.'

'You have been to Side?'

'Yes, yes, and to Egypt of course.'

'Arranged by your patronne?'

'But naturally — who else?'

'Wonderful, wonderful,' he murmured and resolved to be more careful how he spoke to these ardent acolytes. He looked at Wilhelmine with new respect, yet, on the face of it, he found it difficult to accept her as a woman of culture; her conversation at dinner was entirely frivolous. It was all most intriguing.

The meal was good and the wine excellent, all specially laid on as he already knew.

'Do you always travel in style like this?' he asked her.

'Oh no, only on pilgrimages — but there are so many pilgrimages — the money goes pouf!'

He pondered the word — so this was a pilgrimage: in whose memory, to what shrine? He soon had the answer. At the end of dinner Wilhelmine rose, glass in hand:

'And now my friends the moment has come to drink with me to the memory of the great, the immortal poet whom we honour to-day.'

They stood up and all save Otto raised their glasses and chanted:

'To the great, the immortal poet, Lamartine!'

Otto sat down stunned, oblivious of some curious glances as he had failed to drink the toast. But Wilhelmine did not appear to have noticed or, if she had, gave no sign. He felt a sudden revulsion, he could not go through with this foolery; he was here on false pretences, like Burton in the Ka'abah at Mecca. he must slip away at the first opportunity, even if it meant enduring the knowing smiles of Babar Bey at the Palace Hotel. At least he would be able to wear the Duke of Ragusa's nightgown, even if there was no longer the possible attraction of a 'beautiful lady'.

Someone shouted that the full moon had now risen over the Grove. There was a general rush for coats, wraps and rugs. He slipped up to his room. The fleecy rug was spread on his bed and, on the rug, neatly folded, a pair of coarse grey woollen pyjamas. He was touched by the woman's kindness. What sort of an acknowledgment would it be to fade away like a thief in the night. He sat down on his bed to think. He was fully resolved not to rejoin Vilma's travelling circus. But it now seemed childish to run away, cowardly to be deterred by these harmless young people, he had gone to so much trouble to see. And then there was Wilhelmine. He had only seen her alone for a few minutes; he was still full of unsatisfied curiosity — or was it something more than curiosity? He decided to compromise. He would let the nature lovers move off and then follow discreetly and sit somewhere apart where he could watch without being seen.

He heard a woman come up the stairs and enter the room opposite. She came out in a minute and called his name. Feeling utterly ridiculous he hid under the bed. There was a knock on the door and then she came in. She came over to the bed and stood for a moment:

'So he has become an eremite,' she said aloud. 'The poor, poor man.'

There followed a giggle, inspired no doubt by the pyjamas. He wanted to burst out laughing but judged the situation too humiliating. To his astonishment she lent over the bed and he could have sworn she kissed his pillow. He heard her go out and run down the stairs to join her friends. He waited for ten minutes and then followed, taking the rug. He had no difficulty in locating the pilgrim party, they were sitting towards the upper end of the widest glade, facing down the grove and still chatting vivaciously. He circled widely uphill behind them and chose a large tree against which he sat out of the moonlight with the dark rug further helping him.

4.

He had almost gone to sleep — not surprising after such a heavy day and dinner — when he heard someone approaching. He heard her voice first and then saw Wilhelmine. She was quite close and reciting some poetry aloud. He sat very still and listened. She walked into a patch of bright moonlight; on her present course she would pass within two or three yards of him. Her progress was punctuated by stops, apparently necessary for recital to her own satisfaction. She was so absorbed she would probably never notice him. The gestures were familiar — also the poem — by Lamartine, of course. She looked quite absurd but enchanting as she postured and declaimed:

> Voilà le sacrifice immense, universel!
> L'univers est le temple, et la terre est l'autel;
> Les cieux en sont le dome; et ces astres sans nombre,
> Ces feux demi-voiles, pâle ornament de l'ombre,
> Dans la voute d'azur avec ordre semes,
> Sont les sacrés flambeaux pour ce temple allumes.
> Brillant seul au milieu du sombre sanctuaire,
> L'astre des nuits versent son eclat sur la terre,
> Balance devant Dieu comme un vaste encensoir,
> Fait monter jusqu'à lui les saints parfums du soir.

She walked right past him, oblivious to everything save the words of the poem. Her sudden apparition had fascinated him. For a moment he felt he had indeed seen the goddess Artemis. If only she would give up reciting that ghastly poem! She had passed him but her voice flowed on in high ecstasy. He felt sick — but now also with renewed apprehension. She had made a circle and was coming back the other side of his tree. Had she in fact seen him and was now punishing him for his revolt and flight? Whether she had seen him or not, the punishment continued:

> Et ces nuages purs qu'un jour mourant colore,
> Et qu'un souffle léger du couchant à l'aurore,
> Dans les plaines de l'air repliant mollement,
> Roule en flocons de pourpre aux bords du firmament,
> Sont les flots de l'encens qui monte et s'évapore
> Jusqu'au trone du Dieu que la nature adore.

She stopped three yards from him. He could see her face and on it a look of distress. She took a small book out of her cape and started to search through it. She had forgotten the next lines — was it possible! An imp of mischief possessed him; he would forestall

her. In the most sonorous tone he could command he took up
where she had left off:

> Mais ce temple est sans voix. Où sont les saints concerts?
> D'où s'élévera l'hymne au Roi de l'univers?
> Tout se tait: mon coeur seul parle dans ce silence.
> La voix de L'univers, c'est mon intelligence.

He stopped. She had dropped the book and was looking straight
at him, her eyes wide and traumatic as in a dream walk:
'Otto! What are you doing here, why did you disappear?'
He rose and bowed:
'Aegipan at your service, dear madame! My intelligence told me
to come alone, but nature has conspired with you to defeat my
purpose.'
She stamped her foot and spoke in a low tense voice:
'You mock me, as you always did; you are insufferable!'
'I did not seek out your company,' he said gravely.
'Then you deserve to be suitably punished,' and she came and sat
down beside him.
'Now,' she said, 'you will recite the rest of the poem while I
listen.'
'I have forgotten the rest.'
'Then I shall have to remind you.'
'No! No! — anything but that!'
Suddenly she was overcome by laughter:
'Still the same Otto!' She peered up into his face:
'Now, tell me truthfully why you have come here at all?'
'I will tell you the truth — I do not know.'
'But that does not satisfy my curiosity at all — think again. You
came for solitude, you are an eremite — we have disturbed you
with our lively company? You have become a disciple of black
magic? You mourn a dead wife or daughter like our poor Lamartine? Tell me something, anything! 'And she put her hand on his
arm.
He told her then of the visitors' book, the photo of Lamartine,
the spell laid on him by the cedars, the mention by Babar Bey of
the harvest festival and the dancing that night. He did not tell her
about the 'beautiful lady', nor of the private test he had set
himself.
'My dear Otto, it is enough — a truly remarkable manifestation
of spiritual telepathy. No wonder you are bemused. It is the more
extraordinary because I cannot think of anyone who would be a
more unlikely subject than you!'

He groaned inwardly 'Spiritualism as well! What other surprise I wonder?'

She had one up her sleeve:

'I am tired of my companions, they are too frivolous and noisy; I shall stay with you to watch the dancing.'

She snuggled up close to him. He pulled some of the rug over her and, when she leant against him, put his arm round her shoulder.

'Pan and Artemis,' he said gaily, 'a strange and unlikely combination, waiting to be entertained by the handmaidens of Ceres!'

'I did not know you were a classical scholar — you never taught me anything like that in the bad old days.'

'I taught you other things which I then thought were more amusing. But, of course, I was wrong. And I am not a classical scholar — it is only some manifestation of telepathy appropriate to the occasion.'

'Go on,' she said. 'I am eager for some other appropriate manifestation.' And she turned her face up to his invitingly.

'Vilma!' he said with mock reproval and kissed her.

As if at a signal a fanfare of trumpets sounded from the lower edge of the grove. They both sat up and watched a silent procession of men and women file into the glade and sit down on both sides of it. In the bright moonlight they could see that all wore their best clothes, the women with bright shawls and fancy jewellery, the men in their black suits.

Nothing further happened for a while. The moon rose higher and flooded the whole glade; they were only half in shadow now themselves. And then, suddenly, from nowhere, the dancers were in the glade. They seemed to float on the moonbeams without sound; their movements were executed with perfect timing and the sheer pace of their dancing was breath-taking. The girls wore wide pleated skirts in dark colours which swirled above their knees as they danced; they had gold kerchiefs on their heads, tied below the chin. Their tight-fitting bodices of black satin were trimmed with white lace down the front and round the neck; they wore silver slippers. The men wore black knee-length breeches with white stockings and black shoes. Over their open-necked white shirts they wore loose unbuttoned black waistcoat jackets; on their heads they wore crochet-worked silken string skull-caps variously embroidered with bright coloured threads. The group of dancers, thirty or more, floated up the whole length of the glade and down again three times and then disappeared as suddenly as they had arrived. The effect was eerie and absolutely enchanting. The silent spectators stirred and clapped and broke into conversation. Men appeared with beakers of wine and women with trays of food.

Wilhelmine had sat entranced through the dancing, her hand on his arm so tense that Otto felt the ache for some time afterwards. When it was clear that the dancing had finished she relaxed and sighed. In hardly more than a whisper she said:

'It was beautiful, unbelievably beautiful, the most beautiful thing I have ever seen. Oh, Otto was it not divine?'

Suddenly she was in tears and in his arms. He was not holding a woman who he knew was thirty-five but the young girl of twenty who had bewitched him in the Vienna woods. 'How absurd,' he thought, 'but how delightful.' And he kissed her without restraint until she stopped sobbing and lay contentedly in his embrace.

'Oh, Otto' she said 'what must you think of me?'

'Never mind, my dear, my thoughts might horrify you.'

'Really? I have never been horrified — it is my strength and my weakness.'

'Your weakness is your strength — you are a witch!'

'I find it too easy, it does not amuse me now. But this has been different; say it has been different, Otto!'

He was silent. It had been different but he did not want to admit that it was over, that it had all happened under a spell not of their own making.

'Why are you silent? What are you thinking?'

Gravely he quoted:

> 'In such a night
> Medea gather'd the enchanted herbs
> That did renew old Aeson.'

'I am thinking it is time we returned to the inn.'

'No! No! Let us stay here longer.'

'It is becoming damp where we sit — I have cramp.'

'You have spoilt everything,' she said in disgust. 'You have no soul.'

Otto started to get up; she rose reluctantly. He was as certain as of anything in his life that, given any encouragement, she would have slept with him under the cedar tree.

They walked back arm in arm, mingling on their way with the villagers who were now grouping under the direction of some Maronite priest for an open air service.

'We are intruders here,' he said. 'This is no place for two pagans.'

To his surprise she meekly agreed. Lamartine would never have missed the service and the opportunity to draw from it some obvious but elaborately illustrated moral. But Lamartine seemed to have been forgotten. What did this woman really believe in, if anything? For that matter what did he believe in himself? Wilhelmine was right — he was bemused; this was no time for self-analysis. To feel was sufficient, to feel was to be young again. 'O call back yesterday, bid time return' — he had not spoken the words, but the gods of the wood had listened and obliged.

Of Wilhelmine's party there was no sign until they reached the inn. They were in the parlour, loud in some discussion.

'Wait for me here,' she said. 'I must go and say goodnight to them.'

When she came out she said:

'They are arguing the comparative merits of the Spanish and Levantine styles of dancing. They are foolish, these intellectuals, they attribute nothing to the divine spark.'

'Perhaps they have never felt it,' he said.

She turned to him:

'Kiss me again, Otto! I am a depraved woman in search of truth, but I have not found it in all my wanderings. But I have found you — I do not want to let you go.'

The long, full-savoured kiss bridged ten years of separation. Afterwards, holding her at arms length, gently but firmly, Otto said:

'You are deprived, not depraved, my dear. There is nothing so dangerous as a woman deprived.'

'Oh!' she said 'if you like running that sort of risk, it is yours for the taking!' and she ran laughing up the stairs.

He went to his room and slowly undressed. He looked at the pyjamas with some doubt and then put them on. He did not dare look in the mirror. But, after all, he had not looked exactly romantic in his shooting clothes. He heard the banging of doors downstairs and the sounds of people departing. He remembered then that Wilhelmine had told him that the rest of her party were returning to Besharre. They preferred their creature comforts and, in any case, there was no room for them all at the inn. Someone came up the stairs and then knocked timidly on his door. He guessed it was the proprietress.

'What is it?' he called.

'Your bag, Effendi — it has not arrived. I took the liberty of lending you night-wear of my late husband; it is all I have, I hope you will not be too uncomfortable.'

He thanked her politely, suggesting apologetically that the muleteer must have misunderstood his directions. When she had gone he went over to Wilhelmine's room and knocked softly on the door.

'Come in,' she said.

He opened the door. Opposite him was a long mirror and reflected in it Wilhelmine in her nightgown standing beside her bed. He shut the door and turned towards her.

'Oh — you look so funny! 'she said giggling. 'Pan in goatskin pyjamas!'

He smiled foolishly:

'Pan, if you like, but as for the pyjamas. . .

She interrupted him, striking a classical pose:

'And I am supposed to be Artemis — you said it yourself — goddess of chastity was she not? I fear you have no business here.'

'Then I think it would be better if I leave now.'

'No! If you take so much as one step towards the door I will scream the house down and accuse you of entering my room unbidden,' and very deliberately she started to take off her nightgown.

'You have not changed, Vilma. I do not know how many men you have slept with in the capitals of Europe; in Dante's Italy, Goethe's Germany, Byron's Greece or the slums of Verlaine, nor do I care. I found you before all that and you are still as desirable as ever, though to be honest a trifle fatter.'

'You beast!' she said indignantly. 'O you beast!'

Otto grinned as she climbed into the bed:

'I may have forgotten a trick or two but I think, with your help, we can manage. With these goatskin pyjamas I throw off the respectable Count Otto of Ksara! Let us see, too, if we cannot lay the ghost of Monsieur Alphonse, Marie, Louis de Prat de Lamartine!'

'That is blasphemous,' she cried, shocked.

'But your body is divine — thank your creator!'

'That too is blasphemous.'

'I cannot please you — have done with words! 'and he climbed into bed beside her.

Words were soon forgotten, but not the memory of that night.

5.

Otto woke early. Wilhelmine was still sleeping peacefully. The morning light was not yet strong enough to be unkind but, even making allowances for that, he decided she was still a beautiful woman. And what now? The bridge had been only a temporary one into cloud-cuckoo-land. Reality seemed ugly, however he looked at it. He could not support her as mistress or wife; he was sure she was as extravagant as ever. He had heard that after she was ordered by the Emperor to leave Vienna, she had lived in lavish style in other European capitals. Even this pilgrimage must have cost a pretty penny. Her own wealth was a wasting asset; he could not imagine her investing any of it wisely. Even if she were prepared to let him manage it, he was not prepared to live on Leopold's or any other men's money. He was heavily in debt himself on account of the confounded railway line. But if he left Ksara he would be bankrupt. And Wilhelmine? Was she not the same light-o'-love who had left him without a qualm when he was young and handsome, attracted by the glamour of a Ducal title and wealth? By what power could he hold her now? Would she be prepared to give up her present way of life for him? And, even if she agreed to do so, how long would it last? There had been other women with whom he might have been prepared to take a chance but not Vilma. She would make a fool of him again. Better to treasure the whole incident as an illusion, an aberration of time and space, a bitter-sweet memory. Better to leave now before she could see him again. Babar Bey had been right — he was still susceptible; he must act at once or he would be lost. As for Vilma he would like to believe she would be upset but he thought he knew her well enough to know she would not grieve for long — it was not in her character. She was older, yes, it might make a difference, but he had seen nothing in her to justify entertaining such a possibility. He told himself that he had made a sensible decision though his heart refused to be comforted.

He got out of the bed with infinite care, went to his own room and dressed. Then he went downstairs as quietly as he could. Early as he was, the proprietress was already up and insisted on giving him breakfast of coffee, bread and fruit. Before he rose to leave he said:

'I would like to buy your rug — as a memento of a delightful visit.'

She was flattered and made no demur. The price she asked was ridiculous; he paid her double. He went upstairs and listened at Wilhelmine's door; there was no sound from within. At thirty-five, he reflected, she cannot have the same resilience as a girl of twenty. He went to his room and wrote a note. Then he went into her room and with infinite care spread the rug over her bedclothes and put the note under the rug. He pulled the sheet back and kissed her lightly on the breast. She stirred slightly and smiled in her sleep. He pulled the sheet up again gently. He never saw her again.

Babar Bey was surprised to see him so early but maintained that he was not surprised at all to see him back. He had a fine room and good food. . . Otto cut him short:

'Not this time, my good fellow — perhaps some other time I will sample your hospitality. All I want now is a mule.'

'But, of course, I will see to it at once. What happened — where is your friend — did you have an accident, or did the muleteers desert you?'

Otto said nonchalantly:

'Well, yes, I had a chance accident with a beautiful lady.'

'I knew it, I knew it!' Babar Bey beamed and then suddenly looked concerned:

'You slept under the stars?'

'You disapprove? — as a good hotelier, of course.'

Babar Bey threw up his arms in horror:

'Mon Dieu, the moon, the dew and so cold!' and went off to round up a mule.

Otto avoided the Grove altogether after discovering that there was a more direct route to the Col des Cédres. When he reflected later on the whole affair he did not regret a moment of it. He was owed this at least from the past, though, had it been practicable, he would have preferred repayment in longer instalments. And the test he had set himself — had he passed or failed? Surely he had failed with flying colours! But it no longer seemed of any importance.

Wilhelmine woke gradually, savouring for as long as possible the delicious moments of semi-consciousness. She heard someone moving in the room and murmured sleepily 'Otto'.

'I beg your pardon, madame?'

Wilhelmine woke fully and was about to sit up when she realised she had nothing on:

'Oh — it is you Maria!'

'Yes, madame, I was tidying the room. Would you like me to bring your breakfast now or after you are dressed?'

'Now please, I am ravenous.'

'I am afraid it will not be a very tempting meal, madame; this is a very simple inn. I will do my best.'

'Thank you Maria — and, oh — will you find out whether any of the other guests are still here?'

'Yes, madame.'

When she had gone Wilhelmine suddenly noticed the rug. So — he had not gone yet, she need not have said anything to Maria. Humming happily she put on her nightdress, dressing gown and slippers and went over to look at herself in the mirror. What she saw was obviously not too displeasing for she smiled. Nevertheless, she paid considerable attention to her face and hair; she knew from experience how important this was the morning after. She opened the window and leant out. It was a beautiful morning. She gave a little cry of pleasure and took a deep breath, the air was cool and heady as wine. The roofs of Besharre glowed in the sun; behind them a light mist hid the Kadischa gorge; far away the Mediterranean sparkled like a sheet of silver. She was happy with the whole world and more particularly with herself. Reluctantly she closed the window, went out onto the landing and listened, then tip-toed over to his room and knocked. There was no reply. She went in; the room was empty, the bed had been stripped and the bed-clothes neatly folded on top of the mattress. On top of the bed-clothes lay the grey woollen pyjamas. She decided he must be having breakfast downstairs and went back to listen at the top of the stairs, hoping to hear his voice. But the only sounds that came up were of the two women moving around, the clatter of a cup, the exchange of trivial remarks.

She went back to her room, puzzled and disappointed. She started to make excuses for his neglect — he was observing the proprieties, he was waiting until she had had time to dress — there were Maria and the proprietress of the inn to consider. Somewhat comforted, she pulled back the bedclothes at the top, punched the pillow and tried to prop it up, without much success. Her eye fell on the rug — of course — it would make an excellent prop. She pulled it off the bed and a piece of paper fell out onto the floor. She picked it up with trembling fingers.

Otto's note read:

'My dearest Vilma,
        I have thought long and agonisingly about our chance meeting and its delightful sequel and have decided it is best that we should never see each other again. Forgive me for whatever pain this may cause you. I could never offer you the life you want and, I believe, need.

'A little fire is quickly trodden out,
Which, being suffered, rivers cannot quench.'

We should be consumed in this fire, not by the romantic flame of love but by the suffocating smoke of disillusion. I am sure I am right, Vilma; in a little while, I believe, you will agree with me. By parting now you will keep your liberty — no need for you to escape from a cramping cage. You would find me and my life unutterably boring. As for myself — I shall be spared the sharp ache of disap-. pointment, which I fear. Yes, I am a coward in my affection for you — you had better know it now rather than later. I am no purblind pilgrim ready to follow wherever you lead.

But I shall treasure for ever the memory of our night together. Please keep the rug as a memento of our magic journey of escape from reality.

Adieu,   Otto'

Mechanically she folded the rug and propped it behind the pillow and then got back into bed. She felt sick, she had no appetite for breakfast now. Men were all the same, all selfish and calculating. She had come to this conclusion many times before. But this time she had dared to hope it would be different. Well, she knew better now. Otto did not trust her; he had neither forgotten nor forgiven — perhaps he was right. And yet, and yet. . . She started sobbing convulsively, her head between her knees . . . her whole life seemed to be a hollow mockery.

However, it was not in Wilhelmine's nature to be sad for long. She was angry with Otto for his cold-blooded analysis and this drove out any self-pity she had felt at first. She heard the maid coming up the stairs and pushed the note under the pillow. Maria came in and apologised for the time she had taken in getting the meal:

'Theresa — that's the proprietress — had to milk the goat before I could bring your breakfast.'

'Ugh! Maria, I cannot stomach goat's milk and cheese so early in the morning; please take it away.'

Maria removed the tray. As she was going out she said:

'I have asked Theresa; she said there was only one other guest — the gentleman left early this morning,' — there was a slight pause and then she added — 'Theresa spoke very highly of him.'

Maria smiled innocently but Wilhelmine was not deceived. She remembered that Maria had helped to serve at supper; she had, no doubt, heard Wilhelmine murmur his name when she was waking; she could hardly have missed noticing Wilhelmine's nightdress on the chair beside the bed. Oh well! — it did not matter, especially now that the gentleman had gone. Come to think of it, she had never tried to hide any of her 'affairs' from her servants — she was not that sort of person.

'Maria.'

'Yes, madame?'

'I have had enough of this barbarous country; we will return to

Beirut at once. Please start packing while I get dressed — oh — and be sure that this rug is packed in the large hold-all; I have acquired it as a souvenir of my visit.'

'Very good, madame; I will go to warn Theresa and the muleteers.'

When she returned, Wilhelmina had not even begun to dress. Instead, she had been thinking and planning:

'Maria, I have decided to visit Spain. I hear it is a most romantic country, where the men have perfect manners and ride like gods on proud horses. Yes, we shall go at once to Madrid. How do you think I will look in a mantilla, Maria?'

'No-one will be able to resist you, madame!'

'Then away, away!' and seizing Maria round the waist she danced wildly round the room. When they stopped, exhausted, Maria said:

'See, madame — I too have acquired a souvenir,' and she produced a delicate sliver of wood cut in the shape of a heart.

'What is it, Maria?'

'It is a piece of cedar wood from the Grove,' and she gave it to Wilhelmine, who held it up to her nose and smelt. Then she took a deep breath, inhaling the fragrance.

'It is divine, Maria. I should like. . .'

'It is for you, madame; I shall pack it with the rug.'

'And I have a present for you, Maria!'

Wilhelmine ran out of her room laughing and came back with the grey woollen pyjamas. She danced round the room, holding them at arm's length, then threw them at Maria and collapsed, laughing hysterically, on the bed.

It must be said to Maria's credit that she did the right thing and returned the pyjamas to Otto's room before they left.

1975

THE LAST ENEMY

1.

After their long ride up the rough mountain track through the
forest and biting chill of the autumn evening, the simple wooden
hunting lodge was more welcome than a palace. Two peasant boys
took their horses off to the stables; the old caretaker was waiting
on the steps to greet them and show them into a room where there
blazed a great log fire. The four young officers were glad to relax
and thaw themselves before the fire. They were all Gunners from
the Austrian garrison town of Przemysl in Galicia, on leave for a
ten days' hunting trip in the Carpathians.

The lodge, in a wild and remote spot, had been built in 1820 for
a Hungarian nobleman. It was owned now, in 1912, by a wealthy
banker in Vienna. His younger son, Georg, was one of the four officers of the shooting party which had just arrived. He was the only
one who had been to the lodge before.

The old man came in:

'Will the gentlemen be pleased to take their baths first or a drink?'
he asked.

'Has our luggage arrived yet?' Georg asked.

'It has just arrived, Master Georg — the bags are in the hall.'

'Then it is baths for all, I think, Stephan, and drinks afterwards.'

The others nodded their assent. In the hall a huge unsmiling peasant stood by their bags. Effortlessly he picked up all four bags and
followed the caretaker to the rooms the officers were to occupy.
The grave young giant poured hot water into the zinc tubs while
the officers unpacked their bags. The lodge had never been moder-
nised — Georg was apologetic, but the others thought this was the
essence of its charm.

Kurt von Fellner, at thirty-three, was the oldest of the party, tall,
good-looking, a highly intelligent and sensitive man. His family
was of the minor landed aristocracy with an estate in Moravia. He
had joined the army rather later in life than was usual for his class.
Before that, as a young man, he had been given an opportunity to
enter into the life of high society in Vienna. He could have bought
a commission in a smart cavalry regiment and prolonged his gay

life in the capital. But three years of that had been enough for him. Instead, he joined the Artillery at the age of twenty-three. Now, ten years later he was still only a captain but likely to attain his majority soon for he had worked and studied hard and was marked out for promotion.

Like other intelligent young men at that time, and many of their seniors too, Kurt knew that, despite the outward pomp and circumstance and the iron control maintained by the old emperor Franz Joseph, politically the Empire was dying on its feet. The time had long since passed when some radical measure of reform — autonomy for the widely differing provinces and races, federation for the whole — might have saved the Austro-Hungarian Empire from ultimate dissolution. The army seemed to him to be the only hope, the skilful balancing of conflicting fears and hatreds under strict discipline tempered with paternalistic care for and good relations with the men of the Imperial armies, Teutons, Czechs, Magyars, Serbs, Slovaks, Croats and Poles. And basic to all hopes of maintaining this precarious balance and the territorial integrity of the Empire was the German alliance, undisturbed since 1879.

Kurt's companions were considerably younger men and all lieutenants. Frederich Waldstein was twenty-eight, short and tough, the best shot in the party, the best poker player in the battery, a professional soldier through and through. He believed the future lay with bigger and better guns and that the Austrian heavy artillery was second to none in Europe. He was a bachelor like Kurt and professed to be frightened only of women. Gunther von Altenburg was twenty-five, slim and elegant — the very antithesis of Frederich, always gay and joking. He was already married to a noted Viennese beauty, but nothing would induce her to join him at the dull and outlandish garrison town of Przemysl. Georg Wontner the banker's son was the youngest member of the party, but very much a man of the world. He was probably the wealthiest man in the regiment. Though generous he did not flaunt his wealth and was universally popular.

Back in the living room after their baths, changed, relaxed and glowing, the young men sank into their comfortable old-fashioned chairs. Georg was congratulated on the efficiency of his arrangements.

'I take no credit,' he said. 'Old Stephan has been doing this for years.'

The old man came in:

'Your drinks, gentlemen,' he announced.

A girl came in carrying four large tankards on a tray. The other three officers had their backs to her but Kurt was facing her as she came in from the kitchen. Her beauty stunned him — he could not take his eyes off her. Though plainly dressed and without any make up or affectations, her entry was like the invasion of a goddess from the woods. She moved with a natural grace that could not be matched by any of the society beauties he had known in Vienna. Georg gave her a cheerful greeting which she acknowledged with a flashing smile:

'This is Katerina,' he said. 'Our sweet Cinderella of the forest.'

Katerina gave them all a bright smile of welcome. The others took their beer without moving from their chairs but, when she reached Kurt, he stood up politely and bowed:

'Thank you, Fraulein,' he said.

She gave him a half curtsy and ran out of the room laughing. Georg and Gunther were indignant, Frederich merely grinned.

'Now then, Kurt,' said Georg. 'You are old enough to know better! Once is enough, or we shall all be jumping up and down like puppets.'

Kurt smiled:

'You are a clever boy, Georg — reserving the best till last.'

'Where did you find her?'

'She is the daughter of a poor Ruthenian hill farmer in the village a mile down the road, some relation I believe of Stephan's. She and her brother Anton — that's the hefty young man who carried our bags in — help old Stephan to look after the guests here. Yes, she is a charming girl — but you all mind your step, especially you, Gunther, and Kurt who has reached a dangerous age. She is a young woman who knows her own mind — not to be trifled with, and Anton watches over her like a mountain sheep-dog.'

Georg wagged his finger at them as he added his final caution:

'Above all, my friends, we rely on the goodwill of the peasants and farmers for the success of our sport — so — behave yourselves comrades in arms.'

'Well, Georgie,' said Frederich in disgust, 'if you have finished firing your warning shot for the benefit of the Casanovas in our midst, what about discussing something serious for a change — for instance the programme for to-morrow's sport?'

They were soon immersed in this more serious topic.

Katerina waited on them at table and served them more drinks after supper. Kurt did his best to pretend she was not there but every now and again a kick under the table from Gunther reminded him that he had allowed his eyes to stray. By the time their holiday was up after eight days of excellent sport, Kurt was head over heels

in love and decided that his obligations as Georg's guest and
towards his friends had been fulfilled; he must speak to Katerina,
even if he made a fool of himself. On their last night, after supper,
while her back was turned, he picked up a tray of dirty glasses and
carried it into the kitchen. He waited for her there. She came in and
shut the door behind her. When she saw him he noticed at once the
amusement in her eyes. She opened the door again. Kurt bowed
politely:

'Before I go,' he said, 'I want to ask a favour.'

'It is an honour — perhaps?'

'It is honourable, at least. Will you take employment with my
mother in our country house near Brunn? She will pay and treat
you well: this is no life for you here.'

She gave him a long quizzical look:

'I thank you, honourable Sir,' she said at last. 'I do not know if
your mother really needs me, but my duty lies here — with my own
mother and father. They need me.'

'So do I, Katerina!' he said, casting discretion to the winds.

She laughed happily:

'You are a very honest gentleman! But it cannot be — surely you
understand it cannot be?'

Her reply was gentle but resolute and kinder perhaps than he had
expected. He did not press her further; instead he said:

'If you will not accept my offer, may I, at least, be permitted to
see you again?'

'But, of course — I trust you . . . and the other young gentlemen,'
she added hastily — almost, it seemed, as an afterthought, as she
gave him a warm open-hearted smile. Kurt bowed, took her hand
and kissed it, as he would have done for a lady at court or salon,
but with considerably more fervour and walked out of the kitchen,
shutting the door behind him, his head in a whirl. He was greeted
with hoots of laughter by his companions. Gunther came up to
him:

'Let us see your face,' he said. 'Wonderful! — not a scratch, not
even red! How did you escape so lightly?'

'It is not a laughing matter for me,' he said angrily.

'Come on, Kurt,' said Frederich. 'A hand of poker will do you
good.'

Somewhat reluctantly he agreed, on their promising not to rag
him further. He could hear Katerina singing happily in the kitchen
as she washed up.

Next morning she came with Anton to help load the farm cart
they had hired to take their luggage back to civilisation. The horses

were brought round. Kurt was the last to mount. As he turned to wave goodbye, Katerina suddenly broke from the little group of peasants and ran up to him. From behind her back she produced a small posy of mountain wild flowers and presented it to him. As he bent down to take it she stretched up and kissed him lightly on the cheek.

'Katerina!' he exclaimed and leant over further to catch her up by the waist. But she eluded his grasp and ran back laughing into the lodge. Kurt caught a glimpse of Anton's face — he was smiling broadly.

2.

On his return to duty Kurt was posted to the Austrian Military Mission at Constantinople as a gunnery expert and was unable to obtain leave till the next autumn and then only a bare ten days. He returned to the hunting lodge alone and unannounced, leaving his uniform behind. On the way he called in at Stephan's house in some trepidation. The old man would know why he had come and might resent it. But Stephan welcomed him warmly:

'I will come with you and open up the lodge,' he said.

'I have brought food with me,' said Kurt.

'Then we shall only need bread, milk and eggs for the present,' and Stephan went off to collect these in the village.

On the way up to the lodge Stephan seemed to have something on his mind; only after he had opened up the lodge and lit the fire did Kurt learn what it was.

'It is a pity, Sir, you did not enquire before coming. Katerina's father died last week — the funeral is to-morrow. I am afraid she will not be free to come up to the lodge for some days.'

Kurt apologised and explained that he had no time to write and no choice of dates:

'If it is permitted,' he asked, 'I would like to attend the funeral service.'

Stephan was pleased:

'We shall all be honoured,' he said simply.

At the funeral service he had no opportunity to speak to Katerina but he caught her eye and she gave him a sweet smile. Afterwards Stephan told him that they would all be rising early next day to continue with the harvesting, interrupted by their bereavement. But if he cared to come up to the farm in the evening he would be welcome.

Very early next morning Kurt presented himself at the farm and

offered to help with the harvesting. Katerina's mother refused with
courteous dignity:

'It would not be proper,' she said. 'He would not have agreed.
We cannot afford to pay you. Besides, you would kill yourself —
it is not fit work for a gentleman.'

'A soldier is not afraid to die in a good cause,' he said smiling,
'and an apprentice does not expect to be paid.'

The old woman looked uncertainly at Katerina:

'Give him a chance, mother,' she said, trying to keep a straight
face, 'he looks strong enough,' and she came up and pinched his arm.
They all laughed.

'Very well — he will be your responsibility,' the old woman said.
'We want no accidents,' and, turning to Kurt, she said:

'Anton will find you suitable clothes.'

In the fields he was aware of curious glances but no hostility.
Anton, appointed to look after him and to show him what to do and
how to do it, was even friendly. Kurt soon discovered that Anton
had been adopted after the old couple had lost their only son. On
the second morning Kurt ached in every limb but accepted the chaff
with good humour. That evening he was invited to come down and
stay at the farm. There was no bath tub but Anton brought hot
water and apologetically produced a pig-swill trough meticulously
scrubbed clean. Kurt could not remember any bath he had enjoyed
so much. At the end of a week he felt he was really beginning to
pull his weight on the farm. They all accepted him as one of
themselves. Their simple courtesy and friendliness astonished and
pleased him; Katerina's mother treated him almost like a son. As
for Katerina herself he did not know what to think. She seemed
pleased that he had returned; in the fields she treated him the same
as all the other men working beside her; off duty she was gay and
pulled his leg. But when it was time for him to go she allowed him
to kiss her goodbye. He made the most of that and she was
unashamedly responsive. he left promising to return the following
spring.

When he went back in April the next year — 1914 — he received
the same warm welcome. But he was distressed to find how hard
Katerina had had to work, without her father's help, and with only
Anton's support, to maintain the farm. At this rate she would be
old and worn in a few more years. She seemed changed too — no
longer the gay and naive young girl who took him for granted,
unaware of her power over him. She was a young woman now, shy
and emotional by turn. One evening, when they were alone together
and he was telling her about his life in Vienna, lightly mocking the

parties and picnics and balls which had amused him at the time, she suddenly burst into tears and ran out of the house. He followed and found her sitting on a bale of hay in the barn. She did not move when he came up. He sat down beside her and started to apologise for his tactlessness in tantalising her with descriptions of a way of life which must seem to her a foreign and unattainable world. She put a finger on his mouth:

'No, Kurt, no — please.'

He kissed the finger. Suddenly she was in his arms, sobbing her heart out. He knew then for certain what he had only dared to hope — that she loved him. Nothing else mattered or would ever matter again.

The last four days of his leave flew by in idyllic bliss. They spent most of the daylight hours walking in the woods. Vienna and the past were never mentioned, the farm work was sadly neglected. On his last night they slept together. If her mother or Anton knew they said nothing. But Kurt had made a decision. When the time came to leave he took her mother apart and formally asked her permission to marry Katerina.

'What can I say?' said the old woman. 'She loves you — who are we to stand in her way? But you are a good man — can you honestly say that such a marriage would be right? How can she possibly fit into your life and society?'

'My society is crumbling' he said 'already I despise it. It will not last much longer. You will see — when the old Emperor dies, the present order will die too. I will resign from the army; we shall make a new kind of life, Katerina and I — in the country, on my estate. I promise you.'

She looked at him squarely:

'If you do not act up to your word you will break her heart, — and mine.'

'You shall be my watch-dogs, you and Anton. Look, I will buy the farm and lease it to others to run. You and Anton must come with me to my home. There will be work for you both but it will be an easier life.'

She shook her head:

'I am too old to move now. Anton and I will manage and the others will help. But you must bring Katerina to see me from time to time. I will know if she is happy.'

He pressed her hand:

'Of course we shall come — every year.'

It was arranged that they should be married in the village in October, after the harvest was in, according to the rites of the

Orthodox Church. Kurt insisted on paying all the wedding expenses.

On 26th June Kurt arrived at his home on fourteen days leave to break the news of his engagement personally to his parents and to make arrangements for bringing Katerina to live with him on the estate in November. His parents took the news well, though they were doubtful of the wisdom of his choice. But when he told them that the marriage was to be under the rites of the Oorthodox Church, they were upset and made him promise that when he brought Katerina home they would be married again according to the rites of the Roman Catholic Church.

On 28th June the Archduke Franz Ferdinand and his wife were assassinated at Serajevo. Kurt decided that he dare not risk awaiting the outcome; it was prudent to assume the likelihood of war and to marry Katerina at once. He had eleven days of his leave still left; he might be recalled any moment. He set off at once after sending a wire asking for a week's extension of leave, if possible. When he reached the farm all was peaceful, no rumour of the assassinations or the tensions following had yet reached this remote corner of the Empire. He explained the situation, that it was not safe to wait till October for the wedding, that he would not be able to resign from the army until the war, if it came, was over. He must marry Katerina at once without any elaborate preparations. They were bewildered by the news and its implications, which they did not properly understand, and disappointed to be deprived of the traditional and more ceremonious wedding planned for October. But Kurt was insistent and so the simple ceremony took place in the little village church on the fourth day after his arrival. Stephan gave Katerina away and Anton was Kurt's best man. They spent their five day honeymoon in the hunting lodge. On his last day Kurt received a wire, forwarded from his home, to say that extension of leave was not possible in view of the critical situation and that he must return to duty as soon as his leave was up. On their last evening together Katerina was tearful but proud:

'I bear our child,' she told him. 'If a son is granted, I shall call him Karl after my father; if a daughter, you shall choose her name.'

'She shall be Liesbeth,' he said. 'God willing, I shall come back after the war to claim you and the child.'

They knelt down in prayer together.

3.

On the outbreak of war, Kurt, now a major and commanding a

battery, was posted away from the fortress of Przemysl to the 1st Army under General Dankl in Galicia. Kurt's second in command was his friend, Friedrich Waldstein.

The war started disastrously everywhere for the Austrians. Their expeditionary force was thrown ignominiously out of north west Serbia by the end of August; Lemberg, the capital of Galicia fell to the Russians on 3 September. By the middle of that month the fortress of Jaroslav on the river San had fallen and Przemysl itself was besieged. The Russian general Brussilov captured Czernowitz, capital of the southern province of Bukovina and his advanced posts were at the mouths of the eastermost passes leading through the Carpathians into Hungary. The Austrians had lost 350,000 men. On 28 September the Germans, diverting large forces from their northern front, came to their rescue. There was a general advance in Galicia, Jaroslav was re-taken and Przemysl relieved on 9 October. After that there was a bewildering see-saw in the fortunes of war on the Eastern front. In the centre the Germans advanced to within thirty-five miles of Warsaw; further south the Russians advanced to within thirty-five miles of Cracow. Winter conditions froze all the combatants into immobility from the end of November till the end of February 1915.

Kurt naturally felt great concern for the safety of Katerina and her relations, and in January a keener edge was added to his anxiety when he heard from Stephan that Katerina had borne a son, duly named Karl. Their farm was on the southern slopes of the central Carpathians. Though it was far from any of the vulnerable passes, Kurt was faced by a dilemma. If Brussilov were to break through the Magyarweg pass into the plains of Hungary in the spring, they would be behind the enemy lines. But if he was able to persuade them all to move to his father's estate in Moravia, they would be in the direct line of advance of any successful Russian push through the Moravian Gate. After agonies of indecision he decided that the lesser risk was for them to stay put and he wrote accordingly. Stephan wrote that he was not to worry, they were all well, their hardships endurable. Anton was still with them as the authorities had done no recruiting in their area, being uncertain, apparently, of the loyalty of the Ruthenian population.

When spring came the Russians stepped up their pressure in eastern Galicia; Przemysl, which had been re-invested, fell with the loss of the whole of its garrison of 120,000 men. Again the Germans came to their rescue. At the cost of postponing the great offensive planned on the Western Front, Ludendorff was sent enough reinforcements to mount the spectacular Gorlice break-through in

May. It was only just in time. The Russians had advanced one fifth
of the way across the Carpathians. Now, in fourteen days their
Galician front collapsed, Lemberg was recaptured in June and only
the far south-eastern corner of Galicia remained in their hands. On
4 August the Germans took Warsaw and shortly after that Brest-
Livotz. The Eastern front was stablised on a more or less straight
line from Riga in the north to the Dniester river and the northern
border of Rumania in the south and remained static until the collapse of Russia in 1917.

In this offensive Kurt was slightly wounded. At the end of his
convalescence he was able to obtain a few days leave and to join
Katerina at the farm. They were all overjoyed to see him. He spent
many happy hours with Katerina and playing with Karl. But it was
over all too soon. When he got back to duty he received orders
transferring him to the staff of the German Command in the Middle
East. He owed this to the fact that while he had been with the
Austrian Military Mission in Constantinople he had learnt some
Turkish and Arabic. As a soldier he was pleased with his transfer.
The war seemed to have reached a stalemate on both the Western
and Eastern fronts but on the Turkish front in Asia there was promise of plenty of movement. In August the British started to advance from Egypt into Sinai. Kurt was posted to the command of
the German general Von Kressenstein whose daring raids right up
to the Suez canal had held up the cautious British for several
months. His only regret was that he would be so far away from
Katerina with little chance of leave to visit her. However he was
now relieved of any fears about her safety. During the next three
years they exchanged letters, it could hardly be said regularly, but
often enough to keep in touch until June 1918. After that all communications ceased. Kurt was not unduly worried, he put it down
to the worsening war situation. He himself had served with distinction first with Von Kressenstein in Sinai and later under Generals
Falkenhayn and Liman von Sanders in Palestine. But there was no
disguising the fact that the Turkish front was crumbling; the 6,500
Germans of the magnificent Asia Corps were the only reliable
troops on whom Liman von Sanders could count. After Allenby's
resounding victory at Megiddo Kurt was taken prisoner by the
British. He did not get back to Austria until 1919.

4.

Kurt returned to a world turned upside down. His own home, as
well as Katerina's, was now in the new state of Czechoslovakia.

His father had died during the war, his mother was in hospital dying of tuberculosis. He stayed with her till the end and then hastened to the farm in Ruthenia. He found it a ruined shell, the fields untended, the village almost uninhabited. But Stephan was still there, a very old and broken man. He told Kurt what had happened. In October 1918 a band of Magyars, part of the 40,000 deserters from the Austrian army in Galicia had come roaming through the slopes of the Carpathians, looting and burning. They had burnt the hunting lodge to the ground and then attacked the village. Anton and others who resisted had been killed. The women and children and some of the older men, including Stephan himself, had taken refuge in the church, where they had not been molested. After the Magyars had gone most of the survivors, terrified and homeless, all their worldly possessions lost, had decided to leave their own country and take refuge either in the Ukraine or in Poland where there were many of their own race. They had been speeded by rumours that Ruthenia was to become part of the new state of Hungary — false rumours at the time, though they came true twenty years later. Katerina, her mother and the baby had gone with them. No word had come from Kurt since June, they feared he had been killed. Stephan had refused to leave, he was too old and received a small pension fron Vienna which, with pathetic loyalty, he believed would still continue to be paid.

'Where did they go?' Kurt asked.

The old man was vague:

'I do not know for certain. There was talk of Lemberg or Cracow; some letters have come from the Ukraine, but no word has come from Katerina or her mother.'

Kurt saw his own misery reflected in the old man's eyes.

'Here is some money, Stephan — all I can spare at the moment. Promise to write to me if you hear: if Katerina writes, tell her to write to me at once and that I will come to fetch them, wherever they may be.'

'I promise. I am an old man and may die soon. But I will leave instructions that any news of Katerina, or any letter from her is to be forwarded to you at once.'

Kurt went round to the two or three villagers who had heard from some of the refugees, but none of these had mentioned Katerina. Heavy-hearted, he returned to his home. He had no inclination and insufficient means to live there now. He sold the house but kept a small cottage on the estate. He went to see the head postmaster at Brunn, a new man unknown to him, anti-German and unsympathetic. Kurt had no confidence that he would

forward to him any letters that came for him addressed to his old
home. He would have to come himself to enquire.

His next step was to resign from the army. As a colonel who had
served with the German Corps in the Middle East, Kurt had no difficulty in joining the German Police Service. At his own request he
was posted to Breslau in Silesia. Before taking up his appointment
he went to Lemberg and Cracow and made enquiries for Katerina,
but without success.

Once every year for five years he went to Brunn and enquired
personally for letters. He also visited the War Department in Vienna and made enquiries from the police in Lemberg and Cracow, but
all to no avail. In 1923 he heard that Stephan had died. After that
he gave up hope; he was convinced that Katerina, Karl and the old
mother must be dead.

And then, one day in 1936, towards the end of October he
received a batch of letters forwarded from Brunn, with a brief
covering letter of apology from a new postmaster to say that they
had been found stuffed away in a drawer and forgotten. The hand-
writing on the envelopes was Katerina's, the date stamps showed
they had been written between the years 1924 and 1930 and sent
from Warsaw. There was a separate letter of more recent date,
September the 4th 1936, also sent from Warsaw but not in
Katerina's hand. With a sense of foreboding he tore it open first.
The letter inside, dated 3 September, was from Warsaw but no further address was given. It was written in Polish, of which he knew
enough to read its brief contents: —

'My mother died yesterday and is buried in Warsaw. On her
deathbed she asked me to write and tell you of her death, even
though she had given up hope that you were still alive, for she has
sent many letters but received no reply. She told me that you are
my father. I know nothing of how this is so. I too believe you must
be dead — but I promised to write. We have lived in great poverty.
But my mother sent me to school when we came to Warsaw. She
said that, if you were still alive and I could find you, you
would help me. But now I have a job and can look after
myself.

                                        Karl Adamowitz'

After a while, numb with misery, he turned to Katerina's letters the
earliest, dated April 1924, was also the longest. He became absorbed in the story of the tragedy which had overtaken her.

No 14 Block IV
Potocki Building, Warsaw   11 April 1924

'My beloved Kurt,

I write in very great distress; there is no-one to help us in our misery. But, thank God, I still have Karl. I have not been able to write any letter to you or anyone else for five and a half years. This is what happened. In the autumn of 1918 a band of Magyar deserters attacked our village and burnt down most of the houses, including our farm. They killed Anton and all the other young men who tried to resist them. They also burnt down the hunting lodge although it was built by a Magyar nobleman. The women and children and a few older men, including Stephan, took refuge in the church, where we were not molested. When they had gone, we held counsel for our future. Stephan advised us to stay — no-one, he said, could do us any further harm here in our village — who knew what might befall us if we left. But we could not rebuild our houses without assistance, we had no seed left for our fields, no cattle or other livestock — the Magyars had taken the lot. We should have starved had we stayed. I remembered your words "if you are ever in difficulty, promise me that you will get in touch with my parents in Moravia". But there was no longer any postal service and no-one was willing to come with me. I dared not travel alone with Karl, not quite 3 years old. So, very reluctantly, I decided to go with the others who planned to make for Lemberg or Cracow, or possibly the Ukraine, in all of which places there were considerable numbers of our own people. We reached Przemsyl safely, where we were told that the whole of Galicia was unsafe for travellers because of large groups of freebooters roaming everywhere and terrorising the inhabitants. The police could do nothing — law and order had completely broken down. So, instead, we turned towards the Ukraine, which we heard had been occupied by the Germans on the outbreak of the Russian Revolution. This was the first I had heard of any revolution. There were also rumours that the war was over. I did not know whether to believe this, but I prayed that it was true and that you would be able to come to look for us.

'When we got into the Ukraine we soon found out that the Germans were only in control of the towns, not the countryside. Our little party was stopped by rough-looking Slavs who called themselves the Russian Social Revolutionary Party, whose aim was to stir up savage guerilla activity against the Germans. We were searched and questioned. When their commissar examined my papers he found our marriage certificate which seemed to show that I was married to an Austrian Army officer. I knew enough Russian to realise he suspected I was a spy. O Kurt, Kurt, the document that meant so much to me, has led to my undoing! The others were allowed to go, but I, Karl and my mother were arrested. I pleaded to be sent back to my own village, but they would not listen. We were taken to Moscow and handed over to the Cheka, the dreaded Russian Secret Police. We were imprisoned after the briefest enquiry.

'I was in despair; I knew no-one and even if I had known anyone I would not have been allowed to get in touch. We heard the most dreadful stories from the other prisoners. It seemed that our fate was to lie in prison forgotten and unknown till we died of despair or malnutrition, for the food was unwholesome and revolting — I will spare you the details. After a year my mother died. She had been splendid, courageous and unselfish. But when she became so ill and pitifully weak, though uncomplaining to the end, her death was a merciful release. Karl too was suffering from malnutrition and would have died, but I was put to work in a labour camp and was allowed to take Karl with me. There a kindly supervisor took pity on us and managed to smuggle in some vegetables and milk for Karl. This dreadful time lasted for five years. I will say no more about it to save your further pain.

'After five years Karl and I were suddenly deported to Poland in mid-winter and arrived destitute in Warsaw. The Polish police picked us up, ill and starving, and put us both in hospital for six weeks. When we were well enough to be discharged the police treated us as enemy aliens. I had to report to them once a week. I could not leave Warsaw without their permission and in any case I had not the means to do so. But at least we were no longer in prison. I was able to obtain employment in a factory and to rent two rooms in a residential block for workers.

'You would not recognise me now. I remember you were once concerned lest I should become old and worn from working too hard in our fields. Now it is much worse — I look like an old woman of fifty. I am warning you, dearest, what to expect when you come to rescue us.

'As soon as I got out of hospital I went to the Austrian Consulate. But they refused to believe my story — how could I, a rough and poor peasant, be married to an Austrian field officer? I had no papers, the Cheka had kept my marriage certificate. In the end, on my frantic insistence, they promised to refer the matter to Vienna.

'My first care now is Karl. He is nine years old. I have sent him to a school, knowing how important you consider schooling. I can just afford this with careful management. The neighbours have been kind and one or other of them look after Karl until I get home in the evening. I have had to take out Polish naturalisation papers in order to get Karl admitted to school. I thought it safer to take my maiden name — Adamowitz — for myself and Karl. I am sure you will understand and forgive me. But Karl knows what his real name is and I will never allow him to forget that he is your son.

'Now that I have been able to write to you and to start enquiries in Vienna, I feel happier than I have done since I left home. I feel sure that you will come and take us away. All our misery will be forgotten and we shall start life again.

Your adoring   Katarina'

Kurt put the letter down and buried his head in his hands. After a while he read it through again slowly, the words burning into his soul. After that, knowing the end, he had no heart to read more but forced himself to do so. The other letters were shorter but even more distressing. The next one was sent six months later.

Warsaw
10 September 1924

'My adored Kurt,

'I have heard nothing from you, but obedient to the promise I gave you, I do not abandon hope that you are still alive. Perhaps you have moved from your old home, but surely you would have arranged for letters sent there to be forwarded to you?

'My news is not good. After six weeks I had heard nothing from the Consulate, so called there again. They told me that my enquiry had been referred by Vienna to the German Consulate in Warsaw. When I called there they knew nothing of my case but promised to write again to Vienna and to Berlin. It seems they cannot or will not help me.

'Karl is making excellent progress at school. At first some of the boys made fun of him, but he soon put a stop to that and I think he is happy now. He has learnt Polish and is full of admiration for the heroes of Polish history and condemnation of the foreign powers who have subjugated Poland for so long. Unless you come quickly I fear he will become a Pole. We are both well. Please write quickly — I still have faith.

Your beloved   Katerina.'

She wrote again in 1925 to say that her enquiries had come to nothing. She gave news of Karl's progress at school. Though she still wrote cheerfully, it was not difficult to understand that her whole world depended on Kurt being still alive and Karl continuing to remain with her.

In 1927 she wrote from a new address in Warsaw and from a different address in each of her remaining letters. Reading between the lines, he guessed that each move had been to a cheaper and meaner tenement.

Bravely she continued to believe that he was still alive — until the last letter written in 1930. It was a letter of despair.

'My darling Kurt. I am ill — too ill to work any longer. The doctor says it is tuberculosis. Karl has been looking after me devotedly. In warm weather I can still sell flowers in the market.

After years of loyal hope, I now fear you must be dead. If so, perhaps someone will open my letter and write to tell me, though I do not want to hear.

I will not write again. Karl is now the only joy I have left in the world.'

So, it had all ended: Katerina was dead and her son did not want to know his father. In the circumstances it was understandable that he did not even want to take his father's name — he was a Polish citizen now.

Dry-eyed now, he folded the letters and put them away in his wallet. A great anger filled his heart and raged in his head. He would go to Brunn and find the man responsible for this outrage, for the death of his wife and the estrangement of his son, and choke the life out of him, whatever the consequences. When he was calmer he realised the futility of his anger. Instead, he went to Vienna. No-one in the War Department could recall any enquiry from the Consulate in Warsaw twelve years ago. But, if such an enquiry had ever been made, it would have been forwarded to the Police Headquarters in Berlin, for he was now in the employment of the German Reich. He went to Berlin. It was not surprising that again no-one could recall receipt of any such enquiry. He demanded to see his personal file. Yes, of course, they had a file — but it was confidential; he could not see it without the permission of higher authority. He was told his request was most irregular; it was most unlikely that it would be granted. He asked to see the Chief Police Commissioner. Kurt was now Chief of Police in Breslau and an ex-colonel; the Chief Commissioner knew and respected him and an interview was arranged for the same day. The Chief was a genial man, himself an ex-general of the German army. When Kurt told him his story he rang for his secretary and told him to bring Kurt's confidential record. When it came he read it himself and then, looking up, said:

'You say this girl you claim you married is now dead?'

Kurt nodded and, taking it out of his wallet, handed the Chief Karl's letter. The Chief read it and handed it back. He had an unpleasant task and a difficult decision to make; he was not sure that he had the moral right to make any decision:

'And the proof that you were married to this woman?'

'Do you doubt my word?'

'I do not doubt your word, but in this file you are still entered as single. When did you marry her? Have you a certificate?'

Kurt began to understand the reason for the Chief Commissioner's questions; he was in no position to resent them.

'We were engaged in April and were to have been married in October 1914. But because of the imminent threat of war we married in July, in great haste, in a remote and tiny village in the Carpathian mountains under the rites of the Orthodox Church. I have a certificate but I am doubtful of its validity. We had intended to be married again at my home according to the rites of the Roman Catholic Church and to register our marriage with the civil authorities. But there was no time for that, I had to rejoin my regiment at once. I saw my wife only once again — for a few days in July 1915. When I returned in 1919 she had disappeared, with our son Karl. I have already told you the rest.'

'Why did you not report the marriage — at least in 1919 — so that it could be recorded in your record?'

Kurt sighed, he did not like to remember that time:

'When I could not find my wife and son and resigned my commission to join the German police, I was sick at heart, I wanted to keep my grief to myself. Rightly or wrongly I decided that it would be time enough to report if and when I found my wife and the marriage could be regularised if necessary. When, after five years, there was no trace of her, I resigned myself to the belief that she must be dead. I could see no point then in reporting the marriage.'

'I see. You told me, I think, that she was a poor Ruthenian farmer's daughter?'

'Yes, I am not ashamed of the fact.'

'I believe you — but perhaps things were a little different in 1919?'

'No, never! She was worth any three Viennese dolls.'

The Chief looked at him compassionately:

'Then you made a mistake, my dear friend, in not reporting your marriage. If you had done so, you could have commanded the help of the German authorities in tracing your wife. It would have been their duty — just as it was considered their duty, in your own interest and in that of the service to which you belong, to protect you both from the possible consequences of what might have been thought some youthful indiscretion.'

Only then did Kurt fully understand. He looked with horror at the other man, saw his kind and sympathetic face and slumped forward in his chair, burying his own face in his hands. The Chief felt supremely uncomfortable. After a while he said gently:

'I imagine you will not want to see your file now?'

'No — you have told me enough — thank . . . thank you for your understanding: I do not deserve your sympathy.'

'But I am really sorry,' said the Chief, as he closed the file and rose to shake hands with Kurt. 'We Germans are sometimes too matter-of-fact and cautious; we are also sometimes too romantic. You must not blame yourself too much. There have been others before you with similar problems, there will be others after you.'

The Chief was rather pleased with himself, he had observed the rules and preserved the confidentiality of the personal record but conveyed the purport of the embarrassing entry of 1924 only too effectively. But, as Kurt left the room, bowed and grief-stricken he was shocked at the change in his appearance. Had he done right? Should he have lied outright to save this man's sanity and self-respect? He reflected that a Chief's task was not an easy one. He had to combine the firmness of authority with the tact of a diplomat and the wisdom of a father confessor. He sat down and wrote a confidential letter to Kurt's immediate superior.

5.

In the weeks following Kurt went through hell. He cursed the rigid and priggish mentality of the German bureaucrats who assumed to themselves the sole right to judge the morality of a question without consulting the individual concerned. But most of all he blamed himself. By his selfishness and stupidity he had ensured that Katerina's enquiries would be ignored as the audacious claim of some country wench whom it was supposed he had once seduced. His omission has been as effective as signing her death warrant. He would never be able to forgive himself. Now there was only Karl. Somehow he must find him and win him back from oblivion, convince him and the official world that he was not a bastard.

As soon as he could obtain leave he went to Warsaw. But when he found the street where she had last lived, all the houses had been pulled down in a slum clearance scheme. Despite long hours of enquiry and search he failed to locate Karl or where his Katerina was buried.

Sadly he returned to Breslau. And now in 1937 even his work and career had become distasteful. He had watched with astonishment and dismay the spectacular rise of Hitler and the Nazi party machine. Their agents were everywhere, infiltrating and usurping the functions of the police. The rape of Austria in February 1938 filled him with foreboding. In April of that year, at the age of fifty-nine, he requested leave to retire in March 1939 when he would be sixty. His intention was to retire to the cottage he had kept on his old estate near Brunn. By living in Czechoslovakia he hoped to avoid contact with the Nazi regime. But when, later in 1938, Hitler started to put pressure on Czechoslovakia, Kurt saw the writing on the wall. He had no wish to be 'liberated' along with the three million Germans living there. Hastily he started to make plans to emigrate to Switzerland instead. But before the papers could come through sanctioning his retirement, Hitler's bluff had succeeded and Czechoslovakia submitted to his demands on 30 September. Kurt's application to be allowed to retire was refused and he was ordered to hold himself in readiness for a new appointment. These orders came to him while he was on leave in Moravia. He returned to Breslau. But no-one seemed to be concerned to move him elsewhere and after ten months he came to the conclusion that the warning had just been a piece of bureaucratic officiousness, or had been forgotten in the feverish preparations for further aggrandisement of the Reich. With Hitler's triumph over Czechoslovakia, the French and the British, the opposition of the German Army High Command collapsed. He had become an outsize magician, a puppet-master, a heroic figure. In Breslau it was only too evident, as the year 1939 wore on, that Poland was his next objective. Men, weapons and armour poured into Silesia for the main thrust towards Lodz and Warsaw. On 1 September Poland was invaded.

On 18 September, without any warning, he was ordered to proceed at once to take up a police appointment in Warsaw. This was ten days before resistance in that heroic city of lost causes was officially declared to have been overcome. He never discovered who was responsible for his posting. He supposed that his eighteen years in Breslau, close to the Polish border, was regarded as a qualification for service in Poland itself. He was still fit and active but obeyed the order with extreme reluctance. He knew that, if he refused, his pay and his pension would be stopped by the Reich government. There were more ominous possibilities.

But why Warsaw? At his age it would have been more sensible to have left him in Breslau, or to have sent him to some other provincial city in the Reich, in Austria or Czechoslovakia, in order to release a younger man for the war front. Any appointment to serve under the Nazis was distasteful but, if he could not retire, he consoled himself with the thought that it might be more tolerable under active service conditions in Poland than under the sly and suspicious observance of the Gestapo, busily witch-hunting on the home front. But Warsaw itself was not a pleasant prospect, it would be a city of hate and fear, a city of the dead.

Warsaw — the dead? He remembered. He went to his desk and from a drawer took out the photograph of a young girl. For a long time he looked at it until it became cloudy before his eyes. He filled himself a glass of brandy. Holding the photograph in one hand, he raised his glass in the other and drank a silent toast.

When he reached Warsaw, the Chief of Police, a younger man than himself, but still a regular Police Officer of the old school, explained the situation to him:

'Warsaw lies in ruins; there are no police, no fire services, no medical services, no refuse collections. Electricity, gas, and water are all cut off. It will be our business to organise all these services, without which the city cannot be brought back to life or made habitable for the occupying forces. It will not be our business to round up guerillas and arrest suspects; this will be done by the army and the Gestapo. In short, my friend, we are responsible for a general tidying up. As my most senior officer I allocate to you the most urgent and important job , the establishment of a properly distributed police force. Here is a map on which all the key buildings are marked in red. You will tour at once with a military escort to take over and man all the police stations. You will have authority, of course, to requisition other buildings where the police stations have been destroyed or too badly damaged to be repaired quickly. You will draw up a report on the situation and what you will need. Remember, take every precaution possible, there are still groups of desperate Poles in hiding.'

Kurt soon discovered that resistance was by no means at an end, even in the outer suburbs. His party was sniped at twice in the first hour he was out and one of his escort was killed. When he got back he reasoned with his Chief:

'By all means let us make plans, but we have not yet sufficient men to implement them under present conditions. Either give me stronger escorts and more police, or the army should complete its task before we are asked to move in.'

The Chief of Police was unsympathetic:

'I know we are undermanned — but we have no time to wait. The Fuhrer will enter Warsaw within a week. Fierce street battles are still raging in the centre of the city; there is not another soldier to be spared. Moreover, we are not "asked" — we are ordered and it is our duty to obey. You should regard it as an honour to be so commanded.'

'I trust you do not think I am concerned for my personal safety?'

'No, no, of course not — you have been a soldier, I understand, and with a distinguished record?'

'You have read it no doubt?' The other nodded and said:

'Then you will know your duty — I will forget your protest,' — there was a slight pause and then he added in a more friendly tone:

'I can understand your feeling resentment at having to serve under a younger man. Shall we say it is an accident of war? We are both members of an honourable profession whose origin and traditions go back to happier times than the present. You and I have reached our present positions by very different roads, but I hope we can be friends. There is nothing in your record which will influence me in any respect against you. Your private life is no concern of mine.'

'So the damning record had never been corrected,' thought Kurt bitterly. But all he said was:

'I bear no resentment whatever against you — only against fate. I shall serve you faithfully and by all means let us be friends.'

The Chief smiled: 'Good,' he said, 'then we understand each other. I like a man who speaks out what is in his mind. You can speak freely to me, but I advise you to guard your tongue before others.'

Kurt understood. Looking squarely at the other man, he said:

'I cannot help feeling concerned. I served through the First World War I saw how the Reich over-reached itself. I very much fear the same thing is going to happen again.'

There was silence in the room. The Chief of Police pursed his lips and looked grave. Then he said quietly:

'I think it will not be the same, provided the U.S.A. remains neutral and our leaders resist the temptation to invade Russia.'

'Our leader, you mean,' said Kurt bluntly.

'I trust our Generals,' said the Chief and rose to his feet to signify that the interview was at an end.

'I wish I could be as confident,' said Kurt.

On the afternoon of 28 September, the day when it was officially announced that all resistance had been overcome, Kurt set out with ten policemen and a small military patrol, consisting of one light armoured car and a truck carrying nine soldiers. The police followed in a second truck. Kurt travelled in the armoured car with the patrol commander. Their objective was to take over and man a large warehouse on the Poznan road to accommodate police transport due in two days' time. They proceeded uneventfully through the empty and shattered streets of the western suburbs till they reached a small square forming a road junction, on one side of which stood a large and ugly church, surrounded by a fairly extensive graveyard. They were still about a mile from their objective. There they had to stop. All exits from the square, except the road by which they had come, were heavily barricaded, though the barricades did not appear to be manned. But, when the soldiers in the front truck jumped out and started to remove the obstructions, they came under a murderous fire from the houses overlooking the square. Taken unawares, two soldiers were killed and two wounded. Seeing two of his men starting to lift the body of a wounded comrade, the patrol commander, through his loud hailer, ordered all the survivors to leave the casualties and get back into their truck. He was pretty sure that the Poles would kill his two wounded men, but unless they took immediate action, none of them would survive. He looked at Kurt who knew what he was thinking. He was quite a young officer in a very difficult situation; a word from an older man would re-assure him. Though it went against the grain, Kurt said quietly:

'You did right in the circumstances, you really had no choice.'

The street in which they were halted was narrow and they were suddenly subjected to a hail of petrol bombs. The patrol Commander, realising that they had run into a planned ambush, not knowing how many their assailants were and not having the right kind of vehicles with which to ram and demolish the barricades, gave orders to reverse since the road was too narrow for the trucks to turn in quickly. They had only just started when the last truck, now leading in reverse, was set on fire. The driver with great courage and presence of mind drove the truck forwards to the extreme edge of the road to allow room for the other vehicles to get past. The policemen in this truck scrambled into the other truck, though one or two were wounded while doing so. The second truck just managed to get past the burning truck before the latter's petrol tank exploded. The patrol commander in the armoured car decided that his best chance of getting past the raging inferno, was to turn and go through at speed. This was an awkward manoeuvre, during which he sent a message by radio transmitter asking for reinforcements to be sent. The car was almost round when the driver was hit and fell forward over the wheel. The armoured car, out of control, ran over the kerb, hit the parapet of a house and overturned, killing the patrol commander. Kurt and the remaining crew escaped unscathed and ran to join their comrades in the one remaining truck. This had halted and turned across the width of the road to meet a new menace — a crowd of Poles charging towards them from the direction in which they had been reversing.

The situation was extremely ugly. Kurt took charge:

'Into the Church,' he shouted. 'It is our only hope. You sergeant will stay with six men to hold back the crowd, while I take the rest into the churchyard. As soon as we are in a position behind the wall to give you covering fire, I will blow my whistle. If you do not hear it after two minutes, follow us all the same. We shall then retreat together into the church.'

Kurt lost two men killed from his party, including the wireless operator from the armoured car, whose transmitter was also smashed. The sergeant's party lost one man killed, but were able to bring another man slightly wounded with them. One more man was wounded in the dash from the churchyard to the church. As Kurt had hoped, the great West door was not locked and the key was inside. They locked it and dropped the iron bars on the inside. Two other side doors were similarly secured. They dragged two heavy coffers and the alter tables from the two chapels of Mercy and piled them against these doors; they wrenched the stone font off its base and rolled it against the main West door.

Seventeen men had survived out of the original strength of twenty-four; of these seventeen, four were wounded, one seriously and one more had minor burns.

Kurt made a quick survey of the church. Most of it was modern but substantially built; the east end was older and had a rounded apse. The wooden roof over the single nave was of a simple king-post construction. Above the main windows on each side of the nave were narrow clerestory windows. He guessed that the wooden roof boarding was probably covered with lead and then tiles. The ante-chapel directly behind the west door was flanked by two towers; there were staircases in both towers, leading in one to the bell-ringers' chamber and in the other to some sort of office above the robing room for the choir. At the west end of the ante-chapel there were three large rectangular windows. He noted with some satisfaction that they had all been boarded up on the inside. The ante-chapel was vaulted in stone and there were no side windows here. There was a massive gilded iron rail enclosing the whole of the chancel. Kurt reckoned this would provide their last defensible position if they were driven back. The apse, stone vaulted with only three narrow slit windows contained the two chapels of Mercy; he put the wounded in one of these. Except for the choir stalls in the chancel there were no pews but about thirty wooden chairs in the nave. Though wired for electric lighting the church was without current; there were no oil lamps and no candles. The altars were bare, but whether this was because all valuables had been removed to safe hiding, or had been looted, there was no means of telling. It did not appear that anything else had been removed — except for the chairs; he recalled now seeing a number of similar chairs in the barricades outside. He sent men up the towers to see if there were any windows or balconies which commanded a field of fire, but all were useless for their purpose. Luckily there were no side entry box doors in the church. Kurt hoped that the strong wooden doors would hold out until a relief party arrived. The ante-chapel seemed the best place in which to post his small force. From there they had a clear view of the main windows in the nave through which the Poles might try to break in. He detailed two men to be ready to ring the bells, if and when he gave the order, to guide the relief force to the church.

During the time it took to make this survey and complete his dispositions the Poles made no attempt to attack them. Kurt was just beginning to wonder if they had decided to break off the engagement, satisfied with their partial and, indeed, considerable success, when the silence was shattered by the crash of broken glass. To their surprise it was one of the clerestory windows which had been smashed. They waited anxiously for the next move; it came almost at once. Another clerestory window was broken on the opposite side of the church and long poles, their tips wrapped in sacking which was burning fiercely, were thrust through both windows up into the wooden roof beams.

Kurt had already issued provisional firing instructions, mainly to conserve their ammunition. Their attackers on ladders were below the trajectory of any bullet fired through the bottom of the windows. Moreover, the ladders were not directly below the windows for, to reach the roof beams which were spaced out between the windows, the poles had to be thrust through at an angle. So the ladders were clear of the main windows as well which were directly below the clerestory windows. He ordered the first party to fire at the shafts of the poles as close to the windows as possible:

'Free drinks, when we get back, to whoever breaks a pole or makes the holder drop it.'

Light was rapidly fading inside the church but the torches gave them all the light they needed. One pole was splintered and the ball of fire fell onto the floor of the nave. Two men ran to extinguish it but Kurt ordered them back; it could do no harm there and they needed the light. The broken pole was quickly re-placed. Meanwhile, with devilish dexterity, the holder of the other pole had managed to wedge it so that the ball of fire was lodged firmly in the acute angle between a vaulting rafter and one of the cross tie-beams which spanned the width of the church. They heard the ladder being moved and presently a third clerestory window was broken and a third flaming pole appeared.

They only had three hand-grenades left, the rest had been used outside. Kurt had intended to reserve them for use only if the Poles broke into the church. He decided to risk wasting one in an attempt to stop this ingenious fire-raising stratagem:

'Who is our Aunt Sally champion?' he asked.

They nudged one man forward:

'Willy is the best thrower here,' they said. Kurt placed him so that the angle of his throw should carry some of the fragments of the grenade and glass of the window towards the ladder on the far side of the latest broken window.

It was an excellent lob; the grenade hit a section of unbroken glass, burst and carried some of the glass and of its own fragments out onto the man at the top of the ladder. They heard the ladder fall and a man screaming in agony. The pole fell into the church. Willy volunteered to throw another grenade but Kurt restrained him; the other pole was being rapidly withdrawn — the man holding it had seen and heard what had happened on the other side of the church.

Though they had gained some respite, they still had to deal with the pole wedged in the angle between rafter and cross beam. Kurt had already sent a man to the bell loft to cut one of the bell ropes. This was now thrown over the tie-beam and with a man at each end was worked into the angle to dislodge the fire-ball. But they were too late; the rafter was already burning and the flames were being fanned by the draughts coming in through the broken windows. Smoke started billowing down into the church. Kurt knew it was only a question of time before the whole roof would be ablaze and fall in. He ordered the two men to ring a tocsin and evacuated the wounded from the lady chapel.

The little group in the ante-chapel watched helplessly as the fire spread. Kurt had no illusions about the nature of the ordeal before them. He had been ambushed once in Syria by Arab guerillas and had shot his way out of a burning house. Unless help came soon they might be asphyxiated by smoke or roasted alive. Of course they could try the desperate alternative of trying to break out. The Poles would probably expect them to do this only as a last resort; if they went out now they might catch the Poles unprepared. On the other hand, even if they succeeded, they would have to find some other sanctuary and hold it until relief arrived. He thought the chances of finding any other tenable position were very dim and decided it would be better to stay where they were for as long as possible in the hope that they would be rescued before the church became untenable.

For the moment smoke was the most dangerous threat. They had found a can of water, providentially left beside the font. Some of it had been used for the wounded but there was still some left. They tore strips off their shirts to make gags ready to be soaked in the precious water.

The enemy's next move was not long delayed. They heard men on the roof tearing off the tiles and lead and soon they had set fire to the wooden boarding below in two or three places.

And now a new danger threatened. Kurt heard an exclamation and turned to see flames licking under the great west door. Petrol had been poured against the door; they had probably piled wood and straw against the door as well. He could hear the flames burning fiercely on the outside. Those inside were quickly extinguished. The door was tough, it should burn slowly. Dense volumes of smoke were now pouring down from the roof which was ablaze everywhere. Kurt ordered men to fire and break all the remaining clerestory windows at the risk of accelerating the destruction of the roof. After the volleys and the extra rush of cold air which resulted, the flames roared up to the apex of the roof and through the holes made by the Poles. The burning church would be a landmark for miles. But some of the smoke was lifted too, giving them welcome relief. Kurt ordered the men out of the bell tower. The Poles' latest move was to pour crude oil on the fire outside the west door and thick black suffocating smoke was seeping under the door and in at the sides. He ordered his men to soak and tie on their gags. They retreated as far as they dare from the door, keeping in mind the risk of being crushed and burnt by falling beams and masonry when the mainroof of the nave collapsed. The west door was now burning fiercely. When the roof fell they would be caught between two walls of heat. The sergeant suggested ascending one of the towers but Kurt rejected this temptation. Once up, they would be trapped up there; the floors of the two towers were of wood, highly combustible. Moreover there was a chance that when the main roof collapsed the towers might fall too.

Kurt could not help admiring the desperate determination of the Poles, the planning and timing of their assault. God knows they had had enough practice over the centuries, poor devils. They were the victims now of another brutal aggression, for which he could see no justification but in which he had become involved against his will.

'Listen,' he said to his men. 'Whether the door or the roof collapses first, the Poles will employ the same tactics — they will wait to see what we do. They know that we have only three alternatives — to try to get out, in which case they will hope to mow us down — to retreat to the apse at the risk of being cut off by the roof falling in, or to stay where we are, if we can. But in any event they will not wait for very long — time is no longer on their side. So, if we stay where we are, and this we must do, they will eventually try to rush us, hoping to find us roasted alive, or to finish us off inside the church. We must, therefore, make a barricade of chairs across the main doorway and some way back from the door. We shall not man it but form two single files one on each side of the doorway and as close to it as we can get for the heat. When they attack towards the barricade we shall throw our two hand grenades. In the confusion we will run out round the sides of the barricade and the doorway and round the church, one file round each side and rejoin at the back of the church. With luck we may be mistaken for Poles, at least until we can re-group at the back of the church. After that we must act as circumstances dictate. But, before we have to face that unknown, I am confident that our relieving force will arrive. One thing more — we do not abandon our wounded.'

Kurt had spoken with assurance, but he was not so certain now that any relief force was on its way. They were a small party and might be considered expendable; though he felt sure that his Chief of Police would not take this view if he knew of their predicament. They set to work at once and built a barricade of chairs. They had hardly finished this when, with a thunderous roar the main roof collapsed into the nave. By some miracle the towers stood firm. The church was sturdily built and very little of the masonry walls supporting the roof fell with it. None of the debris reached them, though some flaming rafters bounced towards the chairs. Luckily they broke up into hundreds of small balls of fire and red-hot cinders which they were able to stamp out with their rifle butts. But the heat was now terrific on both sides of them and huge volumes of smoke billowed across the floor of the church.

It was at this moment that the great west door disappeared in a roaring sheet of flame, leaving only three twisted and red-hot iron hinges, drooping grotesquely across the doorway. They were driven back by the heat to the extreme corners of the ante-chapel. The entrance was an inferno of glowing embers over which even professional fire-walkers would not have dared to pass.

Kurt thought: 'They will see the barricade and think we are behind it; until they can get in they will only fire or throw bombs.'

But no bullets or bombs came. Instead, they heard through the hiss of the flames, faintly at first and then with growing insistence, the sound of sirens and then of machine-gun fire.

Kurt ripped off his gag:

'We are saved!' he shouted and the others removed their gags and cheered.

'Now,' he said, 'I will go, and you Corporal Hans with me, to contact the relieving force and guide them here. No-one else is to move until our comrades arrive. Sergeant, I leave you in charge — be careful of those hand grenades.'

He shook hands with them all. Willing hands pushed away as much of the burning rubble at one side of the doorway as they could with rifle butts and chairs. They both got through unscathed and were halfway across the churchyard when they ran into a hail of bullets. Kurt dived to the ground; out of the corner of his eye he saw Corporal Hans do the same. Simultaneously he thought 'it can't be the Poles, it must be our own men; they have mistaken us for guerillas'. He shouted to Hans to stay where he was until they could identify themselves.

He had fallen across a grave and laughed at the bizarreness of his situation.

'Where are you, Hans?' he called. There was no reply. He half turned to see if he could locate the corporal and at that moment a searchlight swept across the churchyard. By its light he saw Hans and, by the way he was lying, that he was dead. Kurt cursed aloud. He had not lost a single man since they rook refuge in the church, and now he had led this man to his death — killed by his own side and all quite unnecessary. The searchlight swept back across the church; he saw his men waving their arms and what looked like a shirt tied to a rifle. There was no more firing. They were safe — the relief party would surely be here in a few minutes. Why had he lost his head? He should have stopped with his men. He had seen other men behave foolishly in the sudden reaction from great stress and danger. 'I am no better myself,' he thought wryly 'though I am old enough to be wiser.'

He decided to rejoin his party and had half risen to his knees when the searchlight swept round again. It rested for a moment on him and on the headstone of the grave across which he had been lying. The inscription was new and clear, the name leapt out at him and was gone as the searchlight swept on.

He rose to his knees and found the small pocket torch which he always carried. In front of him the church was outlined against the flames and a rising moon but he himself was in shadow. As he turned the torch on, a figure rose from behind the headstone. Kurt saw the flash but never heard the report. The bullet hit him between the eyes; he was dead before he hit the ground.

A young man came out cautiously from his place of concealment and kicked the dead body:

'German pig, dead pig,' he said quietly. He bent down quickly and took the dead man's revolver. As he stooped to pick up the torch he heard men approaching and fled into the shadow of some yew trees. From there, seizing his opportunity he escaped out of the churchyard. The relief party had arrived. They found Kurt lying across a grave facing the church and beside him his torch, still on and focussed on the foot of the headstone. A few paces away they found Corporal Hans, also dead and still holding his rifle. They were puzzled by the position of Kurt's body and the nature of his wound. Instead of lying facing the square, like Hans, he lay facing the church and the bullet which killed him had been fired at very close range from directly in front of him. Also his revolver was missing. They guessed he had been ambushed by a Polish partisan. The relief party had come prepared to clear the square, if necessary by storming or firing every house, but they found no-one — the Poles had withdrawn. They found the two men wounded at the barricade — one had died of his wounds, but the other was still alive though unconscious. The Poles had probably thought he too was dead. They decided to bury all the dead in the churchyard. Kurt was buried next to the grave beside which he had been found lying, his escort commander beside him. The rest were buried in a mass grave a few yards away. The last shots fired that day were fired in the funeral salute.

The Chief of Police, searching through Kurt's wallet, but in vain, for some address of next of kin, found a letter and inside it a photograph, a little faded, of a singularly beautiful young girl. Beneath the photograph in Kurt's own hand was written 'Katerina' and a reference to I Corinthians XV, 26. He read the letter. It was dated September 1936 and addressed to Kurt. It had been sent from Warsaw but no other address was given. It was signed by Karl Adamowitz and told of the death of his mother. He guessed that the photograph must be of Karl's mother and the letter showed that Karl was Kurt's son. It was only too probable that this was the liaison referred to in Kurt's confidential record. What an irony that he should have been sent to Warsaw! He put letter and photograph back into the wallet, with a guilty feeling that he had intruded, albeit unwittingly, into the private and personal life of his late assistant.

He could not recall the Biblical reference; luckily his wife had insisted on packing his Bible. He found it and looking up the reference, read:

'The last enemy that shall be destroyed is death.' The Chief pondered: 'The Great Mystery,' he said aloud, 'where death is only a barricade for the living. I hope so, I do hope so and especially for these two.'

Next day a working party was sent out to erect over the graves of the men killed in this ambush the simple war-time wooden crosses which would probably be all that they would ever have, and on which were inscribed the names, ranks and units of the dead men.

Two days later the Chief of Police himself set out with a strong escort to complete the task which Kurt had been unable to fulfil. He took with him some of the survivors of the ambush and they stopped at the church to reconstruct details for an official report. They were astonished to find a fresh wreath on the grave beside which Kurt had been buried.

The Chief of Police looked with curiosity at the headstone of the grave carrying the wreath and read:

'Katerina Adamowitz, died 1936.'

1982

GLOSSARY (Alphabetical Order)

Alaknanda	the main river flowing through Garhwal which, lower down, joins the Bhagirathi flowing through Tehri Garhwal to form the Ganges.
Anna	one-sixteenth of a rupee (old coinage).
Bania	merchant.
Beldar	Irrigation Dept. official who measured the water supplied to cultivators.
Bhot	the name, shown only on old maps, for the area immediately south of the Tibetan plateau in the central Himalaya. Home of the Bhotias.
Bhotias	a hardy mixed race formed by intermarriage between Tibetans and hill Rajputs, who used to hold the monopoly of all the border trade.
Bhusa	Chopped fodder — the universal cattle fodder in India.
Biri	hand-made, often home-made cigarette rolled in brown paper. Smoked all over India.
Bungalow-wallahs	people living or staying in a bungalow.
Chatti	Pilgrim rest house.
Chota Peg	small whisky and soda.
Chick	split bamboo door curtain, used to keep out the sun's glare, birds, animals, large insects and some of the dust. If close fitted some deterrent to reptiles, effective to provide privacy against all save Peeping Toms who lever two bamboo slats apart and apply an eye to the resultant gap (very rarely happened).
Chowkidar	night watchman. Chowkidars were engaged by the police, were often ex-convicts and this was supposed to provide some insurance against burglary but sometimes acted the other way.
Compound	enclosure e.g. servants compound within the garden of a private house, where all the servants lived.
Dacoit	member of a gang of professional robbers. Dacoity is endemic in India.
Darzi	tailor.
Dhauli	river rising north of Niti near the border with Tibet and joining the Alaknanda at Joshimath.
Dhobi	washerman.
Dhoti	white nether garment (cotton) worn by Hindus of both sexes. Tying it is an art soon acquired.

Dotial	the Dotials were professional porters from western Nepal who had almost the complete monopoly of carrying loads in the central and eastern Himalaya.
Ekka	two-wheeled, horse-drawn, springless hackney carriage. Passengers sit under a canopy on a woven string floor, directly above the wheels — the cheapest and most uncomfortable ride — will negotiate any track.
Ganesh	the Elephant God — patron of literature.
Gartok	the Capital of Western Tibet.
Gujar	itinerant nomadic Muslim herdsman of N. India.
Guru	Religious teacher.
Hanuman	the Monkey God.
Hardwar	a town and site of Hindu pilgrimage on the Ganges just after it emerges from the hills. The mountain section of the pilgrimage to Badrinath and Kedarnath starts from here.
Jan	fermented barley brew.
Jemadar	in the Indian Army an N.C.O. equivalent in rank to a Corporal, but also widely used in Civilian services. Here = senior Forest guard.
Jodhpur	in the present context — riding breeches (but the wearer need not necessarily be a rider) worn without boots, the legs below the knee fitting close to the calf and down to the ankle, as worn by Rajput Thakurs of Jodhpur.
Jongpens	the two Tibetan Governors of Western Tibet.
Kali	consort of Siva, goddess of death and disease
Kanungo	Revenue Inspector, the immediate superior of the Patwaris (see below) He also had the powers and duties of a Police Inspector in the Hill Districts. There were six Kanungos in Garhwal.
Khan Sahib	The lower of the two commonest 'Honours' bestowed by the British on loyal and deserving Muslim citizens. The higher 'Honour' was Khan Bahadur. The equivalent 'Honours' for Hindus were Rai Sahib and Rai Bahadur.
Kharak	an open glade in Himalayan forests used for steading and grazing cattle.
Khassiya	Rajput, so-called, but distinct from Hill Rajputs who emigrated to the hills from the Plains of India. The Khassiyas are thought to be Aryans who invaded from central Asia, (c.f. Caspian, Caucasus, Kashgar, Hindu Kush, Kashmir, the Khassia Hills in Assam).
Khazzaks	a Turkomani tribe of Muslims now under Soviet rule in central Asia.

Kshattriya	The Hindu Warrior Caste.
Kukri	short broad-bladed curved knife used by Gurkhas Garhwalis and other hillmen.
Kurta	close-fitting tunic type short shirt with open neck.
Kuti	single cell stone hut or rock cave dwelling of a hermit or holy recluse.
Langur	Black-faced, long tailed hill monkey with silver grey coat.
Lakh	Indian Currency term. One Lakh of rupees was worth £10,000 up to 1873, re-valued after 1873 to £6,667.
Lathi	thick bamboo staff, brass-bound at thicker end, a formidable weapon.
Maharaj-ji	a polite form of address to a superior or person of authority.
Mali	gardener.
Mantri	a prayer.
Manu	a famous Indian Code of Law put together between 200 B.C. and A.D. 200 — much misinterpreted.
Mynah	the brahminy mynah (Temenuchus Pagodarum) a relation of the common starling, with black crest and white-tipped tail. A good songster and mimic and favourite cage pet bird in India.
Neem	a tree whose leaves when dried and crushed are widely used in India as a base packing for boxes storing clothes, books etc., giving good protection against damp and insects. Also used medicinally. Carpenters value the wood for furniture.
Padhan	headman of a village.
Panchayat	Council or Court of five elders elected by villagers — India's age-old form of rural democracy, sadly neglected by the British.
Pandit	Priest (in context used here).
Pani	Water.
Parganah	an administrative area composed of a number of 'pattis' or 'patwari' circles (see below) There were eleven parganahs in Garhwal.
Pariah	outcast, commonly used to describe stray dogs.
Pasi	an occupational caste name for grass-cutters.
Patti	a land settlement area in the hills (see below), the smallest administrative unit in the hills, generally co-incident with a patwari's circle. There were 93 pattis in Garhwal District.
Patwari	a Revenue Accountant responsible for keeping records of crops and of all rights in land, and, in the hills, also having the powers of a police sub-inspector. There were approx. 75 patwaris in Garhwal District.

Peepul or Pipal   *Ficus religiosa*, whose leaves, like those of the
                   aspen, are always quivering. The similarity suggests
                   some relationship between the Hindi 'pipal' and the
                   poplar (populus) of Europe. In Kumaon there is a
                   species of true poplar so like the pipal that it is call-
                   ed ghar-pipal (house peepul) or perhaps gir peepul
                   (mountain peepul). It is a noble tree, attaining a
                   girth of 10ft. or more and held in great esteem, The
                   Hindus stand the scarlet images of their gods
                   against the foot of this tree.

Pindar   a river whose source is the Pindari Glacier on the
                   western slopes of Nandakot in Almora District. It
                   flows through Garhwal from SE to NW and joins
                   the Alaknanda at Karanprayag.

Punkah   ceiling fan. Before metal electric fans came into use,
                   the punkah was made of cloth hung from a cross
                   pole and hand pulled by a coolie sitting outside the
                   room by means of a rope which went through a
                   hole in the wall. The coolie's task was a thankless
                   one and sleep inducing and by midday his pull
                   became lethargic or creased altogether.

Ringal   a species of thin feathery bamboo used for making
                   baskets.

Rishi   the seven Rishis or Sages of Hindu Vedic
                   mythology were attributed powers of locomotion
                   unrestricted by time or space.

Sadhu   Hindu holy man or mendicant.

Samadhi   a state of suspended animation.

Sarpanch   chairman of five man village court.

Seer   Indian weight equivalent to 2 lbs.

Settlement   periodic review of Land Revenue levels (Land
                   Revenue was 39% of all central Govt. revenue) Set-
                   tlement was permanent in Bengal and, in all, in
                   one-fifth of all British India.

Seven Sisters   the rusty-cheeked Scimitar Babbler birds.
                   Himalayan variety. The Indian name is 'Satbhai',
                   the seven brothers, but the English name seems
                   more appropriate.

Shikari   hunter.

Shilpkar   the hill name for all the depressed classes, mainly
                   Doms but including other artisans. They were not
                   allowed to draw water from the wells used by the
                   'Biths' (upper castes). They were only tenants-at-
                   will, many of them serfs of the landholders and
                   farmed only 5% of all cultivable land.

Siva   god of destruction, death and reincarnation, one of
                   the supreme Hindu Triad, Brahma, Vishnu and
                   Siva. His cult very popular in the Hills.

Tahsil	an administrative area composed, in the Hills, of three or four parganahs (see above) under the immediate charge of a subordinate Indian officer called a Tahsildar, whose next superior was a Deputy Collector called a Sub-Divisional Officer. There were three Tahsils, co-terminous with the three Sub-Divisions in Garhwal District. The Tahsil with its resident officer, the Tahsildar, could well be called the basic unit of rural administration in northern India.
Tamta	Low-Caste blacksmith (in the Hills).
Tendal	canal gatekeeper or gang foreman.
Terai	the sub-montane belt of hardwood, bamboo and shrub jungle forest which divides the plains of northern India from the Himalayan foothills, once the home of plentiful wild game, tiger, leopard, elephant, rhino, bison and various species of deer, peacock, jungle fowl, various kinds of pheasant and partridge, bear and wild boar. Some of these sadly reduced by indiscriminate slaughter.
Tilak	ritual caste mark on forehead, white for devotees of Vishnu, red for certain extreme devotees of Siva.
Trisul	'The Trident' — a Himalayan peak, 23,406 ft. on the south-western flank of the Nanda Devi massif in Garhwal. First climbed in 1907 by Dr. Longstaff, two Swiss guides and a Gurkha Jemadar and at that date the highest summit in the world undisputably climbed.
Vaish	the merchant caste.
Zamindar	landowner, landlord. Zamin = land, dar = holder.